AMERICAN MADE

Shylah Boyd
American Made

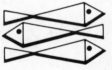

FARRAR, STRAUS AND GIROUX | NEW YORK

First printing, 1975

Published simultaneously in Canada by
McGraw-Hill Ryerson Ltd., Toronto
Printed in the United States of America
Designed by Dorris Huth

Parts of this book have previously appeared in *Viva*

Library of Congress Cataloging in Publication Data

Boyd, Shylah.
American made.

I. Title.
PZ4.B7918Am [PS3552.0879]   813'.5'4   75-5624

To Frank Adduci, Jr.

BOOK ONE

1959–1963

'Twas brillig, and the slithy toves
  Did gyre and gimble in the wabe:
All mimsy were the borogoves,
  And the mome raths outgrabe.

"Beware the Jabberwock, my son!
  The jaws that bite, the claws that catch!
Beware the Jubjub bird, and shun
  The frumious Bandersnatch!"

1

"Where's Mummy?"

"Don't know. How the hell . . . try the living room, for Christsake . . . the rec room—probably passed out in the rec room. Goddamned lush. Get her up here, Shylah, get her up to bed . . ."

"Relax, Perdie. Jesus, put your pants on, put your teeth in . . . you aren't such a great ad for sobriety yourself."

"Don't you talk to me that way. Don't you dare . . . You're the cause of this, you know. You're the spoiled little bitch that drives us both nuts half the time. Christ, the insolence. Go on, go find her. Don't know what to do with either of you. Hear about your mother's latest trick—mind you, at the club dance last night, absolutely marvelous— Your mother picks her moments, doesn't she? Doesn't she, Shylah? Right with the Hogarths there . . ."

"Yeah, tell me."

" . . . Her life story, complete with histrionics and falling over the table . . . food everywhere, soup on Mrs. Hogarth's lap, dishes broken. You know, I simply can't go back there now. Your mother's drinking has cost me my name—at least there—

my club, for Christsake. I couldn't look the Hogarths in the eye again . . ."

"Screw, Perdie, why dontcha. I've never seen Mr. Hogarth when he wasn't juiced anyway. You know, you could have been nice to her, nice to Mummy, you could have taken her home right away—you know when those moods come on. You know as well as I do by now."

Another repeat, I should have thought of it before, when I had gone babysitting last night. Mummy and her "little stallion," as she referred to new husband, Perdue Wanamore III, had had that usual head start on martinis. And the fighting, she and I, but I can't remember . . . no, I remember, her dress; we argued about her dress, the length of it, and we argued over Perdie . . . that little prick, with his back copies of *Playboy* and his social register prominent in every room.

The house was large but not that large. There were only four or five places she would go: the bathrooms, the kitchen, the recreation room, the garage. Pills, knives, laundry rope, or gas . . . Mother's imagination in extremes. And I knew her habits so well, I even knew the special expression—the slight droop of lip, the sloping eyes—she'd wear on those miserable occasions. I could tell by looking at her how much and what she had been drinking, the depth and type of her depression.

Yet there were the days when she'd be up, cheerful and up. And we had our mornings together, Mummy and I . . . when I'd be hugged, brought to her by her thin arms, and called Mrs. Tiggywinkle My Own and she'd be cracking dirty jokes over the bacon sandwiches before driving me off to school, to Miss Staunten's, still dressed in her flannel wraparound robe and bedroom bunny slippers. And there was that time on the way we were laughing so hysterically Mummy had to pull the car over till we eased up a little. Then deciding, well, what the hell, it was such a terrific sunny day, we'd forget about school and go shopping together. Our times were morning-bound and Jesus, I hated the nights.

When I found her, Mummy was lying across the front seat of the car. Methodically I turned off the engine. There had been so many dress rehearsals I had no reason to believe this could

4

be more. I believed that somehow the rehearsals were a necessary part of her life and that they would go no further, they would stop upon my appearance and they would cease till the next occurrence. Except now. Her color. In her cheeks the capillaries seemed more apparent, a certain transparency that shaded her purple, violently purple. Sharp, hard pats to the cheeks, not slaps but quick brisk . . . then shaking her, grabbing the shoulders and bringing them forward . . . Dear God, Mother, stop the acting.

"Come on, Mummy, wake up, just help me a little, huh; come on, please, Mummy, please, please. Goddamnit, come on. Don't worry, I'll draw you a bath; wake up, I'm getting tired of this; at least help me—hold on to me. Mummy, for Christsake, M-O-T-H-E-Rrrrrr."

I couldn't get her out. The space between car and garage wall was too small. And this time she gave nothing back, no support, and I could not carry her this way.

The neighbors. I ran across the street to get the young couple who had been so sympathetic in days past. Only it was the babysitter, alone this time, who started to scream and fall apart, who then called her parents, who called the police, who called my stepfather upstairs, and I sat then, cold in my white spring dress, cold in sweat, an arm over the dining-room table, cold. Nothing but cold. And a medical examiner, a young one, saying, bending over me and saying, "You were just a little too late, maybe twenty minutes or so, you know, honey. It's hard to tell about these things."

Death was an event. There were things to do. I called my stepbrother, who came with his wife to take care of Perdie and get me out of sight, to place me in their new guest room with copies of *Life* and *Look*. Because certainly, even at dawn, I would not sleep.

Later in the morning I returned to the house, to tie and untie boxes, to choose Mummy's pearls and favorite cocktail dress and to demand they put her bunny slippers on. I knew it was nonsense, but if they were going to go against her wishes for cremation, the least I could responsibly do was to think in terms of her comfort. I asked again but Perdie wouldn't hear of burn-

5

ing her up to cinders, thinking it was anti-Episcopalian or something.

By afternoon, I called Mummy's sister, Aunt Samantha, who was concerned we not disclose the cause of her death—I was to say she had "passed away suddenly." On Monday, my older brothers returned—Zoe from Boston, Rick from overseas. Then the question of what to do with Shylah was resolved. Our family lawyer disclosed that I was to be the ward of—not my stepfather—but my aunt, Mummy's only sister, who in turn hastened to phone my real father and stepmother on some island and to beg his nuclear kinship. I wasn't, truth will out, in high demand.

Sorrow never really comes at the moment of loss. It seems to need a jelling time. I gave out little grief, wept tears occasionally, but out of confusion not reflection. I had lived through the pain of my mother's death years before it happened, just as I had wept for my beloved shepherd because he was over twelve and I knew he would soon die of old age. And when he did die I had done all my grieving beforehand, there was nothing left to give out. And Mummy was dead, the practicality of that thought kept me busy and in shock. At fourteen I had been running after her, following her suicide rehearsals for three years now. Remember, Shylah, remember the bitterness. God. Lonely, lonely, lonely.

The big colonial house felt as if it had been suddenly gutted . . . to be filled up again by faces and flowers, the mailman bringing condolence letters from the girls at Staunten's, notes that were carefully scripted. I imagined the mothers and nannies dictating what was to be said and what flowers were appropriate for a fourteen-year-old mourner, consulting etiquette books and flower shops for advice. I stayed angry when the phone rang, answering questions bluntly. I had nothing to hide, never gave a shit about hiding, in fact hated hiders. Screw 'em. Then the packing and throwing out, Zoe, Rick helping . . . "You know you can't keep all of this, Shy. Let's give the stuffed animals to an orphanage or something. You're too old for them anyway."

The funeral in that dreary church with the drone of eulogy

6

and Mummy enclosed in mahogany casket in her blue dress and bunny slippers. No blood, no nothing, no evidence to mourn except the mourners, Rick's loud inhalation of grief, Zoe's words of comfort, their blue suits and responsible faces. And who was I that I could not even muster a gasp?

The faces behind me as I turned around from the front pew, high cheeks and small pillbox hats that had been to our house for drinks, looks of determination on Perdie's sons and relatives, perhaps embarrassment, disgust? Were they disgusted, these fine, level-headed Philadelphians? And behind them, the face of the woman whose kids I babysat for, all colors of warmth in dyed orange hair and green dress, whose presence occasioned a dirty look from Perdie's son and his sable-heavy wife. She who brought Mummy homemade babka cake during her frequent illnesses, crossing our property lines from the so-called Jewish section, named because of the modern split-level architecture that burgeoned there on small plots of land. She of the concerned, plump, maternal face that said, "Stay over, why don't you, when things get rough?" She had come, that was something.

When they buried her, I cried. Out of anger, my cheeks tensed and hurting, I cried. This procedure, the embarrassment telling on the stepfamily.

Suicide implies a lack of organization, something social climbers abhor. Giving up that piece of the action strived for. Poor Mummy. What a trap, this phony funeral. In Italy at least everybody knows it's for show, they just go out and hire professional mourners. I had read that somewhere. I had read that.

So I clung for those moments of burial to the arms of my older brothers, intelligent young men who had, at least in part, broken away, who had returned and yet had something else, jobs . . . the responsibilities of intelligent young men . . . giving them the benefit of distance. And I felt they worried like intelligent older brothers, worried about Shylah going off to live with the father in the Florida Keys, both of which sounded somewhat risqué. They had survived him as I had survived him . . . scarred. I knew they knew it was risk. What to do with Shylah concerned them and frightened Shylah. Shylah was not a good girl, she was not a positive girl, she was not a clean and neat girl, she wasn't even a quiet girl, and she was no prize for the living.

★

"I know this is terribly embarrassing. I just keep bursting in tears. I don't understand. I don't understand."

"It's O.K., Perdie. Good for you. You've been through a hell of a lot. Drink, Perdie?"

Mr. Simpson, the lawyer, my stepfather, my brothers, and I sat in the formal living room, the room I knew least, with its newly upholstered formality of red velvet and expensive antiques. Mr. Simpson had been reading the will and dispensing good will in the manner of hired-professional-who-doubles-as-best-friend-when-the-occasion-arises. He poured Perdie a drink from the side bar, slipping the ice in with prongs from the silver bucket, talking simultaneously, as though addressing the ice.

"Shylah, you understand I'm going to keep investing the money for you as executor until you're of age and then you can do as you wish. What we call the dividends, the interest on the money, the money we make, will be sent to your father as acting on your behalf. Now, your Aunt Samantha will keep the antiques and jewels for you, as well as your mother's silver and china. You understand, dear, that your mother wanted you to have these treasures, just as she had them, when you have a family of your own or, legally speaking, when you reach the age of twenty-one."

"Yeah, I understand."

"Boys, after this is finished, I'll need information as to your addresses and bank accounts. Perhaps a drink at the club . . ."

The reading continued, reminding me of a hideous tableau of the Magi in reverse. All the gifts of the dead and my weeping stepfather wondering how the hell it had all come to pass.

★

"Shylah, hurry up. It's time to go," Zoe yelled upstairs.

"Wait, I can't yet, I'm on the john." I had terrible diarrhea, aching diarrhea, and every time I stood up I'd feel my gut pull me back to the toilet.

"I've got some paregoric for you. It'll help. Try and hold it. You gotta make the plane."

"O.K., O.K., wait a second, I'm coming."

Zoe, my older brother, was pegged as the responsible one; Rick—two years younger—the lighthearted brother, seemingly more distant from the chaos. I listened from the confines of the toilet, listened to the familiar and often-missed tones of their voices.

"We'll just have to see how it goes. Maybe Dad has mellowed. I don't know. If she acts up or if he does, I think we should consider a boarding school."

"Yeah, Zoe, but I'm going to be in Europe for at least another two years. It'll be hard for me to keep in touch that way."

"No, I understand that. I can do that part and of course keep you in touch. Who knows, maybe his new wife has calmed him down."

"We'll see how it goes."

"You all set kid? Here, take a swig of this. That's right, it'll constipate you. Everything's in the car ready to go."

I walked out and placed myself in the back of the station wagon. My stepfather and I had said awkward goodbyes, both of us relieved to be out of the presence of the other. Poor bastard, he had led the most conservative of lives. Once.

Rick drove while Zoe talked.

"Look, Shy, you know how rough Dad can be. You gotta be aware of it now and keep out of his way when he gets on a mean drunk. None of your remarks . . . but, listen, if things get beyond you, rough, I mean, if he goes after you or anything, you're to call me. Understand? I want you to call if you're frightened or anything. On the other hand, I think this could be a marvelous adventure for you. The island is Gauguinic in, you know, romantic tropical beauty . . . I'll bet you can swim out the back door . . . you'll be going with a whole different bunch of kids, boys, thank God, none of the rich-kid stuff like around here. It's all hot and lush. Shy, you know how you like the summer best, well, it's always summer . . . lots of boating and swimming and walking around. Think of all the pretty pictures you'll draw down there. Just be cool about it all."

"Will you come for Christmas? Please come for Christmas. It'll be strange without Mummy and without snow. But you'll be there, right? Both of you, you'll be there?"

Rick, who had been driving silently, answered, "I can't get back this year, Shylah, I'm too far away . . . but maybe next year, maybe we'll be together next year."

"I'll come, Shy, I have a teaching break for a month, so I'll drive down, we'll have maybe two weeks or so."

"Oh, what am I talking about anyway? It's only March. Mother's dead, the whole thing's blown to hell anyway. But Christmas was, well, you know, it was so great, wasn't it? I guess that part of it's over now."

"Nervous?"

"A little. I keep wanting to barf and shit at the same time."

Zoe and Rick raced me through the airport. I had to go again, so that took another ten minutes. We didn't have much time. The DC-6 was loading.

"Everything's going to be fine, Shy. Everything's gonna be OK. Give my love to Dad and call when you get home."

"Yes, no, I'm O.K. I'll call, I'll miss you. Be careful, O.K.?"

★

The line of travelers moved through the door and onto the field. I looked back from the plane to catch a last glimpse of brothers, but there was nothing now, just the freshly painted wall of the terminal building. An airfield is a monstrous place to feel alone or lonely in—the large flat spaces, a "terminal"—the name implies death, not vacation to sunny climes. When we took off, the speed on the runway gave me a kind of lift. I asked the stewardess for gin, two little bottles of it and tonic on the side, as I had seen it done in the movies. I knew I could drink gin— Mummy had given it to me herself, for the curse, she said, to take away my cramps. I wanted to get a little high. I saw no reason, since I looked a lot older than fourteen anyway, why I shouldn't begin on a plane. The stewardess didn't either and brought me the two little bottles of gin, tonic water, and even threw in two slices of lime.

We began hitting air pockets, "turbulence," the captain said, over South Carolina, which woke me from an effusion of daydreams and replaced them with confusion and tears. I did not want to be jolted any more; the hard drop of plane underneath me triggered things. My parents, before the divorce, all glamour and misery and violence—the fear of beatings and the jokes. But somehow growing up that way, with their fighting, drinking, his violence, her sanitariums, was the way I thought or assumed everyone grew up. Then Mummy, bandaged ribs, smiling from the hospital, with the cut yellow roses and the lawyer and the messy divorce . . .

The end of her had already begun.

We lost all the jokes and peculiar family traditions. It became harder to be lighthearted, even without the sight of Daddy's fat fists and the brothers gone and growing in colleges and jobs. Then suddenly a past tense on good times and Mummy got more anxious, more depressed, more into the bottle, and I got angrier and fatter. We fought. My grades dropped from scholarship level to C's and D's; Mummy couldn't hack the teacher meetings, and my antisociability became a monster neither she nor I understood.

Perdie arrived to pick up the pieces. Perdie—the safe bet, secure in blue chips and completely lacking in the dangers of a sense of humor. They married and we packed up for Philadelphia, ironically a month after my dog died. A clear path. Mummy cheered up, and I cheered up because she cheered up. I grew slim and adolescent and she enjoyed my sudden physical acceptability by buying me clothes and expensive jewelry. But Perdie I never liked. I never liked him because basically he was neither funny nor adventuresome, and possessed not the tiniest ounce of savoir faire. We, the Dales, were loaded with savoir faire; it poured from us like a staph infection. We entertained. But not Perdie. Perdie was a bore, not even obnoxious— just a guaranteed sleeping pill for any kind of funny conversation. And who needed that? So Mummy began to slip into a kind of depressed, alcoholic narcolepsy around him. It was not, she found out, enough to be secure. And there was no joy in this marriage, only pretensions and his family, which we both loathed.

The truth was, more or less, that her heart still belonged to brutal old Daddy. Poor Perdie, it was all too much for him, with not even a joke or two to fall back on. The drinking bouts began again; Mummy lost herself in nostalgia and I retreated to my room with a box of crayons. And then the attempts began again, a heavy preference this time for monoxide and knives held to her breast. I sort of figured the latter were for show and the former more in earnest. In the knife episodes I think she even liked making me force the knife out of her hand . . . she'd start to smile and get that hard glitter in her eyes. Then it would pass into tears and collapse, which made me crazy—crazy to help her when I knew I couldn't.

I hated playing emotional housekeeper, taking her upstairs, peeling off the clothes, putting on her now-shallow body one of the long, elegant nightgowns, tucking her in, seeing the contortions in her face when she passed out, at last . . . wiping the drool off her chin with the linen hankie she kept by the bed. This lack of organization, her hysteria and wavelike illnesses, infuriated Perdie. I couldn't really blame him. It stood against everything, every earned rung in his social climbing. So, at times like these, he left her to me. And I felt I could do nothing that would not fail her.

Shylah, stop it, don't think that way. I don't want to think I failed her, I don't want to remember her look of vacant pain—that glitter—that cut me out and killed her.

This terror stayed in the back of my mind, but now it lost space to anticipation. Hey, Shylah, you're on your way. Daddy, Daddy, the Eastern life left behind for an island. New life, like new toys, something to play with, to look at, maybe something nice. Maybe something excruciatingly nice.

Daddy. What about Daddy? Last I saw him I was being taken out for a goodbye dinner on the town with a corsage pinned to my smocked dress. And two records, two 78's "Rock Around the Clock" and "Hearts Made of Stone." 1954. And I had diarrhea before and after—"nerves," the doctor said. I didn't want him leaving, bastard that he was. Though he really wasn't a father to me, that kind of blanket giving was not Daddy's strong point. I could remember how he sometimes hated me—once sitting on the bed in his blue shorts and T-shirt, smoking Luckies, he yelled at Mummy, "Betsy, you take that kid away, you take that brat away or I'll kill her, you hear me. I'll kill her." So we stayed with friends that night, me taking the two dolls I called Daughter I and Daughter II, wrapping them in a blanket, making them safe for the getaway. Now this man had been assigned by death to play Daddy again. Daddy, I wanna be loved. Please be mellow. Please, please.

The plane circled Miami Airport. Four hours now, was it? I looked down at the squares of water, the squares of pink-stucco houses, the viaducts, and the ocean. What looked like open banana peels dotted the landscape and emerged as palm trees when we descended below the last bunch of clouds. I took out my forbidden compact and forbidden lipstick and forbidden eyebrow pencil and began painting. The palms of my hands were soggy again and the makeup job suffered from streakiness. Looking into the mirror brought out a vague feeling of disgust. Mummy had had that long, graceful look that made others call her a beauty, at least once they did. Seeing myself now, the changing contours of my face with nothing of Mummy evidenced, the eyes almost pretty but with a cast to them, the too big jaw, the too short nose; at least the mouth was O.K. and my skin was good. I'd never felt myself to be more than awkwardly attractive, especially now, all five foot nine inches of me squashed into my seat. I gathered myself together and went to the john and whacked my wiry hair into temporary submission, making spit curls at the ears and temples like the latest movie mag picture of Gina Lollobrigida. I returned to my seat and buckled up, and bit my nails till one of them, the right thumb, exposed pink flesh and bled in a line over the fingernail's moon.

We hit the runway.

"Good afternoon, ladies and gentlemen, this marks the termination of Flight 304. The temperature in Miami is a sunny 83. Please remain seated with seat belts fastened until the plane comes to a complete stop. We hope you have enjoyed flying Delta and will join us again. Please check to see you have all your belongings before you depart. Thank you, and on behalf of the crew and myself, we wish you a very pleasant stay in Florida."

Hot air surprised me as I walked off the overly air-conditioned plane and down the steps onto the pavement. The landscape around me seemed to have been sandpapered into brush flatness. It could have been Mars and I could have been a time-traveling amnesiac. Some Brillo eraser had polished off the retentive points of my brain. Good. Reinjected with new patterns, perhaps I could even finesse the scars.

2

"Hello, Daddy's little baby girl. How's my precious angel, how is she, huh? Yesssss."

"Hi, Daddy. Hello, uh, Alice."

"We're just sooo excited to have you here, sugar, honest-to-God. I know we're gonna hit it off, and you know, there's no one in the world who missed y'all more than your daddy. In't that raght, Corky? Did y'all eat on the plane, cutie, huh? We got this great Bar-B-Que place we gonna go to tonight."

Jesus, I couldn't even understand what they were saying. Four years ago my father had worn J. Press suits and talked like Ronald Colman. Now, in his fuchsia linen jacket and string tie, with a new flaming-red mustache, he looked like an advertisement for a Baptist crusade.

And Alice, Daddy's bride, was not at all what I knew about mothers and womanhood. Something new and totally foreign. I had been trained at Staunten's to recognize good taste as opposed to bad taste. It was always assumed a person showed one or the other. But all taste? Alice bloomed like a Sunday-night smorgasbord. Matter-of-fact-looking, wearing a perfume I used to buy on the sly at Woolworth's, Cuban shoes, matronly hippy in a pleasant way, short, tightly curled hair, harlequin sunglasses, and a plastic pocketbook with a felt turquoise monkey in the side. I giggled. Flamboyant, a word used by Philadelphia matrons when they wanted to put down nouveau-riche ladies encroaching on the society page. The kind of thing I envied. And Alice talked. A non-stop talker. The words blew out her nose, giving her Southern slur a hard cast. I could tell in the first five minutes that Alice's only sworn enemy was silence.

Between them and the airport I was amazed by the bizarre pinwheels of color everywhere—like looking into barrels of tutti-fruitti and raspberry sherbet in an ice cream shop. Men in fluorescent shirts passed, women in mink stoles and toreador pants with wispy wheat-like hair passed; the shops gleamed with rainbow clothing; Southern voices filtered down upon the ears like butterscotch sauce. And then I almost went in a colored ladies' room, on account of my bladder, but Alice grabbed my arm, steering me into the door marked WHITE. Inside the room everything had been painted powder pink. Even the toilet bowl was pink and the women fixing their hair were dark tan and wore that same pink with fluffed and spun coiffures and spike heels and thin-strapped sundresses, and there I was in my regulation navy linen suit, white gloves, and a garter belt that assaulted my legs with metal fasteners. But mostly it was the array of eye makeup that fascinated me. The blues and greens and mauves, and the thick black lines over and under the eyes. Philadelphia for me was best described in navy-blue terms, with an occasional yellow knee sock or red blazer, and women wore specially blended powder and Fire and Ice lipstick, and that was it. It was the same monochrome scheme of loose twills and tweeds, support shoes, John Frederics slung hats, and a jungleful of dead animals thrown over the shoulders.

Alice went and got the Cadillac, while Daddy and I waited with the baggage. I'd never ridden in a Cadillac. Rollses and Packards, yes, but Caddies flunked Staunten's taste test, except perhaps for black limos. They were acceptable. But not *this* Cadillac . . . powder blue with royal-blue interior and automatic everything. I thought it magnificent, like owning your own Ford bubble-gum machine. Jesus, the toys they had down here. No wonder Daddy spoke Southernese so fluently. I'd just have to practice.

"You just relax and enjoy yourself, sugar, we gotta long ride ahead."

"How many miles away is Lime Island?"

" 'Bout hundred forty; it takes a while but it's the prettiest ride. We're gonna make a few stops in Homestead first, though."

"Do we have to take a ferry or anything? I mean, it's an island, right?"

"Right, lambie. But the Keys're all connected up by the overseas bridges and Highway 1. It's really sumpin, Shylah. Why, we got a bridge seven miles long."

"Seven miles, you're kidding?"

"You just wait, sweetness. It boo'ful. Right, Father?"

"Raght, Mother, you gonna see the prettiest view down here, daughter. Ah mean the prettiest. Ummmm uhhh. We stoppin at the liquor store in Perrine, raght. Yah and I want to check out those shirts we looked at."

"Yes, dear, and maybe we get baby something to change into, little outfit or sumpin. You must be frying in that navy blue. Be more comfy in some nice Bermudas and a little top, and I'll bet you could use a pair of flip-flops—that's sandals, hon. Then we go to Piggly Wiggly and stock up. You just tell me what y'all eat, Shy dear, what special candy and junk; you like pizza and spaghetti and steak and hamburger and . . ."

"Turn off here, Mother, you piss-awful on that turn, woman, goddamnit, every time."

"I missed it on purpose, Corky, they're doing construction. Can't you see? Easier the long way."

"Oh yeah, I do see, look at those black sons of bitches sweat. Jeesus, thank God for convicts."

The stop in Homestead, last town on the mainland before the beginning of the Keys, took an hour and a half. Daddy spent twenty minutes or so in Johnnie's, the local pub, a couple of quickies, and Alice took me around, Bermudaed, topped, and cheap plastic-sandaled me. For the car ride, she took out four Royal Castle hamburgers with fried onions, french fries, a strawberry shake, which she explained I might munch on the way down. Perched on what looked like a Parker House roll, they were the smallest hamburgers I'd ever seen. I wondered if hamburgers in the tropics were built smaller—like the size of large chocolate drops. But the best thing was the toothpick topped by a rebel flag that stuck out from the bun. Well-saluted hamburgers. Toys, Shylah, toys.

★

Below Homestead and Florida City lies twenty miles or so of mangrove swamp with occasional views of ocean. Highway 1 travels the tangled monotony in practically a straight line, the two-lane traffic speeding to get out of its boredom. It frightened me, this stretch. The sameness of it and then passing trucks and cars at seventy miles an hour is a trick on two lanes with no real shoulder to the road, just marsh. Alice drove, Daddy looked around, and I was in back—I looked around at the back of their heads and at the clothes I had on from the discount store, clothes I had never known before, some new uniform of location.

Jewfish Creek is one tiny drawbridge, a motel, café, and boat basin. It marks, rather a sign just beyond it marks, the beginning of the Florida Keys, a scorpion's tail of islands running to the southwest for 130 miles or so. The transparent aquamarine water looked mostly shallow, dotted with mangrove and sandbar. Coral rock and small prefab or stucco houses, some built on stilts or just built-up solid slabs of concrete called, I was told, Hurricane Houses, stood visible to the highway after the first mangrove-laden miles of North Key Largo. Little bars, superettes, a school, a Spanish-style church, a police station, motels with names like Mullet, Tropicana, Sailfish, Turtle, and Palm lined the road in small clusters. Now and then both the Gulf of Mexico and the Atlantic could be seen when the islands were at a particularly skinny point. None was over a few miles wide anyhow.

In contrast to the stark white of the coral and architecture and the sometimes-aqua, sometimes-green color of the water, the bush flowers, climbers, and plants that abounded seemed almost noisy in their beauty. Red, pink, yellow, and tan hibiscus vied with the orange-crimson combined to make frangipani;

purply bougainvillea hung on fences surrounding Bidy Tropico–type motels and trailer parks. Towns passed us with names out of Robert Louis Stevenson . . . Tavernier, Plantation, Isla-morada, Matecumbe, Indian, Vaca, Duck, Big Pine, Marathon, Bahia Honda. From the seven-mile bridge and from the added height of the Bahia Honda bridge, I could see the direction line of the islands and the clear expanse of indefatigable blue-green waters meeting, so rich upon eyes accustomed to matte grays.

Lime Island lay below Bahia Honda. A separate little off-road from Highway 1 led to a bridge that connected the smaller finger of land to the bigger key—about a quarter mile in distance. It was, of course, what everything else was down here, a resort paradise—but with a slightly higher economic level of ac-tivity—the best fishing guides, the best fish, the best fishing, the best swimming, that kind of thing, and the local residences reflected their affluence. Three movie stars had homes here, one President got drunk here, the world's most arrogant and superb golfer lived here, Alice said. It was when we traversed the tiny bridge with its flared curve and Lime lay emerald and sculptured before us—it was then that I began to have that won-derland sense of things—as if I had stepped into a 2:00 a.m. movie starring Dorothy Lamour and a cast of a thousand motels.

"Here we are, Shy. Can't get much closer to the water than this, can you, honey? Yourrrr newwww hommmme, dear, wel-come, welcome."

"Jesus."

"Y'all can do better than that, daughter."

"Yeah, but . . . I guess I'm a little overwhelmed. I mean, I've never even seen half the flowers in the yard before— Oh, that boat over there, that yours? And, and this grass. What do you do to it? It's like a trampoline and—"

"You know what that tree is over there, Shy, the one at the far end with the brown balls? That's a . . ."

"Brown balls to you too, Mother."

"That there's a sapodilla tree and inside those brown ba—in-side the fruit is the most delicious-tasting pulp. Just you taste this, baby."

The apple-size, rough-covered ball separated to reveal pinkish flesh, sugary and delicious; she was right. Next to it were limes, and next to the limes, guava, coconut palms, hibiscus, jasmine, frangipani. On the ground, Japanese mat grass sucked in my feet and sprung them back again, like a marshmallow trampoline. And then the house that rambled around on one story, a white-stucco structure with kelly-green shutters, glass partitions, terrazzo floors—it stood there, close enough to the ocean to cast a line out from the Florida room.

"And here's the baaaby's room."

Alice's voice, oozing coated baby talk, was beginning to make the edges of my lip curl. It flowed from her, the endless chocolate vocabulary. We moved my luggage into the pink chintz teenage decor she had or must have had designed. My twin beds were flounced and bolstered, my beauty table wore a long pink skirt, on the walls were two Keene prints of children with hydrocephalic heads and eyes like the dogs in "The Tinder Box" fairy tale. It was dreadful, and for that reason and for her efforts on my behalf, I liked my new room, was delighted by it. Newness, Shylah. A different taste to things.

"And here's Joe Joe and Tootiekat come to greet you." Alice's basset hound and tomcat were encouraged through the door.

"Say hello to the baby, say hello to Shylahgirl, boys, idawid-dawiddawidda."

The animals surveyed me with their noses, the basset I immediately saw as sympathetic friend.

"How 'bout a swim before dinner, dear? Daddy and I are going to take a dip."

"O.K., be out in a minute, gotta find my suit."

The water proved thick, very salty, and warm, at first slowing my attempts at a breast stroke to a crawl; then picking up again, I swam to the first sandbar and watched the meanderings of a crawfish directly in front of me. The five o'clock sun mellowed and soothed. I lay back on the sand a while, listening to the new and distinctive sounds of life on Lime.

"Time to come in, lambie, come on—we'll have some drinks on the patio. Maybe you meet some of our neighbors, huh?"

Too good to last. I swam the short way back to the dock, where Alice and Daddy stood toweling themselves down. Paradise. Looking out from the sandbar into the changing colors of sun-struck water had been paradise. I resented Alice's big mouth blasting its way into my first impressions, resented it even while obeying the call to join them.

An inboard motorboat whipped close and across from the sandbar, bearing a boy and girl, my age or a little older, I guessed. They slowed and waved to us, then cut the motor and tied up on the dock next to ours.

"How y'all, Miz Alice. Hi, suh."

"O.K., boy, how you doin? Hey, my girl's down, come meet Shylah."

"Be raght over, suh, gotta get this stuff in first."

Alice had gone in the house to return with Cokes and bourbon, crawfish meat, smoked fish, lime slices, and potato chips. Daddy and I sat in the deck chairs on the dock. The two kids moved slowly over toward us from the property next door.

"This mah daughter, Shylah, she goin' to be livin' down here. This is Luanne and C. J. Cooper. Luanne, ah think you two in the same class, in'it eighth grade?"

"Yes, suh, hi, Shylah; you gonna be at Palm View too?"

"Uh . . ."

Alice broke in. "That's your new school, honey; yes, she's starting Monday."

"That's sure nice. Guess I'll see yah at the bus, Shylah."

"Guess so."

"Coke, anyone?"

"Yes, please, Miz Alice."

"Yes, please, Miz Alice."

"You're in eighth, huh? I'm in tenth," said C.J.

"Oh yeah."

The sun was setting now, commanding what little attention I had left. Purple, black, orange, and red off the changing waters. There were no interruptions to this view, just the grandeur of solid horizon. Seemed to me like fingerpainting on the sky, the thickness of the sudden onslaught of dying day. A scorpion wandered across the dock in front of me.

"Another one of these bastards, look at that." Daddy stamped out at the thing and demolished it.

"Ooh, Jesus, are there a lot of those things?"

"Waaaallll, you just gotta watch where you step. Best to cover up your feet."

"Nuther bourbon, Corky?"

"Jus pour a little in the glass, dear."

"A quick one, Daddy, we gotta think 'bout feeding Shy, that new Bar-B-Que. I don't know how crowded it's gonna be."

Luanne and C.J. and I kind of sat and stared at one another. It's so awkward when parents instigate friendships for their kids. It went against the grain, made me feel nervous and slightly asinine.

Delicate, with down-sloping eyes and bobbed brown hair, Luanne was pretty in a compelling way. Her brother, C.J., however, was antihypnotic, the tenth-grade smartass with Vaselined DA hair who exuded a puslike repulsiveness. And he had the habit of looking me up and down so that I'd know what the score was. Only I didn't know what the score was. I forgot him instantly and focused my attention on Luanne.

" 'Lowwww, Corky, Alice, hi, kids. That Shylah? How you get such a pretty thing, Corky, y'old son of a bitch? Goddamnit." Bobby Jay Leads, our famous neighbor, hung over the fence of his property, showing perfect white teeth in broad winning smile.

" 'Lowwww, Bobby Jay, come heah, boy, have a drink. Been fishing?"

"Yeah, went out for some bonefishing with a bunch of sportscaster stiffs. Jeesus, I do earn my liquor."

Luanne and lugubrious C.J. excused themselves on account of dinner at home, left us, walking the six hundred feet back to their place. Alice and I went in to change for dinner.

"Bobby Jay, you wanna join us at this new Bar-B-Que place? Thought we'd have a look, take the daughter."

"Meet you there, Corky, gotta tend to little bizness first."

★

The Bar-B-Que restaurant and bar hung over the water at the far side of the island. An organist played "Love Is a Many-Splen-

2 2

dored Thing" and "Theme from *The High and the Mighty*" and others, but they all sounded like the first two. Crowded. Lots of bright-colored sport shirts, lots of bleached-blond, curly hair. Everyone knew everyone.

From the gathering I could tell how much people down here liked Daddy and Alice, the way they came up in clusters and laughed and joked and cooed over them. I was by far the youngest at the shindig—populated by older adults mostly, a few young married couples. Then Bobby Jay came in and took the sport shirts and curls, the kisses and backslapping, upon himself and away from Daddy and Alice. Even if he hadn't been able to tell a putter from a number 4, he'd still stand out as slightly heroic. There was that bigness, that tanness; even when everyone else was burnt umber, he appeared burnt-umber velvet. Movie-star handsome.

And Bobby Jay moved through the sport shirts and curls to where I sat, remained there for the duration, attentive.

I didn't know about men—I didn't know how to distinguish between fathers and uncles and step-related men and men's reasons and boys' reasons. I was inclined to be nice to anybody who was nice to me, to anyone who sounded as if he wouldn't hit me. So I talked a lot to this man, this gorgeous-but-ancient Bobby Jay Leads, who must have been at least thirty-eight or so, watched him drink rum, watched him keep me in Cokes throughout the greetings and We-gotta-new-little-conch-down-heah-meet-Shylah-Dale business. "In't she cute, uh huh?"

"Shylah, you're the sexiest li'l thing, wait till all those yokel boys see you. They'll be creaming, scuse mah French, but you better watch yourself. Corky says you been to an all-girls school—it's a little different down here."

"Yeah, I see. These ribs are really great."

"They got a smokehouse out back, that's why. Here, why don't you taste these shrimp— Ah mean it, Corky, you got yourself a li'l angel here."

"She's no angel, this'un."

Daddy was drunk; I remembered the look and the slur— So, I guessed, was Bobby Jay—with the drinks replenished and the mounds of food brought by platinum-blond waitress with the irritated ass my father kept attending. A certain mean tightness showed on his face, while Bobby Jay just became more physical, touchy, and affectionate—looser.

Alice was stone-cold sober as Alice was always stone-cold sober. The quintessence of the drunkard's wife, driving the car, picking up the food and booze tabs as if she had invented responsibility. Workable and in control. Now, why didn't I like her, why didn't I? I was predisposed to, I wanted to, but she put me off. All that cooing affection, which left me with a queasy feeling that she had no real responses, no responses at all. I felt myself to be a walking, exposed nerve. I could do without her power of control then, beneficial or not.

God, Shylah, tired—all bombarding of faces and scenery when nothing fits together to make a whole—I wanna go home.

★

From where I lay upon the bed, I could look out through the glass-slat windows onto the yard. The breeze fluttered the curtains, subtle, just a little disturbance in the air, soothing, like a slow waltz rhythm upon everything it touched, always there— lightly tender. Mummy, Shylah, the mother in the breeze. I played with the thought. Nothing of the day stuck yet, nothing I wanted to think about. I heard Daddy coughing, sometimes uttering gibberish in the snorting of his sleep. Pushing my head between two pillows, I concentrated on crotch and thighs, the wind's intrusion there, warmth, and refused myself any more excursions into personal history.

★

"Shyyyyylah, Shyeeeeelllaaahh, baby lamb, you alive in there? Come on out and have some sticky buns and fresh papaya."

"Morning. What time is it?"

"Eleven-thirty . . . somebody was a tired girl last night, uh huh."

"Oooohhh, look who's here, the Duchess— Hello, daughter."

"Hi, Daddy. God, it's hot out."

"Daddy and I have some errands to run and then we're going to stop over at friends'; you make your bed nicely, dear, and then maybe you'll want to scout around. We'll see y'all later on."

"O.K."

I sat awhile at the glass table in front of the glass windows that stared at the water. I had not eaten papaya before and picked my teeth of the stringy fibers, retasting the sweetness. I poured out the last of the buttermilk, absentmindedly petting Joe Joe the basset on his long-distance snout.

"Hi, boy. Hi, Joe Joe; come on, Joe Joe, don't be sad, aw, Joe Joe."

The dog was nonplused, sniffing over at the door.

"Me too, Joe Joe; wait, I'll put my clothes on."

Brushing my teeth with the funny-tasting tap water brought in on a pipeline from the mainland, I squinted at my reflection in the medicine chest. Ugh.

Outside, the close-to-noon sun was a broiler. Sweat sprung from my jersey underarms and the crotch of my Bermudas. Joe Joe followed me about the front yard, sniffing. I pulled down a coconut, too green and hard to be ripe— I put my nose into the buds of jasmine and hibiscus. Garden spiders, huge in span yet delicate, gleamed, their webs holding the sunlight off the garage. Oh Jesus, everything so damn wild, I could burst with it.

"Hiya, Shylah. How was your first night on the Keys?"

"Oh hi, Luanne, it was O.K. We went to that restaurant, you know, the one that opened last night?"

"Wanna go have a Coke at Treenie's. Thought y'all maght lahk to come."

"Yeah, sure, sure I wanna come."

I took Joe Joe back in the house, heard him baying from the screen door as we walked down the small road.

"How old are you?"

"Fourteen; how old are you?"

"I'll be fourteen in October. I'm the youngest in the class."

"You look older though. What's Treenie's?"

"It's a Coke and hamburger place, you know, a hangout, ah

2 5

guess. Ah'm gonna meet my boy friend on his lunch break. On weekends he does construction over at Boca for Orville Reese. Thought you'd like to meet a couple of the guys. He's in eleventh grade; they all juniors and seniors."

Treenie's, the homemade banana ice cream and Key lime pie, thatched-roofed base for teenagers. A place so convivial in the Southern way, a sixteen-plus could opt for eating in his or her car and still talk to the people seated at the two umbrellaed tables outside. When we arrived, the boys were there, standing outside their cars—strange-looking animals with slicked hair and pointed shoes, a look of boredom upon their faces and the gift of the monosyllabic for conversation. I was terrified.

"Hey, Luuuuuuuannnnne."

"Hey, Luuuuuuuannnnne."

"Let's sit down."

"Whaddoyuhwant?"

"Who's your friend, Luanne?"

"This is Shylah, guys. She's Mr. Corky's daughter."

"Hi yuh."

"Hi."

"Howdy."

"Hi, everybody."

"You in eighth with Luanne, Shylah? . . . You wanna Coke or somethin?"

"Yes, in eighth grade; O.K., a Coke."

The four boys went in and ordered our Cokes and their lunches. Giggling, they looked back at us, gesturing about the new action that had come to the island.

"Well, you've given them something to gossip about, it'll be all over the island before the afternoon's past. Watch out for the oldest, Johnny, he's a make-artist. Ah heard that Lena, that's a girl in our class, went all the way with him at the luau."

Sounds of dimes in the jukebox inside played the Shirelles, "Will You Still Love Me Tomorrow?" I contemplated escape. I didn't know anything about Lime decorum. I didn't know how to be monosyllabic. I didn't know anything except from dancing class, and there the boys wore white gloves and appeared docile—in dancing class the girls ran the show. But these guys,

2 6

they might as well be a meeting of Einsteins—they'd say things I didn't catch—they'd make-out and I wouldn't know how to kiss—they'd crack jokes I wouldn't understand.

It made me think of my recent past in Philadelphia, where I had ritually turned on the TV set every afternoon after school to watch American Bandstand, envying those kids their tight sweaters, flats, bleached hair, as opposed to my uniform, and ultimately their coolness, the network of friendships and new dance styles they invented. Damn you, Luanne, damn you and your slow-talking ease.

"Shylah, you wanna double with Harry and me tonight? We're just goin to an Elvis picture; *Jailhouse Rock* finally worked its way down here. We're the boonies—yah gotta go to Miami or Key West for anything new. Anyhow, Mick, that's Harry's friend, the blond one, he'd be your date. Well, you want to?"

"I don't know if I can. I mean, I've got to check first."

"And if your folks say it's O.K., you can stay over at mah house."

"That'd be great. I'll ask, O.K? I mean, I don't know if they want me or anything, for tonight, I mean."

"O.K."

The boys filed out of Treenie's with trays of food and Cokes, somnambulatory and good-looking, and shining like the french fries.

"So tell me, Shylah, y'all must have just gotten here. We would have known for sure—seen you around—so where you coming from— Mah name's Johnny, by the way."

"Philadelphia."

"Well, you sure a nahce addition to the palm trees, I'll tell you that much."

"So what's the plan, Harry?" said the male indicated by Luanne to be Mick.

Luanne replied, "She's gotta check first for time and stuff." (Referring to me, as if I were somehow out of the picture— Luanne, my lawyer.) Mick nodded to me evenly. I guessed people didn't usually do this first-dating thing head-on.

"Well, Mick, yah beat me to it."

"Yah, nice try, creepness."

"Hey, Bert, wanna do some running to Marathon? We got turtle races down here, Shylah— Hey man, Shylah. That's some name. Anyhow, you know what a turtle race is?"

Luanne cut in, "Don't pay him no mind, Shy, he's got his nigger's mind on things besides turtles."

The other boys laughed.

"To you too, Luanne. Come on, Bert, we gotta get moving."

"Yeah, I s'pose. S'long, Luanne; uh, s'long, Shy, Shylah. See yuh."

Harry and Luanne had been holding hands under the table. Mick stared sullenly at me while I wore my best wet-my-pants smile.

"So maybe I'll see you tonight?"

"Well, I have to ask my parents first."

The boys went back to the job and we walked up the road. Heat—certainly the hottest sun I'd been under. There were already sweat half-moons in the armpits of my jersey. I kept my arms down, self-consciously trying with my nose cocked to see if I smelled bad. Luanne talked steadily about Harry and school and colored people known as "niggers" and anyone peculiar to her called "queers." She used expressions I could understand only from context. I liked Luanne, though she wasn't very kind about colored people or queers or whatever. Maybe I could go tonight and it would work out O.K. and I wouldn't vomit or get raped or have a bugger in my nose or anything gross. Maybe it would be O.K. We parted for the day at our properties' divide. I said I'd come over later whether I could go or not.

The house was cool, refreshing, as I entered it. Feeling an especially strong need to go lie down in the bedroom and play with myself, I begrudged Daddy and Alice's presence, sitting in the Florida room, back from wherever.

"Heeere's the baby. How'd it go, Shy? Did'ya meet some of the boys? Daddy and I passed Treenie's and saw y'all there."

"Yes, it was O.K. Luanne wants to know if I can go to the movies with her and Harry and this boy, Mick, and then stay over at her house. I said I had to check."

"Sounds like fun, doesn't it, Corky?"

2 8

"You watch yer ass, sister—behave yourself."

"I will. So I can go, right?"

"Of course you can, dear, of course. Raght, Father?"

"Raght, Mother."

My father had been sitting in his rocking chair, eyeing me, a little into the afternoon drunk, one and a half sheets as opposed to three sheets to the wind. I thought, then . . . he had spoken little to me, a few public words here and there, not a word about Mummy, and he had not touched me or looked at me straight on, at least not when we were alone. It was, to him, as if nothing had happened before the phony Southernness, not even me. So it was to be Alice who handled, Alice who took care, and Alice who decided my concerns. I grit my teeth, went in, and lay down, thinking that as long as events kept happening at this pace, I'd be kept too well entertained to grieve. Joe Joe came up to my bed and propped himself vertically against the mattress with his stubby paws, his snout to my face.

"Aw, Joe Joe, good boy, good boy." I wondered if we didn't look somewhat alike, or if we didn't give off the same feeling of graduated chaos.

"Shyyyylahhh, telephone."

"Hullo . . . oh hi, Mick, yeah, I can go, yeah, she knows. Seven-fifteen, right, at Luanne's."

"Was that Mick Buckbee, dear?"

"Is that his last name? Yes."

"Isn't it nice y'all have a date already. My popular little lamb."

Shove it up your ass, Alice, how can you, how can you call someone you barely know by all those revolting names, like I was three years old? How can you talk this shit to me? Why, what's the point of doing it? You don't even put it together, bitch, that possibly I don't know what to say to that boy or how to kiss or anything. And you, Alice, you want everything to be comfortable, and I don't fit.

I walked back into my room and brought out my baby-doll pajamas, toothbrush, makeup, and then I didn't know what people wore on dates . . .

"Allllicccce, what should I wear? I don't know what to wear."

"Shorts or capri pants. We're very informal down here."

No kidding. My round-collared, circle-pinned shirts and tartan Bermudas didn't fit in, dumb Yankee prep-schooly Shylah. There was that red and blue pair of capris, the ones I had picked out myself at Bonwit's, and I had one appropriately little top. I put all the stuff in my overnighter and set off for Luanne's. I wanted to get out of the house before dark.

Luanne's parents were entertaining company. Like Daddy and Alice, they were always entertaining something or somebody. Cal and Juna Cooper came toward me, all solid and relaxed-looking. I liked them.

"Why, Shylah, Cal and ah have heard sooo much about you. C'mon in, girl, let's have a look. Have y'all eaten? Luanne, Shylah's here."

"Hi, Luanne."

"Wanna have some turtle steak and Coke?"

"Turtle, real turtle? Yes, sure, I guess so."

Luanne filled two plates full of food, motioning me into her room. The turtle steaks turned out to look like and taste like breaded veal cutlets, thank God, something that wouldn't make me gag. While we ate, she kept a running conversation about how nobody on the Keys except the older conches was from the Keys, mostly from northern Florida, Georgia, Alabama; going on to theories about what a good reputation meant and getting felt up and the niggers and the queers and the dirty Cubans and the cute boys from Marathon and next year trying for cheerleader. Later we showered and dressed and brushed and penciled and perfumed and Odoronoed our armpits. I was watching Luanne all the time, her easy panther slink, elegant in nonchalance, her tight little tits, her arrogant hip swing. I had loped my way through three girls' schools, had much to learn for survival.

★

Mick's arm hung on my shoulder in sweat and silence for the two hours of movie, news, and raunchy cartoon. Afterward, we raced in Harry's car, winding up at Submarine Beach—Southern bedroom to the unmarried high-school set. Here the experts at above-the-belly surrender necked furiously till the eleven o'clock curfew. Luanne and Harry centered themselves in front of the sponge dice cubes hanging from the rearview mirror. They began. Slow, arduous kisses, arms about each other, shifting smoothly back and forth like the tide, occasionally whispering secrets, occasionally the only answer a persistent growl from one or the other's stomach. I sat mute in the back seat, Mick's hand holding mine, capturing in our joined palms a lagoon of sweat. It was too much, the assumed feasting of each other's lips and arms when I hadn't yet begun, except in dreams. I suggested a walk on the beach, something, anything, to delay or at worst get comfortable. Mick, I guessed, was a decent-enough guy, though the breed was still a little foreign to me. Good-looking, boyish, quiet, laughing at everything because it seemed easier than articulation. I guessed he was O.K. We walked, kicking the sand, his arm again on my soggy shoulders. At least we could talk if we wanted—but not in the car, not in Harry and Luanne's love chamber.

"So how y'all like the island?"

"It's pretty down here; beautiful, I guess. And I like the water, warmer, clearer than up North."

"Yeah. You're a nahce girl, Shylah. Ah like you."

"Oh, thanks. Thanks, Mick. Umm, what grade did you say you were in?"

"Eleventh. Thinkin about quittin though. My daddy's a fishing guide. Just bought another boat. Says I kin have the old one if I want it. Thought I'd go into business."

"But you've only got one more year till you graduate."

"Yeah, ah know, but ah gotta make some money. School's for shit anyway. We don't really learn nothin practical. Be one thing if ah went to college but ah'm not—not to be a guide, that's for damn sure. Ah totaled mah Chevy two weeks ago or else we wouldn't be doublin with Harry 'n Luanne. So ah need to save some money. Why dontcha cum heah, Shylah?"

I puckered my lips and closed my eyes. It was awful. That wasn't the way you did it at all. Mick's open mouth swallowed me, so that I came away from the embrace with a saliva mustache.

"You shakin? You cold or sumthin? It's O.K., ah really lahk you."

"No, I'm O.K., I like you too."

The second time we kissed I didn't pucker but opened my mouth as if to say "how." It was better; this time we matched up, Mick closing his lips a little. Since the second worked, I liked the third kiss and relaxed in his arms, feeling the little hairs on them brush mine. When he tried for the fourth kiss, I declined, deciding it was better to part from this experience on the promise of more kissing. Mick acquiesced. I guessed I had responded in the proper way for someone learning the language. We returned to Luanne and Harry, who were making an acute angle now in the front seat.

"Hi, you guys, guess it's about that time, huh?" Luanne chirped and reached for her lipstick and hairbrush. I copied her, reaching for my comb and compact. Harry went through the weight-shifting process of the sexually aroused, finally working himself into the driver's seat. He patted his DA with his hands, glancing into and adjusting the rearview mirror. It seemed O.K., this kissing business, once the terror had subsided.

I critiqued the evening, the new kissing, with Luanne as soon as we were safe behind the closed door of her room, then slept the night in the other twin bed, comfortable in my knowledge and reprieved.

3

Palm View School rested near a bed of mangroves beside the ocean. Pink and green stucco with a series of outdoor corridors leading to classrooms and offices, the school serviced white girls and boys from ages six to eighteen living on any one of six islands south of Marathon. That first morning, under careful tutelage from Luanne as to makeup, crinolines, cinch belt, sundress . . . all borrowed from her . . . freshly shaved armpits exuding Odorono, I mounted the school bus and traveled the ten miles to compulsory education.

"Y'all, this is Shylah Dale, Mr. Corky's daughter."

"Hi, ah'm Cindy."

"Ah'm Selma Annnne."

"Rosemary."

"Everina . . . well, mah nickname's Bubbles."

"Cause nobody can stand her name."

"Thanks, Luanne, ah need you, ah really do, huh."

"How come they call you Bubbles?" I asked.

"Cause she's got a bubble butt," interjected Cindy, blond-cheerful and dwarfed by at least four petticoats.

"You know what ah heard 'bout you, Cindy Lee, so ah'd button mah old nigger lips if ah was you."

"Ha ha. Least ah don't wear mah green petticoats on Thursday lahk you, girl."

"Naw, you don't wear em on Thursday cause you never change what you got on to begin with, yoh queerness," replied Cindy.

The bell for homeroom and the beginning of the school day brought the easy banter, barbed but seemingly playful, to an end. Flanked by the girls nodding and saying hi's—sometimes desultory for upper-class kids and sometimes regal for seventh-graders—we walked or swayed to the classroom.

Mrs. Letitia Gladstone wore sandals and crooked eyeglasses, which she used to spy me over. Luanne introduced us, calling her Miz Letty.

"So you're Alice's child. Well, you'll be over there in the third row."

"No, I'm Corky Dale's daughter. Alice is my stepmother."

"We say ma'am around here, honey. Well, Miz Alice is a good friend of mine, she already told me about you. You jes settle in now, take a few days to find out where we are . . . all right there, Duke, Clarence—siddown, you hear me . . ." Miz Letty was off, calling attention to classroom order. I took my seat, my five foot nine inches towering over the parallel heads of my peers.

"Intercoms on. Stand and pledge." We stood and pledged our allegiance to the intercom, the little brown box below the clock that clicked, and next to the flag. After that we bowed our heads or played with our pencils while a quavering male voice over the box repeated the morning prayer . . . The end of it signified by our aaaaamens and a static signal that the intercom had terminated its morning function.

"All raghht, class, settle down raght now. Ah guess you see we gotta new student's gonna be with us. This is Shylah Dale from Lime Island. I 'spect everyone, ah said everyone, to be helpful to her, her first days at Palm View. Stanley, ah see your mouth flap once more you get the paddle, ah don't wanna see any you boys foolin round, you know what ah mean . . . O.K.! Open your civics books to page 38. Shylah, here's a book for you. Sometime today Luanne can take you to the office and get your permanent books and supplies. Everina, start readin from the second paragraph . . ."

The boys, leering through their sweet-faced cherubicality, glanced at me and giggled. On the backs of their pants was the single little belt; their hair carefully pulled into one solitary drip of lock launched on the center of their overworked foreheads. They crossed their legs into a 90-degree angle and fidgeted. The girls crossed their legs, secretary-style, and flapped the supported leg back and forth in an off-rhythm with each other. Desks creaked, Miz Letty droned, the bell rang . . . filling me with a nasty feeling that I had fallen into a nightmare of manner and gesture and language which I was incapable of grasping. It left me terrified, and it continued, the terror, throughout that first awkward week.

★

Lena, affectionately called the "class whore," had it in for me. I didn't know why. There seemed to be no reason; I even liked her. I liked her because of her studied sullenness, her estrangement, things I felt too—but because of my parents' prestige, I was more acceptable, at first, that is. It didn't last for long. I committed the faux pas of nervous conversation. I argued in home ec about niggers being called Negroes, I talked about the girls from girls' school—how Eloise had had a crush on Judy. It got around. The transplanted Yankee amid the flowers of the eighth grade.

"Hey, Yankee bitch, we don't want no nigger-loving queer Yankee bitch around here. Why don't y'all get the hell back up Nowth with the rest of the nigger lovers?"

Lena's grudge, as it turned out, was that I had ignored her for the more acceptable girls, by her way of thinking. Actually, it had been a feat of proximity—that Luanne lived next door and these were her friends, the clique. I thought I was being nice to Lena. Hell, I didn't know anything. I didn't think anything I could have done in such a short time was enough to have her carry on this way.

Now, at two-thirty in homeroom on my fourth day in this

crazy school, this wild bitch, Lena, was punching me. Her insults brought the upper-graders passing by in the corridors. The boys wisecracked, the girls tittered, and Miz Letty kept saying, "Let 'em alone, y'all stand clear." She liked this fight, Miz Letty, it gave her something to do, something to break the monotony—and I hated her for it.

"Ah heard yoh mama done gone and killed herself. That true, Shyyyylah, huh, that true? Ah bet she did it on count of you. My mama heard Miz Alice talkin. That true?"

Wham. I made a fist, connected it to the side of her lip. I pulled her hair, got her to the ground, and started slapping. Grabbing my leg, she brought me flying to the floor; then bit my arm and tore the straps off the sundress. The revelation of my strapless, boned bra brought animal roars from the boys and clucks from Miz Letty. Our faces and clothes were gory and disheveled.

Two male teachers grabbed us, lifting me in the air. Lena spit. My chest was killing me. As they marched us at opposite sides of the corridor down to the office, the students applauded—that is, except Luanne, whom I had caught sight of, standing apart; who looked into my eyes, compassionate and without laughter.

Lena's mother and my stepmother arrived on the principal's phone call. Alice had the edge all the way. Lena's mother, a pretty woman—too young for maternity, at least compared to any of the mothers I had known—was on the attack.

"And ah don't want that girllll of yours anywhere near mah Lena. She acts lahk a tramp, look at her! Ah don't want mah daughter around anyone as violent as her. Look at what she did to Lena. Look at that! You better teach that girl, Alice. Heah."

"Simmer down, Gertrude, ah haven't heard from Shylah yet. Ah'm sure there's an explanation for all this."

The principal gave his official "grim" countenance. "Gertrude, you take Lena home now, and you keep her home tomorrow, understand. Ah don't want this happening again—ah don't care what the reasons."

"What about this'un, Conway, y'all wanna little brat like this causin trouble?"

"Gertrude, ah think that's enough now. Y'all go on home. Ah'm gonna have a few words with Alice here."

Mr. Conway took us into his office. A landscape of palm trees painted on velvet vied for space on the wall with the rebel flag and a certificate from the University of Florida.

"Shylah, we gotta have us an understanding. Now, ah know you're down here under extenuating circumstances; your mother here told . . ."

"My stepmother . . ."

"Told me, don't-you-interrupt-girl, about your circumstances. Now ah think you ought to be a little more grateful, behave yourself. We do things our way down here. Y'all settle down, ah know you're a bright girl, now act like a lady. And stay away from Lena. She and her mama have a bad reputation in these parts, real trouble. The Dales are respected by folks down here; ah think you ought to try and live up to that."

"Why the hell'd you have to tell everyone about Mama, Alice? Huh, why? Why? Oh Jesus, I'm going to puke."

Mr. Conway pushed me through the nurse's area into the john, where I retched sour pizzaburgers and milk. Feeling better, though my chest still hurt, I rinsed my mouth and walked back to the principal's office.

"Feel better, baby? Now, the reason ah told some folks about your . . . mother . . . was so that they'd understand, you know, if, well, if you acted sad or anything. Unfortunately, well, things get around here quick, hon; we live on an island, you know, and Gertrude, well, she isn't the kind of person we want down here, she and her daughter. But you can't go busting people up again, no matter what, Shylah, you understand?"

"Look, Alice, I don't belong here, you know I don't belong here, I can't even talk right. I mean, look, I have to borrow Luanne's clothes to be right—everything's crazy."

"You just wait, lamb, everything's gonna be fine, real fine."

"Can we go . . . can we go home now, *please?*"

"Yes, we'll go home and you can wash up and rest. That's right, baby, we'll go home."

★

"What the hell this ah hear 'bout? Huh? What's this ah hear 'bout? You been fighting with that bitch whore, huh? Listen here, kid, we get along down here, unnerstand? You stay away from the tramps around. Some fine lady with Betsy's fancy schools, huh! And ah don't wanna hear 'bout this sort of thing again. You unnerstand, you UNNERSTAND that Shylah?"

"Naaaooooowww, Father, the baby was . . ."

"And you can stop that, she gotta learn if she gonna stay here with us. Ah'm sick to hear 'bout it—Susan Lee over talkin 'bout it soon's the first bus got back."

"Leave it alone, Corky, now ah mean it, ah don't want to hear another word."

"Well, *look* at her, woman. Jesus, she looks just like an alley cat. Pull your damn dress up, Shylah, ah don't wanna look at your damn titties."

"Corky dear, shut up. Shylah, why don't you go and fix up a little?"

Daddy wore the same brittle stare, the wet leer I had remembered as a child—when he would come home drunk and beat Mummy or threatened to strangle me—a look given at disciplinary times that meant "untouchable." He had not mellowed. He had simply grown less firm.

Joe Joe got up from under the rattan table and loped behind me into the bedroom.

"Hey, Joe Joe, don't you give me that look too, hey, doggie; aw come here, Joe Joe."

I took off the ripped, blood-spattered dress and crinolines, leaving them on the floor, and turned on tepid water for the shower. The area around my bite surfaced red and black; the upper arm ached. I washed it then, putting Bacitracin and gauze on the wounds. I brushed my hair into respectability, picked up one of the new textbooks, and sat down upon my bed.

The dress being ruined upset me. It was, after all, Luanne's, and I didn't want to hurt anything of Luanne's. Maybe I could replace it. Zoe had given me fifty dollars before I left. I'd give her the emergency money—or replace the dress if I could find out where she had bought it. I didn't want to lose Luanne, I liked her. She had surety and normalcy, and that was it. She was normal, her parents were normal—even if old C.J. was an animal—they, even he, exuded a kind of mental well-being. I wondered if she and Harry and Mick and I would double again, or if I was out now, persona non grata on the island. I didn't want to be left alone, not now. Not that Mick was terrific or anything, he sure wasn't Clark Gable, and it had been difficult to talk and to listen to his grunting language, but I had liked that third kiss; that was nice, that kiss, and it felt "normal" getting dressed up in capri pants and trying on lipsticks and stuff like that with Luanne. Even if she didn't want to be a friend any more, I'd still pay for the dress or buy her one.

"Shy, Shylah, can ah come innnn?"

"Hi, Luanne, hi. Listen, I'm sorry about the dress. Where'd you get it? I'll buy you another one, honestly. I'm really sorry."

"Oh for Lawdsake, don't worry 'bout it. Shylah, you should have told me, ah had no ahdea. Honest, ah was rootin for you. Lena's a tramp, she's always screwin up, that is, when she's not screwin. Listen, we were—you know, Bubbles and Cindy—we were on your side. But, Shy, y'all gotta not talk that way. Ah mean, lahk about niggers and queers, ah mean colored people. Ah mean, you're different, but the girls lahk you, least us, but you just gotta be cool—ah mean, you've been through a whole lot, y'all should have told me about your mother, honestly. Lena oughta be lynched for that."

"But I sort of like Lena. Look how rough it is for her, everybody calling her a tramp and all that."

"She'd go all the way for a nickel, and the word is, her mother had the . . ." Luanne clapped her hands twice.

"What?"

"You knowwwww, a social disease."

"Oh yeah." I laughed. A social disease was about the most exotic thing I'd ever heard of.

"I guess Mick won't want to go out again or anything."

"No, he lahks you all right, maybe we'll double this weekend, but now, well, now you gotta make sure he doesn't try anything, cause, well, the guys think you're pretty sophisticated and stuff, and that fight . . ."

"Oh God, yeah, I know; O.K., I'll be careful."

"Look, get dressed, we'll go over to Treenie's and have a Coke and play the jukebox for an hour; c'mon, put on those red and blue capris y'all got."

★

Treenie's was jammed. Outside the quadrangular bamboo structure a line of Chevys and Ford convertibles, two couples to a car. I was still terrified.

"Well, the rumbler, how you doin, Shylahhhh?" An older boy laughed from his car and the girls tittered their frustrating little squeaks.

"Hey, Luanne."

"Hi, Luanne."

"See you brought the Union Army with you."

"Shut up, Al."

"Oh, ah just love that song,

> "Many a tear has to fall
> But it's all in the game
> All in the wonderful game
>   They call love
>
> When I kiss your lips
> And caress your dainty fingertips
> Then my heart just flies away."

"Oh Lawd, ah know what you mean."

"Yeah, me too."

"Hey, have you heard that new one, 'Poison Ivy'?"

Luanne carried on the usual three or four conversations at the same time. I stood beside her quietly, half smiling, aware of the position of my mouth and praying it would be O.K. and that I looked all right.

"Hi, Shylah."

"Hi, Mick."

"I seen yah slam into old Lena, holyyy shit. You get around, girl."

"Yeah."

4 0

"Whatdoyouwanttoeat?"

"Um. An order of french fries and a Coke." That seemed to be what was found most on the tables and on the dashes of the convertibles. I figured if I couldn't act acceptably, the least I could do was fake it as a normal eater.

An older girl, maybe a senior—still in her crinolines, waspwaisted and honey-blond—sauntered by.

"Well, hi, Luanne, how's it going?"

"Hi, Sunshine. Oh, O.K."

"Who's the wild wonder?"

"Oh, this is Shylah, she's Mr. Corky's daughter. This is Rita, but everyone calls her Sunshine on account of her hair."

"Hi, Sunshine."

"Well, y'all sure do get around. Lawd. Hear you down from the Nowth."

"Philadelphia."

"People get around up there."

Sunshine meandered away, the bitch. Luanne leaned over secretively. "She's a senior."

"I guessed."

"She used to go around with Mick."

"Oh oh."

Mick returned with a tray of bar-b-que sandwiches for himself and french fries for me.

"So how about Friday night, huh? Maybe me and Harry and y'all can go to Key West."

"Great. But we gotta be cool. Mah folks'd fall outta trees if they knew we went that far. Shylah, don't tell yours either, O.K.? Lotta sailors and cheapy places down there; we're supposed to stay in town."

"Yeah, sure, O.K."

"O.K., so the way we'll do it is pick you up for the show, round seven, and then take off," said Mick. "Ah'd better go pay that nigger and buy me some rum."

I got through the hour with Luanne fencing and being charming, while I nursed the french fries and Coke. A breeze struck up over the declining sun as we dawdled back, stopping to look in Islabelle Sportswear at the mannequins draped in sunglasses

4 1

and pants and straw hats and Aurora Borealis crystal jewelry. Roots, like the island, Luanne had roots. Something permanent to grasp.

★

The day passed quickly enough, new textbooks and names to learn. Nobody gave much to education at Palm View—English, civics, health, P.E., arithmetic were conducted more for the deportment of the class—like one teacher wouldn't let the girls cross more than their ankles—spent most of the fifty-minute period lecturing us on virginal postures. Learning or competitive learning was kept at a minimum. I liked art. The teacher, Miz Tallulah, and I hit it off at my first class with her. A small, plump woman, she had a prettiness about her and could love anything—almost anything. Even yelling at the boys, she came off as slightly angelic, doing it for show—because part of a teacher's job is to yell at males.

I enjoyed using the large sheets of manila paper, drawing endless numbers of profiled girls with bouffant coifs, all colored and shaded in her special pastels. She'd come and look at my work and smile. "Why, Shylah, that's a real pretty picture. Whyn't you fill in the background with something, huh, think you could do that? Ah'm gonna send some of your pictures to the state contest"—and by Friday she had asked me if perhaps I would like to help her with first- and second-grade art sometime, that she'd get me a principal's pass. On the other hand, Miz Letty had paddled me twice for talking—had pulled my hair—had lectured me on the importance of a young lady keeping a decent reputation. It was only because of my desire for peace through acceptability that I did not tell her to stick it— answering instead with the newly acquired "Yes'm" and "No'm" which appeared to work like dope on grownups.

Daddy and Alice and I had quiet dinners, except for his nasty drunks—and even those were mostly on a verbal scale now. Besides, Alice had the upper hand, except perhaps in creative intelligence. And Mummy's name was avoided. Instead, Daddy took much of his anger out in the common practice of local prejudices. So he'd swear about the Negro gardener—talk about places he thought were restricted and therefore respectable, till he noticed they were taking in Jews; and the wops, spicks, and dirty Cubanos could be brought in for a snarl or two. Still, he gave me few words—no explanations—no sympathy conversations. Nothing would upset his masculine distance or equilibrium.

Uncle Bobby Jay, as I was told to address him, came over almost daily for bourbon and talk, one time bringing me an autographed photo of himself and one of those huge, cheesy, polyester-stuffed elephants—said it was given to him during a publicity campaign, thought I'd like it. He greeted me via bear hugs, lifting tall body-up-helpless like a small toad, yelling something about "How's the Princess today?"—all that kind of stuff I wished would come from my father, not some damn golf maniac. My father accepted that Uncle Bobby Jay was a great American and a great guy and so on, and even I thought he had something exciting and infectious about him—certainly he was gifted with the loudest voice of anyone I had ever heard, including Daddy in a rage.

I had wangled a certain chuminess on the usual telephone-after-school basis with Selma Anne and Cindy, Rosemary and Bubbles, and of course hung out with Luanne as much as possible. Alice took me to Paula's, the local beautician, for a hair set, outfitted me at Islabelle's in crinolines and full-skirted sundresses. I took comfort in visions of future conformity, where I would appear so unobtrusive as to be invisible. Things had slowed to a busy but numbed pace and by Friday I had gotten into a certain spirit of adventure for our night out in Key West, with its forbidden sailors and all those artists they talked about and honky-tonks. I slept well, dry-eyed at last, with an ear to the lulls of an island put to bed.

★

"Hereyahgo, Shylah, a Roman Coke special." Mick played bartender with the Treenie Cokes in their paper cups taken in the car and mixed and drunk upon the way to Key West. The rum had turned the amber cola to a kind of topaz translucency in its 75:25 proportions.

"Uhhhyaaaaa, God, that's kind of strong."

"Aw come on, girl, drink up. This the way we make'm down here."

The twenty-five miles or so went slowly. Harry was afraid to speed, with all of us drinking and the weekend highway patrol out looking for arrests, and the Friday-night traffic swelled with the expectation of nightclubs and glimpses of Hemingway and Williams out drinking. We passed the naval base and adjacent submarine station—guys lining the highway with thumbs out, pointing to Key West proper or the other way to Homestead, where they had the air force base, or Miami if they were rich gobs and could afford the expensive women and hotels.

I couldn't be positive when we actually entered the city limits. The action ran the length of two islands instead of one, with highway expanding to accommodate roadside bars and liquor stores. At some point I realized we weren't tied to Highway 1 any more, that there were little streets and boulevards with thick flora and Spanish stucco houses, two-story affairs, when the rest of the Keys supported mostly one-story built-ups or ranches.

We drove down Duval, the town's main drag, past what looked like a Hollywood set for a Jane Russell picture; past cheap strip-show bars with live semi-Dixieland bands, smells of frying fish, crafts shops, little five and dimes—past sunburned artists displaying driftwood sculpture on chicken-wire fences— the narrow asphalt culminating in a residential section before the ocean—past large houses with hanging trees and just before the end and the water, the Hemingway house—huge in its encompassing veranda and royal palms, the lazy Spanish and colonial architecture inviting, lovely, certainly grand. Strange to move slowly in a car down Duval—going from the honky-tonk to the crafts shops and finally to the large homes—interconnected by the narrow strip of sidewalk and unstoppable tropical brush. Oh, I loved Key West. I loved it—tiny little streets and shrimp boats and people speaking Spanish rapidly, sounding like one long aching word, and shrubs and vines and the mystery of where we would go tonight. And this twilight, the look of Southernmost City in the rum-blurry, end-of-the-world hodgepodge under beginning eight o'clock purples.

I felt the rum inside me. Warm—nicely warm, furry. Something to cuddle. This drinking business—Luanne getting giggly in the front seat, voice rising in staggered pitch from the liquor.

"Harry, where we goin? Let's show Shy the Dunes. Think we can do some mixin with the Key West roughies?"

"Key West has dunes?"

"It's a drive-in joint where all the kids go, near the shrimpers."

"Oh, sounds great. Yeah, let's go there."

"Hold on to it, girls, we'll get there. Ah heard there's some kind of party goin tonight, maybe we'll hear something."

The Dunes had the advantage of dancing space with jukebox, as well as numerous things to eat. The under-eighteeners (it still being too early for older fare) looked arrogant and tan, and milled around on the chosen spaces with a certain furious nonchalance.

"Hey, Mick, Harry, who're your tough-lookin girl friends?"

"Hey, man."

"Hey, man."

"Hear there's goin to be a party or something. That true?"

"Yeah, later on, down at the old Terry place."

"Well, that's cool. So what else y'all been doin?"

"Catchin shrimp, keepin in trouble, chasin the nigger lobster-pot robbers, that 'bout it."

"Careful, boy," interjected Harry, "Shylah here's a Yankee, she say Neeeeegrooooo; get that."

"Sheeeeeiiiitttt, well ah'll be goddamned."

"How you lahk the real world, whadja say your name was?"

"Shylah. Is this, uh, the real world?"

"Yes'm, this is the end of the world. Hey, you guys, she ain't bad."

"Oh, cut it, will you, jerks. Let's order somethin or somethin. Ah wanna dance." Luanne appeared to be tight, though it was hard to tell what was real and what was put on. I was getting annoyed and depressed from the effects of the alcohol on my sys-

4 5

tem. Maybe one more drink would take off the edge and transform me into a silly, acceptably girlish version of Luanne.

An hour or so later we drove onto the Terry place, a rambling, once-occupied house and grounds, now up for sale, looking overgrown, as if a buyer had not come for a millennium. Located on the bay side, Boca Chica, where shrubs and mangroves made the little road almost impossible to traverse, it seemed to have its privacy insured. This was not strung-lights-record-playing-hot-dog-eating party, rather a chance for numbers of kids to get together, race engines, drink too much, gossip, make out with dates or flirt with others. It was a stage upon which to be seen, to barter personalities, and to pretend some great adventures.

I wanted to enjoy myself. Everyone down here enjoyed themselves, didn't they? I wanted to turn off my head, kiss Mick, swivel my hips, put my lipstick on, bat my eyes—to join in and stop thinking.

Something was rising with the rum, the sick-sweet cloy of it. Something was rising. Mick and I got out of the car holding hands, he leading me from one group to another of cliqued kids. I mumbled and swayed the best I could. Harry and Luanne had retreated to the car for another acute-angle make-out session. We eventually went for a walk alone on the beach. I thought being kissed would mellow everything, but Mick, the booze, and my diminished or nonexistent reputation brought a differing focus to things, made the overtures automatic, hard.

"C'mon, Shylah, ohhh mannn, ah'm so high. How come you in such a bad mood? C'mon, Shylah. Hey, you want some more Roman Coke? Make you feel looser."

"Yeah, I guess I want some more."

"Wait here, I'll go get it."

The beach lay brambled with blackened wood and seaweed from where I sat looking out. A half moon played like a jump rope upon the water. It should have been O.K., I mean. The kids, I could hear laughing . . . Some car radio playing "Tweedlee Dee." It should have been O.K.

Mick walked back with the bottle and a cup of Coke, laughing at something that had happened.

"Here yah go, kid, try swiggin it from the bottle and followin with the Coke."

"Oooohaaah, yeck!" Some of the rum spilled on my chin. I felt vaguely nauseous.

Mick reached his arm around the upper part of my back to turn me, putting my head at a side angle to his shoulder. He brought his head around and down—my official fourth kiss had begun, followed by others of growing intensity, till he had us lying on the charcoal driftwood.

"Hmmmm, Shylah, uh, nice." Mick's hand made a circle on my right breast, moving down and under the jersey top and finally tugging at the tight band of elastic at the bottom of the bra.

"No, come on, Mick. O.K. Let's not, come on." I put my hand over his to stop the movement. Dizziness, the effect giving everything a bright sheen. And there was this dimensional thing, like I was thinking differently. I wanted or expected something to happen, some kind of end to this, like the camera pan at the end of a particularly melodramatic movie. And it did feel good to be held and caressed this way, excited me—like reading *Peyton Place* excited me. Romance. Being held down, well, what the hell, why not. I mean, if I didn't go all the way, everything else'd be O.K. I couldn't get pregnant from being felt. Thought made me giggle. And Harry played with Luanne, she confided in me. It was ridiculous to think this way while you were doing it, though. I thought people didn't think of anything when they did this, they just sort of turned into cotton candy for the duration . . . they merged into some celestial conglomerate—a batter. But my mind kept figuring things out, talking to itself, as Mick's hands, both now, plotted me. And it felt so soft and everything had that sugary, excited glaze to it . . .

"Oh, Shylah, y'all so sweet, ooh, ah really lahk you—move a little this way."

We were leaning toward each other on our sides, one arm caught under the weight of each other, one arm free to explore. Mick used his to unbutton and unzip my capris. He slipped his hand inside, moving it down until the longest finger touched my crotch. God, felt marvelous, oh God. Just there at the beginning, stay there, just there. I knew how wet I was; my underpants were sticking between my legs. My hand clutched at his bottom and upper thigh, moving up and down, and then moved around to the bulge in his pants in sympathy, imitating him. I remembered as a little girl how a neighbor boy and I had done this—we couldn't have been more than five and it was our favorite game, running off and playing with each other—but this was different.

I shifted, and Mick slipped his hand to the full expanse of crotch, making me move my legs a little apart. The radio played "All in the Game" again as he abandoned the top part of my crotch for the underneath. It didn't work, didn't feel good any more, all the feeling being in my breasts and the top part of my crotch, but Mick had both his hands down under now, keeping my legs apart. He pushed a finger at me, at the hole—stung. It stung. I contracted. He tried again. It hurt.

"Don't, Mick, that hurts."

No answer, just the persistence of that damn finger. I wanted to tell him to lift it higher—but wasn't I supposed to react down there, not up high? Like a plug. The stabbing of that finger made headway—the pain enraged me. It wasn't fun or soft any more.

"Stop it, goddamnit, stop it, Mick."

I grabbed the hand and pushed him away—no good any more. Mick took the hand, the one from my crotch, and wiped it on his pants, wet sticky substance glistening off the fingers in the moonlight.

"You sure some prick teaser, Shylah. Jeesus. After what I hear going round about you— Jesus, c'mon, let's go back, huh? C'mon. Goddamn."

"It hurt, you knew it hurt. Besides, that's not where it feels good. And WHAT have you HEARD about me? I haven't done anything. I've only been down here a couple of weeks."

"Lez go. Well, ah'm goin back. Y'all can stay here, you want to."

He walked away then. I tried to follow, to get up and follow, but fell back with a stagger. A kind of thin glass on everything—I couldn't see to balance myself. Vision kept doubling and swaying and my mind wouldn't connect. Mummy. Where was Mummy? Mummy, Mummy. Why is everything so screwed up? Why glass on everything?—eyes kept picking up the shattered bits, gleam breaking apart. I heard Luanne's voice rising over the babble of the others. Luanne. Luanne.

"Where's Shylah? Where's Shylah, Mick?"

"Sheeiiittt."

"Shyyylahhh. Where are you? We're leavin, Shyylahhh . . . HEY, Shylah, what's the matter? You O.K.? Oh Lawd, what's wrong? You drunk, Lawd, y'all really are. Mick's real mad—Whatdidyoualldo? Shylah, don't cry, tell me what's wrong. We gotta git home. Y'all think you can stand?"

"All . . . the glass is breaking. It's all breaking, I want Mummy, Mummy. I screwed up, Luanne. It's all crazy. I wanna go home."

"We are going home. We are. Listen, trah and act sober. We gotta pass those kids. It'll be O.K. We'll talk about it when we get home. Y'all stayin over, right? Mah folks won't be around till real late. It'll be O.K. Harry, Harrryyyy, come here a minute."

"Oh man, she really gone, how much'd she drink anyway?"

"Help me get her to the car. Lawd, she's actin crazy. C'mon, Shy, try and stand, O.K.?"

"Don't hurt me, please don't hurt me. No, don't let him touch me, please, no, no."

"He's not gonna hurt you. Honest. Let's just get to the car."

"Shit, man, she's no feather, that's for damn sure."

We walked up the beach, past the house where the kids were fooling around, some making out, some holding bottles, laughing and in control. Like walking to the grave past all those goons at the funeral, the careful march of three people, two of them supporting or hiding or embarrassed about the third. I walked as straight as I could, holding my breath, then slid into the back seat, trying to contain some embarrassment, some explosion I was sure would come from me; the whole of me would become a pile of shit if I didn't control . . . Goddamn. Control.

"Where's Mick, Harry, we gotta git home."

"He's not comin. He—ah—he's with some guys, you know, Luanne, let's just go."

Harry gunned the engine. I was leaking from everywhere. I thought I was leaking—felt the wetness around my mouth and on my cheeks and under my arms, the backs of my legs and between them. I couldn't focus. Please, let me focus, please. It was rising now, it was all rising. Car flying up highway, air from the open windows catching at my face, blowing at the wetness. I inhaled deep into me, and it caught; it caught and came up in a retch, gag sound of rising, followed by the push, the backward push of food soured by digestion and rum spewing out.

"Oh Lawd, Harry, hurry, she's barfing."

"Jesus, ugghh, shit."

Despite her repulsion, I felt Luanne's hand reach back and touch my shoulder as I sat bowed from the waist, glass breaking behind eyes, exploding. She kept it there; she kept her hand on my shoulder. Where it touched, there could be no broken glass, no confusion. On that part of me where she touched, something, something safe.

"Help me, Harry, help me get her to my room."

"Where's your folks?"

"Out, ah told you before. Shylah, come on, y'all gonna be O.K. C'mon."

My hands clenched. Everything still cracking fissures. Why was I wrong? Why? Nothing worked. The dizziness was gone after puking, but nothing worked. Fragments. Crying. Why didn't all the wetness stop? Like my eyes were swimming. Mummy, Mummy. Just let me go, let me go, huh, no more. The bathroom. I wanted to go to the bathroom. Clean, sanitized, spotless tiled bathroom. I could clean myself. Take a shower. It would go away then, with the water and gleaming spigots.

"Let me take a shower, Luanne, I'm all dirty."

"Yes, O.K. You O.K.? Can you take off your clothes and stuff? Ah'll get y'all an aspirin and some coffee and you can sleep after, huh."

I tumbled out of the top and pants, soggy panties and bra. Water sounds inside, the water, like Mummy crying. Stop it,

Shylah. I was slipping, hard to keep balance on the porcelain, slipping. My hand caught a large glass bottle of shampoo on the tub's edge—splattering next to me, my feet. I lost balance then with it, sitting back hard on the edge of the tub, the broken pieces of glass covered with soapy white goo. Strange how glass breaks, how it is reshaped in sharp points, the refracted light at breaking edge. And I took the largest slice, the dagger sliver, fondled its distinct, perfect edges. Like an answer, like a yes or no, something definite to hold on to.

"Shylah, Jesus, Shylah, let go, let go of the glass. Harry, help me quick." Luanne had run in after the shampoo bottle broke.

Then a trickle of blood—my arm—me standing naked, shampoo filming over feet, playing with the glass, feeling good about the glass, raising it to my cheek. Harry grabbed my wrist, and Luanne took the glass away, becoming enemy, becoming Mick, becoming Daddy. I ran into the living room, tired now, getting tired.

"Here, Shylah, here." Luanne rubbed me down with a beach towel, put the cotton nightie over my head. I sat on the straw couch while she administered, finally undoing the Band-Aid and putting it on the bloody cut on my arm.

"C'mon, Shylah, lie down now. Let's go in the bedroom, that's raght."

"Goddamnit, Luanne. Barf in the car, blood and shampoo in the pisser. Man, she sure wild, that ain't no ordinary lush."

Cool. The sheets were friendly on Luanne's other bed. Skin had that softened puckeredness from the onslaught of shower water. Things now nicely straight again, smooth with no glass, no bright slices behind the eyes. Luanne brought me coffee and aspirin. It didn't matter that she didn't understand. She took care of it. She didn't run. Luanne took care.

★

I woke up late, with Luanne making noises of hair whacking and squeals at painful eyebrow tweezings.

"Ohhh my God."

"Good mornin, how you feel?"

51

"Shitty, I'm sorry. Oh God. What did I do?"

"Lawd, were you ever wild last night, Shylah. I have NEVAH seen anythin lahk it; ah mean you kept cryin and moanin about your mama, and when you got that glass piece in your hand, I lahk'ta died on the spot."

"I don't remember. Oh God. I blew it, didn't I?"

"Listen, I made Harry swear not to tell. Honest, he in't goin to say anythin 'bout what happened. But what happened with Mick?"

"He tried to finger me, and when I pushed him away, he called me a prick teaser."

"Yah, I sort of figured that was it, or somethin lahk it. There's a rumor round you aren't a virgin, ah mean, ah told people you were real nahce and stuff, and things were a little different for you now and stuff, but some those upper-class girls, they lahk to make up gossip. Ah betcha Sunshine's behind this. She don't want Mick any more but she don't want anybody else to have him. Don't you worry, Bubbles and Cindy and Selma Anne and Rosemary and me are who count in the eighth grade and y'all are in. Don't worry, Shy, ah'm glad you're here, really. O.K.? Seriously, ah lahk the other girls and stuff, but we're different— ah can't imagine anybody else bein mah best friend, you know what ah mean? You don't talk same as me but, well, we get along, yah know, we get along."

"Yes, I know. You've been really great. It's better now, Luanne, really; I mean, I feel better now, well, you know what I mean, and you're my first and always best friend, so that's good, even if other things are shitty. Guess I better get home. Listen, thanks. I'll see you later, O.K.? Honest, you are my best friend. I want you to know that."

4

Daddy. Big man Daddy—Daddy of belly bluster, the 42-inch, 230-pound flesh artifact of pleasure, Daddy the head-back laugher—of the angry sumo's paw; fat-fingered, bowlegged. Daddy the decorated, the drunkard, the entertainer—the take-over, the talker, hunter, golfer, fisherman. Daddy, the long-distance, rocking-chair receiver, the war without end, the whore-master, the guardian, the beloved and uninvolved. Daddy meticulous, Daddy patron. Clean rows of monogrammed linen hankies with the prophylactics (3) in plastic stacked beneath them. Daddy custodian—the moans, ripping snores giving way to farts in sleep and dreams; the self-inflicted master, the eagle, the crippled bull.

And daddy of an offspring—the girl-baby to be lapped on state occasions, to be brought in and excused, to be endured, not to be endured, to be cowed by command, to be chased—annoying, like hemorrhoids, like lice, like a seed caught between the molar and bicuspid. Daddy the remaining, the other.

Daddy, be for me, be a daddy-daddy, a walkie-talkie daddy, a no-hit daddy. Be, goddamnit, Father of Daughter.

★

"Hi, Daddy. Hi, Alice."

"Jesus, girl, what the hell you and Luanne been doing, beating on each other? Y'all look lahk death over toast. Do something with yourself, brush your hair, something. Y'all a mess."

"Go clean up like Daddy says, baby . . . and then come sit down, have a little breakfast."

Despite my headache, things had seemed so light I had forgotten my appearance—puffy face, red pockets under nose, hair sticky with hair spray and matted at one side, flying at the other. I washed and brushed, reapplying thick liquid makeup base and as much eyeshadow as I dared before presenting face at the eleven o'clock breakfast.

Daddy sat before the glass table in the Florida room. Upon it, a plate containing three fried eggs, four stacked pieces of toast, Canadian smoked ham, and grits. A pot of coffee and a container of orange juice stood before cup and large tumbler glass. My father ate like a surgeon performing an appendectomy. One slice of toast buffeted the incised white and yolk while he made the slow, clean sweep of laden fork to mouth and back; then he replaced the toast to pick up knife from its one o'clock position on plate and proceeded with a two-way, precise cutting rhythm. He looked up then, looking at me looking at him, grunted, indicating the opposite chair. It meant I had clearance to join him.

"So you been down here a week now, y'all settlin in, huh? Allliccce, we got any buttermilk left out there . . . Uncle Bobby Jay, he thinks y'all a real humdinger, he's been mighty concerned about you . . . Consider yourself lucky, Bobby Jay's an important guy to have around. Real nice he's taken such a special interest in you."

"Alice, may I . . ."

"And that's another thing, this Alice business. Alice, come on in here, ah wanna say something now."

Alice came through the kitchen doorway, in her left hand a container of buttermilk, her right hand wiping itself on the cotton apron.

"It just doesn't seem right at all you calling her Alice—ah don't like to hear that, don't like to hear it one bit, gnaws at me. You growing up now—you show some respect to grownups. Ah don't wanna hear you call her Alice any more, understand? She treat you like her own, bought you outfits and took care of that bullroar at school, and she been wunnerful about having you. Y'all hear me, Shylah. Wunnerful, and ah think you could call her Mother now . . . because . . ."

"My mother's dead. She's my . . ."

"Don't you talk back to me; certain person not around now put up with that shit. Y'all don't seem to realize how wunnerful Alice . . ."

"Now, Corky, ah don't mind. Baby can call me anything. Maybe when she gets used to being here longer, she'll call me Mama; won't you, Shy, lamb?"

"Now y'all wait, Mother, ah'm serious about this. She got to learn, and ah don't want someone who's been so wunnerful to her to be disrespected."

"Well, a lot of the people, at least a lot of the kids down here, say 'ma'am' all the time. How about if I call her ma'am in public, that way everybody's happy. Is that O.K.?"

"That's a good idea, Shy. That's a good idea, in'it, Corky? Come on, drink your buttermilk now. Y'all yelled for it. That's enough of this talk, O.K.?"

Alice retreated into the kitchen. Daddy grunted.

"God, Daddy, everything's so different down here, you know. Remember how you used to talk with a Northern accent, wear those three-piece suits, and . . . Well, no, no, I just mean it's different. I hadn't seen you in four years till last week and . . . Oh yes, I liked the presents; remember, I wrote you . . . Oh, she did? . . . Yes, very good taste and, oh yes, I liked her letters, interesting. Remember how . . no, I do remember, last Christmas, you got on the phone. No, I picked them out myself, Mummy just gave me the charge plate. But remember the last time I saw you, you took me to the athletic club and I had that hamburger with the sauce and clown cone for dessert and I kept getting sick and you gave me those two records. 'Hearts Made of Stone' and 'Rock Around the Clock.' I still have them, honestly. I thought, maybe today you'd take me . . . Well yes, some homework in English and civics but not much. It's not hard, you know . . . Oh, I didn't mean it that way. Anyway, well, we really haven't had a chance to . . . and I missed you, you know; four years is forever. Oh yeah, they're both fine. Oh no, Daddy, you know, you said it yourself, that men don't write . . . that it's unmanly to write a lot of letters and they've been real busy, you know. Oh no, Zoe isn't a Communist or anything . . just very intellectual. What? Oh yes, very funny, Rick's got your sense of humor. Well, yes, it's too bad about the divorce . . . she was there at the funeral. Don't say that, Daddy. She was terrific, really. Talented, you should've seen the picture she drew of Mummy and me and . . . That's not true, even if it didn't work out with Rick, she was still very fond of Mummy. After all, you and Mummy got divorced too . . . No, I didn't mean it THAT way; well, you know what I mean. She said it was just better this way. Anyhow, I thought maybe we could go— Oh, what's wrong with the boat? Well, maybe you and, uh, you and Alice would take me out sometime? Yeah, I like Uncle Bobby Jay. No, really, I have been polite. Please, Daddy, I'm serious. Don't give me horse bites again, it hurts, it's not funny . . . Please, no, I just wanted to—uh—talk. Oh yes, I'll be here; yes, I'll help Alice with the hors d'oeuvres. Yes, O.K., no, never mind. I just thought, well, no, never mind. Yes, I'll do my homework now."

I knew it wouldn't work out, I knew it. In my room, I took out the manila paper and the pastels Miz Tallulah had let me have. Shit, if he'd just say something to me, anything, anything directly without going through his channels— Maybe I really was a mess. I sat before the flounced dressing table and looked into the mirror. Some of the swelling had gone down already; I didn't look as good as I had yesterday morning, but I was presentable. I reapplied the baby-pink lipstick till it thickened on my lips, and sat on the floor with paper, pastels, pencils. I was copying a picture-book painting of Jesus the child, the one with the lamb and the dove. Miz Tallulah had asked me for something religious for the first-grade bulletin board. He stood amid primroses in the book picture, but I made the flowers hibiscus instead, taking a fuchsia pastel and a dullish yellow in my hand and filling in one color on another. Then, with my fingers, I blended the two shades into shadows of each other, and did the same with blues and greens on Jesus's smock. I put Beethoven's Fifth on my phonograph since the *Pastoral* had been scratched to death, getting an electric shock, so I tried again, using the rubber flip-flops as handles for the arm.

Outside, in the Florida room, Daddy had moved to the rocking chair and turned on the quad-band marine radio to hear the stock-market reports. The tinkle of ice against old-fashioned glass signified the beginning of his drinking day. Later, my Jesus in the Tropics finished, I heard Uncle Bobby Jay's voice describing his new glass-bottom boat, and would Daddy and Alice like to try it out; no, they couldn't; well, how 'bout the Princess, bet the Princess would love to see this boat open up out there.

"Shyyyylahhh."

"Never mind, Corky; ah see her in there."

"Hey, Princess, how 'bout some boating this afternoon? How 'bout coming out for a ride?"

"Oh thanks, Uncle Bobby Jay, I'd like to but I've got this . . . well, no, Daddy, but tomorrow we're going to Cutler Ridge and I don't know . . . Oh yeah, I'd really like to go but . . . well, O.K., I guess I can finish my homework later. Where are we going?"

"How does Traitors' Island way sound to you?"

"Oh, really terrific. I've heard so much about it. That's the place where they kept—uh—they tortured those political guys, right? O.K., well, give me ten minutes. I just have to get my stuff together and put my bathing suit on."

Shit, Shylah, I don't want to go. I don't want to go with Uncle Bobby Jay, despite the new boat and Traitors' Island. If it had only been Daddy. And it seemed peculiar, his doting on someone too old to be a daughter and too young to be a sister or whatever. Not that Uncle Bobby Jay wasn't funny and entertaining. And it was pleasurable sometimes to be in his company—I mean, I guess, that nature works on the eyes, doesn't it?—he had all that beauty going for him. But I wanted my daddy, and my daddy threw me over with orders to accompany this stranger—to be charming and polite, as he said. Daddy pimp.

The sun at one o'clock was almost sheet-white, clear, small, defined, like a core of something. Perfect speedboat weather, and Uncle Bobby Jay's new red and white craft cut through the water like a spatula through frosting. We kept to the channels mostly so he could open up on the throttle, zipping around small, gnarled mangrove cluster-like little islands in the otherwise uninterrupted horizon of blue on chartreuse ocean. A half hour out, he slowed the engine down to a lull as we moved between two mangrove islands, finding an obscure, deep channel lagoon.

"Hotter than a son-of-a-gun. How 'bout we hop in for a little swim, Princess?"

Uncle Bobby Jay took longer to undress than the queen, sliding the white jersey with the little alligator on it over his head, slipping out of the Bemudas to reveal a pair of 3-D Hawaiian boxer trunks, blinding to the naked eye. I had already swum the small lagoon twice, chasing a school of mullet in my wake, when I felt him underwater, pulling my toe—something I hated.

"Hey, you quite a little fish, honey."

"Yeah, well, I practice."

"Keep yah in shape—lot of the girls down here pretty enough but they aren't built lahk you. Y'all wait, Princess; you grow up a few years, well y'all know what ah mean. Ah told your daddy ah keep an eye on you. You just let me know y'all have any trouble with the boys."

"Sure."

I saw my first two porpoises about two thirds of the way to Traitors' Island. Uncle Bobby Jay had bait on him, which I threw out as a greeting, hoping they'd come visit. There were two of them, friendly fellows, each with permanently fixed sparkle and smile like they were in on an endless anecdote above human comprehension. Probably used to the traffic of tourists and guides, they came easily to the side of the boat as Uncle Bobby Jay cut the motor—close enough that I could coo to them and graze my hand over their sleek, blue-gray-black hides.

"Hey, Uncle Bobby Jay, they don't bite or anything, do they?"

"Doesn't look lahk it, does it?"

5 8

"Let me go in for a moment, will you? They seem terribly loving and wanting to play."

After patting the two little snouts, once to the left, once to the right, I slipped carefully into the water, not wanting to scare them away by a splash. I put my arms around the bigger of the two, indicating a desire for a free ride by wiggling my arms. He or she, I didn't know about porpoises, glided or skimmed the deep-water channel, so I had no need to hold my breath; its buddy following parallel and occasionally circling us.

"God, this is terrific."

"Y'all got really tame ones here, used to people feeding them and stuff. Wonder if these the porpoises got loose from the aquarium. Hey, Princess, tell your funny friends goodbye, we gotta get going. Hotter than a pisspot out here."

"Why don't you do it, Uncle Bobby Jay? They're terribly nice about rides, really."

"No, ah got more of a bang just watching you, Princess."

Uncle Bobby Jay helped me into the boat, toweling my back for me, starting the engine. The porpoises followed us for a mile or so, then dropped back to other pleasures. A giant ray leaped nearby; jewfish moved slowly beneath it. I was getting burned but didn't care, the sun obliterating my hangover while reddening my skin.

Traitors' Island maintained its two-hundred-year-old fortress; only this time it was for tourists not prisoners. There were shoals alternating with channels just before it and a criss-crossing of shark fin just beyond our boat. The local island official, out of deference to Uncle Bobby Jay, gave us a personally guided tour of the local island horrors. Later, someone snapped a picture of us eating conch salad, the famous-golfer-with-drink-in-hand at our table close to the pirates' pub. A parrot said, "You go to hell," while flowered shirts chuckled into their clams and turtle steaks. I was enjoying being sun-drunk, relaxed from the heat and the bar and Uncle Bobby Jay and the island in the middle of nowhere with its motel, restaurant, and sharked-in ex-fortress for political prisoners.

After our lunch, we were treated to tiger and blue and hammerhead sharks swirling in the basement pit in the small amount of water. Tourists were allowed to feed these predators with fish provided by attendants. It did seem slightly absurd, this show of shark power, with them surrounding the island anyway. I almost pitied the monsters their overcrowded living quarters.

"Oh come on, they didn't really throw those guys to the sharks."

"Once in a while. It kept the prisoners cowed. One thing to get shot trying to escape and another to get devoured."

"Jesus, that's disgusting."

"That's what the prisoners thought, honey."

"Aw, let's go back, huh, Uncle Bobby Jay?"

"Princess squeamish? Sure, I can understand."

"I'm not squeamish. I just think that's a shit way to attract tourists."

"Hey, watch your language. Who taught you that word? You, a young lady; now, goddamnit, Shylah, gotta watch that stuff."

"Yeah, O.K. My burn hurts."

★

Tuesday night was Bubbles's surprise birthday party. With Luanne's approval I had bought a new sheath dress for the occasion, had dressed in my room in the early evening, had gone to sit politely with Daddy and Alice at sundown before being picked up by Luanne and Harry.

"Shit. Y'all look like a damn whore, that thing on. Get in there and take that dress off. Hear, Shylah, N-O-W. See your godddamn ass here to Georgia. Go on, git."

"Why, why, Daddy? Everyone wears sheath dresses . . . it looks O.K. Stop being so damn cri—"

"You heard me, sister. Y'all get out of here if you wanna act lahk a harlot. Ah don't want to see that under mah roof; y'all git your ass in there now."

"Better do what Daddy says, baby. Whyn't you put on that nahce pink two-piece, Shy, you put that on."

"I don't wanna put on the two-piece. For Christsake, will you stop telling me I look like a whore all the time. You leave

60

me alone, Daddy. You used to say that to Mummy, you stop saying that to me. What the hell do you care anyway? You never take any interest in what I'm doing. I'm tired of this shit. If you don't care, then leave me alone in general."

"Alice, tell that bitch where she can get off. Tell her how she was sooo wanted by her aunt that she couldn't wait to get to the phone to beg us to keep her . . . You thank God, sister, you gotta home, y'all hear. That mother of yours, as you call her, didn't do such a hot job. Now ah don't want to hear you cursin and back-talkin me again. I'll show YOU a little discipline, tootsie, y'all keep this up. Now get in there and change that dress, it makes me sick."

"Don't you say that about my mother; you know why she got that way. You oughta know, huh, Daddy, you oughta know . . ."

"Yah dumb little tramp, y'all gonna get it now. Get outta the way, Alice—Jesus, are you gonna feel it now."

"Leave me alone, I'm sorry, just leave me alone; don't hit me."

Daddy's trusty old cavalry riding crop whistled as it broke across my breasts and stomach. When I tried to move, he'd pin me against the side of the bed or throw me at the bedpost. The sting got worse, more painful, and he still wasn't through, until the broken glass came back behind my eyes; then black with white spots, like a dying TV picture tube. I was going down.

"Stop it, Corky; y'all hear me, stop it. Y'all want the neighbors over here? Get back in the living room, and don't you raise your voice to ME—not to ME—now, get back in that room."

I lay on my back, the welts rising off my newly acquired suntan like a relief map. It was so still after the beating, I could hear my body, the heart, the lungs, the movement of skin.

My dress lay on the floor in a pile with my shoes. I had kept my blue panties and bra on to view the damage. Luanne would be over soon; I was too tired to get up and I was a mess, my hair, the streaky makeup, a mess, everything, even the blood. He'd killed my mother, Daddy'd killed my mother, and Alice didn't give a damn about anything except her shitty sense of propriety. He'd kill me too, he hated me— All he cared about was Uncle Bobby Jay liking me—all he cared about was my polite behavior to Uncle Bobby Jay. Oh Jesus, Luanne, I'll be the only one of the group not at Bubbles's party. And the slumber party afterward; there'd be talk.

"No, Luanne, Shylah can't go now. Yes, ah know, but that's the way it has to be. No, she has work to do and Mr. Corky and ah feel it would be better if she stayed in tonight."

"S-h-y-l-a-h, Shylah." The whisper from my window was Luanne.

"Listen, ah heard the ruckus. Y'all gotta get out of there. Crank open the slats and slide out. Hurry."

I moved slowly because of the beating. It made everything ache tremendously, sliding out from the wide-slatted window a torture.

"Oh Lawd, Cal, look at those welts, just look at that. Here, honey, let me put some of this ointment on you, it'll make y'all feel better. Y'all have a sip of this."

Miz Juna had put her bathrobe around me, opening it now and again to apply ointment to the welts. Mr. Cal stood in the doorway pumping Luanne for information. The excitement, the beating, were pulling me away from everything now—so tired, hurts. I went into a kind of twilight sleep then, vaguely listening to the sound of Mr. Cal's voice on the phone cursing my father.

★

When I came home, which after all was only one house away, a week later, Alice, by means of her special brand of diplomacy, made it possible for Daddy and me to inhabit the same room without speaking to one another. She fenced, kept up two-way conversations, joked, and entertained. The loneliness of it choked me and I lived more now through my friends. I avoided him for the rest of the school year, festering inside for a real father to come and close the wound.

★

The beginning of our freshman year at Palm View meant an excuse for numerous celebrations. The first smattering of Chevys and Plymouths made their way into the possession of the oldest boys in the class, who made runs to Key West and Marathon, even as far as Homestead if we had some special action in mind, like drag races or the rodeo. Our skirts were shorter, bosoms fuller, boys creeping up in height from our navels to our noses and beyond into full flytrap acne face of puberty.

It was a time for obsessions—any would do—usually related to sex or gadgets or liquor or cars or boats or speed or size, and political thinking too found its way into our constantly critical banter under the smoking tree. A man named Kennedy was a nigger lover, and it was thought that the freedom riders and Martin Luther King ought to be lynched or, from some of the more moderate voices, tarred. Cape Canaveral became a familiar name and Vietnam, the boys dreaming of their moments of glory with the sanctioned genocide of the yellow races.

And my girl friends were beginning to think in terms of getting pregnant by their now-steady boy friends, so that they might marry and gain a kind of status. Mostly though, these things were still at the slumber-party-discussion stage. But already our compulsory home ec classes were given over to lectures on the danger of premarital sex. A French kiss was O.K. after engagement; petting—well, petting was dangerous but sometimes unavoidable. For most of us going on fifteen, as with the even younger original Juliet, it was time to give oneself totally to love, or at least to have a reliable squire with whom to pretend or hop into a back seat once in a while.

★

"Hey, Moose, when y'all shave those legs last? You got a five o'clock shadow from last July."

"Stanley darlin, I see you're wearing your green again. How clever, right on the teeth, who'd have thought to look there?"

"Did you see that, guys? While she was mouthin off, two palmetto bugs and a scorpion just keeled over from the smell of her breath."

"It was your jock actually that did the trick. I just saw a whole family of cooties fall out of your pant leg."

"Y'all oughta know. You put 'em there."

"Oh, stick it in your nose."

"Y'all offerin again, Shylah Moose?"

Stanley, my six-foot, half-Seminole classmate, and I had a kind of mutual crush, and this was our way of making love. But it went beyond just talk and into action as well. If we happened to pass each other on soft grass instead of in the corridor, one or the other would stick a foot out to tackle or be tackled. Both of us had gotten the paddle on account of this, while we provided our class with recess humor. But Stanley never went beyond our touch-tackle foreplay. He had an intense shyness because of his home life; the mother who deserted them, the drunken handyman father, the slow sister. And Stanley took care. Stanley fed. Stanley cleaned house, but Stanley did not ask girls for dates, nor did he initiate anything except the educated tease. And Stanley—Stanley had something shining to him—big, hulking, sometimes clumsy out in his leaky skiff fishing after school, diving for conches and selling them, taking his father out of bars at night. Stanley was Huck Finn, American patriot, wistful bull, gentle, awkward, supreme . . . the island's beloved, good citizen and the poor but honest dream of the four hundred mothers living on Lime.

★

When Miz Juna offered Luanne a party for her birthday, my immediate silent prophecy was sex.

The party was to be in the back yard, which ran down to the dock. I helped Luanne string lights while C.J. reluctantly set up the hi-fi. Hot dogs, potato chips, potato salad, marshmallow salad, and a huge one-layer Holsum birthday cake were placed on a card table to one side. Her parents were out with my parents for the evening, an unspoken politeness shown island teenagers by parents on special nights of entertaining. Luanne and I had bought enormous quantities of Coke for the rum that would soon join it, and I was responsible for the dozen draw-

6 4

ings of Polynesian maidens Scotch-taped to the palm trees and sapodilla. A bamboo shade hut took care of extra beach recliners for couples.

We dressed slowly, ritually, sipping pre-official rum from Dixie cups, bathing, perfuming, slipping carefully into the perfectly ironed capri pants, brushing each other's hair. Lipstick, the last tweezed eyebrow hair, the perfected eyelash. Jumping up and down—squeezing each other for some mystery, some unaccounted perfection that could happen only to us. Because we were us—friends, confidantes, saved seat on school bus, social insurance.

Selma Anne, Rosemary, Cindy, and Bubbles came early to sit on Luanne's twin beds and talk, Luanne doling out the celebratory Bacardi as I passed the Dixie cups of half-filled Coke. The group—advantaged in prettiness and proximity—the beauties, the clique, the full night of first party, seriousness, and grandeur. We sat in our varied, colored capris, our bamboo-pink and soft-orange lipsticks; hot coral in our cheeks and sex. We believed that a three-quarter moon and the warm breezes and our queenly stature would bring us that mystery—perhaps someone would go halfway; perhaps someone would get secretly engaged; perhaps the pubescent boys would grow into Frankie Avalons and Elvis Presleys under Artemis's moon, hopefully somewhere between the third and fourth Roman Coke.

"Hey, Shy, y'all look sharp . . . Did something to your hair?"

"Luanne fixed it. You too; where'd you get the new capris?"

"Richard's in Cutler Ridge. Hey, y'all wanna hear what Sonny Lee told me . . . he said the guys invited some guys from Marathon and Key West."

"Too much! Damn senior girls think they're gonna see all the action."

"Remember the Big 6; we're the only class Palm View's ever had that is this tough, man—we're the toughest," laughed Selma Anne, who choked on a giggle, throwing her head into the pillow.

"Come onnnn, Bubbles, damn y'all, stop makin that face; ah can't stand it, ah can't stand it."

We were dropping under the momentum of rum and party

like a card house, laughing over nothing, loving our silliness together this night.

"Aw, Shy, ah'll never forget when y'all slammed into Lena. Man, the Keys never seen a girl fight that way; y'all sure was a different sight to behold." Rosemary was rolling around on the throw rug, streaking her makeup with laughter-tears.

"Honest, Shy, y'all gotta be weird with—with like everything you been through and your vocabulary and drawing and stuff, till you came down we weren't like we are now. Ooow weeee-we are sooopreme!"

"Yeah, I wish the boys in the class could get that into their heads."

"Aw, Shy, y'all know how those things go, damn older kids just ruined you . . . Look, you're the most popular girl with the Marathon and Key West guys, the ones that talk fancy and stuff; we don't get a chance, you're the one who . . ."

"Yeah, but I want to, you know, be liked like you all, by the boys in my class. They terrify me with their teasing."

"Oh Lawd, y'all crazy. They're babies."

"Not all of them. Oh, drop it, you guys; listen we're the tops, no sweat, so let's go outside before the boys give up on us."

Luanne's front yard began to fill up with the automotive droning of Chevys and Fords and an occasional Plymouth convertible customized beyond recognition. The Key West and Marathon boys, nineteen- and twenty- and twenty-one-year-olds, confident in their red and white upholstery—the pressed open-to-the-new-chest-hairs knit shirts, the tight pants, the fifths instead of pints of adult drinking nobility. They came and we swiveled—my flat ass and hips swaying in hopeful imitation—my shoulders thrown back—my expression of carefully studied vacancy. The six of us paraded the yard, the best of local produce—paraded and received the adulation of these visiting hotrod dignitaries, confident in the power of our poker faces. This accomplished, we resumed hysteria and compared notes. Then the younger kids—our classmates—arrived, piled into the three cars owned by the oldest members. And the rest of the high school in their cars, filled to capacity and freshly waxed (the cars) and shaved (the drivers).

"Hey, Shylah Moose, y'all look pretty good for an animal. Ah figured you and the other lips be around getting a little head-start on the rum."

"Thanks, beauty, I guess you're focusing for once. Wanna Coke?"

"Yeah, O.K.; so how's it goin?"

"It's not yet."

"Get fresh again, Moose?"

"Begging again, Stanley?"

"Think we could go and sit down on one of those things without y'all getting spastic?"

"Depends on whether you can contain the gorilla underneath that Old Spice . . . Oooh, Stanley, I do believe you used deodorant tonight. Knocks me out."

Stanley and I managed to hold hands without side effects as we walked to the farthest beach lounge chair under the bamboo and frond canopy. C.J., looking as if he had emerged from the sacred pools of grease, had charge of the records. Thoughtfully he put on the slowest, most agonizing ballads he could find, like "Teen Angel," which always put me off, as I kept thinking about what her body looked like after the big train engine had run over her, his high-school ring or no ring—and "Town without Pity," which was a little too autobiographical not to depress me. C.J.'s selections were all geared for instant sex, not for any desire to get on the concrete patio and dance.

It was coolish near the water. A Northeastern due, the beginning winds picked up paper plates and cups, scattering them about the lawn. Rich moonlight shone in streaks, with clouds closing in and passing in front of its path upon the water. A few of the kids came in their speedboats, the lights making patterns closing into shore and the whirring motors had a certain gritty, romantic lull to them. I was surprised that Stanley had come. Usually he kept to himself at night or stayed with his father and sister. Rumor had it that he tutored her in reading and spelling, which seemed both amazing and peculiar . . . peculiar because Stanley could barely handle more than Classic Comics. Not that he was particularly stupid. But unless a student pursued independent study, Palm View presented a pretty raw source of learning—nobody read or wrote particularly well, including the faculty.

Stanley and I squeezed into the deck chair together, our combined bignesses pushing our skins against each other. Nothing happened for a while, except our sweat. So we sucked on our Cokes—mine fortified with rum—still holding each other's damp paw. Short of me kissing him first, which I thought would make it worse, he needed to be budged into initiative. So I waited and squeezed myself into advantageous positions like a rutting python.

"Ah don't mean to insult you, Moosie, but y'all really look good tonight, ah mean for a leper; y'all know that, don't you?"

"So you finally noticed. Well, you're getting there, Stan Bear; maybe in the next forty years you could . . ."

He kissed me. He finally did it . . . softly, like eating bananas, like satin quilts. With the windiness and the kids dancing, we just stayed kissing crammed together, our arms pinned by each other's weight and falling asleep, we stayed biding, the longest unexploring, matter-of-fact kiss.

"Y'all wanna go for a walk, Shy? This is embarrassing, huh. Whyn't we take a walk?"

"O.K., down the old road, I guess."

Vertical again, still holding soggy hands, we walked down the little-used road that was the first to cross the island in its pirate days. Toward the end of it was the Tanya Lovel place, with its expanses of mat grass and Spanish manor house with the heart-shaped pool (or ass-shaped—that being the local joke about her risqué movies). She used it rarely, keeping the house for occasional visits away from Beverly Hills and Rome. We climbed the head-high stone fence—nobody took security very seriously on the island—and jumped to the other side. We skirted the pool and gardens to the main house and around on the other side to the water, with its filled-in, perfect little beach, pinkish sand turned blue under the moon.

I kicked off my sandals and Stanley his pointed old loafers and smelly socks, approaching the shore fill of water, squiggling our toes. Stanley hugged me, a squeeze that would have flattened my smaller, more delicate Southern girl friends but seemed appropriate to my bigness. Unlike Mick, who was merely eager, Stanley had tenderness built into the clumsy caresses. And because of the awkwardness—the absence of false finesse—it felt better, much better, and I could participate more, moving my arms in different positions upon his back, rubbing it, gently grasping the generous wrinkles that flesh makes.

We lay down with our toes resting together at the shoreline and kissed again, and he moved his lips to other places now, to different parts of my face and neck—acquainting kisses to the ears and neck and cheek and eyelid, eyebrows, chin; and mine to the side of his nose and just above his upper lip, and this too was constantly beginning things. My hands slid about—he was laughing a bit—we were tying each other up with the contortions of rolling around. And when he stopped he lay at an angle to me, one leg between my two and moved around to the kiss, more open-mouthed now, more directed, his tongue pushing between my teeth. I could feel the ridge of his erection against the top part of my leg, comforting for some reason. We lay sweat-soaked, becoming embarrassed again at the newness and at our bodies.

He felt me. Tentatively at first, unaccustomed to softer places, different places, rubbing my breasts on top of the material, then under and over my bra; then one hand traveling down to crotch and touching, curious and cautious, touching—light, with open hand slightly inclined, pressing at different points, while I pressed hard on him, hard.

"Ohhhh Shylah, oh Gawd."

"Hmmmm."

Stanley had been momentarily confounded by the technology of bra, trying to undo the impossible hook in back, struggling with the possibility of instant success. I put my hand around to help, bunching the material until his hand brought one side over and loosened it; then pushing the shirt and bra up too quickly, and stopping as if to question, and the hands finally brought forward over the breasts and around, startling me, then withdrawing, then returning, then dying a little over the expansive, loose, sloping lemon-shaped nipples, then kneading the breasts whole, then particularizing to nipples again as they grew rigid; then traveling to the waist, the fingers more confident on the familiar turf of button and fly, then downward to where the hair sprouts sparsely, to the pubis and to the ridge of lips, and back up to pull the pants and panties down, out of the way.

At some point his clothing and my clothing were at the extremes of our bodies—pushed up to the neck, pulled down to the knee; naked except for this binding at extremities. It was funny to us, this bondage, so I left his arms long enough to remove the remainder of my clothing, and he his. It was altogether quicker than helping one another.

When we were naked, I mean, completely so, it seemed initially less arousing, less sexy than before, with the gradual unfolding of flesh to be quickly encompassed within the other's flesh. We were separate for a moment. And the embarrassment returned, then was replaced by a kind of objective curiosity. Stanley's arms and trunk were suggestive of two ages: straight, soft fleshiness of child, and bulges here and there of labor-induced manhood-muscle, at the upper arms and chest and around the ribs. Only a half dozen wispy hairs were scattered around the two flat nipples, and down below a line of dark fuzz that expanded into sparse soft hair, making a nest out of which his prick sprang, I thought at first, like some grotesque egret off a hair nest of testicle eggs. The sight was an ambiguous one; I was unsure if it should be viewed or obscured—there was something initially just a little too obvious about a prick. I wasn't sure if I thought it funny or frightening, pleasant or repulsive. I was used to the hide-and-seek aspects of my own apparatus. A prick, however, begged confrontation. And it was kind of bizarre, sort of crippled-looking—sort of freaklike at first. Poor Stanley, poor baby. It went against everything I had been taught about aesthetics. I wrapped fingers around it then, to blind and to reassure, trying not to laugh. Yet the strength of it, comfortable pleasure in my hand like a smooth sea rock or waxy cucumber—I felt less compassionate then and more interested in what I held and now fondled.

7 0

Stanley shifted to his side, his arm crossing my hip and moving so that the flat of his hand caressed the hairs over my pussy. His fingers opened the lips and closed them—opened and closed—until one finger slid between and back and in and again, the familiar front part getting fuzzy and excited better than when I did it to myself. Better than that. Softer, then harder, then softer. On my back, feeling the particles of sand in the crack of ass, feeling the breeze and seeing the few visible stars through the black-cloud clusters, feeling the finger and yet not feeling, pleasure—the tension of my legs beginning to shake with it, responding into him and apart from him. His finger lowered and pushed against skin, and pushed lower against skin again, until it found the opening—pressing, pushing. It stung and I jumped.

"Oh Shylah, ah'm sorry, ah'm sorry. Did ah hurt you?"

"Yeah, it's O.K. I guess you have to be pretty gentle there. It's O.K., really. I like it, do it again."

"No, ah don't wanna hurt . . ."

"No, really, Stanley, I want you to."

Again the wet hand moved down, his face inclined to it as if watching for pain, bringing his lips up again and down on my face, kissing me again and this time the fingers were barely felt in pressure, me enjoying it even more in suggestion, until the forefinger went farther, while the remaining ones spread the lips—extended them to open me a little more. The finger approached, and pressed rather than butted this time, pressed and remained there till I felt my pussy open enough of itself to give entry. Although the sting was there, it wasn't so bad this time, and I grew wet with gooey stuff like Vaseline, which let the finger go in farther . . . in a kind of whoosh of wet, a little way, then a little farther, until I jumped again, so he drew the finger back a little and went in again, while I stroked his prick, holding it just below mushroom top and moved my hand back and forth, imitating him, imitating the way he moved while his other fingers caressed the button. We went on this way awhile . . . building, building, until he pushed abruptly away from me, making throat sounds.

"Oh, Shylah, ah gotta . . . ah don't know, ah don't wanna hurt you, but ah mean, ah wanna do it . . . you know . . . ah can't stand it any more . . ."

"We can't; I'd get pregnant and stuff and, oh God, if we got . . . maybe if you had a rubber or something."

"Uh, uh, no, it's O.K., we won't, ah guess, but ah want to be there, ah want to be with you. Oh Shylah, ah really love you. Oh Shylah, please."

"We'll do it this way, Stanley. Won't it be O.K.? I know, I know, I want you too but . . . Show me how to, you know, rub you and everything, show me . . ."

Stanley held me to him with one arm around me and with the other brought his hand over my hand, which was holding his prick. He moved my fingers to a spot just under the head of it, and directed my hand back and forth over a prescribed area. I held it close, tightly against my belly, and gently tugged as he directed, and he returned his hand to my crotch, playing with the top part again until he was moaning and my legs were shaking; then he pushed his prick hard, straining, into my hand, until the stuff spurted out of the valley in the top, then more—a stream of it exciting me, feeling my own contractions, shivering, rolling into him and back, and everything let go, and there was nothing except the feeling, the feeling of rolling in sugar on a mountaintop, afterward coming down the slope of it, legs loosening, tired, and Stanley's eyes watching me, respectful and soft. Ah, nice Stanley, nice Shylah. Nice and protected. My hand came awake to itself again, felt the sticky globs of mucous stuff, his sperm, milky and lumpy like flour dough, and on my stomach more of it, sticking there, gelatinous. I took the messy hand and put it around him and held, half on, half off each other, held and we almost in sleep but not asleep, and I kissed his cheek and he mine.

"You awake, Stanley? We better go pretty soon. But I don't want to leave, Stanley, ever."

"Let's swim, Shylah, let's go for a quick swim. There's a net out there . . . it's safe. Want to? C'mon."

We stood up, brushing off the sand that stuck to our wetness, and slipped into the quiet little bay. We swam to the net and back a few times, just long enough to wash ourselves and cool off . . . I had to be careful to keep my hair dry to avoid later explanations. And then, where it was shallow, we embraced. No excitement—peaceful—and the water made the skin new and puckered and pleasant.

"Ah love you, Moosie, you know ah love you, even when we talk that way."

"Yeah, I know; I mean, I guess I know. Me too, you, love. We'll come back here soon, honest. I— It was good, yes? Please?"

"Oh Lawd, yah, oh Shy, Shy Moose, ah wouldn't hurt you. Ah don't ever want to hurt you."

"I know, I believe you. Oh shit, how are we going to climb back into our clothes when we're this wet? I forgot about towels and stuff."

We raced each other back and forth on the beach to dry off, jumping up and down, skipping, until the excess moisture had left us and we could climb, sticky from the saltwater, into our clothes again and not give ourselves away.

When we returned I was ready to plunge into the nearest bed. Tired and without many thoughts, my last interest was more party or dopey conversation.

"Shylah, where y'all been, you missed Bobby's elephant imitation . . . Bubbles is really bombed. Y'all can see by the bodies the party was a success."

Luanne reflected her age and the community. She was not nearly as tight as she pretended—most of the kids weren't either—but alcohol served as an excuse to act in a cute, crazy way without repercussion. Certain abnormal behavior was permissible, even laudable, as long as the person was assumed reasonably shit-faced.

"Wallll, if it isn't the two lovebirds, y'all been missed by us common folk." Selma Anne cackled as Selma Anne always cackled at others' attempts at bliss. Bert and Jack smiled with their teeth in Stanley's direction.

"O.K., you guys, shove it."

"Whatcha yawnin for, Stanley, y'all ain't seen that much party, lez y'all and Shy been havin a private show."

"Shut up, Jack. Who needs your mouth, huh."

Another hour of the party and relief when Luanne's parents returned and kids squealed out in a cordon. It was difficult for us to be alone again, and Stanley was much too shy for any display of obvious affection. We kissed briefly out of sight before he went home. If we could have slept together, like on Tanya's beach, that would have been perfect—to go back and fall asleep with our toes in the water—to be that close and unconscious.

★

Zoe drove down in December as he had promised. It would mean Daddy and I spending more time together with him; it would mean our first Christmas without Mummy and Rick. But Zoe was here, Zoe would make it O.K.

"Zoe, Zoe boy, goddamn, Alice. Allllicccce, Zoe boy's here." My father bestowed the paternal bear hug, a wallop to Zoe's wiry back.

"Hi, Dad; hey, Shylah."

"Hi, Zoe. I . . ."

"Zoeee, ah've heard soo much about y'all from Corky; oh, Shy's just been waitin to see you these past few weeks, sooo excited, mah goodness. It's really a treat to have you here, in'it, baby, in'it, Shy?"

"Oh yeah, how have . . ."

"Baby's been an angel, Zoe, gettin good grades and . . ."

"Oh for Christsake, Mother, let the boy sit down and have a drink, he been drivin the whole damn day."

"Absolutely. Shylah, you and me, we'll go fix some nice nibblies for the boys. Corky, how 'bout we take the children to the Old Lime Inn for special treat. Have some nahce cream of peanut soup and turtle steak and Key lime pie and . . ."

"Yes, yes, settle down now, Alice, wanna talk to Zoe here, now."

Daddy's conversation with Zoe was essentially private, as it was with all returning males over the age of ten. Though we pulled out the crawfish meat, the crackers, the onion dip, the scallions, the cheese, though we served, though Alice freshened drinks, though I smiled—it was not a time for me to talk to Zoe. See but not speak, until after the paternal lecture and question period, till after the consummation of shared liquor, till after the pleasure of seeing a piece of one's blood had diminished to small talk, the public-ness of dinner at the island's one prestigious eatery. And Daddy got drunk and by dessert had moved from small talk to nastiness, challenging Zoe: "How does being a damn intellectual affect your sex life? Been to any Commie rallies lately? Not much money in teaching, is there? How come you never write; but we're proud of our smart boy, yessuh, we're proud," etc. Awful!

Awful for Zoe. Awful for Shylah. I couldn't speak; the words came out like wet laundry. Nothing worked. Nothing at all. Daddy struck out. He had to. Other parents would have welcomed their children, fed them, and given advice. It was Daddy who made war out of emotion—unendurable to his own feelings of tenderness. Terrifying. And Alice, Alice could not endure what was raw. It must be kneaded into an acceptable explanation; it must be cooed into obeisance; it must be mollified and controlled; it must be separated from itself and made into an article. While Daddy grew sodden, attacked Zoe and me, then attempted some connection to love, Alice explained, interpreted, propagandized in translation. By the ride home, dream talk and conversation had merged. Daddy raved quietly amid snorts and questions; he left the zone of returning son to wander amid the ruin of his daughter, repeating to himself, "Piss poor, piss poor, piss poor daughter. Not worth a shit," and dozed off in the back seat. At home, he balanced himself while removing the bulk of his stomach from the Caddy. He stepped carefully, deliberately avoiding a stagger. Once in his rocking chair, he turned on the radio, catching the Miami news station in competition with Cuban jamming and Radio Nacional—unintelligible buzz. Then, ordering a snifter of the older brandy from Alice, went into a loud nasal snore, punctuated by farts.

"Jesus Christ, Shylah, that was rough, you know."

"Yes, well, I guess the excitement. It's good in a way. At least he can't hold it and cover the territory like he used to. I thought maybe things'd be O.K. when you . . ."

"He doesn't mean . . . Oh Shylah, you can't take his ravings seriously, I mean when he says things about you . . ."

"Why the hell not? Am I supposed to kid myself?—he hates me. You can't tell me he doesn't hate me. Neither one of them gives a shit about anything except that I don't disgrace them and that I'm nice to their famous friend, Leads, Jesus. Alice, she controls everything; I mean, she's nice about stuff but she's always acting, you know, unreal, insincere, and oh God, she talks to me like I'm some sort of cretin. They never discuss Mummy, you know. It's like the plague, and Daddy blew up when I wouldn't call Alice Mother. Mother! Can you imagine asking something like that, just so I'd be more respectful to her. I don't know. Aw shit, I thought things'd be different, good and easy, for your visit, and I wouldn't be saying these things. I'm sorry. And the Christmas trees, I could have screamed; she bought those little plastic things instead of a good solid pine, and she supervised what I could get everybody, and she made me buy her mother this obnoxious cheap perfume, and I've never met her mother, right. I mean, I can't help feeling contempt for her, Zoe."

"Yes, I had an idea you did. I know we couldn't really talk over the phone. What about school and the kids down here? Is it all right, do you like it?"

"That's the terrific part, I'm different and everything, but I've some close friends, a group actually, and dates, stuff like that. It's a completely different way of living—all this color and different values, shit like that."

"You getting along at school, Shylah?"

"Well, yes and no. It's real Southern-cracker living, with all the bigotry. School's kind of a joke in a way, but I like it—I mean, nobody really learns much. The older kids give me a lot of lip and I don't get along that well with some teachers, but it doesn't matter some way. I mean, I guess I really love Lime, even with Daddy and everything. I really love it, the island, the way people are and live. You know. It helps me forget the sadness. When things get really rough with Daddy, I spend the night at Luanne's next door, she's my best friend, her parents are pretty understanding."

"Well, we'll see how it goes. I don't know, Shylah. He's pretty dreadful this way—difficult for anyone."

★

Stanley and I met in secret at the Lovel house Christmas Eve. It wasn't exactly that we couldn't hang around together, but then again, if Daddy suspected what was going on, I would be grounded. So we kidded around at school and after with the kids, and when we wanted to be lovers, to feel we were in love, to act accordingly, we met in secret and played out our dreams of domesticity.

"Oh Stanley, thanks really, yeah I love Friendship Garden, no really; and it's a whole set, powder and cologne and soap and everything; no, it's just great—I really love you, Stanley— No, it's better than expensive. Besides, you had to really save for it, right? I'm glad you like the shirt; you like blue?— Oh good; no, that isn't it—I have more money than you. Oh, I wish you could be with me on Christmas Day; it'd be great just to sleep together through midnight into Christmas. What are you going to do? Oh Stan Gorilla, don't say that, you'll do something. What about your sister? That's really a nice dress you bought her. Look, I have some extra money; why don't I give you some and you all can go and have a big Christmas feast at . . ."

"No, Moose, ah'm O.K. and ah'm not takin money from YOU of all people. Y'all wait, Shy, we gonna have Christmas together one of these days, and everything and everybody else can go shove it. Soon as ah get a payin job and stuff, we can get married and have Christmas and Easter and birthdays—all that shit. Mr. Bob said he'd let me apprentice-guide for tarp and he's the best in the business."

"Oh shit, c'mon, that's four damn years. I want us to have this Christmas. Hey, my brother's down, by the way."

"Yah, ah met him. Your daddy acquainted us; we was working on the yard, Terry and me. He's sort of nahce, brainy guy, right? Plays a fiddle."

"Viola actually, oh Stanley . . ."

It was chilly on the Keys this time of year, getting down to 60 sometimes, even below, cold when you weren't used to it, wet wind getting into the flesh. We wore sweaters, Stanley and I, burrowing under each other's to feel and to touch and to hold. We had not yet gone all the way, following the best alternate imitations we could think of to get to one another. I had been frightened about it, and because I was frightened, Stanley felt responsible and we waited. Even as I knew him like this, he was growing and reshaping, slimmer now, more muscular, the baby fat draining from his cheeks and jowls, replaced by hard Indian ridges and a slanted jaw. And I had in turn grown slimmer, and now it was different the way we fit together, a little harder, more definite, more accustomed. And we grew this way. We grew.

★

"Wellll, Bobby Jay boy, good to see y'all, Merry Christmas. C'mon in, Shylah, look who's here—it's Uncle Bobby Jay, in't she pretty-looking? Alice got her that little bathrobe she's wearing, in't that the damnedest thing. Hey, meet my boy Zoe, down with us a couple weeks; yah, he's the skinny one. How 'bout some coffee and little morning snort, huh? Alice, y'all wanna bring out a pony glass for Bobby Jay here."

"Hello, Princess; come here, angel, Merry Christmas." Uncle Bobby Jay produced a small gold box with an outsize red ribbon.

"You too, Uncle Bobby Jay, gee thanks. I've got one for you. I hope you use this stuff, it smelled the best."

"English Leather, why it's just what ah use, honey; now y'all open your little present. You open it."

I knew before I opened it that it was expensive, and by the size of the box, some piece of jewelry— Uncle Bobby Jay liked expensive things; it was part of him to order the most expensive of everything.

"Oh Uncle Bobby Jay, it's, uh, nice really. A real Arlene Francis heart necklace. Thanks, thanks a lot."

"Bobby Jay, oh, that's much too much, really; why y'all just the most generous . . . Shylah lamb, in'it just boo'ful, ooooh, real diamonds."

I hated Arlene Francis hearts. They reminded me of Shirley Temple on a middle-age chest. I wondered how many hundreds of dollars he'd spent, maybe enough for a secondhand car for Stanley or a trip. I tried to be gracious, but I thought the repulsive little diamond heart needed a quick pawnshop. It would have been one thing if Stanley had bought me a little paste heart, I could accept and love it then, but Uncle Bobby Jay and his monied presents were a little too intimate, a little too much like payment on a lease or something.

"Shylah girl, ah hope you appreciate what a fine gift you got here. Honest to God. Bobby Jay, y'all joinin us for Christmas dinner, boy? Lots of good food; Alice been busy for a week."

"Corky, y'all know ah can't stay away from Alice's cooking. Ah got a whole slew of fancy French champagne we're gonna open for it. Hey, Princess, come help me bring over some bottles, hear."

"Go on, daughter, make yourself useful."

Uncle Bobby Jay's excuses for intimacy out of parental eyeshot made dirty old men in a park look discreet. And yet Daddy and Alice encouraged it. Inside his house, with the glass bar and the two hundred photographs of himself and the eight-foot sofas, he picked me up as he always picked me up and smooched, as he called it. I chortled, pulled, made jokes, as I always did, to get out of the squeeze—as if I had rabid eczema or something and needed to scratch every time he touched me.

"Princess, you look damn nahce these days, y'all know that; lost all your baby fat. Tell you what, before we bring the stuff back, let's you and me, as a special treat, split a bottle here in the house, huh. Nahce and cold. See, this one's Dom Pérignon, best there is."

The champagne tasted like 7-Up with lemon added and the sugar taken out. Delicious. We sat before the glass bar while Uncle Bobby Jay talked about the old days and about how pretty he thought I was becoming and about going fishing with him one day that week.

"Come on, Uncle Bobby Jay, we better be getting back; they'll wonder if we fell off the pier or something. Really now, be serious, don't you think we better get going, huh? Oh, come on now, that tickles, no, really, please don't; no, I don't think . . ."

"Aw, Princess, relax now. Just a little affection; now, be nahce."

O.K., bastard, one big kiss and out the door, payment received. And actually it wasn't bad really, he being very gentle in his boozy way and good-looking and all that. And he knew everything about mouth placement. Jesus, but why me—why not some movie star or something? Seemed silly, a silly thing to do. But it had its sexiness, kissing him. I wished it had been my idea instead of his demand; that made me sort of hate him at the same time.

"Y'all wait, Princess, y'all grow up and ah'll marry you and we'll go travelin all over the damn place. Y'all just grow up lovely and pure . . ."

"Yeah, sure. Here, let me help you with those; no, I can take three. Hurry, Alice'll want me for the kitchen and stuff."

Wanting to see Stanley or just to talk to him, but there was no phone at his place, no way to get away. Anyhow, we were busy now—mashing potatoes and pouring bourbon and cutting cranberry loaf and setting the table, while Zoe and Uncle Bobby Jay and Daddy did nothing, sat, drank, and talked. Joe Joe hung close to me, licked my bare feet after I'd given him tastes of cranberry and stuffing. Sweet Joe Joe.

Champagne and dinner, with me a little drunk and excited. I couldn't get myself to do less than drain anything that tasted like doctored 7-Up. Luanne came over, had some champagne, and we exchanged presents. Harry had given her an engagement ring, a new secret to keep. She wore it pinned to the inside of her bra, as was the custom for unannounced engagements. I guessed that she'd be trying to get pregnant soon, so that things would be official. That was the way to do it.

And then it was over, first Christmas after death, and it had been nothing, nothing much. Zoe went North, I started school again. Even in the tropics January and February had that dull, frigid cast, dangerous months for depression.

5

"Hi, Shylah bird."

"Hi, Selma Anne."

"Ah'm havin a slumber party Friday night after the game. Just the group— Y'all coming, right?"

"Oh sure, sure, why not."

"Mah folks'll be up in Illinois; only mah dumb sister and the maid'll be around. Man, we'll have a blast. Got the whole motel to ourselves practically."

"Want me to bring anything?"

"Uh uh. Guys are gonna get us some rum, and Mom's makin potato salad and stuff for us before they leave. Just bring your Yankee, nigger-loving soul, Shy."

"Negro-loving, Selma Anne. Negro-loving."

"Oh, pahrdon me, your High Queerness, hoohah. Hey, Shy, did'y'all hear about Verona, ah can't believe it."

"No, clue me in."

"Sandy said she's pregnant. You know, she's been acting odd lately; ah mean, she's always been a little weird, y'all know, depressed and stuff, that horrible father and brother she has. There's even a rumor—sheriff came to her house—that her daddy, well, you know how he is, that he raped her. But officially ah guess it's Custer; ah mean, ah knew she wanted to marry him and everything and . . ."

"Oh God, poor Verona. Shit, Selma Anne, she was crying in art class last week and I thought, you know, it was just one of those times when she gets depressed. What's she gonna do? They're all so dirt poor . . . Besides, she's not, uh, very stable, you know. Like I like her a lot but sometimes, well, I guess she has emotional problems. Who wouldn't in her place? Maybe there's some way we could, you know, make her feel better, like, why don't we invite her—no, I guess it's a little out of her turf, but well, something we could do. She's really sweet, you know, and . . ."

"Well, we can be extra nahce to her, but frankly, she's so . . . Well, they lead a different life, Shylah, she'd feel funny, me askin her to the slumber party."

"Yes, I guess. I don't know. I've been helping her in history with the answers and maybe I could ask if she'd like to go get a Coke or something after school. Jesus, Verona doesn't deserve all the shit she gets."

"O.K., Florence Nightingale, O.K. Y'all mahnd if ah ask you what the hell you wearing to the game or if you would consider going with Ma and me Homestead way to buy an outfit, lahk Wednesday after school?"

"Sure, if Alice'll let me have some money."

Selma Anne was built like, and moved like, a hard-boiled egg. Wherever she went, she tilted and sloped, her head elongated, her shoulders rounded, her little belly pushed out, her arrogant buns, her baseball-bat thighs and those incredible calves. Really like an egg. Her strawberry-blond hair always pulled back into a perfect ponytail, sloped under, page-boy-style—again like a nice strawberry-blond egg. Selma Anne was too much. Came off the cutest of us but not the prettiest, the funniest but not the wittiest, the most energetic but not the most active, the bitchiest but not the nastiest, the most jovial but never content with herself. To get into Selma Anne's sync was a little like putting a needle on a record blindfolded. Either a person got along with her or didn't, and it didn't matter if the personalities were sympathetic or not, it had to do with the

rhythm of Selma Anne's moods. We had shared rocky times of
insult hurling; now, as long as we kept it light, we were buddies, and when you were buddies with Selma Anne, unless she
did a little backbiting, which was her style, if anybody else attacked you, old Selma Anne would let fly.

On Thursday Cindy called a meeting of the six of us to
discuss tactics for the slumber party. Not that there was ever a
tactic for any slumber party, or any party for that matter, but
Cindy called group meetings for what Cindy felt was important—which we all dutifully attended under our smoking tree
by the schoolyard. Cindy was Cindy, the oldest child in a struggling family of plumber and local singer. Cindy was responsible. Cindy was in control. Cindy was a natural sophisticate,
smart but not brainy, unique-cool but diplomatic, and certainly
no rebel. Cindy, a mother's choice, always the one who would
win the civics award for citizenship. If there was business to be
done, she took care of it.

"Who's in charge of gettin the rum, Selma Anne?"

"Johnny and the other guys paid some nigger to get us Bacardi."

"How long we gonna let the boys stay? Ah mean, don't y'all
think it'd be a good idea if we made a rule that they'll have to
go by twelve or something?"

"Cindy, if you think ah'm gonna kick Harry out by twelve
when it'll be the first time in ages without parents . . . Aw shit,
we'll just go to the beach then."

"Y'all made your point, Luanne," Selma Anne placated.
"Look, why'n't we say no boys in the unit we're gonna use after
twelve and boys can stay in another area with girls until one or
so. That way Harry and you . . . and, oh wait, let's also say no
boys except boy friends can stay, O.K.?"

"What about the boys comin up from Key West, y'all sayin
they can't come over? Danny said they maght come, aw c'mon
. . ." Rosemary moaned. "Besides, ah'll be comin late anyway
with cheerleading and stuff. We got a meetin after school."

Rosemary was our jock, the one ninth-grader on the senior
cheerleading team, the upper-class girls' favorite. Rosemary had
the loosest style . . . about books, sex, anything . . . the group

cracker, a real, pure Southern backwoodswoman, her Alabama granddaddy being some super mucky-muck official in the Klan. Rosemary wore her race hatred like a new white dress, and her Holy Roller mama did the best she could to nurture the quirk. Yet in her way Rosemary appeared the most adventurous, the most daring, the most laissez-faire to others— Perhaps it was that Rosemary was not very bright, not very bright at all.

"Oh, y'all know there's no sense in making too many rules. Whyn't we just keep our unit to ourselves and have the kids elsewhere? Ah mean, what's the fun if we don't have some guys around, specially if they're from Key West and Marathon?"

Beautiful Everina. Even with her dumb nickname, Bubbles, nothing detracted from the doll-like prettiness she carried with her. Delicate, delicate—something slightly hysterical in her, easily excited, fainted on whim. Hers was never to initiate; she went along, she laughed a lot. Everina the belle, to be taken care of and given things. Everina had no meanness, no creative intelligence, no ambitions. Everina moved as water moved, oblivious to the shores she touched or the weather.

When all of us had gone through the attitudes and points of view, we wound up with a better idea of what each person wanted and rules were then unnecessary. So it was understood the unit would be off limits and girls could make out in the numerous other available places. Cindy's sense of organization was replenished, while Bubbles's lack of it also fit in.

★

The big-toe sandal had come into style and I wore my new pair in a mild amount of pain that Friday night, the leather cutting into the skin between my big toe and the one next to it, a piece of raw flesh being rubbed in confinement. Palm View played Seminole, down from the Everglades, and we lost as we always lost to the other team. Stanley, our star basketball player, functioned as a salvaging agent for the raunchy team, making twenty of our twenty-four points to their eighty. Key West males hung around, slicked hair and all that garbage keeping us on our sexiest behavior, a little more bored in our pretend-bored look, a little more vacant and uncaring, the way they expected us to act—silent beyond everything—objects of immense value but useless. Except me, I wasn't silent and I wasn't bored, not really, just contemptuous now that I had Stanley. And they especially liked me because boys like the girls they can't get close to. I didn't like them.

Stanley and I were still unofficial sweethearts, which offered me no protection at these events. He wouldn't be caught dead near our slumber party . . . not with the older, affluent boys, the boys with convertibles, who traveled distances and wore cuff links in their shirts. Stanley would not come, would not speak of it.

"Hey, Rod's got 'Handy Man' and 'Cathy's Clown' and 'Now or Never.' Lawd, ah love 'Handy Man.' C'mon, Shylah, help me hook this thing up." Luanne had hold of the little record player and I obeyed by moving the chest of drawers to get at the socket. Rod came up from behind, putting a hand on the small of my back.

"Jesus, Shylah, where y'all been? None of us seen you for ages. Y'all got some action on the side?"

"Nope. Been busy."

"With who, Luanne? Y'all so thick, ah mean . . . Johnny says as how he saw y'all kissin. That true, huh, Shylah, you turnin a little bit queer?"

"Oh, shove off, snotnose. You're just pissed cause I couldn't go out with you last week."

"Maghty peculiar, y'all turnin down a big party in Key West. The other girls would . . ."

"Kick you in the nuts. Look, smartass, next time ask them, not me, why dontcha?"

"O.K., O.K., didn't mean to make you mad, beautiful, ah was just kiddin."

For some reason, though it had nothing to do with common sense, we changed into our sleepwear immediately—that is, the standard baby dolls, hip-length cotton pastel tops and oversize bloomers. Slumber-party uniform. The boys were around—that made no difference—it was perfectly respectable to run around and dance in transparent attire as long as it was within the confines of an official night together, even though none of us would risk contempt by sleeping before the sun rose. Once the baby dolls covered us, we were free to swig Roman Cokes, listen to nothing, listen to everything, or listen to something that would inevitably occur, we thought, if we listened hard.

"Where's Luanne, Shylah? Ah haven't seen her in over an hour." Cindy wore her concerned look.

"With Harry, I guess."

"Ah just came from the beach; they're not there and his car's gone."

"So . . ."

"So, fruitcake, she been drinkin pretty heavy and last ah saw her, she and that guy Lee were makin a case for themselves in his car and ah think Harry must a seen 'em too. Since y'all so hot and heavy, ah thought y'all maght lahk to know."

"Oh God, now what? I just thought they . . . well, you know."

Rod drove me out to look for her, to the two beaches where kids went, then up and down the Highway 1 strip. Nothing. Aw, Luanne, Luanne. I couldn't stand this. I couldn't stand not knowing where she was. Why didn't she tell me? She never did that, never left without telling me, never.

"Take a run up-island to the Palm View beach. Please, Rod, don't argue; something's weird. No, I mean it."

Rod begrudgingly swung the car around for the ten-mile ride to the school. Harry's blue Chevy stood parked just off the little road that led to the beach behind the old gym building. I was the first to hear her.

"Luuuuuannne, oh shit, Luanne, what'd he do to you? Jesus, Luanne. Does it hurt? where? Wait till I get my hands on him. Oh, Luanne, be still, will ya. Just let me—let me hold you. Here, I've got some Kleenex, let me wipe your face. I'll take care of you. Luanne, it's O.K. Yes, I know, it's all right, that's still no reason to get slapped around; you were sort of drunk, it happens, and . . . Jesus, that cut looks mean."

Good old desperate Luanne, moving into my arms like liquid cement . . . tightening when she got there, howling her outrage in forced tears, still a little drunk, her freshly rolled hair hanging in clumps. We sat holding each other, the bottoms of my baby dolls and her capris soaked with the incoming tide.

"Rod, did you find Harry?"

"Uh huh, he's O.K.—just pissed off. C'mon, let's go, Shylah."

"Luanne, try to stand. Here, I've got you. Listen, the girls are worried about you, c'mon. You'll feel better after you get cleaned up. Really, it'll be all right, Luanne, I'll take care of you."

Rod drove Luanne and me back, leaving Harry to follow. She kept up a steady weep, sniffling, choking, and heaving, her soggy face laminated to my soggy lap. Arriving at Selma Anne's, the boys dispersed quickly under command of Cindy, who rose to the occasion. In a short time, the group was sitting on beds in the spacious motel unit, eating potato chips and comforting Luanne. After all, a girl could get drunk sometimes too and get carried away with a Key West boy and it didn't really mean anything against Harry. Yes, we decided, Harry had a right to be pissed off and carry on a little, but not to beat Luanne up, certainly not that. Even if he only slapped her a little, the intent was the same.

Colors—the light through window slats had changed from blue-black to off-pink, hazy and indefinite. It was after five, and earlier crosswinds had calmed to a whisper-breeze. We left the room then, walking out to the dock, silent except for an occasional fish leaping or beating the water's surface. A quarter mile out, the pastel sun highlighted a large finger-shaped sandbar, a sandbar we had used often for swimming because of its deep-water channel, sparkling green now inside the darker blues of seaweed flats.

We took the larger of the two boats, the one with the 75-horsepower engine. Selma Anne squeezed the gas line while I took the ropes, shoved the boat into deep water, and started up. Luanne wore her two Band-Aids with I've-been-through-it-all pride; she had returned quickly to the group equilibrium; unlike me, she walked through her emotions, emerging cleanly for the next event.

I cut smoothly through the water, it being too short a ride to bother opening up; besides, noise disturbed dawn. It was pleasant to move slowly, glancing at the early activity of life under the clear waters. When we approached the long, narrow strip of coral sand with its fresh assortment of sea shells, I cut the engine, drifting until the boat stuck upon the shore. We pulled it up and scrambled onto sand, carrying the bottle of rum, cigarettes, and a box of potato chips.

Crabs, making their way for food in the early light, were to be stepped around. Starfish lay dry and bleaching out, thrown on their backs by the last tide—a conch shell lay with its dead tenant decomposing inside the pristine satin lip. I picked it up, managing a strong throw to the first seaweed flat.

We had finished the last possible gossip and conversation with the dawn, and our quiet took the form of physical movement—a dance—a circle, holding hands at first, our soggy baby dolls flapping against skin, then stretching raised hands, then twirling heads back around and around again, feeling out perimeters of sandbar, laughing, then doffing the baby dolls for tan-line nakedness, throwing them up like dancers' veils. And then, when we had sweat enough, when our bodies sweltered under the opening heat of the day, when we tired of dancing—there was the channel running as drop off from the brief shoreline.

Rosemary dove in first, moved easily in breast stroke, cutting a streak through the unrippled water, proceeded around the sandbar from point of departure, and back and around. We followed her then, splashing in the warm saltiness more than swimming, holding noses and somersaulting, diving at unsure objects on the bottom, bringing up shells and sea cucumbers. Then back on the sandbar, remembering our nakedness, scrambling for bloomers and tops, sticky—anxious in full morning to get back into the convention of motel room and shower, hair rollers, bobby pins, lipstick, and orange juice. And Luanne, Luanne with her perfectly rounded body, with her two Band-Aids and her straight streaky hair. Luanne. Luanne.

★

"Hi, Verona."

"Hi, Shylah."

"Tomorrow's the history exam, you want to go over the questions this afternoon? I could get Ace to pick you up and we could work on the dock. I've got this sheet of all the stuff he covered and . . ."

"Naw, ah cain't, Custer and me goin to Marathon, ah guess. He wants to look at his cousin's new boat."

"Hey, Verona, come on, we've got that test tomorrow; you're barely passing this course. They're not just yes and no answers this time, he's really cracking down. Don't you think . . ."

"Aw, Shylah, ah don't give a damn 'bout no stupid class. Sheeit. What difference does it make? We're gonna get married and stuff, hell, ah don't need good grades to do that, ah don't need school to do what ah want. Ah mean, ah 'preciate it and everythin, but school's shit. And the teachers, they never lahked me, big pains in the ass . . ."

"Miz Tallulah likes you, Verona, she really does, she says you're a very good stylist; she told me she liked your imagination. Really, she likes you. Besides, the other teachers aren't exactly fond of me either; they just put up with me because I grade their damn exams—I do their stupid work. But you like other things about school, I know you do, Verona. And the group, I mean Luanne and Bubbles and everyone, they like you a lot. You just don't get out enough with us, you know. It'd make you feel better, really. Why don't you come stay at my house this weekend and we'll go to Treenie's with Luanne and . . ."

"Yah, maybe, maybe ah'll do that. Mah daddy let me, that is, then ah will. There's Custer's car, gotta go meet Custer. Thanks, Shy, really. See yah, huh?"

"Sure, O.K."

★

April and early for hard rain, the kind of fast tropical disturbance that brings water spouts inland and gale winds. The ninth-grade class had been let out early for the funeral. Six of our boys, the bigger ones, served as pallbearers.

Luanne and Bubbles and Stanley and I went in Harry's car, my plain navy mourning suit offsetting the pinks and blues and crinolines they wore. Vestiges of Yankee taste; I resurrected the proper attire from Mummy's funeral for Verona a year later, who lay in her open casket like a wind-up doll, the usually pale face made up for this final display with ruby bowed lips and orange theatrical powder. Long blond hair too perfectly arranged about her shoulders, when she had always tossed it back sloppily. Her favorite turquoise dress, freshly pressed and cleaned, worn over the cavern she must have made leaning into the shotgun.

The Baptist minister based his eulogy on the word "beloved"—voice struggling for resonance over wind sounds, tossed branches hitting the small Key West church. What could anyone say about fifteen years of life? Suicide was for grown-ups, for people who had borne children or risen in business or joined local clubs or held political office. A fifteen-year-old girl can't commit suicide, can't really die yet. There just isn't enough happening or to say except, Gee, it was plain shitty she hadn't time to marry Custer, to get out from her stinking trailer life with her stinking father and her brothers, and her frequent depressions. She must have been playing, trying to dramatize a point, probably thought it wasn't loaded. Girls had to go to measures with boys to get what they wanted, if the need for it was strong enough. If Verona was pregnant and Custer didn't react to it right away, she had to show him her desperation, didn't she? She had to make her point, didn't she? Verona didn't die on purpose; it was a mistake, had to be a mistake, a dirty trick.

For a moment I saw Verona getting up out of the white-satin-lined box, rising up out of that ludicrous pose, dragging her hand hard across her lips, wiping off the lipstick, brushing off the orange powder, shaking her hair about to release it from the false confines of bobby pins, getting up out of that box while the minister told of how "beloved" was the deceased; getting up, lifting her arms, throwing out the flowers from their artificial-marble encasements, extending that finger— Go on, Verona, shoot us the bird. You never did get mad enough, that was it; you never told anyone to go to hell; you never got the taste out of your belly before you blew it out. Oh Jesus, Verona, your last move, so goddamn dumb.

9 1

"Oh for Christsake, will y'all shut up, Shylah. Ah mean, you weren't *that* close with her either, yah know, why the hell you cryin that way?— Luanne, make her shut up now, will yah. Jesus, ah can't see or think for shit in this rain and she ain't helpin."

"Drive the car, Harry, y'all never any good at thinkin anyway. It'll be O.K., Shylah, hush."

Harry was right. I hadn't been that close to her. It had been only the excuse of the funeral and the road-sweeping rains that brought on my weeping. And Luanne, Luanne brought it on, prattling about the prom that was coming up in a month. I hated her when she was like this, when she was so dumb, when she acted as dumb as the older girls she sometimes hung around with, vicious and stupid but pretty and acceptable, purveyors of the status quo. Oh Luanne, don't be a dopey bitch, not today, I can't stand it, not today; don't talk about tulle over silk after your classmate's funeral. Oh God, no wonder you're so capable of going from mood to mood quickly. You don't think much, do you, Luanne? You're all loveliness, but you don't think much at all.

Then screw Lime and the Keys, screw all redneck dummies with their customs that fit me like a shroud, and screw Luanne for her limitations; and Daddy for his phony accent and phony propriety, pimping a little for daughter, for daughter and the golf pro. Screw everything, everything except Stanley and me and a boat and the water and the midday annihilating sun if it ever came out again to hold me.

6

"We're not doing anything, Daddy. Just listening to records and, see, I'm doing this sketch of Stanley's head."

"Fifteen more minutes, sister, and with the door open. Stanley boy, we're havin company and Shylah gotta be on hand to entertain, so ah want you out of here in fifteen, understood?"

"Yessuh, Mr. Corky."

"What entertaining, it's miserable weather. We goin somewhere?"

"Uncle Bobby Jay's taking us all out for dinner, raght nice of him. Ah want you to get cleaned up, look decent before he gets here, understand?"

"Do I have to, Daddy? Verona's funer—"

"Yessss, you havvvve to. What the hell does that have to do with dinner obligations? Just don't say any more, Shylah, hear, fifteen minutes. Stanley leaves and you clean yourself up. Ah'm going to the post office. When ah get back, y'all be getting ready. Gonna have a fine dinner tonight."

"Jesus, your old man sure doesn't lahk me." Stanley moaned into my armpit as Daddy's car took off down the road.

"He's that way about people; really, it isn't personal. I don't see why I've got to go everywhere Uncle Bobby Jay goes. Really stupid. Shit, all I want to do on this lousy day is fool around with you."

"Yah, me too. Come here, Moosie, don't be sad, huh, ah love you, even if y'all got the world's weirdest old man."

Stanley took our rationed time on my twin bed—me, sprawled-legs-in-a-covering-V over him, kissing, sucking on each other's tongue, squirming around each other, clothed crotch to clothed crotch, fondling breasts and ass, humping for nothing but the pleasure and limitation of fifteen minutes alone. And after arousal, Stanley scurrying to pat and shake down his erection and me doubled over with gas pains, standard side effects whenever we made out and didn't have time to get some blessed relief. Daddy was becoming restrictive with us. As Stanley grew, as his acne cleared up and his body trimmed down, became more obviously muscular, Daddy hung around more, talked critically, gibing about his poverty, his family.

"Ah don't want you seeing so much of that boy, Shylah. Bad business y'all seein so much of him. They piss-awful people, real tramps. Jesus, your taste's in your mouth—ah begun to think you need a keeper. Besides, you're growin up, that's a nahce little outfit Alice bought you, very nice, shows off your finer points, uh huh; y'all watch your weight, keep that nahce figure."

"Come on, don't do that, that hurts. Don't, Daddy."

"Hello, ah'm home— Why, lamb, don't you look pretty, wait till Uncle Bobby Jay sees that nahce new outfit. In'it nahce, Corky? Whyn't you brush your hair a little more? Just brush it down a bit, Shylah dear, that a good baby."

"Look, how 'bout I stay home tonight, uh, ma'am? You know, what with Verona's funeral today and school tomorrow. And I'm not feeling that well. I mean, you don't really need me. You're all adults and everything. Really, I don't know why . . ."

"Now, don't pull a pout, Shylah. You know how Uncle Bobby Jay feels about his princess and we wouldn't think . . ."

"Yeah, I DO know; every time you're out of earshot he tries to . . ."

"Now, you shut up, ah don't wanna hear that crap. Y'all shut up and behave—damn lucky girl, Shylah; now, start actin decent or ah'll . . ."

"Corky, that in't necessary, Shy's gonna come and everything be fine . . ."

"O.K., O.K. You don't care what that guy does, do you? You think he'll drop you if I don't tag along. Why don't you try and see what happens?— I mean, is it worth dragging me everywhere?"

"Shylah, ah don't want to say this again. You move your ass in there, brush your hair, and come on out when he comes in. Y'all understand, girl, you understand? You do as you're told, quick. Now move, bitch, you move."

I questioned myself: Was this always the way, or an offshoot of the way, or maybe somehow I was not seeing something clearly. But it seemed to me, from viewing Luanne's parents or even Stanley's father, that I had the all-time turd as paternal seed. Stanley had the advantage of being at least needed, loved and needed—I remembered his father falling-down drunk once, putting his arms around his son as a brace against keeling over, shouting, "This's my son, gotta great boy, my son, Stanley. Take yer old dad home, huh, take him home." And Luanne's father, always calm, bringing her tea and gin when she had her period cramps, smiling at us a lot, approving. But then Verona's father had to be a bastard, right? And most of the class complained in some way about their fathers' nastiness or withholding something. Not so much mothers, though; mothers were sort of buying kids things, mothers were givers, fathers restrainers— But there was leeway at least, not like this, not like my father's constant judgments, not that eternal no.

And Alice. Alice the baby-talk machine. Unbelievable in her affected affections, as Daddy was believable in coldness. I did try not to hate her, stepmothers were always having a rough time. But the woman was just an assault on my need for occasional reality, a shithead, a manipulator beyond my most grotesque dreams. Yet I wished I could love her, throw it her way from the frustrated daughterdom I bore that resembling face— Dadda, Dadda, Father the Prick.

9 5

Hating parents was tiresome. It made me sick—diarrhea, headaches—made me see pieces of glass behind my eyes again—prismatic daggers moving against each other, crowding me out.

"How's your lobster, Princess?"

"O.K."

"O.K. what, daughter? She been in a bad mood all afternoon, Bobby Jay, you give 'em everything and they have moods. God-damn, when ah was a kid . . ."

"What's the matter, Princess, why such a pretty girl in a bad mood, huh? Why you in a bad mood?"

"I feel lousy, that's all, my stomach aches, I guess."

"Verona's funeral was today, Bobby Jay; in'it raght, Corky? It's a shame about that family. Ah don't think she was ever very well, certainly not a bright girl, terrible father though, really disgusting that Sam, ooh, real island trash. It's a shame 'bout that girl. Baby here was terribly nahce to her, used to help her with her studies. In'it so, lamb? Girl in trouble that way, what a shame—should've kept her legs crossed, but you know, some of these kids are grown at twelve. Shy's our li'l artist, aren't you, baby? Very sensitive to others' problems."

"Here, Princess, have a little wine. Warm you up."

"Stop this crap, daughter; you're making me lose mah famous appetite."

"No, really, I'm O.K. Really."

A group of tarpon guides, their wives, and the tourist parties they had taken for the day came in to celebrate their catch. They joined us, pushed two tables against our one, the sun-burned Yankees anxious to talk and sit with Uncle Bobby Jay—ordering drinks, ogling the photograph-strewn walls—compilations of famous guides with prize-winning catches, photos of Daddy, of Uncle Bobby Jay, graduating-class pictures from Palm View. So we hung around while they ate, having more drinks, talking to the wives who had stayed behind to have their hair styled, their bodies massaged, their nails painted, their eyebrows waxed. Successful folks in their forties, kids in college, banks and insurance companies and shoe chains taken care of for their vacations . . . who would return tan, have a small cocktail party, showing slides, telling the story of dinner with the greatest golfer, a nice guy, a fine American, and who would come again next year to Lime because they had been shown such a good, sunny, hard-drinking, sandy time in the Florida tropics.

The tourists picked up our tab with theirs, followed us back to our house for Brandy Alexanders and Daiquiris; everyone, excepting Alice and myself, a little tight, a little loud, the women now flirtatious, moving the line of conversation away from sports and onto the hours of prepared beauty that had been utilized for this evening, bringing them to the peak of middle-age controlled loveliness. I prayed for a better maturity for myself.

It was already after eleven; the conversation wilted me to compulsive yawning. The group had been talking about jaunting up to the Tampa Bay area to do a little Gulf fishing, renting a yacht and cruising up and back for a few days. Would Corky and Alice join them? Would Bobby Jay? Wouldn't it be fun, wouldn't it be a lovely time? Daddy and Alice were sure it would be. Already Alice was talking arrangements aloud. Uncle Bobby Jay regretted, but some businessmen, promoters, were coming down, he had to stick around, but he'd certainly watch out for Princess, take her to dinner. And Daddy thought that was just so lovely of Bobby Jay, and daughter better appreciate what a special person old Uncle Bobby Jay was, what a special guy.

I lay in bed, Joe Joe's soggy snout within caressing range. The conversations in the Florida room had dwindled to gasps of laughter and squeaks of remonstration at Daddy's dirty jokes. Raining again, this time without the lashing winds, just the soothe of downpour, like tap water running in a tub. It'd be better now for a few days. They'd be away and I could see Stanley more. He'd come over and I'd draw and listen to records, and we could be alone and quiet. Maybe, if we made the necessary discreet cover-ups, we could sleep one night together; we could play house, make dinner together. And I'd report in to Bobby Jay that things were O.K., that I had to study. To organize time

9 7

around myself, to make him leave me alone enough, to do it
right.

★

"Lawd, it's quiet without your old man, know that, Moosie; ah
don't have to worry 'bout him kicking me out."

"Yeah, I know. Hold still—I just want to do your jaw over
again, I can't get the damn line right."

Stanley squirmed back into pose while I erased the pencil
line and eased the pencil back into contact with the jawline
again, making it wider now and shadowing in under the ear. I
did it right this try, laid down pencil, hugged him hard. In our
months of learning each other, Stanley had lost some of his
quirky shyness; he could manage serious talk now without
stammering or looking down at the floor, or he could hold me
without it being at the point of desperation.

With his head down, aiming toward the bed, Stanley butted
me, while I maneuvered my hand under and up to his balls. He
pushed my top up so that it hung like rope about my neck; then
tugged at my bra, unfastening the back expertly, better than me,
burying nose into the cleavage my breasts made when pushed
together. While I unzipped his fly, feeling rise of prick in my
hand, kissing, laughing, shaking into each other's mouths,
the goddamn phone rang.

"Oh shit."

"Don't answer it."

"I better, it might be Alice. Let me answer; then I'll take it off
the hook . . . Hullo, oh hi, Uncle Bobby Jay. Nothing, doing
homework. What? (Cool it, Stanley, I'll get rid of him.) No, I
can't, got this work to do. Oh, he DID call, hmmm, what'd he
say? Oh yeah, I see, promised. Oh well, no, no, I appreciate it
really, just a second . . . (I can't, Stan, he talked to Daddy already. I mean, what can I do?) Yes—yes, it sounds exciting; I
hear the food is terrific, uh huh. So early? Well no, I mean, I'm
just used to everyone going out around nine and stuff and . . . A
dress? That fancy? Oh you—we are? But just drinks, O.K.? Yes,
I'll hurry, it'll take about an hour, I've got to take a bath and
stuff, yes sir. O.K., bye. Screw him."

9 8

"Shit, that guy's really pumpin away, Shylah, ah don't care what your old man says. Couldn't you have said you were sick or something?"

"Sure, so he'd have a goddamn excuse to sit by my bed and feed me aspirin and bourbon. I gotta go, Stanley; if I make waves, it'll get back to Daddy. And he's been really nice in a way, I shouldn't complain. Weird huh. And I thought we could have supper by ourselves and make love. Look, don't worry about him, Stanley, he's O.K. I don't think he'd get really, well, you know."

"O.K., Moosie, keep it tight. Ah know, ah know, ah better go, so y'all can put on all your shit. Sheeeiiit, a dress, what the hell you gotta have a dress for to go and eat?"

"He says we're going to have drinks with some people first. It's part of that promotion deal he's doing."

"Ah'll call y'all later from the phone outside the Laundromat, O.K.?"

"Yes, good, O.K."

"See yah, jail bait."

"Bye, Bear, I love you."

"Yeah."

Goddamn him with a putter up his ass. I had given up saying no to Uncle Bobby Jay. He either heard it yes or used my father for intervention purposes, the latter being worse.

I filled the bath full of Alice's bath oil, lay back to soak, in extra-hot, skin-reddening water. Poor Stanley. I wouldn't want to be kicked out of the house because he had a date with a woman old enough to be his mother. And then he was so sensitive about his poorness. I had to be careful about that, careful not to be too generous. Painful for him. Couldn't stand it when he hurt, worse than confronting Daddy. Had to be protective, gentle with him. It would be all right. If I was careful it would be O.K. Oh God, Shylah.

I stood to dry myself while the water drained, wrapping beach towel around me, sarong-style, walking to dressing table. On my right lay the hardware—bottle of liquid-makeup base, Sunny Goddess shade, Mumble-Jumble pink lipstick, stick of Positively Purple eyeshadow, dark-brown eyebrow pencil, eyelash curler, black brush-on mascara. My mother's silver hair-brush set lay positioned on the left, the ones I never used but looked at respectfully while I whacked my hair with the plastic bristles of the Rexall fifty-nine-cent brush.

"Well, Princess at her toilette." Uncle Bobby Jay walked through the open door and sat on my bed.

"C'mon, Uncle Bobby Jay, get out of here. I still have to get dressed and stuff. Why don't you go fix yourself a drink? Take me ten minutes. Please. I can't get ready with you here. It'll just take a minute, go on."

"Yesss, ma'am. Kiss first, c'mon, then ah'll go 'way."

Uncle Bobby Jay crammed his arms around the towel while I held it together, hands pinned like a mummy to my chest. This was his sizing-up embrace, when the long arms moved up and down and around my back from ass to hips to shoulder to neck, squeezing each part before moving on. He had recently become more the suitor—the suitor-keeper, making some mystical transition from keeper–Dutch Uncle—now with mouth sliding from edge of my cheek over to my mouth, turning lips this way and that in graceful gestures, while I turned mine inward like an old woman without teeth.

"Come on, Uncle Bobby Jay, pleasssse."

"O.K., O.K., y'all look so edible in that towel, ah hardly wanna go leave you." My ass received a last swipe, sort of cross between a slap and a fondle. Then only the safe noise of bourbon poured over ice, the distance of three rooms to the kitchen bar.

★

The promotion people had rented the old Sky Villa outside Key West. A landmark built by Gatwick in the early twenties, the days of the old overseas railroad and Miami nobility coming down on yachts to gargantuan parties in the old man's house, it had fallen to lean days with his death and bare superstructure with the 1935 hurricane and tidal wave. A motel combine had bought it with the surrounding land, dredged, restored, planted royal palms, imported furniture, and kept it as a super-rental for visiting millionaires and advertising affairs for citrus magnates and the like.

Alice and I had driven to see it on our way to Key West a month ago, taking the private road off Highway 1, past stone gates and sculptured Greek girls with flamingos. Like everything in southern Florida, Sky Villa was mostly pink, with occasional bits of white stucco, and black grillwork on the verandas, then pseudo-Corinthian columns, a way of hanging out the dollar sign for very rich house owners. A filled-in beach adjoined it, with docks and boats, a Spanish-tile swimming pool with porcelain flamingos on each corner, four or five smaller houses in the same decor for the staff, a nine-hole golf course, and two clay tennis courts. And then the formal garden I thought was so idiotic . . . Who could imagine such a thing in the tropical brush, with azalea and hibiscus bushes in the shapes of lions and elephants. Frangipani and imported vanilla and ginger orchids, their vines making flamboyant modesty out of the naked women with their accompanying springs of water gushing too close to the genitals to deny implications. Sweet opulence, tropical-style, lushness out of lushness, circus-like, grand and absurd.

There were twenty or so waiting for Uncle Bobby Jay with back slaps and presentations and good liquor. These were the middle-aged, paunchy, business-corporation men. And women. There were five of them—all pouffed and gorgeous; too young and silent, I thought, to be wives; more like the furniture or the red velvet drapes in the mirrored reception room. And, oh my, they had not expected me. So obvious. They had not expected Leads, the unmarried golfer, to be accompanied by a teenager, daughter of prominent islanders, a liability to serious chat and the glamorous movie star–looking ladies, who frowned at me. And I thought he enjoyed it, Uncle Bobby Jay, that is, enjoyed having me as niche, this paternal excuse to stay only a little while and keep his business short and sober.

"Well, how delightful, a young lady. What's your name, dear? Shylah, what an unusual name, like S-h-i-l-o-h, no? Well, hmm, what can we get you? I think we could find a Coca . . . Oh yes, sure we have it, we have some very nice French champagne, as a matter of fact. Perhaps one of the ladies would show you around Sky Villa. Oh, you have, oh really, hmmm. How old are you? Oh, and you're a freshman. Oh, that's just terrific, honey. When I was your age . . ."

"Hey, Princess, how y'all lahk this place? In'it though; could really git lost in it, huh? We can't stay too long, fellas, she got school tomorrow. You know, ah thought 'bout buying Sky one time, thought seriously 'bout it, impractical though, without twenty-five children or something to fill it up— Married at the time, yah; thank God, ah didn't. Whew, what an alimony hound, ah'd never a seen it again. Well, O.K., you wanna bring a crew down here, ah don't see why it wouldn't do, even if it is only nine holes, good for demonstration purposes at least. Use Shylah here, she pretty enough, don't y'all think, bring back the pure American girl, huh?"

Uncle Bobby Jay moved with the men over to the bar while I stared at the women. Fantasy women, everything seemed so perfect about their appearance, except, of course, they hardly spoke, which I thought peculiar. They wore cocktail dresses, with deep, movie-magazine cleavage, and spike heels showing off slender ankles, and false eyelashes. I had never seen women up close that wore eyelashes. And those hairdos, just done, not the way Miz Paula did it down here, but very high on the head and smooth like a new hat. Like the pastel girls' heads I drew, working the colors with my fingers till they emerged vague in prettiness. The women stood off to one side, occasionally whispering or almost whispering to one another. It was pleasant to be in their company, with their perfection and elegance. I went over to talk, nervous about talking but curious—maybe I'd find out some things about how to look that way, how to be so perfect-looking.

"Hi, I'm Shylah, do you all live in Key West?"

"No, honey, Miami; we came down here from Miami."

"Oh sure, I should have guessed. You're in show business there or something . . ."

They smiled. "Well, sort of, we model and things. My name's Marilyn. How come you asked that?"

"Umm, well, because you're all so, you know, lovely and perfect-looking; you could never get that look down here with Miz Paula, that's our beautician, I mean, she's good and stuff, but you could never look, well, you know, like a movie star. See, I experiment a lot at home with setting my hair and makeup, but it never comes out right, I mean, like the magazines, and you all look like the magazines."

"Why, in'it sweet of you to say, honey. Yes, it takes a lot of know-how and time. But I like the way you look, Shylah, you don't have to think about glamour yet. Would y'all lahk some champagne? Doesn't look lahk we're gonna be on call much now, maght as well make ourselves comfortable."

"Oh yes, yeah, I would; look, I'll just get the bottle from the bartender and we can talk. See, the reason why I wondered how you get to look that way is, well, partly the reason, is that I draw, I mean, I do pastels, girls mostly, when it's not religious stuff, and the girls come out looking the way you do, you know, with big dark eyes and hair that's smooth."

I brought back a couple of bottles from the uniformed bartender, who shot me a half-assed look; maybe he thought I was too young for champagne. The men scurried around Uncle Bobby Jay; one took notes while they talked business. Maybe if the women could just explain how they got their hair that way, I'd copy their instructions, arranging my own— It'd be incredible to look that way, like my drawings, it'd be something enviable.

"Well, first you set it in the *big* rollers, you know, the really huge ones; then, when you take it down, take each curl and tease it. No, that's when you comb it back till it's all frizzy. Hey, Sherry, whyn't we all go to the powder room and do it on Shylah-here's hair. We'll show you how honey; it'd be fun, not a friggin thing doin here."

When we had assembled in the wall-to-wall-mirrored, velvetized room with Kleenex in gold boxes and bottles of Joy and Chanel already there, Sherry bringing out her overnighter full of paints and sprays and hair stuff, the women placed me in one of the satin-cushioned swivel chairs and surrounded me. Marilyn had brought the champagne and someone ordered a tray of hors

1 0 3

d'oeuvres. Sherry, who, in addition to her other assets, had the longest fingernails I'd ever seen, painted bright powdery pink, like my lipstick; who had white-blond page-boy hair, unmoving, like a French glaze, took charge. I bent down a little while she brushed my hair forward and over my eyes, brushed it for ten minutes or so while I tried to bring my mouth and the glass of champagne together without making contact with the hair. The other women made suggestions whether it would be better to brush full back, make a wave, a French twist, or what. After the initial cold stares they turned out to be warm and friendly, called me honey a lot, fed me hors d'oeuvres through the dark forest before my face while Sherry began to separate parts with a comb, then comb back hard till my head was haloed by a circle of hair fuzz from the teasing. Then she brushed and patted, brushed and patted, spraying each section. The other women handed her pins to place at certain points while she brushed the strands over the fuzz, and down and under at the nape of the neck. When she had finished, my largish head peered back at me from the mirror, dwarfed by shining bouffant playing down from the top of my skull, sloping into a wave, over one eyebrow and close to the eye. Smooth, smoother than I had ever seen it, gleaming after the final administration of lacquer—my perfect hair. I had made it into the ranks of the truly glamorous—as long as the magic spray worked.

"Jesus, it's gorgeous, don't you think? Don't you think it looks good? Thanks, Sherry, everybody. Damn, this is really something. You could make a lot of money fixing this kind of hairdo down here, really. I wish Luanne, that's my best friend, I wish she could see this. And wait till Uncle Bobby Jay sees it. And I thought when I got here, I'd be falling asleep with boredom; you know, all that business talk, and those guys are sort of weird, don't you think?"

"You're telling us, honey. You do look real nahce, Shylah, a real pretty young lady. Wait'll Mr. Leads sees you. He your uncle or something?

"Well, not exactly. He's my father's best friend and we live on the same island. So I'm supposed to call him Uncle Bobby Jay and stuff; he sort of looks after me. Hell, he's not always so uncle-like either, if you know what I mean; seems peculiar going around with him like some sort of mascot."

"Listen, don't knock it. He'll take good care of you."

"Yeah, well, it's a problem. He gets in the way of my seeing my boy friend. My father pushes us together, know what I mean? It's stupid, the guy's old enough to be my father, and it would be one thing if it was just once in a while but now it's like I'm on call. It's really hard on Stanley, that's my boy friend. Don't you think it's peculiar?"

"Look at it this way, honey. Bobby Jay Leads's a real important guy. He can take y'all places, and you won't be stuck or broke, lots of fun things while you're growing up. Go ahead and keep your little boy friend, but you can't just ignore someone lahk Mr. Leads. Just be real ladylahk, that's what they lahk, just lahk you are, angel."

"Yeah, well, I'm enjoying myself more with you all and Stanley."

"Pays the bills. When y'all get older, you'll understand how it works."

We walked back then, to the reception area, with me pausing before all the mirrors I could find, looking at the unfamiliar coiffed hair, basking under the hair-spray halo. Uncle Bobby Jay glanced up at our parade.

"*WHAT* the Sam Hill did'y'all do to your damn hair? JEEEE-sus, Shylah Dale, what is this, huh?"

"I asked them to fix it for me, Uncle Bobby Jay. Isn't it amazing?"

"Yah, amazing. Come on, we gotta get on to dinner. Spent more time here than I thought . . . Fellas, fah's ah'm concerned, it's all O.K., 'cept of course for the stuff we discussed. Y'all can talk to Bert for the particulars. Sounds good. Shylah, you got everything? So long, boys. Shylah, come on, girl."

"O.K., Uncle Bobby Jay, just let me say goodbye to the ladies. Just a second."

He was driving a little too recklessly for comfort, remaining silent till we drove up and parked in front of Oceanview, one of the older restaurants in the town, down by the shrimp boats.

The maître d' led us past lobster, crab, and shrimp tanks through a large dining hall to a window seat overlooking harbor and boats just coming in, nine o'clock twilight.

"What's the matter? You're so quiet and mad-looking. Did I do something?"

"Look, when y'all get home, you brush that shit out of your hair, hear. Aw hell, you didn't know, Princess, it's O.K. Ah never would've taken you if ah knew those whores'd be around. Guys didn't expect me to bring a young lady. Ah just don't wanna see you dolled up that way. Cheapens you. Hell, you didn't know, ah shouldn't have let you alone with those broads . . ."

"But I wanted them to do my hair; they all look, you know, like movie stars, and really they were terribly nice once you got to know them. Frankly, Uncle Bobby Jay, it was your friends, you know, those business guys, who I thought were weird and stuff and . . ."

"Look, let's just forget it. Ah'll help you with your hair when we get home, 'n ah won't be taking you to that kind of thing again without checking first. Jesus, Shylah, how'd they do all that junk to your hair in such a short time? Oh well, never mind, guess the experience made you wiser. Now at least y'all know a chippie when you see one."

"THEY WERE GODDAMN NICE, DON'T YOU SAY THAT ABOUT THEM."

"Ah, don't wanna hear any more, nothing. Now, what you all want, how 'bout that jambalaya for two, y'all like that, Princess . . . We'll share it from a big pot and . . ."

"I'm not really that hungry any more. We ate a lot of hors d'oeuvres."

"Come on now, don't y'all be in a mood, just that ah want you growin up nahce, ladylahk; ah want y'all to be just as pure and sweet as ah know you can be. And ah'm responsible for your behavior with the folks away. Ah don't want you round the wrong people, that's all. Those women, if you can call them that, are tramps, Shylah. They get paid to be all dolled up so guys will wanna go to bed with them, that's all, just give 'em what they want and get paid for it, cash on the line."

1 0 6

"But, really, they made my whole evening, Uncle Bobby Jay, and what was I supposed to do, it was boring. Those guys didn't want me around. I thought they were idiotic, stupid, asking me stupid questions."

"Aw poor thing, poor baby, it'll be all right. See, it's all over." Uncle Bobby Jay kneaded my hand with his own, then leaned across the table to stroke my cheek and neck, careful not to get near my lacquered hair, my infamous hair, which I adored now more than ever, which I knew looked disgustingly elegant and chic, and screw everybody else. Maybe men got paid for it too. Maybe there were divine-looking men who got paid to go all the way. Pissed me off . . . Stanley and I playing cat and mouse with our bodies while the adult world paid each other to get laid.

★

Driving home, Uncle Bobby Jay and I battled with hands for possession of my knee, a battle I won by threatening to crash-dive out the door. Talkative and a little tight, he explained what a mean bitch, money-loving tramp his ex-wife was, how she'd had an abortion without him knowing it, what women were after, what it was like to make par; about when he met the President, when he had his clubs cast in gold, when his name was placed in the Hall of Fame, how he supported his widowed mother, how he made things comfortable for her at last, how fast his boat ran, how when I got older he'd take me to Europe; wouldn't I like to take a big boat first-class to France, wouldn't I like that?

He turned the car onto Lime's residential roadway, but instead of dropping me off, he passed my house and continued on straight through the stone-gated drive of his own property. It was after eleven, breezy and clear. I had been fighting sleep in the car. Now the air and water hit, and I caught myself in a series of yawns, one pushing out another. For a guardian, Uncle Bobby Jay seemed little impressed by my need to sleep. Instead, he wanted a nice talk and a nightcap for himself in my presence. Tired. Please, let me go home.

"Really, I'm pooped. I've got to go home and get some sleep. I can't keep my eyes open. Please. Come on. Oh Christ, O.K., O.K., a Coke. That's all, promise. Then you've got to let me get to bed. I have to be up by six."

Upstairs Uncle Bobby Jay poured himself a brandy and reached in the bar icebox for Coke and ice cubes.

"Pretty quiet over there, with your folks gone. Doesn't it bother you, Princess? No, you're so brave, ah know that. Worries me though. In't raght, young girl staying in a house alone. Y'all never know, all these crazy bastards around."

"No, I love it, as a matter of fact. Peaceful. Besides, there's Joe Joe. He'd bark if anybody came around."

"Christ, that dog's useless as tits on a bull. Y'all need a couple of big shepherds, Princess."

"I hate shepherds."

Uncle Bobby Jay moved in with the drinks, placing himself next to me on the endless sofa. Please, oh please, God, not this baloney. Leave me alone. Find someone, you're so in demand, but leave me alone. Jesus.

"Yes, all right, one hug, then I gotta go; really, Uncle Bobby Jay, I gotta go."

"Oh, Shylah Princess, ah won't hurt you, ah won't hurt, come on, give a little, relax, let me hold you, there, lahk that. You know, for a big girl, y'all very delicate, really such an angel, such a pure angel. Oh baby, y'all know your Bobby Jay loves you, y'all know that. Let me touch you. Let me, no one else; ah wanted you here lahk this. Ah remember when Alice said y'all were coming down and showed me that photo of you in a horrible uniform; even so you were so sweet-looking—ooh Shylah, Shylah. And the first time ah saw y'all in a bathing suit out at your dock, y'all remember that, Princess, you remember the first time, huh? Lawd, a lot of trash down here, girl, but y'all were somethin special, so elegant. Oh, ah was crazy for you that first time. Let me touch you."

"Uncle Bobby Jay, stop, cut it out. I mean it. Please, let me go home. Look, I'm really getting pissed. Daddy would blow his top if he knew you liked me like this."

"C'mon, honey, of all people, old Corky wants his girl along-side me. He doesn't want you running off with island trash either. Oh Shylah, ah know all this stuff is new to you, but things are different here. Girls grow up faster, pace is slower, more uh . . . romantic. There's so much we could . . ."

"Look, you're a really terrific guy, honestly—I'm sure of that—but you seem to forget I'm only fifteen. I mean, I'm not a baby, right, but you're almost forty. Let me get to know boys my age, for Godsake. I've got college to think about, shit like that. Really, I want to do something, all sorts of things, I don't want to settle down. Jesus, maybe I'll become an artist, and I need time to do that. I'm too young for you. Why me? Well, look, you've got to leave me alone, no matter what, I'm not . . ."

"What is this? What about a home and the caring of children, in'it a career, Princess? Can't you paint in the house? What's this crap? Y'all screwin up all the real values. Ah know, ah've been around. Y'all want to become hard lahk those whores you seemed to enjoy so much? Do you want to become lahk that? Aw, let's stop this, come here."

He reached out, turning me in his arms on the sofa, pushing me back a little so that my body made a kind of angle, half lying, half sitting. He kissed me, sliding lips again over to my mouth, kneading it under his own, now with his tongue against my teeth, weighing me down; then his head against my cheek, mouth against my ear, "Oh Shylah, oh Princess, so pure and nice, just for me, just for me," and the hands coming forward to my half-covered breasts in the T-strapped sundress, pushing flesh upward from the built-in boned bra. "Let me, let me, oh baby, baby princess . . ."

"No, please, please, let me go; please, Uncle Bob—"

"Ah won't hurt you, ah wouldn't hurt you; mine, it'll be mine."

He stood, the bulge of erection under summer trousers looking enormous even with his height. He stood and picked me up, trying to carry me fainting-lady-style, making two holders of his arms but changing as I protested, putting me over his shoulder before the seven or eight steps into his bedroom.

"Aw Shy, don't fight, ah won't hurt you, ah love you, you're my own, you'll learn; please, don't fight me, ah want to, uh, possess you, to make it lovely . . . Oh Shylah . . ."

All right, you bastard, do it, do it, shithead. Screw me. It's going to happen anyway. My asshole father'd think it was an honor. But I hate you for it, pig bastard . . . I should've taken chances with Stanley. Oh Stanley, I miss you so. Luanne. Luanne. We'll see, son-of-a-bitch; if you die while you're inside me, it'll all be worthwhile.

"Oh, touch me, touch me here. Oh Shylah, sit up, baby; let me take this off. There; oh you're so pretty, pure baby."

My dress lay on the floor by the big double bed, only pink stretchy panties remaining on me, half tugged down anyway. I closed my eyes, so damned tired; maybe I could sleep through it. I couldn't have fought, it wouldn't pay; who could I call against Bobby Jay Leads, pig? He unbuttoned his knit shirt and pushed it over his head; then slipped off loafers, white athletic socks—stupid jock—then unbuckled belt, undid, unzipped the fly over that obscene prick. Oh God, make it go fast. What can I concentrate on, besides killing him? Need to kill my mind. Shylah, help.

"Get me something to drink, I—uh—I need something to relax me; please, I'll do anything, just bourbon first, some ice in a big glass and a lot of it, a lot of bourbon. O.K., please, I'll be better then."

"Yes, darlin, anything, yes, sweetheart. Don't move, I'll be right back." While he messed with the bourbon and the ice in his blue shorts, I closed my eyes again, wondering how much money his ex-wife got from him anyhow, smart lady, how much she took him for; wondered if he did it that way to her their first time, if he made up her mind for her, if she had been a virgin or not, what difference? I didn't want my virginity any more than warts but at least to lose it with someone I liked, with Stanley. God, I wanted Stanley. Ummm, sharks, to see that bastard in the water getting it, right up between the legs. I wasn't afraid of anything, not his stupid prick or even him, not like my father; I was afraid of Daddy. But Bobby Jay. Bobby Jay was a kind of pervasive turd to be flushed out with a lot of water and disinfectant.

"Oh baby, here, drink this. Oh, you're so lovely, hmmm; drink it, while I take the rest off."

While I quickly swallowed gulps of bourbon, he moved down on me, kissing my breasts and stomach, pulling the little panties, the last scrap, off, running his hand from knee to thigh, spreading my legs. I sucked hard on the ice cubes. Now he pushed at me with his finger, slid it between the lips and down and up.

"Ow, goddamn it, ow, ow."

"Oh, poor Shylah, ah'll be more gentle now; ah'll make it feel good."

Do that, you bastard, make it feel good; if you're gonna screw me, make it feel good.

I drew my legs together, while he rubbed my pussy, alternating palm with curve of hand, kissing my stomach, then upward to breast again, using one hand to remove his shorts. He had a muscular, lean body; beautiful, in fact. Not like Stanley, who would always be somewhat given to a soft stomach and whose legs buckled, things I loved and didn't mind, because they somehow made him more approachable, more to be cared for and tended. Bobby Jay, though, the prize bull stud all the way, from his barber-shop straight hair on down. I wouldn't mind being well paid for being his cow. Stop it, Shylah.

He had begun examining my parts now, while I semi-reclined on the pillows, supporting neck and head so that I could continue to drink without choking and without looking down at him. He spread my legs again, rubbing at me, trying the finger again and again. I was nearing the end of the bourbon as the finger lodged itself and swung back and forth inside me; the bedside clock said twelve-thirty. Oh Jesus, hurry up, take it, take the cherry and let me run. Don't hurt me.

"Oh, Shylah Princess, let me come in, ah've got to, please, oh sweetheart, pure li'l princess."

Bobby Jay gathered himself to his knees between my own, lifting my legs for me. I was prone. He came down, the muscles

1 1 1

in his arms shaking a little. I could feel his prick, hard and swinging from thigh to thigh, till it stopped, lodged too high at my crotch. He placed his hand down on it, gripped it, and felt for my hole. When he had caught just the tip of it there, he withdrew his soggy hand, placing it on my ass, and pushed, pushed hard, pushed too hard.

"Ow, God, it hurts, please, not so hard, ow." It startled me, I cried with outrage. The thing stung, it stung me, stung and tore, and I hated the bastard, felt contempt, while he groveled around with my crotch and his protestations of love, of purity. Hurry up, please. Jesus.

"Oh, ah, ooh, love youuu, it's good, yes? Good for you?" When he climaxed quickly and slid the length of me, taking with him my blood and mutual spillings, I pretended a Victorian faint, sobbing by sucking in my breath, shaking. My wet eyes he construed as devotion, his very own Miss Chastity Belt . . . Would Bobby Jay get his beloved a hefty snort of brandy? She's so, you know, out of it, weak and stuff, lost blood. He went to the bar while I went to the bathroom, limping bow-legged-fashion. Inside, I splashed cold water on my crotch and face, wiped myself with his white towel, staining it a little, and folded it back on the rack, blood to the inside, just in case he forgot and found himself drying face or arm or balls on the caked blood. I found the image funny; I was relieved that I found anything funny now. I drank my brandy as I dressed, explaining that I must sleep at home just in case someone called or the neighbors got suspicious. He understood, didn't he; didn't want to ruin my reputation, did he?

It hurt like a son-of-a-bitch, my aching pussy . . . and I was mad and I was drunk. I couldn't do it again. I didn't care what I could get out of him. Christ, just seeing him again would make me puke. What to do? I lay on my own bed now, having showered the remains of him off me, I lay there and thought about Luanne and Stanley and Lime, and then about nothing.

It was close to two o'clock. I wouldn't go to school tomorrow. Daddy and Alice wouldn't be back for two more days. I'd be by myself tomorrow. Wouldn't even see Stanley. God, poor Stanley, oh why? I wanted you. I wanted you.

1 1 2

★

"Hello, Zoe; it's me, Shylah. I'm sorry to wake you, but you said in case . . . Yeah, it is, no, they're away, thank God. It's just not working out; no, I'm scared; yeah sure. Sure, it's Daddy. I don't know, I did try. Well, you said to let you know, so now I'm letting you know. I don't want to run away, I mean, there's really no place to go. Oh, you did. You have. Sure anything, yah, even a boarding school. Please, just find one that isn't too strict. No, I do love it here, really; no, it's impossible, he'd just get worse. Yeah, thanks, I wouldn't have called but I didn't know what to do, really. I just didn't know. I will, I promise. Yes, tomorrow, you too . . . Bye."

Shit. Why did I do that? Why did I call Zoe? And what could I do? I can't say, "No, it's not really Daddy beating on me I mind, it's his best friend's screwing." Shit. I don't want to leave this. Mummy. Oh Mummy, you've been dead only a year.

7

"Shylah dear, how marvelous to see you. My goodness, you're tall. The image of Betsy. Have you eaten? Mrs. Sturbridge left a plate for you in the refrigerator. You must be exhausted, just exhausted."

"It's nice to see you, Aunt Snow. No, we ate on the way from the airport. I didn't realize it would take so long to get here. How far is Dickinson from Boston?"

"A good hour. Let me draw you a nice pine bath when you're ready. You need a little time to adjust to the differences in climate. Now, just let me tell you before I toot off, dearie, we have breakfast at eight so Zoe can get off to Cambridge in time. Let's see, let's tend to that tub. So nice having you here. When your mother was just this age, your age now, that is, she'd come visit your Uncle Edward and me, stayed in the same room. Oh my, things become very repetitive with age—try and avoid growing old, Shylah. Try. Tragic about Betsy though. I know you've suffered terribly—I think of it all and shudder, really. But look, dearie, everything's looking marvelously up for you now. Charity Slope's a superb choice of school, you'll love it; certainly as progressive as Putney, if not more—people there are a delight. Small too, only a hundred or so boarding students, the rest day, maybe four or five hundred. I know your headmaster from way back, a dear, really. There now, all drawn, you just hop into that. Towels are on the dresser. Sleep well, Shylah, we'll see you in the morning."

In the tub my mind ran backward to last goodbyes at Miami Airport. They'd all be starting tenth grade soon, late August. I didn't want to go. They knew it and I knew it. Crazy. Why did I call Zoe, why not just be a whore?—was it worth it? Yes? No? Cleaning out, I had given the crinolines to Alice's maid, with cinch belts and any of my more flamboyant Florida apparel. And Joe Joe, dying two months ago on the road. All guts and tongue. That's how they all went down there, on Highway 1 usually; I missed him. But Luanne would write, she'd keep in touch. Stanley wouldn't though, he'd fade after a while. Proximity would count a lot with Stanley, and my arch rival, Lettice, had been closing the gap, playing up to him while I packed my things.

My departure from Lime had been accomplished subtly, with explanations from Alice. "Shylah needs more academic schooling this year, more things for baby. Oh no, she hates leaving, gets along fine with Corky; no, she just needs more specialized courses— Sure, she'll be back, can't wait; well no, not for Christmas, too much doing up there for Christmas, but soon."

I had kept busy and out of the way for the last months— Bobby Jay conveniently went on tour. When it became clear I would leave, neither Daddy nor Alice pushed for mutual entertainment. I spent the summer alternating between Luanne's and Stanley's company. Daddy made no more objections. When the decision sunk in, no one cared to prohibit me as to hours or company. I was polite. I was O.K.

★

Though I had not seen it before, Dickinson was a familiar town, large but not too large, existing for the most part because of the girls' school and women's college, both named after the poet from Amherst, both irrevocably unsuited to the name. But Dickinson was a popular name in Massachusetts just the same and it fit in with the late-eighteenth-century expanses of colonial seven- and eight-bedroom houses and the neo-imitation-colonial drugstores and clothes shops—the kind with white-framed windows that displayed Shetland cardigans and Wee-juns and gold-chain scarab bracelets and circle pins. If I shut, then opened my eyes in Dickinson Square, there all of this would be, with no surprises, only acknowledgment from some-where in the back of my brain. I had asked for this, and even if I had not, a part of this town knew me by tribe.

Two weeks to shop for woolen clothes and fool around before school. Charity Slope—godawful name—only ten miles or so from Aunt Snow's, but I would board just the same. Boarding me took the heat off everyone—I'd be accounted for, with kids, tennis courts, and woods and stuff. And there would be no uni-forms or deportment classes or hard-line lectures from Miss Staunten types. That much Zoe had promised. It'd be more like a college. I'd like it, he said.

★

Snow Grosvenor, my great-aunt, had inherited enough to live like a tight-rich New Englander, to retain servants yet drive a ten-year-old black Ford, to use the scratchy kind of toilet paper and skimp on soap. She had a kind of almost-perverse intellec-tualism about her that grew instead of waned with the years, a drive that got her out of bed each morning at five in order to formulate or review her opinions, scour the newspapers, so that by each breakfast time she could, if she cared to, discourse on at least one new topic that had been mentally resolved since dawn.

Her house—THE house—had come to Aunt Snow early in marriage. Built in 1785, it had been added to in the subsequent century in several modes. There was grandeur, some indefin-able status to it, though the design wasn't particularly unique, traditional yet not tradition-bound. Inside, the antiques were all functional and falling apart, unlike Mummy's Historical-Society-Keep-Off-Queen-Anne shit. An aura of dust and decrep-itude gave the living room especially a feeling of prowess, as if something had been written there or worked out, some great historical event in a thinker's world, yet no one could quite agree on who or what it was and when. To hear Aunt Snow tell it, each stick of furniture, including the tattered Oriental rug, had been placed there with reverence by some theologian, or the Aga Khan, or a poet or historian or doctor. The bookshelves deserved scholarly notice with their crowded-in, cracked, leather-bound books on the Civil War or Victorian gynecology. A couch dominated the opposite side, velvet, heavy, and worn to a slope, just the kind of thing to curl up in with the Encyclopædia Britannica in forty languages—to be removed in the same position a half century later. A comfortable, possessive couch, a couch for flannel nighties and mukluks and sherry.

A distinguished room, a worthy room—whether or not anybody had outdone Turgenev in it—I could be safe here.

★

Breakfast was at the last three bongs of the grandfather's clock. Early risers waited in the music room, reading one of the three dailies, to be accumulated later for weekly paper-drive dispersal. Aunt Snow, who had a knack for wretched amounts of early-morning enthusiasm, introduced me, first, to Mrs. Sturbridge, the cook, then, sitting at the table, to Mr. Fitzwilliams, Mr. Hanover, Miss Arenali, Sister Magdalena, and Mr. George. The boarders, who had been screened and accepted on the basis of their morning habits—their ability to enter into a debate or discussion while eating that first egg. Brilliant folk, differing, but all necessarily intense, ranging from twenties up to a full seventy in the case of Mr. George, who wrote botany books and appeared this morning in lederhosen and woolen knee socks.

Each had an individual napkin ring marking his chair at the table, and within the napkin ring a linen cloth, washed twice a week. It behooved the eater to maintain a certain reticence when wiping the mouth—perhaps a bite of distasteful food that could have been easily hidden would better be swallowed lest it fall out the following morning, some bit of bacon gristle or burned toast rolled into its saliva ball falling on the dining-room rug under the eye of Lady Sarah what's-her-name, circa 1815, whose portrait hung behind Aunt's chair and next to the side table where the table linen was kept.

A person ate one egg cooked to specifications, not two; had margarine on toast, not butter; and there were two dairy pitchers, one of milk and a smaller of pure cream, to be mixed with the milk in modest amounts on the porridge. Aunt Snow served as captain of the bread, an electric toaster situated on a movable table next to her.

"One slice or two, Mr. Fitzwilliams, two, ah—I was shocked to read how much—let's see, how much was it, the Senate appropriated for the defense budget. Really, it goes against everything Kennedy was running on, this business in Vietnam. Slice, Sister, yes, I remember, turn it to light, ah—you see—just as I said—they burned that bus in Montgomery. We're planning to picket, that is, some of us old war horses from the Women's League, with students at Dickinson, do join us. Would you like a little oatmeal, darling, and how about a nice soft-boiled egg? Oh, that damned buzzer, I have to feel for an hour to find it, ah, found it. Yes, the damn thing's under the rug—legs are dreadfully short for this sort of thing. Oh well . . . Oh, you did! Yes, how did you like it, isn't he absolutely marvelous, really, brilliant, so incisive. Here, Shylah, dear, some marmalade for your toast. Off with the Appalachian Club, Mr. George? Really, my heavens, how extraordinary, he did, a red Muscaria, this far east? Well, perhaps a good omen for mycologists. Don't forget me, will you now, if you come upon some *chanterelles*."

Aunt Snow's breakfast salon functioned on levels beyond me. While I sat picking at the soggy egg, she and Zoe demolished foreign policy and went on to a fungi native to the Berkshires. Though debate ran the discussions, it was assumed that anyone who appeared at Aunt's table had to be a civil libertarian, an Adlai Stevenson supporter from way back, and an orator for just causes. This, I thought, was what it was like to introduce order into a lifetime.

After breakfast I returned to my room, to sit at the window desk and begin a letter to Luanne, who would write back promptly, and another to Stanley—briefer, more emotional, knowing I'd get a scrawl, a paragraph or so in return. But to write just the same, to detail my life away from them.

From this desk, large-paned window, I could look down the street toward the town square, past well-pruned grass and lines of old elm and pine. I could admire the odd placement of Greek Orthodox dome, three doors down, with its blue and blood-red stained glass, where rich Greeks came to pray and hear lectures by scholars on Hellenic myth. Straddling the continuing line of stone-wall fence, kids walked in bunches, wearing saddle shoes and blazers and small flower-patterned blouses. End-of-August was a last flame of rich greens in New England, differing shades from chartreuse to kelly and fern, zinnia and snapdragon still blooming—adding ornamental Christmas-tree effect to the front lawns and bordering the green-, blue-, red-, or black-shuttered white houses. Despite myself, I liked it, the block with its seasonal lushness, Aunt Snow's austerity, the regimented life, leaving a first butter mark on me. Maybe I'd enjoy Charity Slope with full autumn coming to the foothills of the Berkshires; the newness—if nothing else, the newness.

★

"Hi, I'm Carrie; you're Shylah, right? We're roommates, I hear. Oh, this is my mother and father, Mr. and Mrs. Plimpton."

"Hi."

"How do you do, Shylah. My heavens, look at all this junk you two girls have brought with you. Can the room hold it? Oh dear, look at that, Philip."

My trunk and two suitcases, stuffed skunk, and smattering of books and drawing pads were a drop compared to Carrie's complement of sporting goods. Skates, skis, hockey stick, lacrosse stick, tennis racket, snowshoes, sleeping bag, a stuffed elephant half my size, books, portable record player, radio, plus clothes and personal things, in a room the size of one of Aunt Snow's bigger walk-in closets—a room containing a double-decker bed, two desks, and two bureaus. Also, Carrie herself stood too large for the room—five foot ten or so of prep-school jock, massive in her red Shetland sweater, unkempt curly hair, and mouth full of steel braces. Her face, for all its giant incongruity, was cheerful enough; smart, with lots of jokes to tell in each expression. Carrie seemed O.K., no sweat; O.K. to share a room with the size of a thimble.

Charity Slope fanned out on four hundred acres of back-road woods outside of Dickinson. Not an old school, not old enough to have consistent jungles of ivy-covered, red-brick buildings set in some prearranged quadrangle, it was the better for it. Instead, buildings appeared in scattered woody places, often with little roads leading up to them; some, like the dining and recreation halls, were rustic-modern, with huge windows and unfinished-looking triangles of wood, meant to be contemporary but snug and inconspicuous at wood's edge next to the three or four colonial houses that stood nearby. The art building lay behind the clustered main buildings in a kind of cul-de-sac. A large log-cabin structure, perpetually messy and well used, with recent drawings tacked on beams in the center of the main room.

We boarded in four houses; two for the fifty boys, two for the fifty girls. Mine was named Pine, because it stood surrounded by old pine trees, a large, rambling, nineteenth-century country house that had been renovated inside to include thirty or so bedrooms, a common room, and two apartments for the faculty. Seniors got official solitude, small cells on the third floor, and they could stay up late; it was their responsibility to inspect our rooms for cleanliness each morning. I had the weekend to unpack and adjust.

Carrie was spending her second year at Slope. She loved it, she said; it let her breathe, she said—especially after the restrictions of Miss Porter's. She said Daddy was a writer, Mama taught at Bennington—she said they were "possessed of a totally free marriage," whatever that meant, and that this was a serious place for serious kids who were into politics and painting, and the student government really *was* an effective weapon against the establishment, she said. And she was a devout atheist, she said—and Sunday night all the boarders met at eight for a lecture or recital or meditation. We had to go, she said, but it was a spiritual experience, not a religious one, none of that Episcopal horseshit. Carrie kept up this instructive talk as she put her things away and we figured out what was what and whose in the room. I wanted the bottom bunk, which was O.K. with her, and I wanted the desk by the window in exchange for her hogging nine tenths of the closet space with her paraphernalia.

Carrie had this brash assertiveness about who she was in our first unpackings together, as if she had done everything in an intelligent way—in a unique way—a stick-with-me-kid kind of way. There was not much to be said for commonality of experience. But one thing we shared was disorganization. When our cubicle stood officially ready for co-existence it looked worse than when things were standing out in the room in boxes. Now the drawers of the two dressers hung half open with sweaters overflowing; legs of jeans, bra straps, and shirts fought with each other. The two desks were unrecognizable, drowning under books, my pastels and sketches, her records and radio. The closet shocked—exploded—when opened. I cracked the door, coming away quickly after a brief encounter with fifty pounds of goalie gear and a suitcase. It would be a crowded year.

The bell rang for us to join in the first house meeting before dinner, where we could meet each other, learn the rules; where the newies, as first-timers were called, could meet the experienced crazies. Since Carrie and I were at the back of the first floor, we hadn't far to go. The old wooden stairs clunked loudly under the weight of girls and two house dogs, as all of us straggled or, for the more gung ho, bounded, into Pine's common room.

"All right, everybody settle down as quickly as possible, please; come on now, pipe down, we've got much to do before dinner. Everybody sit down somewhere—anywhere. For those of you crazies, a big hello, everyone looks just terrific; and for the newies—I see at least three or four here—we'll be spending additional time getting to know each other. I know it's nerve-racking for first day and I think everyone here is aware of that, so let's all be extra considerate and helpful these first few days.

O.K., first of all, I'm Jan Nordstrum; this is John, my husband and your English teacher—at least, one of them—and new among the teaching staff in Pine is Irine Rudd, who will also be teaching English. You will be seeing or most likely hearing our children around, they're off now, but John and I have four girls ranging from four—that's Susan—to ten."

"Hello, Jan, tell us all about it, Jan—yaaaayyyyyyyy." The girls applauded our good-looking housemother, her dog yelped, John raised his hands and patted down the enthusiasm.

"I think first off that we might begin by going around the room and introducing ourselves—no cracks, Elsie—so the newies get to know our names . . . Good. Then special welcome to Nickie, Shylah, and Jane. Oh yes, the new dog around here is Hrothgar, who will inevitably visit you in your rooms at some point. I'd like to move on now to a subject I know you all feel strongly about—the rules. There've been some changes. First off, junior and senior girls or girls over sixteen with written permission may smoke in the common room between three and five and after dinner—or may smoke in designated areas and at times like dances, things of that sort. But that means absolutely no smoking in rooms or outside specified areas. First offense is campusing, second suspension. Yes, I thought you'd like that. O.K., second, lights-out on school nights has been extended to ten, except for seniors, when it's twelve; special permission can be arranged for anyone with a special project or exam. No lights-out on weekends. You are responsible, as most of you know, for orderly rooms, God help us all—I mean, do try a little harder, ladies, this year, O.K.? Inspection is at eight-fifteen, Monday through Friday. I've put up a list for seniors on inspection teams—please check to see if your name is up. Also, a general list for clean-up. Last year we had the dirty-bathtub scandal. Please, I beg of you, in the name of athlete's foot and bodily hygiene, bathtubs *must* be cleaned after each use as well as sinks. Don't brush your hair, then leave stray strands to clog up the works. Now, as for weekends off campus, girls with family here may leave Friday after two and must return before eight Sunday evening. Otherwise, written permission for visits to friends' houses or a blanket permission must be obtained at least a week in advance. There's a sign-out book in the hall; be sure to include name and address of destination as well as time and your own name. Also, newies, you can walk or call a cab for local shopping—there's a Friendly's Ice Cream hangout, which is a mile's walk. But even for weekday-afternoon excursions, be sure and sign out first. Ladies, you might notice the rules have been liberalized this year. Still, penalties remain the same for any infringement. I needn't tell you, no drinking or coming back from weekends with liquor on your breath. Understand? And I guess, finally, no being in boys' dorms except by open-dorm rule, and absolutely never in another boy's room—ever, ever. Also, if a girl's door is closed, knock, don't just barge in. O.K., that's about it. Anyone feel like a general discussion?"

Everyone felt like a general discussion, everyone except me. I clutched. It was too much again, the well-scrubbed intelligent faces, the rules, the ease always, that ease with which the familiar could talk to one another about nothing and feel good about it. And I resented having anything planned out for me as much as I turned off to the purveyors of regulation living. I was fifteen going on sixteen, which meant no smoking, and I smoked; I liked to draw late at night and even that I was denied without special permission. It was my habit to wander for an hour or so, but this too must be accounted for—O.K. for a school day, but living under twenty-four-hour standardization, with no privacy even in the bathroom, meant ultimate claustrophobia. Shylah—different. Shylah—scared. I felt my mouth dry up on me, the awkwardness coming over me, my tongue tying itself up, paralyzed. I checked to see if my fly was zipped up, felt around my nose for stray snot, bit my fingernails, petted Hrothgar, who made his way around, getting affection from the girls, now it was my turn and I stroked him maniacally, because it meant doing something, gave me an excuse to be preoccupied. This place, this place. I had asked for it and I hated it. I didn't know why really—just hated it. Maybe it had to do with jealousy; maybe I choked on affluent girls with red cheeks and lacrosse sticks, or maybe it was the rules—something about those rules made me tighten up, could feel myself—muscles tense. People accepted—like potted plants, you can transplant them into another container, water them, and they'll grow, and while they're growing, you can whip out the Bible or *The Christian Science Monitor* or *Das Kapital* and there's your easy mark; you can just stand there and give them anything you want and they've got to hang in by the roots even if they think you're full of shit, and screw you, I was no damn plant.

The dinner bell rang and I walked up the gravel road to the main dining hall, a little behind our house's girls, to be joined halfway up by the Saltonstall House girls. The dining area itself was Danish-modern, rustic-looking, with blond-wood everything. Assigned seating, wouldn't you know. At my table were seven students and one faculty member. If nothing else, we were eclectic. The boy on my right wore a three-piece suit—appeared profound, scholarly, and humorless; the girl across from me, a rich Texan; another boy—a jock senior green-cord prep Negro—I figured he ran the class—the combination was just perfect for all the hungry-looking liberal faces. And Nickie sat at the table, one of the other new girls living in Pine—tall, pretty. Sweet, I thought. And Haverford the brooder, darkly beautiful and monosyllabic. Finally Sharon, a smiler, followed by our faculty man—known as Bunyans, another nickname to indicate, not the state of his feet, but the fact that he had a working knowledge of the woods and nature. We chummed up as best we could until meditation time—that's what they called it. I did not see the difference between this and any garden-variety grace, except the word "God" had been gratuitously removed. Why have a grace if you don't have a God?—perhaps going a little overboard so as not to offend.

"So tell us, Shylah, what's life like on the Keys? Sounds exotic." Bunyans must have memorized our dossiers for pertinent questions to "bring us out." I relented.

"Oh, O.K., lots of warm water and palm trees. Different. The school I went to was pretty primitive and all, but I kind of liked it."

"Profoundly interesting, in fact. I was down there last year; they have the only underwater state park, Pennekamp, with an enormous variety of coral specimens, perhaps the best in our waters. Fascinating really." That was Bernard the scholar, who had an abiding love for anything that did not noticeably breathe.

"Ah sailed real near there; we all docked Marathon-way before we went off to Grand Bahama, kinda seedy-looking, the Keys." Daisy's accent was craw-catching, akin to grating carrots; she didn't talk, she sliced. A bitch. A rich bitch. A stupid bitch. Shylah, stop it. For a moment I saw the slivers again, listening to her—same old anger. I couldn't listen to certain things, couldn't listen. Nickie was talking now, talking to me, but the conversation came in fragments. We were finishing fudge brownies with ice cream; we were coming to the end of dinner. The headmaster, Steve Ryerson, spoke to us from the announcement platform, welcomed us to Charity Slope, introduced his wife, told us of improvements in the sports facilities over the summer, assured us of having a terrific year, we're the best ever, he said, smoked a pipe, spoke haltingly, methodically. His wife, his gray-suited, fog-horn-voiced wife, embellished for him, talked about the liberalized rules, the spirit of Slope, the meaning of schooling, respect for others. Drowning in their practiced monotones, I fought an attack of yawns. Nickie nudged me under the table. We smiled—a conspiratorial look. She wore her swallowed yawns as I was wearing mine. Bunyans lifted one perfect eyebrow at us and looked back at the glory of the Ryersons. We were requested to stand and sing the school song; newies would listen and learn, we were told. Newies! A shit thing to be called by the progressive eyewash conglomerate. Nickie and I stared into each other's wincing eyes.

"Well, that was a little bit of hell."

"Yeah, Nickie, doesn't pay to be a 'newie,' or whatever/whoever we are."

"Fuck them, I hate this bullshit school rah-rah junk. Really, that's why I was kicking you, I've been to enough of these institutions to know a kindred spirit when I see one."

"God, you know it. What school'd you go to before Slope?"

"I didn't. I was in the funny farm, McLean, for six months. Before that, at Billings School in Eastmont. But I had a bad habit of running away too often. Actually, this doesn't look too bad, considering every one of these places is absurd, I mean, with the now-we-will-wiggle-our-left-ear-in-unison crap. We're all supposed to be pretty smart here, you know, all this individual expression, and if you see a shrink, that's supposed to be an indicator of how artistic you are. I don't know. Nothing's perfect. It's just the rules, and then they pretend they're so bloody progressive. Makes me sick."

"Where do you live when you're not incarcerated?"

"Maine. Well, New York originally, but my parents died, so I live with my aunt and uncle in Bangor."

"I've never been to Maine. Cold, huh?"

"Yeah, you said it, in more ways than one. Aunt Susan has spent the last three years not approving of me. You know, I don't have that cowed-proper look. She's the great pain in my ass. Anyhow, this is my third boarding school, the first 'liberal' one, right? Like what can I do, huh? McLean was the best of the joints. Really, Shylah, if you ever get desperate, there's nothing like it, for four hundred bucks a week."

"Hey, you've really been around. Your auntie sounds like the Wicked Witch of the East."

"She really hates this place; progressive education isn't her style, you know, coed and Negroes and kids being intelligent, not her style at all. But my counselor at McLean gave her an ultimatum and she'd sort of given up on me anyway. So it was just as well. I've only two years of high school left, and if I'm out of the house and out of the loony bin, it's a godsend to sweet Auntie."

"Christ. Sounds horrible. Want to come to my room? I've got a roommate but I think she's probably off with some people. Carrie, the big girl; God, you should see the stuff she brought with her—a superjock, I mean, and what a jock. Hockey, lacrosse, snowshoes, skates—tons of shit."

"My roomie's superquiet. You should see her maman, Shylah, a real number. 'Jessica darling, you be a good squirrel. Daddy and I will call from Madrid. Remember, no rich desserts'— Shit, poor Jessica, a real cream puff from the old conceptual egg."

"Sounds like Alice—my stepmother—she does it all the

time—talks that way—wouldn't be so bad if it was backed up by a little sincerity—couldn't hurt. My mother—she's dead—used to call me Mrs. Tiggywinkle, which was O.K., cause, you know, she wasn't putting me on or anything. I loved it when she called me that—meant for one thing that she was sober—she'd call me that mostly in the mornings."

"Oh, fuck it. when I have kids, I swear to God, it's going to be easy for them. That is, after I've made it as an actress and all that."

"Are you an actress? Terrific."

"I want to go into musical comedy. What are you?"

"Nothing in particular; I draw a lot. I don't know, maybe I'll be an artist if I'm good enough."

Nickie and I sat on my lower bunk. I could hear Carrie with the other girls through the wall, talking about the hockey team. I sort of envied her; I mean, she had something, she could always go whack a puck or throw her net around to blow off steam, or maybe she didn't think all that much. Nickie was something else, more like me, but at extremes. Pretty and pretty tough. She swore like she smoked. Sort of Bette Davis-staccato-nervous. We were a pair, Nickie and I, we'd do O.K. hanging out together. Good to latch on to someone like Nickie, to enjoy each other's company, all new, in a faintly disgusting atmosphere. Nickie wasn't at all like Luanne; Luanne was a rock, Luanne had the life of a well-fed turtle compared to Nickie's.

★

Bedtime occurred when I couldn't stay vertical any longer. Friday night, no lights-out, but most of us were exhausted from unpacking and saying goodbye to relatives. Anyhow, I lay in bed considering the logistics of a basic problem: my roommate. My elephantine jock, who, every time she shifted in the upper bunk, called up visions of a herd loose in the room. But it wasn't that. It wasn't that. It wasn't the noise; it was the privacy. It was being alone at night sometimes that mattered. How could I play with myself with her rumbling in the upper bunk? I liked to play with myself. I slept better. It helped. It was so friendly. And I could dream up Stanley or Clark Gable or anybody. Peaceful. Playing with myself made things more endurable when the loneliness sunk in and started to gnaw like little rats. Mummy long ago said the whole "thing," what she called touching myself, the "thing," was like being born with hydrocephalus. Weird, degrading, blinding. It certainly wasn't something I would have done in dancing class. But it was me, goddamnit, even if I was a sexual worm. I liked it. If I ever got married, I'd have my husband do it to me all the time like Stanley did; that was the best, that was the best of all. But right now I wanted to be a freak in private. I didn't want Carrie around. God, I wanted to be alone. Fuck you, Carrie, jock rhino, fuck you. The NEW word, some of the girls and Nickie used it, like Luanne and Selma Anne said Mahhhh Lawwwd, like that. I liked the word—fuck. Fuck, fuck, fuck. Like hitting a tennis ball against a cement wall—it bounced back at me. Oh fuck, Carrie, get out of the damn room.

I heard her snores finally, kind of a snorting whistle with her braces and stuff. When I had listened until the rhythm of breaths sounded deep, about ten minutes or so, I started by trying not to think. Not to hear her and not to reflect; to clear the head and then to start rethinking, about sex. It would be Stanley; I missed Stanley, so gentle, big, bearlike body, all that tenderness, sort of clumsy, made me wet to think about it. So I thought about Stanley and our first night; I thought about his skin, how it was leathery compared to mine, and his prick, I thought about Stanley's prick, when it brushed my leg—when it came close to being inside me, but never did, only that pig— oh—but then I'd come down if I thought about Bobby Jay— Stanley again, Stanley's hands in my hair and his hands holding my hands straight up and out and getting at me, feeling me over the bra and then naked, and his fingers rubbing my crotch and getting into it, just barely touching. Ooooh ahhh. I imitated the daydream, pushed my hand down from my belly and underneath the cotton underpants to where the hair began, and down, first rubbing over the crotch, then slipping the forefinger in lightly just between the lips, lightly, then a little harder—just until the muscles started to vibrate, and Stanley breathing in my ear and his finger, and my hand on his prick, the top of it, where that piece of flesh was, and my finger gentle again and his kissing me with his tongue in my mouth and the finger, the finger. And I went over—as he was—as the daydream was kissing me. Quick this time, I got very tight to get over. The best being when it's not so tight; the best was with him and occasionally myself, but there were the noises and Neanderthal turnings of Carrie. It was O.K. Fine, I could sleep now. My underpants were well soaked. I could put them under my pillow and rub my crotch on the sheet and sleep. No palm-branch sound. No cross-island wind. Only to move into her snoring, to move with her breath, to sleep.

★

I was homesick. It began a week after classes started. It began when I thought of the slumber parties and Luanne and Lime. I missed them, my racist reputation-manic friends who thought I was totally queer and stood by me. I missed them. Daddy and Alice, I did not miss, not really. About Daddy—he just didn't have it in him to be "Daddy"—and I kept pushing for Daddy-daughterhood, but he didn't—wouldn't be a father to me. He wouldn't be Daddy for me. And Alice—who could know Alice behind the candy superlatives? It was all wasteland and distance.

My courses were advanced and difficult. That is, by Lime standards, which really weren't standards at all. I had been in front, the class queer-brain—and here I was so obviously behind. The answer was to become a serious grind. But except for art and Chaucer I hated my courses. Or maybe it wasn't hate but the persistent dreaming. I had begun to fantasize again. Vague. I would sit down in algebra and go into a world of heroics until the bell rang. I did try. I did try at first. I would stare at one teacher's buck teeth or another's heaving chest or the bulletin board, or compulsively take notes in my book, but it would become automatic quickly. I could write down anything and not be aware of it. Miss Weinstein complained, first to

1 2 9

me, then to my counselor, then to Mr. Ryerson. I had made the mistake of getting an A on my second algebra test; I held the only A for that particular exam. Otherwise my math marks were F's. It was looking at a haze of numbers with nothing connected . . . happened in chemistry too, nothing—no sense. I couldn't study. I wasn't stupid. First, I got called in—they cajoled, asked me if I was having an uncomfortable "adjustment," said I had had a rough time. Then I had after-class sessions; then Zoe was called in and the school psychiatrist suggested. I wasn't in touch, they said. I kept too much to myself and to Nickie. Noisy in study halls. I needed a shrink, I needed help, they were here to help. Poor Shylah; Shylah needed a little push.

Dr. Cassandra Witten was my push. A thoroughly portable shrink, she trekked out from Dickinson to Slope on Fridays for the benefit of us half a dozen unstable boarders. Dr. Witten, with her permanented hair a bit too curly and her clothes a size too loose, reminded me of Mummy in her saner moods. So I naturally wanted to get friendly, but that wasn't allowed. Instead, she sat and listened. It was for me to unburden the burden. But for only fifty minutes once a week, I couldn't really get into it. I mean, fifty minutes once a week is not enough time to zip into the tragedy of my learning problem without feeling somewhat out to lunch. "Oh, Dr. Witten, and then I can't concentrate on algebra because I was unloved by my daddy and I really want to mow the class down with tommy guns, and the kids don't love me because I'm quiet in a noisy way or I haven't mastered the boarding-school dialect, and yes, they really are nice kids, but I like Nickie and Nickie's enough. Involved? Me, involved? No— Oh, yes, in daydreaming . . . Well, in one, but I don't have that much any more—I start a religion in Norway during the Second World War and I lead my people against the Nazis; I risk my life, you know, like crazy, and then I say the most amazingly profound things about love and generosity and everyone is moved and I'm full of love for them and selfless, and I'm totally full of shit. Don't you think I'm full of shit? Now, come on, Witten, you know, really, the Second World War and Norway. And then I'm fat. No, really, I'm fat." And that's about as much as I could muster. I even tried to do a few tears for her, but nothing happened. I felt like laughing. But I didn't want to hurt her feelings. Dr. Witten would feel she wasn't helping me if I giggled all the time and that would sadden a wise doctor; I felt responsible about that, felt it must be especially difficult to be a female shrink with all that Freud business hanging over— I'd been reading a lot of Freud and Jung. It must have been tough. So I went in every Friday at one and unburdened myself as best I could, so Witten would silently rejoice that I was improving.

★

Mid-November and I suffered. For and over nothing. I couldn't understand it. I went daily to the woods to weep. There was this spot with a brush pocket in it, so I'd be surrounded by thicket under a tree. I'd pull out my illegal cigarettes and smoke and cry and put my arms around myself and curl up, and sometimes I'd explain everything to some surprised bird or squirrel. Once a deer came up close, causing me to howl more and louder, and the deer looked at me terrified and ran the hell away. But these things I couldn't tell Witten or even Nickie. This was the darkness. I could not even *say* the darkness. The darkness had no voice. That was the darkness. And once I went out to my thicket and smoked my cigarette and cried and there seemed no end to it. My sobbing kept up until I passed out from it—like falling asleep from pain, when something exhausts you with hurting—like terrible diarrhea, when finally the lull from trips to the john occurs and you drop in your tracks, empty. Nothing left. When I came to, the pitch of night was full on. I raced back. I had missed supper. Ten-thirty—after lights-out.

"Oh shit, Jan, really, I'm sorry. I fell asleep—went for a walk—guess I didn't sleep well last night. Oh no, looking for me. Oh, good Christ."

"Shylah, look at your face. You weren't just sleeping. Look, come here, we'll clean you up, I'll make some nice tea. Better yet, for medicinal purposes, let me give you a little sherry. Dear

God, we've been absolutely out of our minds with worry. Shy-lah dear, what's wrong? You've been looking so desperately pained recently. Can't you tell me?"

Jan had that concerned-mother look, but sincerely that way. She had that look for any of us who were hurting or for her kids when they skinned their knees. Taking me by the hand into the bathroom, she had me sit on the toilet cover while she washed my face with a warm cloth. She put her hand to my hair and drew it back gently. She put her arm around me on the way back to the living room, sat next to me on the big old couch, poured both of us sherry, and patted my knee.

"Nothing's wrong. Well, I mean, I guess everything is, but nothing in particular. Look, you know, I went out and it's been a rough day, I flunked another algebra test—and I just fell asleep, that's all."

"Come on, Shylah. Your eyes are all scarlet and swollen. Look, I know you've been skipping afternoon study hall and coming back here. And I know you've been doing some first-rate sketches in your room. I confess I peeked. Those pictures, they're so strong—but so disturbed. The faces, the crowds, the specter of it, but also the one you did, that pastel of the male and female combined. It's beautiful, really, Shylah. Shows a lot of concentration. I thought maybe your drawing would get you over this rough time. But you've got to try; it'll be so difficult for you otherwise."

"But I have been trying—I mean, you know, like I've been reading the *Symposium*. The idea of people being split apart and then looking for the other half, somewhere there's a perfect fit—you know— I really, well, uh, I'm fascinated by the idea. Aren't you? But, shit, I'm O.K., Jan, don't worry."

John came in then. John, whom I disliked, suspecting he beat Jan, or at least browbeat her. Such a prig, John, whereas Jan was all openness and wanting to fold in everything. He wanted his charges to be rigid sticks. At least, it seemed that way to me.

"Waiting for an explanation. Waiting."

"I fell asleep in the woods, John. Sorry."

"What does that mean, you fell asleep in the woods? Sounds like Miss Dale is playing a latter-day Rip van Winkle. You realize, I'm sure you do, that we were out looking for you with flashlights, time better spent in other pursuits, don't you think? Or don't you think? Look, I'm frankly a little tired of your heraldic moods, do you understand? You stay in your room alone, you deem Nickie your only confidante, and I must say I question that friendship, her toughness, her elusory manipulations. At least her grades have some merit to them. You're disgusting, look at you. When you brush your hair, it's a downright miracle. Do you even bother with your assignments now? I don't like this removal, Shylah, I think . . ."

"Fuck you. What do you want me to say anyway, prick? Man, I said I fell asleep. Stop lecturing me. Will you stop. I can't stand it—don't dictate to me. Hey, listen. I don't have to listen to you, I don't have to listen to any of you. I don't care what you say. Don't scream at me, stop telling me."

"You don't speak to any faculty member that way. You listen to me, young lady. You have a choice at this juncture, Shylah. Either apologize to me on the spot or I telephone Mr. Ryerson and tell him I feel you won't work out at Slope. You're nothing new. We've had plenty of disturbed kids around—we give you a lot of leeway. And I'd like to see a general improvement immediately; do you understand what that means? It means, move your ass, Shylah, to use your kind of language. That's what it means. Now, which is it? Are you going to . . ."

"John, I think Shylah is very upset right now, and maybe in the morning—we could sit down after breakfast and . . ."

"Absolutely not, Jan, not in this case. She's got to learn, she's got to . . ."

"NO, no, no, no, leave me alone, will-when-will-when-will you leave me alone? why are you doing this to me? I want to be alone, please, God. Jan, make him leave me alone. I hate him, I hate him, leave me alone. No, stop it, don't touch me, you bastard, don't you touch me, I'll kill you, leave me alone, leave me alone, oh Jesus, shit, Mummy, Mummy— Goddamnit, why-why-why can't you leave me alone, I didn't do anything. Nothing. And you can shove your threats—don't-don't want to be threatened. Fell asleep. I fell asleep, like what Jan said."

"It's all right, Shylah, it's all right. Here, drink this, just water. Here, it's O.K.; try not to carry on so, calm down. We'll talk about it calmly, won't we, John? Here, Shylah, blow your nose; please, John, she's ill, can't you see—well, upset then. There now, better blow again."

"You can't talk to people that way, Shylah, do you understand— You simply mustn't say impolite things, no matter how badly you feel."

"You attacked me. All you could think of was how screwed up I looked and how much trouble I am and shit like that. For God's sake, I told you I fell asleep. Really, I fell asleep."

"I still want to hear that apology. I'm waiting . . ."

"I apologize then. But I really think you're a vicious prick, and now you know it."

"Again. I want to hear it again, without the addendum."

"You really want the lie, don't you? What's the way you say it, 'Cut the mustard, toe the line'? I'm sorry, I'm sorry. Now, please let me go, please let me go."

"I accept your apology conditionally. The condition is no more sign-out weekends for a month—you're campused. Your room study permissions are suspended as well. You can study exclusively at the monitored study halls both at night and in the afternoon. And I want to know that you are making an effort to join with the other students . . . meaning, I don't want to see you and Nickie so constantly together, is that clear? Is it, Shylah?"

"Yes, sir, clear, absolutely clear. Can I go, please? Jan, make him let me go, I'm exhausted."

"Don't you ask her, you ask me—you're speaking to me."

"Can I go?"

"Yes, get out of here, goon; you may go. Don't forget, Shylah. I want to see a change."

Prick. Prick bastard, shithead. How could anyone live with him? Damn those crystals; damn it, the glass breaking again, slivers, can't make it, slivers. I didn't care, but Zoe, he'd gotten me in. Didn't want Zoe to feel shitty, didn't want this reflecting back, just couldn't stand anything for very long. Oh goddamnit, goddamnit. Why were, why was John like Daddy? Groveling—

Jesus, apologizing to that bastard. Couldn't go to sleep now. Had to talk to Nickie. I stuffed a pillow into my bunk—under the sheets. Carrie slept on louder than life itself. Jeesus, elephant, you got it made with your adenoidal narcolepsy.

Tiptoeing up the back stairs to Nickie's room, the one just left of the stairwell. Could hear their breathing, even sleeping, Nickie in the top bunk. I climbed the ladder, pulled at her shoulder.

"Nickie, wake up, it's Shylah; Nickie, come on, wake up, I've got to talk to you. I'm in bad shape. Please, Nickie, wake up."

"Uh huh, uh huh, uh huh, wake, I'm wake, yah yah sure, outside, shhh, careful, don't wake her up. The asshole. What happened?"

Nickie took her jeans and coat and stuff into the bathroom with me, dressed quickly, and followed me out into the midnight yard. We lit cigarettes. Nickie kept her eye on me.

"I fell asleep in the woods, got back around ten-thirty. Old son-of-a-bitch John really put it to me. I mean, it was gross, really gross. Campused me, took away room study privileges, everything. And he said we aren't supposed to see each other so much. Isn't that unbelievable? That bastard, that's horrible, right, Nickie?"

"Gross. Fuck him, just fuck him—what a pig. Look, don't sweat it, Shylah, I've been through this routine before. Poor Jan, though. God, how could anybody marry the prick?"

"Probably because of it—maybe she got knocked up and had to. Anyhow, I sort of flipped out, you know, like I'm flunking two subjects and I can't study and you're the only worthwhile thing for me here except art and, you know, taking walks. I mean, it's O.K. really, it's just me."

"God, I can't stand it when you do this; stop blaming yourself, for Christsake. Look, you've got to be practical about this, I mean about pricks in power, that's one thing I learned in the funny farm. Avoid him as much as you can—you can override his discipline by going to your brother or the counselor, say it's important to your emotional development that you have your weekends and all that crap. He can't dictate how much we see each other, you know that, and I can read his mind. He's exaggerating everything. He can't pigeonhole you so it screws him up, you know. Some housefather huh?"

"I know, I know—you're right, I'll steer clear of him. It's just that I can't stand pricks like that having power over me."

"Do you feel better now, Shylah, huh? Let's go in. I'm freezing, and you need some sleep; so do I as a matter of fact."

"Yes, O.K. Look, you know, I didn't mean to drag you out of bed, but I thought you should know, like in case he pulls you in and says, 'I don't think you should see Shylah,' and all that baloney. Really though, you've been a big help. I mean it. Like I feel very calm. I can think again."

I put my arms around her then, drew her to me, close enough to kiss her cheek but not to frighten her. Affection was difficult for her; with all her toughness I think she feared touching. So I felt a bit selfish kissing her this time, but it was my way. And she liked it. I thought she liked it. I didn't think she just endured it, the hold, the kiss. I felt her incline a little. Aw Nickie. Nickie.

8

First snow, all that hilly woodland drunk with it. Wet, sculptable snow, and when I walked out, out past the art building and over the half-frozen stream, it was to make things or to fall backward in my ski suit, creating an angel or a monster. There were no more trips out to the brush, to weep and talk and nod. The impracticality of sobbing into fat snowdrifts stopped its function. Instead, I read furiously, read everything—Kafka, Dostoevsky, Frank Yerby, Mailer, O'Hara, *Popular Mechanics*, *The Kenyon Review*, an antique cookbook, Emily Dickinson, Robert Lowell, the Bible, *Das Kapital*. The movement of my eyes over the print, the feel of the books—I enjoyed it, enjoyed looking at the words, the sense of things—seeing them, the stories or resolutions as individual landscapes, like the changing climate at Slope. John had eased off. My chem and algebra grades were still cretin-level, but he had let go, because I was reading, because I spent time in the art room—he left me alone. My production was sanctified.

Luanne phoned me from Lime, called to ask, if she held off her wedding, could I get down during Christmas, to be maid of honor, could I? Pregnant; Luanne knew how to make up minds. Children were irrevocable in Lime and always desired—from conception onward. The other girls got on the wire. We talked and giggled, and for five minutes or so I slipped into their patterns. But no, I could not get down, I said. No, but I'd try later. I wanted to see them, I said; I was excited for Luanne, I said. Maybe after this year, maybe something could be worked out. No, I had not heard from Daddy; yes, Alice wrote. Everything was O.K.; yes, it was a good school, but different. We chatted. Talked about the baby to come, first of us from the group to get knocked up, and we talked about sex, about slumber parties, and then promised to write every week, forever if necessary. I went back to my room from the pay phone and mulled the Southern hick sounds over inside me.

I continued to see Witten each Friday afternoon and continued to make her feel good, though I never saw the value of that fifty minutes out of so many minutes. They let me spend weekends again with Aunt Snow, who would occasionally have little salons on Friday night. I could curl up on the couch and listen, or just read, while attending them.

And Nickie came for one Sunday; we went to the movies and over to some senior day boy's house. His parents had left for the weekend, so we drank vodka collinses at ten above zero and got tipsy; then went sledding near a batch of evergreens on the old golf course and returned by cab to Slope together. Then the dome on the Greek Orthodox church held a ledge of icicles, which gave me hours of entertainment wadding up snowballs to hit them down, the huge three-foot daggers falling into the snow. I liked their feel and something about them, the smooth translucence, like certain jewelry, and the size: big things, it was a season for big things.

★

I hung around the town square thinking up possible things to do. I could eat, go to a movie, go to the library, hit icicles, or hit the party at Pril's—a desperate last choice which I took.

Pril Atwater, the perfect Charity Slopian: a grind, a jock, a pretty girl, a friendly girl, a responsible young citizen. Despite

1 3 8

these obvious drawbacks, I liked her better than most. This pre-Christmas party of hers was an official one, one in which parents and friends of parents hung around and the food was extensive and elegant, and their house, one of Dickinson's finest, used every electric bulb for the event. In June she'd have some horrendous coming-out thing before going on to Vassar, probably to win all possible plaudits and marry a clerk to the Supreme Court. I could see it. Then at thirty-five she'd divorce him, study at the Radcliffe Institute, go nuts, publish a book about mirages, and redeem herself. Pril was O.K.

Once inside her door, having goofed by shaking hands with the chagrined Filipino houseboy, I checked out my source of pleasure—food. I'd go to the worst parties just to see the food lying out buffet-style and the colors, all the different possible tastes between salads and pâté and ham and shrimp and cake and olives, dips, crackers, bread. To look at different breads, especially the kind that comes from foreign bakeries, the kind that's shaped like hair rather than the Holsum-loaf type—bubble-gum bread. The cook came from Vienna, so there was chocolate everything, petits fours, cookies, and little chocolate cups filled with Chantilly. The punch bowl had a meringue swan stuck in the middle and little meringue floating islands. It was enough to make me cry—all that stuff. I had taken one slice of cheddar, one of Swiss, and a piece of cherry gourmandise, then ham and the pâté in the star mold, then cocktail shrimp but jumbos, and dip, French bread, a cold tuna, tomato, and caper salad thing, string-bean salad—then, with croutons, one of the giants—cheesy Newburg in a chafing dish; then olives and carrot curls, a few almonds, a chocolate petit four with a pink squirrel squiggle on top, pink and green mints, a chocolate cup, some fresh strawberries, and cookies. That I would most likely be in the john with one finger rammed down my throat in an hour made no difference at all. Just to have the food on my plate, to play and mix it, to eat shrimp with crumbs from the cookies and vinaigrette from the bean salad. Oh God. Food.

The recreation room in the basement had been arranged for dancing, a band played mostly souped-up fox-trots, Lester

Lannin–style. Grownups clearly got the most out of the dances. They dipped each other around like serving ladles. The Atwaters' St. Bernard sat up next to my chair, looking appalled.

"Would you like to dance, Shylah?"

"Uh, no."

"How've you been? You look terrific, absolutely fantastic."

"Thanks. O.K., I guess. How have you been, Chauncy?"

"Oh great, really great."

"How's Harvard? Which dorm are you in, anyway?"

"Wigglesworth. Oh, you know, it's easier than I thought. I like the other things. We're getting a band together and stuff. Say, really, I'm glad I ran into you, we're having this dance next week in the Union, you know, and I thought maybe you could stay at Binnie's in Harvard Square and we could make a whole weekend of it. Really, it'd be terrific. I know she'd love to have you. What do you say?"

"I should check with Zoe, but sure, why not."

Chauncy Atwater, Pril's older brother, whom I had met and liked at smaller gatherings she'd thrown. Chauncy, graduate of Slope, the smart boy, the early-admissions freshman at Harvard, the least athletic of the Atwaters. Pleasant guy, Chauncy. Sometimes he'd stop in at Slope after school and fiddle around in the art building. We had gotten to know one another that way. Chauncy had a flair for charcoal sketches; he could render anything—crumpled newspaper, a window with a view, me, the beams above us. Besides, it was the weekend we would be let out for the three weeks of Christmas recess. A little freedom, Harvard, dressing up. Sure, Zoe'd look forward to having the weekend to himself, to not worrying about sister.

★

The Pine House girls were in the common room having a farting contest. Sunday night, the last five days before vacation, Friday ahead of us—I put my weekend gear down and tried to sit comfortably with them awhile. Carrie played queen of extremes; she could fart and belch at the same time, a sort of echoing-frog effect. I guess it had to do with her musculature.

"Hey, Shylah."

"Hey, Carrie, sounds like you had a gassy weekend."

"Passes the time. How was Pril's party?"

"Lotsa food."

"Well, come on, you must have done something. Get tanked? Get fucked?"

"No, I ate a lot, though."

"Oh, you're so precious sometimes, honest to God."

"What's precious about it? I answered your question. You want me to provide a tale of orgy to entertain you."

"Delicate flower, isn't she, you guys? On the rag again, Shylah?"

"Go back to your concert, huh. I'm gonna flake out, that is, if you haven't dumped your weekend athletic gear on my bunk."

I walked through to our room. Slobovia to inspection teams. Kicking away the pads and sticks and skates and dirty clothes to make a path to my bunk, I put the suitcase down and opened it. I brought out the Russian cigarettes and guitar picks I had bought for Nickie, who had been feeling bad, and wrapped them in a little drawing I'd done, Scotch-taping the ends carefully, then a hand-made bow with scissor-curled ribbon ends. When I had finished this task, I removed my clothes, threw on the Mother Hubbard and bunny slippers, and trudged up to find her.

"Hi, Nicko, how was the weekend?"

"Oh O.K., I guess. Just hacked around and slept. Not very sexy."

Nickie lay on the bed looking miserable. She tried to smile—I saw her lip curl a bit—which made the misery even more acute.

"You should have called me, Nick. What's got you this way?"

"I don't know, or well, you know, it's that time of the year. Everybody goes and has a big Christmas, and I miss my parents. My aunt just phoned. God, she's such a shithead, I can't believe it sometimes. She's off to Europe, so she wants me to stay here, made arrangements with Jan for me to spend Christmas with her and the Nazi. Oh God, at least I thought I'd have *some* family, you know, we'd have something to talk about together."

1 4 1

"God, a real fuck, isn't she? Maybe it doesn't have to be so dreary though; maybe you can spend Christmas with Zoe and me. I'd love that, and I'm sure if I explained . . ."

"Thanks, but it's all arranged. I don't think she'd let me. The Nazi's had talks—no doubt with words about us."

"Well, I'm going to ask anyway. Maybe we can work something out. Here, look, I got you something. Well, open it."

"Oh neat, Shy, what is it? Oh, terrific, picks and oh, those cigarettes— Shy, thank you, really, thanks a lot. Really great."

"Good, you like . . . oh Nickie, don't cry, aw Nicko— I'll be with you, we'll figure something out. Who would want to spend Christmas without you?"

I went over and closed the door, then climbed up to her bunk, grabbing the box of Kleenex on the bureau. I put my arm around her, lifted her to me, and dabbed at her cheeks with a tissue. The screams and giggles of the Sunday-night rapport downstairs carried. No one would hear her sobbing with that racket. She was a piece of me—Nickie. Rocking her, kissing her cheeks, her tears in my hair—she wanted that. She wanted that because it was what I would have wanted, and part of it, part of the pain, was the same.

"Will, will you, will you get under the covers with me? I'm, I'm cold."

"Sure, sure, I will; just let me throw off these slippers. There. Oh Nickie, your feet are freezing, God—there, that's better, uh huh, now they're warming up."

I eased down and lay on my side, she on her side, facing me. Irregular breathing had replaced her torrential weeping now, the kind that comes after long sieges—all gaspy. The closeness of bodies under two layers of flannel nightgowns heated us up. We couldn't move; the bunk had a nun cell's size to it. Just lay there. Under comfort of female skins—and breasts, hers closing over mine. It did make a difference, the smoothness and rounded feeling. We kissed and stroked one another, pulling up the nightgowns. And easy. Easy to know how and where. Easy.

★

1 4 2

"Hey, Shylah, Aunt Susan said I can go. The whole bit . . . to the dance and to spend Christmas with you all. Jan talked to her and your brother. Jesus, that was terrific of him, really."

"Great, Nickie, I'll call Chauncy then. You get his roommate. Oh, don't worry; you know Chauncy wouldn't fix you up with a dog or anything—he's probably very acceptably cute."

Friday. Exams were over. Pine House was a packing suitcase. Jan had had us all in for punch and Christmas cookies. Even the Nazi managed to nod and smile, though Nickie and I kept away from his path. Dr. Witten had left for two weeks in Nassau, which meant I didn't have to cheer her up with my tragedy and we could go to the train directly from school.

"Oh fuck, help, oh no, what the hell am I going to wear?"

"Relax, look, we'll wear these. Nice huh, none of that flouncy shit." I produced my two new sheath dresses, woolen but dressy. "You can buy high heels in Cambridge, black spikes, right. Everything's O.K. really, wear the red dress."

At North Station, Chauncy and this guy, his roommate, met us. Nickie was enchanted. He turned out to be, in my judgment, too good-looking. We took a cab.

Harvard Square, an impossible clutter of skinny streets, full of alleys, and Massachusetts Avenue's confusing curve. When we arrived at Shelley Mews, where Binnie lived, Chauncy and Redford had us mapped. Tonight we'd go to dinner at the Union; that's where freshmen ate anyway, and then a party in Belmont. Redford, whose name shackled me, had rented a car for the weekend. Then tomorrow we could go to the Bach concert in Lowell; afterward dinner at La Maison des Champignons, where they'd be sure and let us underagers drink, making the big dance at around ten. And Sunday anything went.

Binnie Atwater, the oldest of the Atwater kids—maybe twenty-three even—had a large apartment. Three bedrooms, a study, two bathrooms—very nice. She had set aside the larger of the two guest rooms—with window seat, fireplace, and large bath—perfume and soap all over the place. She gave us a key to come and go—generous with things. Binnie, it was explained, had a "friend" and wouldn't be around much. She *looked* like she wouldn't be home much: all hair and a sweeping walk.

1 4 3

Nickie and I felt a little intimidated by her ultrasecure loveliness. The boys left us to get ready, and Binnie went to her lover, after telling us to make ourselves at home.

"Hey, Nickie, let's strip and dance the Rite of Spring on the pile carpet. Wow, super. Look, I'm a fat Natalie Wood."

"Oh Jesus, how much time have we got to ourselves?"

"Three hours. Let's do something."

"How about a drink? Let's check that out first. Ooooh, this is really grand. Binnie and her ritzy life; give me wine Shylahvsky, give me wine."

"Yeah sure, only let's stay reasonably sober, we've got these guys coming and a whole evening of total glamour. Uhh whadda Christmas, weeee, look at me, I'm Wonder Woman."

"Ah yes, quite right, Shy, Wonder Queer, quite right. Look— all this wine in the fridge. My God, and last week I was over the edge. Spectacular. Hey, Redford is really cute. Makes me nervous, you know, I'm O.K., but I'm no Liz Taylor."

"Don't sweat it. Redford is no Liz Taylor either."

"No, I'm serious, you know what I mean. Hey, let's make each other up and stuff, do our hair, the whole thing."

"Sure, sure, the whole thing. Nickie, I love you. Really, I love you, even if you do become a musical-comedy star and forget poor Shylah."

"Forget you, how could I forget you? A big pain in the ass like you. I can't live without some torture in my life. God, will you look at her record collection—she's got Del Shannon's 'Runaway' stuck in with the Vivaldi."

But I had already become enamored with her old-fashioned porcelain bathtub, deep, with lots of oil and bubble-bath stuff to choose from on the vanity. I dropped four different-colored oil eggs into the hot water and, when it was to the point of overflow, stepped in. Nickie brought us wine. I went into a hot-water-soak think. Luanne would be just about getting married, and Stanley, Stanley's two-paragraph scrawls had stopped last month. If I went home again, maybe it would be the same, maybe. Then again, I had to think of Christmas presents. What could I give Zoe? I turned the water off with my feet and sunk back in the steam. Nickie sat on the john top and talked. I listened to my hand treading the water, to the sponge as I squeezed and rubbed soap on it, to the glass as it clinked against the porcelain when I grasped it. Hmmm, for a while. Just a while.

★

"Shyyyylahhhhh!"

"Oh come on, Chauncy, I'm just having some fun, that's all. I like the dancing. You were, after all, the one who was looking forward to this shindig."

"Let's go. It's O.K. for a while but, look, it's after one. Let's go back to Binnie's and hack around for the rest of it. Redford and Nickie want to go back."

"O.K. Uh, no thanks—we were just leaving, no we're going . . . Goddamnit, I know what it is, you just don't like to dance and I'm enjoying this."

"Yeah, you sure are; well, you've made the rounds, as they say. Let's go, huh?"

"Shylah, come to the john with me."

"Hmmm, Nickie. O.K., you guys, meet you at the door. Back in a sec."

"What's the matter, Shylah, don't you want to go, I mean, you know, be alone with Chauncy? Redford is so totally fabulous."

"Shit no, if you want to know the truth. Oh well, I'm glad that you and the cute one are so enamored, I can see that. Sorry, Chauncy's O.K., but I just don't feel like making out with him or anything. I'm not that attracted. That guy, John, you know, the one I kept dancing with, he's the kind, you know, the kind I like."

"So, what are we going to do with the bedroom situation?"

"Nickie, you really want to fuck Redford?"

"Well, why not, he's so damned fabulous. See—I don't think I'm good-looking enough for him, you know. I don't think he'll want to make a big to-do out of this, and I really want him, sexually, I mean. So might as well act now."

"That's a horrible reason for fucking—why fuck someone you're nuts about if you don't think you'll see the guy again?"

1 4 5

"So I won't go daydreaming about him, you know, wondering what it would be like and all that."

"So what do Chauncy and I do, play checkers?"

"Oh, for Christsake, it won't take that long. Binnie's coming back in the morning anyway."

"It's your choice. I think you're going to get hurt. I mean, if you really like Redford, you'll want to do it again, right?"

"Nah, it won't be the first time. Come, flush the toilet, let's get going."

★

While occasional groans and rustlings came from the bedroom, Chauncy and I sat on Binnie's Danish sofa and argued. Basically we were incompatible and my morals were NOT involved. It happened that my thoughts kept wandering to John at the dance, and every time I kissed Chauncy, I'd muster up the face of John—somehow I felt less than honest.

"Shylah, you're castrating me."

"What's castrating?"

"Means you're deballing me, the way you act. Like you're going to get YOUR way, and you deny me basic affection."

"Oh Christ. What the hell would I do with your balls, Chauncy?" I have enough problems. Look, I just don't feel like it; maybe I'm getting the curse. Let's check out the fridge. I'm tired anyway. I hope they hurry up."

"But I want you to know that I really like you, Shylah, you know, I REALLY like you."

"That's nice, Chauncy, I appreciate your saying so. Oooooh, Christmas cookies. God, she's really got fantastic pickings here. How about we go tobogganing tomorrow? O.K., Chauncy, let's. With this packed snow and everything, be terrific. Really."

"We should check with Redford first, see what he's planning."

Redford limped out at dawn and the two guys left quietly. Nickie was upset. I knew it. Situations like that offended me for some reason. What can you say about it? If I did say anything, she'd tell me how cynical I was about sex, about something so terrific. And I'd agree with her. Yes, I was cynical. Why not? There didn't seem any justice to it. Poor Chauncy, poor me. But then Stanley, that was just—that worked—some things were just.

★

Christmas-tree lights in the windows on Dover Street, the college and the girls' school deserted, fresh snow—Dickinson stood like a centerpiece. Aunt Snow was off at her married daughter's. Nickie and I spent most of our time in the weather, sledding and trudging around. Zoe bought a tree, and the three of us strung popcorn and cranberries and threw on tinsel, and later baked cookies and stollen. Zoe had a marvelous knack for kitchen merriment—we were happy enough, the three of us.

Yet it was always somewhat uncomfortable with Zoe. I didn't know why. For one thing, he had the habit of constant busyness, even when he wasn't busy—a distance. But that wasn't it really. I felt embarrassed in his company. I felt that I was doing something wrong— I felt a little sullied, less than what a proper sister was. His self-discipline, his control, the quiet nervous movements, the extreme asceticism even if he did go out with women. It was something inhibiting. I-never-did-anything-right kind of thing. His occasional criticisms—like he said I had bad breath—were agonizing. I went out and bought two dollars' worth of the strongest mouthwash. If he entered the room, I was sure I smelled as if I hadn't bathed for weeks. And all that business of being the oldest responsible sibling, the one to call in the event of another suicide or beating. Zoe, the Jesus of the Dale family. Seeing him made me dredge up my limitations; hell, it was demoralizing. And Martha, Zoe's friend, was around for the holidays. Too nice, I thought. She fawned over me like a mother gorilla; I sensed a motive—Zoe. Even Nickie saw it.

"Hey, I don't understand your big brother. He's so, uh, stiff, you know, and that Martha, ye gods, what a peculiar combination. Hoo hoo, the strangler of love."

"Yes, I know, I don't understand it either. Guess Zoe does everything on some high mystical plane."

1 4 7

"Aw, come on, you got that thing about the glory of your brother. He's O.K., a good-looking guy actually, little underfed though. But Jesus, he's so goddamned stiff. I could go for him, really. I mean, he's smart and good-looking, but he acts like a crazy Jesuit."

"You think so? I thought it was just me. I always feel like I've just shit on the rug when he's around, but, you know, he really is special. I mean, he's exceptionally kind and stuff. He's always been the responsible one. After all, how many brothers get strapped this way?"

"You're not so bad, Shylah. Cut it out. You're doing it again."

"O.K., O.K. Hey, you want to see what I got him for Christmas; look, a globe. Isn't it great?—lights up too—look at that. A goddamn globe. Don't scholars always have globes—you know the pictures of Einstein and stuff—don't they all have globes? Oh shit, I'm really being stupid; I guess that it's just, you know, I'm not doing well in school, and all the money, and I'm always screwing up and I'm not smart. And he IS. You know, I feel like I've disappointed Zoe and Aunt Snow."

"That's dumb, Shylah. Everyone knows how talented you are. Just because you don't give a shit about chemistry and algebra. Who cares? For Christsake, wow, what an inferiority complex."

"Sure, you're right. Look, I'm just depressed. Maybe we can figure out some bizarre and thoroughly disgusting way to pass the time—rape, murder, grab children and tell them there is no Santa Claus. Anything to avoid that stupid algebra book. Anything at all. I think I AM GOING TO EXPLODE."

★

"Oh, this IS magnificent, Shylah. A perfect Christmas gift. Terrific. I've always loved globes. Do you remember the one we had in the old house? I spent hours turning it, studying for exams."

"You really like it? I just didn't know what to get you. I mean, you do, because, really, you can always exchange it for books or something."

"No, this is a very imaginative gift. I wouldn't think of it . . .

1 4 8

Now for yours. I couldn't put it under the tree because it's too obvious, so go look in the music room."

"Oh, hmmm, how nice. A guitar. Gee, thanks, Zoe, what a great present."

"It's from Rick too. We wanted to get something you'd get some use out of."

"Oh yeah, sure."

"And I've arranged for lessons for you."

"Oh, with who?"

"A colleague of mine, Jack Gunther; you remember, you met him at my office."

"Here, Nickie, this is yours. The wrapping looks shitty, it was hard to do but I tried."

"Here's yours, Shylah, we can open at the same time. This isn't original, just practical."

"Oh, underpants, gee, I needed them too. Mine are dishrags, and look at the colors. Maybe I should just walk around with these on, not bother with dresses any more. Hot pink, scarlet, kelly green. Thanks, Nickie."

"Oooh, Shylah, a portrait. So that's what you borrowed those pictures for. Oh God, it's terrific—man, you are too much. Shylah Dali, hoo hoo. Oh, it's just great."

"Well, if it's surrealistic, it's by accident. I tried to render you faithfully, my dear."

"Ladies, a superb Christmas. I have my incandescent globe, Nickie, you are immortal in oils, and Shylah's underpinnings are uh . . . devastating.

★

Christmas buffet at the Angus Walpoles'. Zoe got around. Mr. Walpole wore his Nobel Prize-winning smile; Mrs. Walpole— his new wife—sooo English her upper lip quivered. What a spread. There must have been a hundred opportunists around every sofa. Nickie and I looked, glued side by side. Wow. We smiled and smiled and smiled. And all the little children wore velvet smocked dresses and Mary Janes and looked like they'd been bleached to perfection. The light conversation centered on large vocabularies extolling one another, describing the food on the buffet in French. Lots of hands shook one another heartily and delicately, according to gender. And the cheek kissing. Mrs. Walpole stood elegantly through it all. Even the maids looked faintly Brahmin American in gray and white uniforms, smiling, passing canapés, and picking up empty glasses.

"Did you ever get the feeling you were a pig accidentally wandering into the king's bedroom?" Nickie made an exaggerated side-of-the-mouth communication with me.

"Yes, this very-very. Well, what the hell, looks like everybody's having a great time, even if we can't understand what the fuck they're talking about. Hey, that bartender looks like Paul Newman; don't you think he looks like . . ."

"Don't look now but somebody's giving you the hairy eyeball."

"Aren't you Shylah, Zoe's sister? Remember me? I'm Jack Gunther."

"Oh yes, hi, Jack; uh, this is Nickie, my friend. I understand you will be giving me guitar lessons."

"Yes, I look forward to it. How do you like your new guitar? I helped Zoe with the selection."

"Oh yes, I like it, sure I like it. Thank you."

Jack Gunther had lovely, intense dark eyes behind the standard horn rims. There must have been fifty pairs in the room and fifty striped ties to go with them. Jack managed to emerge from this conformity better-looking than the others. I sucked on my glass of sherry and made small talk with him. Anyone surrounding Zoe's life I usually considered taboo, like a connecting incest link or something—but not Jack. Jack, I flirted with. I played little girl with big brain. They seemed to like it. Older smart guys liked that. It brought out all the sex they thought was big-brotherly tenderness. And it was a gas drowning my instability in this kind of thing. Made me better in a way. Power. Get them on the old emotional wringer. Oh God, cruelty. Shylah, you whore, you beast. Though I wandered around the room, looking aloof, feeling cretinism converging, and sweat, I know he looked over at me a lot. I could guess and hardly wait for these lessons. It was, in a way, a damn shame about the guitar. I wasn't really guitar material. That murdering word "practice" undermined my interest every fucking time. Scales was an unfortunate skin condition. Not that I didn't appreciate it. It was a superb present, such an intelligent thing to get a teenager, so philosophical. I just couldn't get into it. Maybe that was part of the reason Jack Gunther now seemed a catch. We had to do something at those lessons, didn't we? I'd keel over if it meant three hours of G-7 and occasional sips of Earl Grey. If I could play like Joan Baez and sing like she sang "All My Trials" in a week, I'd get mileage out of the guitar. But not years of G-7. Except, of course, with a leg pressing mine the likes of Jack Gunther's.

★

Two days after Christmas at two-thirty I was trudging over to Jack's house, guitar by the handle, trudging over with my folk-song book and my ironic stare. I had given it a few feeble but sincere plucks in front of Zoe and Nickie to show I cared, then stashed it in the closet. I had arranged myself with care for this appointment. I was not given to a prep-school look but I knew it would please—so I had parted my hair to the side, put on the McGregor jumper and white turtleneck. Lust moved me to superficial conservatism. But underneath I wore Nickie's gift, the hot-pink underpants. The hot-pink, lurid underpants worthy of Sadie Thompson—goddamn them all.

"Hello, Shylah, how nice you look. I didn't think young people were ever prompt. You've redeemed the race."

"Oh, what a terrific-looking living room. Where does that table-that's-really-a-big-plate come from? I've never seen one of those before."

"I bought it when I was in India and these pillows with the mirror glass. Come sit down, there. Can I give you some tea, or how about a glass of sherry? I have this Bristol Cream; my mother presents me with CARE packages every Christmas. This is part of the treasure."

"Yes, the sherry, that would be fine. You read a lot, don't you,

1 5 1

hmmm, and in German too? When did you start playing the guitar?"

"Oh, when I was about ten or so. I had started on the piano but wasn't much interested, so I moved over to string instruments. My favorite's the banjo."

"Oh, can you play stuff like Flatt & Scruggs?"

"You mean like 'Foggy Mountain Breakdown.' Well, yes, but hardly as fast or as well. There you are . . . have a little fruitcake. Zoe says you're at Slope. How do you like it?"

"I'm not exactly boarding-school material, but I guess it's better than most."

"I think it's probably a hell of a lot better than most of them. I went to a military prep school for a while—God, dreadful. Horrible discipline and loneliness. Anyhow, here's to your guitar-playing prowess."

"Yeah, I have a feeling you ought to be drinking to your fortitude."

"Oh, come now, we haven't even begun."

But we did begin. Except for Jack's putting his arms around me—all in the line of musical prowess, of course, showing me how to finger the strings and stuff—it was hardly nirvana. My hands ached. And we DID practice G-7. I thought I'd never draw again. Oh, we were diligent sitting there, before the Indian table.

"Well, let's call it a day for now, shall we? I think that was a pretty adequate first lesson. How do you feel about it, Shylah? Do you like Shylah—or Shy; I keep wanting to call you Shy."

"Shy's fine. My fingers hurt, frankly, but you were very clear. I guess it just takes a lot of, uh, practice before I can really play anything."

"Yes, at first, but you'd be surprised. Another glass of sherry? I have a feeling if you'd ease up on yourself things would come faster to you. You ought not to put yourself down so much. Zoe thinks the world of you."

"He does, really? Well, uh, he thinks a lot of you too. Thanks for the pep talk and guitar lesson."

"Would you like to drive in with me to Cambridge tomorrow afternoon? There's a flamenco guitar concert scheduled for three. We could have supper at the faculty club afterward."

"Yes, I'd like to."

"I'll pick you up at one-thirty then. See you tomorrow, Shy."

He liked me. That was something.

New snow and more coming down. Powdery cold-weather snow over mounds of hardened slush made it hard to walk as fast as I'd have liked. Sort of dream-walking, when the legs don't move in proportion to the effort. Oh Stanley, Stanley who-never-got-north-of-Miami, I wish I could show you this snow. What's a childhood without at least one cold snowball paralyzing the cheek and slowly melting down the neck into the secrets of forty pounds of outerwear.

★

"How CAN you eat a piece of meat THAT rare? Lord, look at the blood."

"Hmm, you ought to see the little children my daddy sacrifices each year."

"I can imagine. Certainly a gourmet approach. Well, did you like it?"

"The steak?"

"No, the concert. Did you like Ramírez?"

"Yes, though I have no one to compare him with. I love the style of playing. You know, the hard, definite fingering and then the way he uses the rest of the guitar, like slapping it and all. Yes, terrific, Jack. Did you, I mean, like the concert?"

"Uh huh, he's a fine musician, one of the best in his way. Very individualistic . . . like you, you're very individualistic and . . . uh . . . feminine. You're very feminine."

"Me! No, come on, I always think of myself as being kind of masculine, I guess. I always think quiet means feminine and loud means masculine. I mean, I know it doesn't work that way, but that seems to come to mind. But then you're, well, you know, you're manly, and still you're pretty quiet and, uh, intense. Oh, hahahaha."

"What? What's so funny, Shy?"

"Nothing, nothing . . . I just thought of a pun about Arabs."

"You're always thinking up jokes and the like. You've done that twice already today."

1 5 3

"Yeah, I really knock myself out."

"How about some Indian pudding? Do you like it?"

"Yes O.K., let's see if we can get extra hard sauce."

The waitress came and cleared our table and dutifully noted the request with the pudding. Jack lit my cigarette clumsily, which provoked my rabid tenderness. When he finally did put his hand on mine, he brushed the tip of my cigarette, scattering ashes on the white linen. Some clumsiness could be sexy—endearing—a sign of self-conscious intelligence. His was. It had begun to snow again when we walked to the car, a stormy snow this time, gray and windy. It would take time to return.

"Dear God, this is hellish weather to drive in. Ooh ah, nice, oh Shylah." Jack had been about to unlock and open my side of the car, had found himself kissing what had been placed so handy. Short of throwing him into a snowdrift, I was being as aggressive as was possible with subtlety. I knew my age scared him. And I wanted him, sort of exotically, I wanted him.

It took us double time in the weather. The Volkswagen slipped and turned and wobbled and rattled. When we got back to his place, he'd calmed down a little; the concentrated drive had done it. Jack took to fire-building in the stone hearth while I poured his mother's sherry for us. His steamy horn rims lay discarded on the table. For an awkward guy he had such a self-assured look to him, I mean, around the eyes. The sheer physicality of Herculean weather had relaxed him. I put my hands to the blaze and then put them to his cheeks. He turned into the half-moon of my arms and stumbled on the tip of the Pakistani rug, which made me brace him tighter with my body.

"Let's sit in front of the fire, O.K., Jack. Here, I poured some of your mother's finest. Fierce out there—you drive very well."

"Oh, that sherry feels warm. Yes, this weather makes us special, don't you think? Rather like going back in time. I guess it's because we have to work harder to have our physical comforts, so they mean more. Yes, Shy, yes, hmm, so warm. Why are you so, uh, mature, you know?"

"Maybe it's the tropics. Didn't you ever read Caldwell or any of the others who describe living in the South—although I guess the Keys are a little different from Mississippi and stuff.

We're all supposed to grow sexier younger. Anyhow, I'm not a real Southerner—that's just the general rationale."

"Really, I thought all that Southern sexual precocity was myth."

"Yes and no. It's the importance given to certain things. After twelve, as far as I'm concerned, everything's either relative or bullshit. You really get nervous about my age, don't you?"

"Very. When I met you that time in Zoe's office, I thought you were in college, at least. I was so attracted to your, uh, your charm."

Jack drew away to pull his heavy black ski sweater up and over his head, struggling a little, then returned to crouch near me—I was lying on the rug wiggling my toes. I brought my head back and looked up and touched his knees with my hand. He came around then, to be closer, to surround me, unsure, faintly nervous, excited, birdlike. Then turning again, lying now at my side on his stomach, on his elbows, drawing hands over my face and through my hair, and down lightly upon my cheek.

Ah, my ear. He kissed the base of my ear and I traced my finger down the back of his. I guided his head around with my hand and kissed him full on, not with tongue but open-mouthed. He held for a moment, then kissed around the lips, quick touches, then back on the lips, long, longer, then tongue, then hands moving down over my sweater, over the breasts, and down in a line and back up. We played for a while—stopping sometimes while he took a sip of sherry and I lit a cigarette—then starting up again, embracing again, while he pushed up my sweater, then stopped, then pushed it up again. Because of Jack's nervousness, it took longer for me to get that slight buzz. I didn't much mind taking time either, maybe a little better that way.

"Uh, I, uh, I don't know what to think. Devastating, well, that is, I desire you, Shylah."

"But that's lovely, don't you think? I desire you too."

"Yes, but, Shy, you're, uh, not even legal, or maybe it's that I'm too old."

"Old? You're twenty-six. Big fucking deal. I'm not Baby Snooks. Maybe you don't think I'm smart enough or some . . ."

"Oh God, no, no, oh Shy, I just want to hold you, well, you know, make love to you. Is that terrible?"

"No, not terrible. Yes, hmm, oh yes, there, right there."

Jack had begun pulling off my clothes in earnest now. I sat up and did the rest myself, while he stood to remove pants and underpants and socks. Because it was definite, because it would happen, he moved smoothly now, passionately but not the jerking motions of before. He was on his knees, then drawing me to mine, touching skins, pushing my head back a little, bringing my breasts up, kissing my neck and shoulders, running tongue across skin, then pushing me back until the backs of my legs hurt. So I lay down and drew him to me with my hands until he lay close by, not quite touching. I ran the back of my hand, like feeling fabric, up and down his body, quickly, then slowly, turning the hand over, to use it—to fondle him. To touch him. If I had started it—the love motions—it was Jack now who moved, who took my hands and drew them up, who reached with his own and pressed downward, kissing my breasts, rubbing the nipples hard between thumb and forefinger, tickling a little with his tongue in my belly button, down to my crotch, pushing my legs a little apart with the other hand. Then moving down until his head hair touched my thigh.

"No, hey, what are you doing?"

"Let me give you—let me lick you."

"I, uh, I don't know, I've never done that much. I mean, I'm kind of embarrassed, ooh, Jack, uhh."

"Shylah, you're lovely, let me look at you." His head back now and to the side, he spread my hair, parted the lips, looked into me, paused, then, bringing his head down again, licked at the spot just at the center of my crotch, then put his head full on and brought his hands up to my nipples and squeezed them. Sugary desire. Better—now a buzz. It was a buzz. The tongue—Jack's tongue slid in and out of my crack, barely making contact, teasing, then pressing down. I shook more, and the buzz just took over everything, and down and up again and down until I didn't want any more and then not thinking any more but coming, loudly coming. After its wane, I yelped and rolled over to my side and smiled, and he looked up, grinning, his mouth and chin all wet with me, and drew up his body by my side. My hand went to his penis, long and slender and hard. He turned me around on my belly, bringing me up by the waist to my knees, and with his hand spread me from behind and entered, moving easily under the soak of my crotch, and rocked me and pushed and pushed and drew out and panted and pushed deep in until I moaned in surprise and he cried out and I could feel it throb and I could feel the push. And then the softening and it made me cry. I couldn't understand it; I mean, why I felt so lonely all of a sudden, so vulnerable, like when my mother left me at summer camp and I was afraid I'd never see her again. I didn't think it would be that way—I didn't think it would be that lonely. I wept without gasping, turning over now in mutual embrace, the tears running off the sides of my ears, wetting the rug. Lonely, lonely, holding him and lonely.

"I'm sorry. I didn't mean to cry."

"Shhh, baby, hush, Shylah, it's O.K. really. So unbelievable, so lovely."

"What you did was, uh, very nice, I can't explain it. Where'd you learn to suck on a girl like that? In the army?"

"What a thing to say, Shylah. I wanted to please you; making love is better if it's giving. Your whole face has that look about it."

"That's because you were so . . . so good to me. Do you still think I'm too young?"

"No; well, it's that your age makes it a little difficult for me to take you around, you know, but I can't stay away from you. I can't."

We drank our sherry. I lit a cigarette and watched the smoke, lying on my back. Jack got up and brought back wet paper towels for my crotch and wiped me while I puffed and daydreamed. He had a sinewy kind of body, Jack did, lean with developed muscles in his calves and thighs and hollows at the sides of his ass. He walked more gracefully now, paced the room a little stretched out; then stood there looking down on me. Reflective. I could sense his mind working between romance and worry, worry about what he was going to do with me—if he was going to do with me. It didn't pose a problem to me. I was content with this. I didn't feel it had to be earth-shaking. The lessons could be lessons and love-making sessions at the same time. I sensed in a way that men did this only with very young girls; they didn't think so seriously at first with women, women in their twenties, women who really were available and who would be able to talk at length about Ramírez. But this, this had a different flavor to it for him, sort of forbidden, making everything romantic and irresistible.

I stood up, stretched, and walked to the window. Quiet now. The harsh blowing had stopped. Street lights illuminated the trees and icicles on the houses across the street. Despite the pleasure we had shared, I felt let down, even annoyed at Jack, who was now talking idly about different things. He had a kind of know-it-allness about him that at first I had enjoyed but that now grated on me. And I had taken a chance—a chance of getting knocked up. Though only a day past my period, supposedly safe, it was dumb to play Russian roulette with my ovaries this way.

"Getting dressed, Shylah?"

"Yes, I better get home, it's getting on."

"I'll take you home."

"No, it's O.K., Jack. I'll just walk it. Really, it's been a big day for us— I guess I just want to be alone for a while."

"Shylah, Shylah, so amazing. Will you call me?"

"Yes, I'll call. I'll call you tomorrow. Really. I'll call you tomorrow afternoon."

9

New Year's Day, 1961; the car radio played non-stop Hit Parade
of 1960. Zoe had been driving through sleet most of our trip
from Boston to New York. The fretful guitar had been dutifully
brought, along with our suitcases and Christmas presents for
Rick. He had come back for a while, Rick had—had come back
from letters postmarked Baden-Baden and Cheshire and Istan-
bul, containing descriptions of stray cats and aspects of rural
gardens—had come back with the great American novel completed to make us all famous. I knew him now only through
loyalty to childhood—remembered our Christmases—the practical joker, good-looking, sort of a jock. Remembered a deep
voice, the sounds of his laughter making me laugh in imitation.
Brothers. Older brothers. Baby sister. The mystique of less than
equal siblinghood angered me, the impotent lamb under masculine protection—goddamn agents of care.

"Shylah, do us a favor, would you, and chew with your mouth
closed."

"Oh, uh, I'm sorry."

"God, that's the fifth time you've said you're sorry. Don't say
it, do it."

"Jesus, Rick, I frankly didn't think you'd notice. You and Zoe might at least talk in English if you want to recognize my presence at the table. You KNOW I can't speak French. I mean, it's like eating alone, I might as well just sit here with my mouth hanging open, drooling strawberry shortcake, while you all carry on with your repartee."

"Ah, the martyr speaks."

"I'm sorry."

"Shit, Zoe, when'd she pick up that apologizing attitude?"

"Hm, don't know."

I lit a cigarette, the best thing to do when I was feeling overwhelmed. I could hide behind the feel of it and the curling smoke screen. The men returned to their conversation, this time in English—something about a town they had both known in Provence. Discomfort, the kind that comes from sitting at the headmaster's table, set in.

"Zoe says things have been rough with Dad, Shy. Is he still drinking heavily?"

"Yes, it's a little different now though; he disintegrates faster, takes less bourbon to do it."

"How'd you like Lime?"

"Loved it in a way. The pace and all that lazy beauty."

"Brainless?"

"No, maybe at first it appears that way. People use their intelligence, and for that matter their stupidity, in different ways. Like they're smart about nature things—'ocean-wise,' I guess you might say. Reading skills aren't too highly cultivated. Anyhow, tell me about Europe. Except for the funeral, you've been away four years. Never could tell by your letters, you kept describing the gardens and those damn cats, not that the descriptions weren't interesting. Don't you have a girl friend or something, and what about all that fantastic food? Hey, what's your book about? Zoe says you wrote a novel."

"Yes, I finished a novel, it's with an agent. And I prefer not to talk about it, O.K.? So where would you like to go in New York? Plays? How about *The Fantasticks?*"

We were together for three days. A reunion of skunks would have been more gratifying than this. Communication with them was torture and silence was torture. I felt judged—goddamn them. So the alternative was to allow myself to be entertained. They took me shopping. They took me sightseeing. We took in plays and arty movies. Anything to avoid conversation. New York stifled me—too much enclosure. We were always going inside places, outside being for transit to more insides. I didn't like gray. And things, my brothers together, the words were all impenetrable granite slabs.

★

"Why? Why do we have to stop seeing each other? Why, Jack? Why don't you like me any more? Don't do this to me."

"Look, I've already attempted to tell you, things just can't work out. It's like a burden desiring you, Shylah. You're too young and there are other things. I just don't think this is very healthy. Look, honey, there are plenty of boys and things for you to do. It would be inappropriate for me to allow us, the involvement, to go on—inappropriate."

I hung up on the second use of inappropriate. Who needed it? Besides, the dorm phone was too public for argument over personal shit. Exams were coming up next week; Nickie had turned into a boarding-school grind for the occasion. I went into my room, mine and the jock's, and put the guitar in its case to stow it forever in that pig-trough closet. It had been an excuse. Who needed an excuse? My books lay scattered over the bed; equations and formulas looked up at me from messy penciled scrawls in open notebooks. The whole fucking thing was that they made no more sense now than when I had first looked at them. There was no surface to this. I picked up the useless notebooks and two texts, turned off the overheated radio with its "Why Must I Be a Teenager in Love," and started the trek up to study hall.

Late January, the freezing winds and no new snow to brighten up the harshness. I wanted to go home. Wherever that was. I wanted to go back to Lime, that was home in a way—the island vistas, Luanne and Stanley, that was home.

Failure to achieve. My mind of late read like hieroglyphics.

1 6 1

Nothing worked, not Nickie, or walks, not symbols on paper for more symbols to occur, not even a workable sketch. It was quicksand.

★

"You know, Shylah, I don't quite know how to interpret all of this. I've never been shown a report card that read two A's and two F's. Your vagueness, this disconnection from the school activities. What is it? Discipline? Why did you fail chemistry and algebra? Why?"

"Because I can't do them."

"Ridiculous. You can't excel in some subjects and suffer from idiocy in others. Doesn't hold. Doesn't hold at all. I remember having problems with my French when I was your age—came from wanting to play football all the time. Maybe you have something you want to do. As it stands, the only output we've seen from you in the extracurricular sense has been in the art realm. Your attitude has been consistently negative from what I see here. You don't mix well, and I understand there's been some trouble with John. And my view, as I've seen you, is that, well—is that you act sometimes less than ladylike. For your own good, and since you lack any discipline to help yourself, I want to see you staying close to school, no more weekends for a while, no trips to the store. We'll work out a supervised study program for you and you can meet with John once a week with reports on your progress. It'll be tough for a while, I understand that, but you need a little toughness, Shylah, you need that."

"Terrific. Can I go now, please, Mr. Ryerson?"

"Yes, of course, you can go, you can go directly to your room and review your examination books. Here you go, fresh from your frustrated teachers. I've also instructed John to check on your being there. I don't feel we can trust you just yet, Shylah, I just don't think we can right now, and Slope operates, as you know, on the principle of self-reliance. So I'll see you next week, O.K.?"

★

Saturday. Almost everybody was off somewhere; Dickinson or Cambridge or visiting family. There had been no school Friday. Faculty weekend, a time for our teachers to hold meetings on new methods, to discuss students, and to listen to lectures. All day they had been sitting in the library before the immense glass windows with their coffee cups and cigarettes. For once I was left to myself, left without the hourly checks of John between enforced study periods. Thank God. The Nazi had something to do. And I had the false spring to myself and Hrothgar, sweetest of large canine friends. Only ten of us ate lunch that day, sitting at two tables, dwarfed by the size of the dining hall. Nickie and I made sandwiches from plates of bread and cold cuts.

"So, how's it going on the chain gang?"

"Today's the first day I haven't felt like shit."

"Rough, huh?"

"Lonely. I haven't really gotten around much, all this fucking enforcement. I could hack it better if I could get to the art building at night."

"When does it end?"

"Last week in March with quarter exams—that is, if my grades in chemistry and algebra improve."

"You think they will?"

"I don't know. Hard for me to think in that way, grasp laws through symbols like that. I'm trying, I think. Nickie, do you think it's possible to be partially retarded when the rest of you is supposed to be O.K.? I mean, they keep telling me I'm a . . . My attitude is lousy and all that bullshit. I suppose it is. I would love to tell them to jump. I call it my self-preservation arrogance. Tell you one thing, I'm not hanging around here next year, I can't. I feel trapped."

"Shy, we're all trapped. Only most of us are too dumb to know it and too scared to take our own freedom if we could. You put too much on yourself, for Christsake. Like John. You know what he is? He's a coward. That's why he can't stand you. Really, he has to control everything because he's weak. Did you know his first wife jumped out of a window? Did you know that? I don't wonder why. He tries to demolish anything or anybody that deviates from his miserable discipline. This school isn't progressive, Shylah. Learn that. There ain't no such institution—because institutions themselves are against progress. See what I mean. It's bullshit. They give us student meetings and smoking privileges, but it's the same old crap. What you need, Shylah, is to learn to keep your mouth shut. Teachers never know what to do if you don't say anything. They can't find a way to hurt you. Fuck. Man, they're so involved, at least some of them, with credentials and gung-ho intellectual trivia, they're beyond hope for anything as basic as simple knowledge. You can't beat it, Shylah, unless you shut up. Especially people like us. Because we're girls and someone like John or that aged jock headmaster of ours expects his 'girls' to be intellectual gumdrops. We hardly fit into anybody's idea of sugar and spice. We challenge them. It's that fucking simple."

"Sure, Nickie, I know what you're saying. I just find it a depressing way to live. Everything I do I screw up. And I can't keep quiet; I can't stand around and let someone mouth off in front of me without wanting to tell him off."

"You'll learn, Shylah, you'll learn. When you feel better about yourself, when you stop letting them get the better of you. It's a question of energy, you know."

★

March and an early thaw, startling—the life noise that went with it. Birds again, the sounds of birds, and a visible sun. I took off my jacket, went out in my sweater and jeans, stretching winter-rubbery legs.

I was supposed to go in and speak to John after he and Jan and the kids got back from church, or whatever they packed off to in their station wagon and white gloves. Today, however, the temperature stood at 65 degrees, sparrows and robins were noising it up outside the house. Just opening the once-frost-stuck window to air out Carrie's jock haven and my solitude in the stuffy room became a dazzling act. Fuck the Nazi. I'd say I had a sudden bout of diarrhea in the library and couldn't show up. I took the two books, the disgusting torn and weathered notebooks, and set out for the little path behind the art building. I hadn't finished a sketch or even doodled in a month and a half. Today maybe.

Soaking, bubbling earth underfoot; a season's accumulation of dead leaves now beginning to disintegrate in the wetness; an occasional early-budding tree and squirrels. Squirrels in full run, I could hear the nails scratching as they raced up trees and onto branches. The small stream was flooding now and picking up speed. Farther on, a half mile of hard walking through soggy underbrush, the forest opened onto a hillside meadow. I stopped then, stopped and treated myself to an unobstructed 180-degree view of valley farmland. Cows in the valley, black and white ones, their mooing echoed back off the slopes. Sitting there, occasionally scratching, humming in monotone, puffing on a cigarette, wriggling toes and squinting, I knew that my smarter part was erasing my dumber part this late morning. Righting myself then, putting myself into a crouch on the slope, I rolled down the mucky ground in a series of snowballing somersaults, thoroughly disgracing myself before the cows, who sniffed their way over to where I lay soaked in mud. Later I sketched them, the cows, but in anthropomorphic fashion, cartoon-like—sketched them with horn-rimmed glasses, in poses of intense concentration. Ooh, the day, feel it. To know it. That was something.

★

"I'm sorry I was late, John. It's not too bad though, only an hour and a half."

"Where were you?"

"Out walking."

"You just took off, didn't you, and willfully missed our appointment? Isn't that it?"

"Oh, come on, John. It's this terrific day, I was out in it. That's positive, isn't it?"

"For those of us who can handle it."

"Well, I handled it O.K., right. I've been studying. See, I've made the effort, wouldn't you say?"

"Then, Shylah, you won't mind staying in this afternoon and studying, in your room, of course."

"Yes, I would mind. This is the first day I've kind of felt healthy. You can understand, can't you? I want to be out enjoying it. What's the problem, really? You go to church and I go walk in the woods. Can't you pass it off as religious preference? How about Slope's credo of individual expression? Mr. Ryerson said . . ."

"Don't give me that. You're in no position to judge, one way or the other."

"That's not fair."

"Shall we call Mr. Ryerson, then? Shall we, Shylah?"

"YES, sure, call Ryerson, do whatever you want. I don't give a shit."

"Get back here, Shylah."

"Fuck you."

If I shut my eyes tightly and rubbed them, it had the same kind of effect. The slivers, the breaking-glass pieces hurrying through, confusing in speed, the daggers sweeping across each other and falling apart. Chaos. My eyes wide now, I felt the sharp rigidity of them as if my body were another shard colliding, going somewhere, hurling to a glass wall. The prismatic glaze of being and looking through sharp angular glass distorted everything, like being drunk, like being able to walk but still being very drunk, rushed kind of drunk that comes before vomiting or passing out or fainting.

I saw John's face through this glass head. Hideous, something in it—the tight muscles in and around jaw and cheek. My hands sweating and clenched while he glowed there. I could kill you, Nazi. I think I could kill in the most agonizing way.

I ran. Kept running. Raced through the yard, past the main buildings. In the woods, didn't take the path, raced through brambles making streaks on my arms below the short-sleeved shirt. I ran to the meadow, and fell, and put my face to the beginning grass. The cold beginning grass, wisps on my cheeks. There was no glass left, no pieces left; it would be O.K. without the shards. O.K. Lay there, coming back now. Yes, I had done it right. The prick. But to not think about it. What would I like to do? What was the first thing I'd do now?

I walked back to the dorm. Someone yelled, but I kept on. What could happen? They wouldn't shoot me—not at a progressive school. We were supposed to be liberal pacifists. I grabbed my little Indian bag with cigarettes and wallet in it. There were some private places—the Nazi with his psychic crowbar—I felt violated, like with Bobby Jay—different but the same.

Ah, something sweet. The full sun of the afternoon. The ice cream shop off campus. Verboten for two months. Hot fudge sundae; it's about time.

★

"Look, Aunt Snow. Really, I'm sorry. I didn't plan to have this happen. I did try. Honestly. I don't want to make it difficult for Zoe. Can't you see? That man was so clearly unreasonable. Flipped me out. I couldn't go anywhere. Had to sit and study all the time—hardly progressive education, do you think? He kept pushing me."

"Oh dear heaven, I throw my hands up, really. I do try and understand. You were rescued from Lime upon your request; you were miserable there—now you're miserable in equal measure here. Just dreadful. One can only say 'poor dear' to you to a point. You're most inconsiderate, really. Zoe has given you every understanding. Your behavior—really, simply astounding."

I moaned inside. Aunt Snow, the paragon of intellectual integrity, of the orderly, reasonable, stimulating mind, was processing me as a female cad.

Zoe, philosophical in his silence, had picked me up that afternoon, and the drive back to Dickinson bore the weight of unspoken pain. If I was to continue there, then it had to be better, better than what the Nazi doled out, problems or no problems. I couldn't do it any more; please, God, I couldn't do it any more. What's wrong? What's wrong with Shylah?

"Basically, I think you're absolutely right, Shylah. But, I

1 6 7

mean, what in the world can I do? I've done the best I know how. Do you *want* to continue here after this year? Or do you want to return to Lime, God help you?"

"Yeah, I guess I want to go back. I'm more—uh—I can function better in a way. I don't know what to do about Daddy. I guess if I just avoid him—there are other things. I never really wanted to leave Lime, you know that. Just that, at the time, there didn't seem any alternative. At least, that's how I saw it. Shit, I'm sorry, Zoe. What can I say? It's the way things are for me, I guess."

★

May. Grass and weeds sprouted over ground no longer sagging with the congealed mush of turning seasons. The woods, the slope with my sitting rock had graduated to a fine shade of green. Mild. A waiting kind of mild. If I could wait out the month and a half left of school. If I could outlast anger . . .

After a round of informal "chats" with headmaster and teachers, Charity Slope had taken its errant angel to the breast again, knowing I'd be gone after this one year, knowing and therefore blessedly leaving me to sniff the spring forsythia and doodle on endless sketch pads. John and I steered clear of each other. My grades actually went up a point. Things were, after all, O.K. The faculty could thank itself and ignore me.

And Nickie. Despite her blasé "everything is shit" routine, old Nick had succumbed to the call of a new drama department, establishing herself as numero-uno actress among Slopians. She had little time to hack around or furlough to Dickinson with me, with Tennessee Williams waiting in the wings. Not that we didn't still share an illegal moment or two. Just, there were other things now. And she'd survive these progressive halls, she'd be a kind of star, and so much the better for her life here. That was the end of it for us. Which was O.K. Except I'd miss the old Nick. Nickie was terrific. Pointless to cry about it.

I was on my way home.

10

Luanne and I took turns kicking the infant nurse shark that stayed close to the sand flats. Harmless by size but nosy in the comatose, stupid way any shark is nosy when there's something in the water, it circled near our legs. Our boat lay anchored on a piece of sandbar nearby. If we were lucky, we'd return with enough crawfish to feed the four of us.

"Oh, come here, you little mother." I had seen one, scooped my hand down, and missed grabbing the body, instead feeling flap of thorny tail. Again, after shaking out the sting, I put my hand above it, and this time got the four-pound rock lobster full on. I brought it up, the tail fanning out, legs wide and struggling, placed my free hand on its tail, and twisted my hands in opposite directions. Water in the tearing flesh made it squeak for a second until body came away from tail—then glutinous flesh hung out, the spine full of black crud. I threw the body at the nurse shark's snout and the tail into the boat with the rest of the pile. Only the tail of crawfish, or rock lobster, as we called it, was really worthwhile. And that was tougher than Maine lobster, more the consistency of sirloin steak than the "butter texture" New Englanders were always talking about.

"We got six now, Shy, that oughta be nuff, don't y'all think, with the stuff—the conches—the guys are bringin for salad? Ah better get back and pick up Loosie. Mom gets perturbed when ah leave her too long. She thinks it in't healthy."

"Yes, all right, I'm getting burned out here anyway."

April 1963, a particularly hot month for some reason. The Keys had been almost airless for a week now, unusual for the tradewinds to subside so completely. We had once again taken Luanne's father's skiff this Saturday afternoon for an outing time together, like in the old days, like before Luanne was married, when we had been ninth-graders and would mess around on the water for the whole of a weekend's daylight hours. Now this was a luxury, our being together away from shore. Though we saw each other often enough for coffee, sometimes supper over with her, Harry, and Loosie, our interests were naturally apart. My senior-class activities, the rush of things, had kept me happy enough, involved at last, preoccupied with my classmates. And Luanne was diapers and pins, installments, clothes patterns, and friends with babies to trade off babysitting with. So to have an afternoon like this was prime. It brought us back in mutual focus.

"Oh shit. Shylah, we're in trouble. Lawd, it's the shear pin, ah think it's the shear pin."

We had cut maybe two knots into shore when the motor sputtered, then stopped, a clog of seaweed and mangrove weed was caught in its blade. I pulled it up and Luanne came back to check.

"O.K., so what now? Maybe we can fix it. Have you got another one?"

"Uh uh. Oh Jesus, we're in the current as well."

"O.K., O.K., we can pole back." I grabbed the guides' pole, the thing they used to steer a boat across flats and into separate channels, but the pull of water made it hopeless.

"No, I'm wrong, the current's too strong and this water's about ten feet or so. If we can steer it over to shallower water, to that flat over there. Hey, Luanne, how long you reckon that tie line is, you think if one of us can swim over there to the sandbar we can pull it in? Jesus, this thing's going fast."

"Ah can't raghtly say, Shylah. There's sharks around here,

you know, this the area that guy, the singer, just got it, mah Lawd."

"It's not that far; look, we're going out into deep ocean. Look, I've got my period, is that the same kind of thing as having a cut, you know, the smell, shark frenzy?"

"Don't look at me, ah got *mah* period too."

"Yeah, might have guessed. O.K., so I'll take a stab at it. Look, try and angle the boat with the pole, and for God's sake, don't throw the rope until I've gotten to the flats."

I jumped far away from the boat with the loudest splash musterable under the circumstances . . . it being difficult to get any momentum off the low edge of a skiff. But the splash would scare them away if there were sharks. We hadn't seen any near the boat, big ones, that is, except before, farther out, we'd seen a couple of circling fins probably picking over a fallen sea gull. I got into my ferris-wheel frame of mind, that is, don't look down and everything will be O.K. I wouldn't think, I wouldn't look down. Everything, all brain power, went to the muscles in my arms and legs, keeping the hand full out and poised, going like hell, while Luanne grappled with the pole. I heard her yelling at me and kept going. There was nothing I could do about anything she might be screaming about except to keep hauling ass. The extreme saltiness of the water, overheated, maybe 90 degrees from the sun, slowed me down—like trying to swim through mud. I knew I was swimming with other things, whether they were jewfish or grouper or barracuda or shark or stingray—all common in the rich life of these waters— I felt if I did not look, they would not notice me either. I kept my eye toward the sandbar. When I had reached the short run of flats next to it, my eyes stung with heat burn and I lay flattened by the gasping wheeze of unaccustomed lung power. Because of the current I had landed up from where Luanne poled the boat, but I could walk over the flats and another small sandbar. I weaved across, sun-drunk, falling a lot and picking myself up; the sun made everything a white dot.

Luanne threw short. It meant, to save time, another swim to pick up the lead line. Just a little way, but still two hundred feet or so. One was out there. The fin cut water like surgery. Not close but visible. And shadow beneath the fin; it could have been a clump of moving seaweed but wasn't. A superb diver, which was something most boys over the age of sixteen were in these waters, would not have so much minded. Oh, they'd keep their eye on its movements, on the surprise inconsistencies that marked the species; no one wanted a sudden meeting with an overbite chock-full of pointed daggers, set beneath those wide-set paralyzing eyes.

The fact that a shark was a shadow until contact worked on my fear of gray things. Choice was no argument. Again the wide jump to gain distance and scare what was around; only this time I had to go under, go under for that bit of rope, and quickly. I knew exactly where it was and how deep and knew the way a rope dropped in water and grabbed it. Luanne had leverage now to keep close enough for slack. I could not have pulled the full weight of the boat, not this way. I wondered, while pacing my side stroke, if anyone really got chased by a shark. Rarely, I thought. Mostly contact, I supposed, like a swimmer would turn suddenly or be in just the right position and not see it looming, or would freeze in shock instead of getting out of the way. The shadow was closing in, still far enough away, unless it wanted to be the exception and make a mad dash for me—pray it didn't care for menstrual blood. The rope kept twisting, slowing me down, and because of that, I had to keep looking, my head in the direction of that fin and the shadow beneath it. Eventually it would pass by. Why shouldn't it? But not now, only a little bit more, only the weight of the boat. I'd drop it if things got hairy, but only a little bit more really.

I stood. Made it—the channel had sloped to a flat. Then I pulled the rope higher and higher, balancing with my heels in the coral sand. And I saw it. A second fin criss-crossed where I had just been, one that had been in back of me all the time, perhaps trailing me. And I had not known. Thank Jesus.

"Shit. Didn't you hear me scream the first time? Mah Lawd, ah can't believe you weren't hamburger meat for that muthah."

"Yes, I see. Do me a favor and let's change the subject. Now look, we're sitting on a sandbar the size of a motel room. Let's hope it's high tide. We've both had a dose of sun poisoning. I think we can walk the boat partly in by following this line.

What channels occur are pretty narrow. Let's try. At least we could get closer in, maybe get help. Fishing parties are bound to come this way—leads into the main channel for Lime. Don't worry, Luanne."

"Hope to hell we don't broil first. Ah'm scared, Shylah."

We walked the flats toward shore, taking turns with the boat. The sunburns were beginning to show up now, even under daylight. We had put shirts over our bathing suits, but our heads, which weren't really functioning well by then, were exposed directly to the late-afternoon sun. About an hour later, having drunk the remaining Cokes in the cooler, which just made things worse, the first sounds of an engine. Highest buzz, meaning a low-powered skiff. We saw it come our way and waved at it, crossing both arms.

"OhmahGod, Shylah. Niggers. They're niggers."

"Aw Jesus, Luanne, don't pull that shit now. All I know is that they're under way and we're broiling to death. Just once, fuck your prejudices, will you, please; don't blow this. I swear to God I'll take you apart . . ."

"Jesus, makes mah skin crawl."

"Do us a favor—shut up. If I was a Negro, the last person I'd want in my boat in fried-chicken land here would be you, honey. It's mutual, so shut up for once. O.K.?"

I could tell that at first the two men hesitated about stopping. I was jumping up and down, waving them in. But they didn't come directly in, passing us by initially, then slowing and turning around, then coming full up to us. Risk. Risk to have contact with whites down here except in the prescribed way.

"Look lahk you done wasted yer propeller. Ummm hmmm. Jimmy, take a look at it heah; ah thinks we maght fix it, huh. You think? Huh?"

"Ah ain't got no tools to do it heah. Needs a pin. Naw, gotta tow it. Y'all live on Lime?"

"Yes, on the out side."

"Well, ah reckon you best git in here with us and we'll tow it. There ain't no way we kin fix it fer you without them tools."

"Thanks, thanks a lot. I don't know how long we'd have lasted.

"Yes'um."

173

"OHMAHGOD, Shylah, Jesus."

Luanne folded into a faint.

"Heah, missy, take the hat, she had herself a wallop of sun. Jes put down center. Put some speed on that thing, will yah? Got some water heah, put a little on her forehaid. Y'all drink a little too, look lahk you beat from it too."

"Thanks. How much longer do you think?"

"We got it wide open, pullin extra weight, li'l while anyway."

The water from the cooler was too cold. My head felt like bursting after a swallow. I poured a little in my cupped hand and put it to my temples . . . Luanne was coming around . . . Both of us sick with the heat . . . Dizzy, had to keep my head down, body reacted—shiverish cold-wet heat, and God, I was tired. Muscles pulled and achy from the swimming. The rest of me slipped into sensory daydream images—boat docking, men talking, being helped out, pain, puking, cool sheets.

When I woke, it was already twilight. Luanne lay on the other of my twin beds. Daddy and Alice and Harry and Luanne's parents stood at the door of my room. Daddy all bluster-laughing, shaking his head.

"You girls make a pair of the biggest lobsters ah ever have seen. Wouldn't y'all say? Damn lucky those nigger boys came by when they did. Whadda way to get saved, hoo hoo."

"Hi, what time is it? We must have fallen asleep."

'Ah'll say, baby; you two been out for four hours."

"Jesus, it hurts to move. Luanne, you awake? Did you hear how long we've been out?"

"Sunburn's killing me; hi, Harry, Mama, Daddy. Ah am STARVED."

"Think y'all can get off those beds of nails?"

"Harry, where's Loosie?"

"Home with the maid."

"I forgot, I have a date with . . ."

"He's here, in the kitchen. We thought, under the circumstances, we'd all combine forces and eat outside. Heat broke, you can feel it. Nahce soft breeze now. Shylah, your friend David's been doing quite a job with the conch, marinating it in

1 7 4

rum and lime and garlic for the salad, hmm, delicious, and we got lobster tail and steak. Real down-home feast. All you girls have to do is get it to your mouths. Now, take a cool shower, get that sand off you, and change. We'll be outside. Oh Luanne, here, Harry brought over a change of clothes. Y'all hurry out now."

Walking to the shower was a little slice of agony. The backs of my knees and crook of the elbow—like being the Tin Woodsman; I imagined a squeak with each step. But I didn't fare too badly in the mirror; just short of sun-poisoning blisters, reddish-brown rather than purple. The salty heat, sweat smell got to my nostrils as we unzipped each other's bathing suit and slow-motioned them to our feet, exposing candy-stripe flesh.

"Mah Lawd, ah know ah'm gonna get it from Harry 'bout those niggers."

"YOU are absolutely insane, Luanne. They saved our lives."

"You'll never understand that all that stuff takes time down here, Shylah. Ah know, ah'm grateful; ah doubt if Harry will be though."

We made our way out of the bedroom after the tortures of hairbrush and shower. David smiled. Lean David. Older. Harry's friend at work. Calm, good-looking, and boring. But he cooked well. He had taste, David did. He bridged part of the truce I had with Daddy—no sweat, David. I wish I could have liked him more.

"Hi, Shylah. That sun lahkta made an Indian out of you. Ah never thought ah'd be thankful for a couple of catfish niggers, sheeiiit. Give me a kiss."

"No way, hurts too much. Later, David. Let's eat. How about some wine, I see the bottles flying already. So it's a real down-home feast, huh?"

"Hey, those niggers, they didn't touch you or anything. Ah mean, y'all were really out of it. . . ."

"Uh, David. Shove it up your ass, will you."

"O.K., O.K., Mrs. Martin Luther King. Everybody's gonna sing and dance for integration."

I left him in the kitchen and joined the others outside. Daddy

1 7 5

had one culinary feat—destroying chicken and beef on a grill. Thank God, it was steak not chicken this time—both he believed in charbroiling, he called it black-ashing, burned on the outside, raw inside. I hated eating pink chicken that still quivered like aspic under the skin.

"Doesn't baby look boo'ful. How's your burn, Shy lamb? Come sit here; ooh, it hurts, doesn't it? Now tell us what happened. You girls must have had yourselves quite an adventure. Glass of wine, dear? Cool you down."

"Oh, you used our lobster tails as appetizers. Hmmm, would you pass them, please?"

"You know, we had to carry you two out of that boat. What'd you do, swim halfway in? Jesus, girls, y'all looked lahk drowned rats. Those black boys didn't give y'all any trouble? You tell me now if . . ."

"No, Mr. Cal. I don't think we'd have made it much farther if they hadn't of stopped. Really, everything's fine."

"Well, had a happy ending—all of us here for supper, in't that raght, Corky? Drink, Cal, Juna? Luanne, a little wine, dear? My, these girls are really grown up. Looka that."

"How old are you now, Shylah?"

"Eighteen. I just turned."

"In't that nahce. Pretty soon you'll be out of school. Ah'll bet you wanna go to college. Y'all know where you want to go, huh? University of Miami or Gainesville? You gonna go to Gainesville?"

"Radcliffe, I'd like to go there. I don't know yet. Palm View isn't even accredited for state colleges, let alone out of state. I did O.K. on my tests though. I'd like to be up there. I applied to a bunch of places."

"Up with the freedom riders and Communists. Preacher was over, that young one, we were talking about Ole Miss, he's a graduate, just loved it, he said—you think this'un would listen, sheeiit, no."

"Well, Corky, y'all know how independent kids are these days. Ah'll tell you though, there is nothin lahk the senior year in high school. It's a real memory-maker. So many things to do. Why if Luanne hadn't . . ."

"Motherrr, c'mon now; half the class is out and married already anyway, and the rest are planning on it. Least some of the girls."

"It's true, Miz Juna. Selma Anne and Bubbles are engaged. They're getting married in a double ceremony right after graduation. I'll bet most of the class will be married before 1964, really. And we're a late class in a lot of ways."

"Soups on, chillen. Gotta eat, married or single, y'all come to the table. Come, Corky, now, raght now. Nuther bourbon, Juna? Here yah are, girls, y'all sit raght there. In'it nahce everybody bein together this way, ah declare."

★

Hurricane Donna in '60 had brought changes to Lime. The smaller bait houses and motels were no longer in existence, anything the government wouldn't support with an emergency loan vanished. What was left and what was rebuilt looked slicker, wealthier; the few dirt-poor trailer dwellers left for other islands in the chain. And the Keys had begun the gradual transition from back land to extension of the Gold Coast—Miami Beach chain. Where there had been miles of mangrove jungle on the upper islands, now long expanses of filled-in coral rock supported Happy Havens and Stuckeys. Then freedom riders replaced "queers" for scapegoating, and dread of integration joined the fear of Communist infiltration. Our class, too, changed—we wore our skirts shorter, one crinoline would suffice—we danced the twist—cars grew sleeker. Best of all, virginity by our senior year was nothing anybody cared to retain. We wore our Balfour class rings as if betrothed to the whole class of '63. Stanley was going steady with Lettice. I missed him, missed him.

I had returned from Dickinson to begin my junior year back at Palm View, progressive education having taught me that anything was better, even lechers and paternal rages.

Daddy and Alice and I kept a certain amount of distance. They weren't very helpful to me and I wasn't very helpful to them. Instead, I became a cheerleader, president of the Latin

Club, prom designer—anything to keep me out and active and with my classmates.

And Bobby Jay. Bobby Jay married a genuine starlet and they were off somewhere most of the time, spending money. It got better, I didn't fall apart; I enjoyed myself, even with Luanne married and no Stanley. I did O.K.'

Senior year, augmented by the Cuban crisis in October, got us off to an active and patriotic start. Good old panic bringing us closer—the Kennedy speech, the endless cordon of military trucks, jeeps, missile bearers, and submarines patrolling the waters, residents fleeing, runs on food, evacuation practice each day from school, Key West under military siege, the boys all talking about how they were going to fight if it came to that, and the drone of jets overhead. And then all the Cuban immigrants escaping in small boats to our shores, and the two Cuban kids who showed up at school, trilingual, with the faculty not knowing how to discriminate against two Cubanos who held the highest averages in all of Palm View's medieval history.

It *was* the best year—the best of all. We bloomed, every one of us—we bloomed high on the same bush. Our class was one hundred percent. We spent our time congratulating each other. The last of the unified islanders. Eighteen was a redemptive age.

★

"Before y'all leave, I'd lahk to go over just a few things we hold by at Palm View for every senior trip. Ah know y'all are gonna have a mahvelous time, do a lot of dancin and seein the sights. Ah know there'll be a lot of drinkin goin on. That's O.K. too. But ah don't wanna hear 'bout any of you gettin drunk and disgracing Palm View by raisin hell. So don't drink any more than you can handle, or ah'll come down hard. Ah want y'all to stay together. Check with Mr. Sal or Miz Larraine you want to go off somewhere once the ship docks. Lotta things to do in Nassau; ah know you'll be wantin to take it all in. Girls, if you take side trips, ah want you to be at least in groups of three. No girl goes anywhere alone—that perfectly clear? Things are different entire over there, so if some nigger asks you to dance, you just politely say no, but be a lady about it. Ah don't want to hear 'bout any race riots caused by some uppity senior girl. Don't accept no cigarettes from anybody, hear—that's very important—don't accept no cigarettes. And, finally, ah wish you the best trip ever; ah'm very proud of this class, you're a fahn and distinguished group. Ah want to see y'all fresh from the boat Monday. Don't go home, come here first. O.K., kids, best of luck, y'all have a good time."

Selma Anne, Bubbles, Rosemary, Cindy, and I were dressed and groomed for absolute surrender. It had taken two days of sleeping over at Selma Anne's with three boxes of rollers, thirty dollars' worth of cosmetics, agonizing decisions to be made over clothes to be pressed and re-pressed by the silent, haunchy laundress. Our new three-inch spike heels buckled and swerved. I felt the garter belt cut through my thigh, and my nylons constituted sacrifice as they clung to sweat-soaked legs in 85-degree weather. But there was nothing quite like this. I walked to Jay's convertible, which would take Selma Anne, Bubbles, and me the two hours to Miami. Pure power. I was unbeatable. The second grade passed in its lunch line and whispered my name reverentially. I was absolutely gorgeous, even if I did have to hold my breath in the merry-widow cincher underneath my sundress and my face couldn't move for cracking the base and powder and my hair had been sprayed with lacquer till it stood like a porcelain vase over my head. I held my shoulders as far back as possible without dislocation, and my bosom made the appropriate Rhonda Fleming crease. I moved my hips to the right and to the left, a cross between the normal walk and parading best of breed in a dog show. Even those natural cynics, the senior boys, looked at me from their low-slung convertibles with a certain awe. Smashing. Worthy of Troy Donahue or better.

"Ohhhh shit. Goddamnit. I ran my nylon on your stupid car, Jay."

"Oh sorry, majesty. Shall we call off the trip?"

"It's ruined. What am I going to do? God."

"Man, women are beyond hope. What now? You're gonna be

miserable, aren't you, Shylah, now that y'all have a tiny little run? Ah gotta admit, y'all look pretty damn good, ah mean, shavin that two-day beard off your legs and yah did something to your hair, lahk comb it. Y'all'd be really something else if you was struck dumb—pull you down from that cloud."

"Drive the car, Jay, drive the car."

The S.S. *Bahama Star* cruised the weekend run from Miami to Nassau and back, one of those package deals. "Visit Nassau for three nights and two days of tropical sun and fun." As we were off-season—after Easter to Labor Day—the cruise ship would be only partly filled.

Our cabins were located on the cheapest deck, meaning the lowest. The five of us took a six-bunk cabin, the last berth for our luggage. We had made our appropriate entrance, impressed everyone, we were sure; the gangplank would never be the same, having known our feet. So now to change into something a little more realistic for hard drinking and the six meals a day we were in for. Capri pants, tops, jeweled flats—the clothes flew around the tiny space as we changed and reapplied goo to our faces and lips.

Ship sailed at four-thirty. We stood on the bridge and looked appropriately bored, though I could never do that one correctly. The senior boys stood with us, a furtive bunch, almost possessed as they raced one another to the main-deck bar. God, they were grown up—I hadn't noticed before—big, muscled, bright-eyed, like chained satyrs; they were all there—even those once-concave chests sported the beginnings of a hair swamp peeking out from their white dress shirts. The little idiots had become mature idiots.

"Hey, let's all go down to the Grotto, that's that bar on the lower deck. They're gonna have a limbo dancer with torches and everything."

"Did y'all see those boys on the bridge, the blond ones? Mah Lawd, beautiful. Let's clean up. Y'all think they'd be goin down there? Ah don't wanna hang around if there's no action."

"Oh, don't worry, Rosemary, y'all gonna get somethin out of all this. You always do."

Only the lighting made legitimate the name Grotto. Dim, faintly pink, a few tired potted palms in strategic places, ten or so tables, and the ever-present bar—slick, and stacked behind it exotic-drink glasses: coconuts halved, pineapple-shaped containers, African-statue containers; plates with gardenias, pineapple slices on skewers with cherries, anything and everything; the tired, lean, blue-black Bahamian in red bolero waiter's jacket bartending, thinking behind the slightly yellowed eyes—"Jesus, not another white senior class, no tips and no way to handle their liquor." Slightly elevated and to the far end of the room a sawdust-covered limbo platform, metal bars and paraphernalia leaning against the wall. Passengers dribbled in, mostly in small groups; more red-coated waiters appeared. The five of us got a table close to the center of the stage.

"What's your pleasure, ladies?"

"Ah'd lahk a Mai Tai."

"Me too."

"Scorpion's Tail."

"What's in a Passion of Nassau?"

"One-hundred-and-fifty-one-proof rum, crème de rose liqueur, fruit juice, and you get something—a parasol—in it. Very nice, ladies. Very nice indeed."

"Ooh, ah'll take it."

"I'd like a Zombie."

Bahamian men, if the waiter was any example, had to be the finest. Big-eyed, sun-mahogany skin, and that voice, a lilt to it like musical instruments . . . singsonging each of his words. He returned bearing the drinks, reminiscent of a children's birthday-party centerpiece—things sticking out of exotic glasses. Amazing things.

"He's got a lovely speaking voice, don't you think?"

"Here we go with the niggers, Shylah; ah maght have known."

"Rosemary, you don't think he's attractive? You're nuts."

"Nah, I guess so, but he's still a jungle-bunny . . . Well, ah, he is kinda cute, in't he—oh hell, things are different with the Bahamians."

By the time we finished our drinks, the band had arrived.

1 8 1

Steel-drum sounds seemed imitations of the people's speech—a lyrical staccato. A pleasure. A sweetness. Butterscotchy. The guys, all young, all shiny-healthy-looking, wore the layered puff sleeves and tight pants of tropical entertainers. Cumbersome, I thought, those puffy sleeves.

Prince Turk, the limbo dancer, was not so encumbered. Naked to the waist with what looked like an African print diaper hiding our obsession, he looked huge, maybe six foot four or so, lithe, in his late twenties, sort of Sidney Poitier with a better physique. Rosemary's mouth fell appropriately wide, which happened whenever she came up against some new heat. I didn't go for guys that good-looking. I told myself it was because nothing that good-looking could hold a brain. More honestly, I thought that nothing so good-looking wanted less than a cosmetic wonder who had perfect hair to graze in. Not so with Rosemary, however.

"OhmahLawd. Ah mean, ah maght just become a Yankee, what a glorioussss piece of ass. Shylah, y'all maght see me integrate to Nassau."

"Immigrate, dummy. You integrate a school and you immigrate to Nassau."

"Ah wouldn't mind eithah way, oooh eeee."

"Will y'all shut up, the two of you. Hey, ah think we need another drink while black beauty goes under the bar-b-que." Selma Anne was unimpressed by these things.

Across from us at the next table sat what looked like Dade County Junior College boys being loudly themselves. While Selma Anne, Cindy, and Bubbles made use of these prospects, Rosemary kept her eye on Turk, and I mine on the steel-drum player—a little less nourished-looking and more intense. It turned out to be a short show, a preview really of what would come later that evening, after we returned from the dining salon, chock-full of overfeeding.

The college boys had picked up our tab and walked alongside us as we left the Grotto. It was time to change clothes again, to shower and reapply makeup and fix hair—the satin capris and flowered blouses, and ribbons in the plastered coifs.

Our assigned dinner seating placed me next to an English gentleman who spoke as if to make a question out of each sentence. Alexander Harley, with his navy-blue blazer and gray-turning mustache, treated us to champagne with the lobster tails. A sort of tired David Niven cast to him. The girls liked his wit. By the time the strawberries and coffee rolled in, the table, meaning us and the others, was in his lap. While the other tables wobbled through the courses, we laughed and sang and listened to Alexander's next name-dropping tale of the peerage. Lucky us. Most of the hundred or so passengers seemed to be taking the trip as a cure for depression and not getting off to a very auspicious beginning.

Nine-thirty's early on a pleasure ship. The dancing and other entertainment really begin at eleven. The time we had between could be spent in one of three bars, in the lounge, or changing clothes again.

We split up. In the deck bar, the one frequented by the older passengers, I ordered and paid for a double grasshopper in an old-fashioned glass, taking it out to the bridge. Oddly, almost everyone stayed inside the ship while the panorama, the activity of the sky, was left to itself. That thick, indelible sky reached to where I stood. It seemed the only thing on the globe, blackness, a velvet drop with a million spangles sewn to it. Clear—for once I could make out the recognizable constellations. I was aware of the ship's voices, some human and some the constant hum of stabilizers or water, wet tongues against the flank hull, iridescent. There. Inexhaustibly black and spoken for. I dragged a deck chair out to the center of the stern, away from its sister chairs—lay on my back smoking a cigarette and drinking the sweet green goo of the grasshopper. Slow breezes combined air with ocean mist. Played on forehead and cheeks. What the hell else was there?

"Shylah, ah should have known. We've been combing the boat for you. Come on, girl, the limbo guy's starting up. You said you lahked the nig—the guy who does the steel drum. Come on, ah need some support."

"So, what's up? I smell an 'integration' in the works."

"Well, not really, y'know, but ah did get a chance to talk to him a little while ago. He's, uh, really nahce, y'know. Listen, maybe we get something going afterward."

"Maybe his friend won't like me."

"Heah we go again. Will y'all shag that ass. C'mon, Shylah, ah need you."

"O.K."

The Grotto was a crush, with people and extra tables now for the main entertainment. Eleven-thirty and another Zombie. I could have slept. I could have.

This time there were dancers to begin with. Women with cloth wrapped up high on the head topped by sewn-on plastic fruit and men in those horrible shirts moved in barefoot leaps. Then Turk. I broke out in giggles. Nice way to make a dollar, greasing yourself up to go under a bar that's in flames—could probably make more doing ads for fire insurance. Turk appeared in gold-lamé loincloth, his biceps and chest greased to reflect the fire. Marvelous feet. He really had lovely ones. Long, slender, straight-toed. The whole procedure of going under again and again—under the gradually lowering bar—repeated perfectly.

Afterward, the entertainers took over a table and mingled with the passengers. Turk and Rosemary exited separately, but subtlety was lost at that point. Selma Anne had a bout of sympathetic hysterical laughter and Cindy looked self-righteous, shooting me the hairy eyeball as I prepared to check out a certain steel drummer.

Timsy Lord, short for Timothy, spoke a more British Bahamian dialect than Turk, whose voice had more thickness to it. His being Jamaican, Timsy said, made the difference. He came from a large family of fifteen children, he said. Wanted to be a doctor, he said. A steel-drumming pediatrician. I liked him.

Rosemary and her jock Othello had disappeared with a bottle of rum. Most of the ship was bedded by now; first night out in the salt air and strong rum inside bellies. Crews were mechanisms of romantic slush for girls, I figured from the stories we read in love magazines about off-limit shipboard romances. And on this ship in Southern waters based out of Miami, what was going on was about as off-limit as shooting a cop. I wondered how much of that forbidden-dark-desire bullshit moved Rosemary's ovaries.

"What ta bout you, Shy-lahh, you're an eenn-tel-li-gent girl; are you going to get mahr-rieed right ta wayee? You ought to go to college. I'll bet yerrr ahrr-tist-ick."

"Well, I draw and paint a lot, you got that right. I've even exhibited. Well, only in the bowling alley and a real-estate office, but still, maybe I'll major in art if I can."

"Let's go o-verrr here by de back boats. We aren't supposed to meeen-gle with the passen-gerrrs, so I don't want to be too dis-playy-ful. Here, I'll take de glasses and we'll have ourselves some rum."

"Aren't you exhausted? My God, you've been playing off and on since eleven."

"I like to look overr and see you there. Twass like a tonic, youu know; I ken sleeeeep eny timmme."

Pleasant being in approximately the same space in which I had been alone earlier in the evening. The sound of his talk reassured me, reminded me of Lewis Carroll . . . that is, the singsong voice made me think of magical worlds. Shylah in Wonderland.

Timsy took the glass out of my hand, placing it at a little distance, Oh God, he's going to kiss me. I panicked about the position of my lips. Since racism in Lime seemed to center on the size of Negroes' lips, they had become exaggerated in my mind. I didn't know how to do it. I mean, did I open my mouth a little to equalize where the four spaces of flesh met? But then some of his mouth would get some of my teeth. I didn't want to ruin it by kissing badly. I didn't want him to suggest we call it a night. Shit, do I pucker or not? People mixed in the islands— How did thin lips and full lips reach the desirable connection? Everything else was negotiable; at least I hoped it was negotiable.

"Wha-tis wrong, Shy-lahhh? Are you ah-fraid of a kiss?"

"No, no. I, uh, well, I just don't think you'd think I do it well."

"Do youuu think it khan bee done not welll if de two people have de desire to?"

"Hey, no. You're absolutely right. So I, uh, don't have to be, uh, terrific or anything."

We were sitting amid the lifeboats, heads tilted up so we

could stargaze. Timsy turned me a little to him. I put my arms around his neck, half to balance and half to just have them there. Like a seesaw that slowly tilts one way when the weights are just slightly off balance, we began kissing halfway to getting full length on the deck. The skin on Timsy's full lips all smoothness to my lined smaller ones and salty warm. Like swimming off Lime, slower, a strength to it. My tender friend was a doctor already if you could heal by strokes—I could have slept that way.

"Why, mah goodness, if it isn't May Britt. How was it with Samb—ah mean, your steel-drummer friend. Ah'm not so surprised about you, but Rosemary—ah just don't believe it, she won't even let her cleaning girl get near her. Mah Lawd, she's still out with the black prince."

Bubbles, Cindy, and Selma Anne had crowded into the bunk with the porthole, sitting there in baby dolls and rollers, painting their toes with Erotic Orange nail polish, talking, giggling, running the critique of first evening aboard ship. Our cabin after only one evening's use was an impressive shithole of clothes and cosmetics and half-filled glasses of rum with cigarettes decomposing in them. Breathing was a challenge.

"Shylah, talk! Y'all so quiet; c'mon, tell us about it. We're the group, remember, c'mon."

"Well, O.K., sure. First, you know his eyes, you know those big, inky eyes, well, they were just so full of fire and he grabbed me first moment we were alone. Why MAHLAWD, I almost passed out from the smell, well, you *know* how they smell, and his lips almost devoured poor little me as he pushed me down, and then, oh God, then, I looked up into those nostrils, straight into that nose and there—up there in that divided highway was this little demon waving at me. I mean to tell you, at first I thought it had to be just an unusually large bugger but no— NOW I knew I was in the arms of black Satan— Ohhh sisters, I struggled against the binds of those powerful muscles and then, and THEN he unzipped; why, I was barely conscious at the time, of course, and there, I mean, I couldn't believe it . . . his

1 8 6

pecker the size of your arm, Selma Anne, and glistening with horrible stuff. I struggled. Nothing would stop him. And then, like this gigantic tornado, he farted. OHMAHGAWD. It was the last thing I remember till I woke up here, at the door, like a lost child. Lost to the ages."

"Uh, we get the point, Shylah, we get the point."

Bubbles rolled on the floor space between the bunks. The rest of us followed in erupted laughter, making enough noise between us to bring Miz Larraine to the door.

"Y'all shut up in there, hear. Y'all makin enough racket to wake up the ship. Now quiet. It's four-thirty in the morning."

Selma Anne and Cindy stuffed pillows over their mouths. Bubbles talked in sign language. When Rosemary came in, the three sets of eyes were bulging with hope of new and serious narrative. Oh Christ, and Rosemary—Rosemary the jock—dull as she was in certain areas, would keep us awake all night. It'd run like a Frank Yerby novel or *Gone With the Wind,* and about as long. Good ole Dixie Rosemary, granddaughter of a white hooded sheet, had discovered, as she would say, "immigration" and I was sure I'd be the one up shit creek when we got back. Good Jesus.

"Hi, y'all. Whatcha been up to, huh?"

"Cut the crap, Roseberries, and clue us in. We ain't been waitin up for nuthin."

"You gotta absolutely promise, ah mean it, Selma Anne, you run your lip and ah'll have your ass, mah daddy'd kill ME 'fore he died of shame. Well, listen, he was just tooo much. Ah wanta go live in Nassau, ah'll tell you. After those drips on Lime. Anyhow, we had to be careful, you know, he'd get in trouble, raght, so we went to this vacant cabin and had some drinks and uh . . ."

"Get to it, beauty, get to it."

"Yah, Roseberries."

"Don't rush me, ah gotta tell it raght. Oh, by the way, Shylah, how was what's his name? He was cute too, sorta."

"Never mind, will ya get to the story, Roso, I wanna get some sleep."

1 8 7

"Well, first we had some, uh, rum and talked, you know, like where he was from and where ah was from and then, well, we started making out. God, he's really experienced."

"Well, did you?"

"Did you go all the way with him?"

"Yup, and it was sooo, um—so exciting. Ah mean, you know."

"Did he force you or anything?"

"Lawd no, he was kinda—ah think he was kinda nervous about it. You know, all that white jail-bait shit. But ah, uh, ah sort of took it in hand. Ah mean, you know."

"Well, c'mon, what he do, Rosemary, WHATHEDO?"

"Well, you know, the same thing anybody does, only better, raght. Ah mean, he kinda played and fingered me and then he stuck it in. Oh yah, ah forgot, his hair made me feel kinda strange."

"Oh God, his hair, did y'all hear that; we wanta hear 'bout his dork and she talks about hair."

"No, ah mean it. You know those kinks, it's kinky down there, you know, around his prick; feels funny, sorta tickles . . ."

"Yah, but his DORK, Rosemary, his DORK, well, was it . . ."

"Well, it was bigger than Clyde's, but that ain't sayin much. Ah don't know, seemed, well, it weren't a baseball bat or anything. Lahk he was built nahce, not too big or small. Ah mean, ah sort of forgot he was a nig—colored—after we started making out. It was just nahce, sexy, you know, exciting. He takes his time, unlike our drippy boy friends, you know, kinda lahk being in a movie. Real romantic. Ah really lahked him, you know. He talks, uh, speaks nahce. But look, nobody say anything, raght? Not about Shylah or me, understand. We gotta be cool 'bout it. Our ass is grass if anybody finds out. Hey, you guys, ah'm 'bout ready for some sleep. How 'bout us goin to bed now?"

"Listen to her, y'all, some nig—some swashbuckling Sammy Davis, Jr., puts it to her and she thinks she can start givin us orders 'bout our sleepin habits. Ah HAVE seen it all, Rosemary, ah have seen it all."

★

Nassau, pink on the early-morning horizon; we were coming in. Passed small fishing boats and yachts anchored offshore for the night—cutting through an all-day-sucker-green ocean—pure, waveless and friendly as a bedroom. I hung on the deck an hour before breakfast, the girls still slightly dead and snoring in our cabin, hung on the deck with sketchbook and hangover, watching the finger of land grow larger.

Smoked fish, scrambled eggs, broiled tomato, coconut juice, buns and coffee later, our group along with the entire senior class went on deck again to view the natives now climbing up the ship and diving from its highest point. The girls had somehow fared better from the first night than had the boys, who looked moribund, definitely seasick, and incapable of drinking so much as a 3.2 beer ever again. Neither Timsy nor Turk appeared and Rosemary bitched but had gained composure by the time we docked—she had hopes of an island full of Turks at her disposal. Mr. Sal and Miz Larraine called us together before disembarking.

". . . And ah expect y'all to handle yourselves lahk grownups. Ah want you back for lunch and dinner. Tonight we go to Dirty Mariah's as a group, understand? Girls, remember, stay together, no less than three in a group. When y'all shop in the markets, beware of getting cheated. Jew 'em down. Girls, act lahk ladies. Stay clear of the sailors and out of bars, y'all understand? O.K., tha's all, see you for lunch."

Pompons of pink, yellow, blue; green straw lined the hats and bags in the market. Wooden tikis, bowls and spoons, scarves and shirts in bright cotton lay displayed. Hawkers and tourists in equal number eyed one another. The market at ten in the morning jammed with life, especially insect life. We got down to serious bargaining, at which I proved a sucker's delight. I knew that for the bookends, bag, and hat I purchased I had paid the maximum price, my toughness a drop of sweat next to their insistence. We walked past the stalls and onto the main street, stopping to buy the five duty-free bottles permitted and perfume. Then Rosemary had the bad faith to suggest we rent this car from a guy that approached her. We did, piling five of us into the small black Anglia, Cindy at the wheel, and we were off on the back roads and to the beach, euphoric until, going down a cobbled hill, the brakes failed.

"Pray. We're in for it now. The brakes caved."

"You gotta be shitting us, Cindy, pump em."

"Too late, hold on, ah'll try getting us clear."

"NO BRAKES, GET OUT OF THE WAY, NO BRAKES." We yelled at the children, vendors, dogs, and chickens along the way down. Cindy skated the car from curb to curb so as not to pick up any more momentum. Locals stared, loping out of the way; small children broke into laughter as if this was a daily and humorous pastime—watching crazy tourists lose brakes in shady rental cars. At the foot of the hill, Cindy made a sharp right and banked it. We were fine. The car didn't look so good, fenderwise, but the beach was just across the road.

"Nahce driving, Cindy. Ah didn't think we'd make it for a second."

"Whew, O.K., now what, we're miles away from anywhere. How about flagging a cop? They're supposed to be pretty good at these things."

"Look, let's beach it for a while. Ah'm in need of a little refreshment. C'mon, we got our suits on under— C'mon."

Rosemary was never one to fret. She made the jump from renting the car to swimming, while it sat there miles from the boat and brakeless, without much to-do. And the beach being right there, all powder pink, how could we refuse?

"This water is delightful. God. Hey, look at the little crabs."

"Hmmmm. Hey, Shy, how'd it go with that guy, you know, what's-his-name? Ah never got a chance to find out."

"Nice—it—well, it was nice, that's all. We didn't do anything much."

"Well, ah presume we'll be gettin together tonight; hey, maybe we can all go out, you know, around Nassau."

"Rosemary, I say this in all fairness, not only are you a sex maniac, but with sex in mind you turn from narrow-mindedness to fair play, generosity, and a genuine feeling for your brothers black and white. Suddenly, after a background of total ancestral

bigotry, you're about to join hands—well, not hands exactly—
with the world. Maybe they could open up a slot for you in
human relations at the U.N. You could be the screwing ambas-
sador."

"Shyyyyylahhhh, y'all shut up now. C'mon, ah'm sorry ah
asked. Let's swim."

We raced each other into the five feet of water close to shore,
working out the remains of hangovers and fear, dunking,
dolphin-diving, and splashing before getting dressed again.
Then, walking up from the beach, we hailed the bobby going
by on his Vespa, explaining the car and nefarious rental, all of
which got straightened out. The man was easy to find under
police escort; we got a free trip back and our money refunded,
with a certain weren't-trips-to-exotic-places-full-of-shady-deal-
ings humor on the part of the law.

Lunch and the beginning of the drinking day. Afterward, as I
was heading toward our cabin, a steward came up and slipped
me a note.

"Uh, Rosemary, don't fall over, but we've got a double date
this afternoon. Look—" The note read: *Dear Shila, Can you and
Rosemary go to Shipwreck Bar down street to the left (1 mile)
—Turk and I will be waiting at three—xx T.*

"Mah Lawd, what'll ah wear? Hey, girls, y'all come down
with us so old Miz Larraine don't get suspicious, O.K.?"

"Yah, what's in it for us?"

"C'mon, Selma Anne, pleeease, ah'll pay you back. You can
borrow mah Impala for the day when we get back."

"Ah swear to God, Rosemary, you smell male and your own
mother'd get the shaft. O.K., O.K., who am I to interrupt the
lovebirds? Y'all wanna be carried down the street so as not to
mess your capris?"

"Eat it, will you, Selma Anne."

Shipwreck Bar was the kind of place tourists would never go
to. The clientele sipped rum straight or with Coke, no parasols,
no tiki glasses, no mucho-poco-type drinking, and the predomi-
nant color at the tables was brown, not white or sun-red—a local

joint. Rosemary shook and, for all that interracial bravado, pushed me ahead of her toward the section with tables and chairs.

"OHMAHLAWD, suppose they aren't there. We'll be scalped."

"They're here, see, Rosemary. Now relax. Pretend you're Swedish."

The two men beckoned us over to the plastic-lined booth, rising to let us sit on the inside.

"Chahrley, would youu bring de lay-deez some rum Cocas. How would you lahk to see some of de islahnd? Turk has a car. So we go motoreeng after a while."

"Sounds great. We tried renting a car earlier but the brakes failed, right, Rosemary?"

"God, ah can't think 'bout it. Scared, uh huh. Ah lahk ta died. We were going down this hill, couldn't stop for shit."

"Haf to be car-full what de merchandise is round here. Some unfriendly people on de islahnd. We go a little out to some country—to nice no-tourist beach. Beeeeg abahn-donned house."

Turk and Rosemary wolfed at each other, making it awkward for Timsy and me to carry on any kind of conversation. The rum came with an appetizer tray of smoked fish, the best I had ever tasted, must have been a smokehouse out back. But Turk and Rosemary were rushing us through food and liquor to get at each other. I stuffed the rest of the fish into a napkin while following them out the door.

"Let's make love."

"Let's not. Let's go swimming."

"You khan sweem eny tihme, Shy-lahhh."

"No, I don't want to go any further. Well, maybe a little further."

"Why don't youu want to do what's naht-ur-ull—lahk Rose-mahr-y?"

"I feel seduced. C'mon, let them make it for both of us. I want to swim. I, hmmm, it feels good, hmmm."

We lay on the littered fish-corpse beach in bathing suits, mine halfway down as Timsy kneaded one breast and with the other hand touched the cloth-covered crotch. Getting excited with someone I didn't know and wouldn't see again seemed wasteful, emotionally wasteful. There was no potential for a one-timer. I hated thinking this way, thinking abandonment. So why was I getting all wet? God, the same old bind. His clarity and my vagueness.

While my thoughts warred with each other, he progressed in an orderly mapping of body. Being attracted to a guy, a guy who wouldn't be there for long, a hit and run—it tortured me. Maybe it had something to do with ovaries; maybe it had something to do with everyone being, every male being, a future father. A girl needed permanence for her womb's sake. Still, he made everything so great, even for an hour. Push and pull. I ran into the water, pulling up the Lastex suit. Timsy followed, swam out quickly into deep water, diving under the ripples, surfacing far out, and returning.

"Shy-lah, you are de great teaser, you know dat? You get a mahn all excited, then you run away from it. It's not a kind thing to do, Shy-lah."

"Well, you were being very persuasive, and Jesus, yes, I sort of want to. But it's a risk for me. Why take it if I know I'm only going to see you this weekend?"

"What ta 'bout pleasure? You cahn't be both ha t'and cold de same time. Dat's silly, girl. Why'd you want to be with me if not for a little of dis?"

"Because I like you. You make it sound like, if I kiss you, why don't I screw you? That's bullshit. Come on, Timsy, there are other things . . ."

"I do not theenk from de white Southern tour-eest girl dere is much else. Deese women, de older ones with der beeg words about keeping demselves special ahnd keeping de colored maids with dem, dey cahn't wait to jiggle de first native mahn dey see. It makes for laughing stories amongst us. You talk one thing and do de other."

"Yes, I see your point, but it's not that. I mean, if I thought we were, well, you know, I don't want to like someone a lot and then never see the person again. I'm not really explaining myself very well, am I?"

"Ah, you want to mahry de one who does it. So serious, Shylah. You know, I do lahk you, funny girl."

"Please, let's not argue any more, Timsy. You're making my trip really great. Look at all the stuff you've shown me. I wouldn't have seen this part of the island if you hadn't been around."

"I'm sorry. I thought dat is what you wanted. Come, Shylah, we drink some rum and forget about it. You lahk dat?"

"No, no rum, all we do around here is drink. Can we walk around the property a little? Hey, what are those?"

"Ginger—here; pretty, aren't dey? I wish now we had more time. If you come to Ja-MAYYY-ca, Shylah, I give you my mother's address. You come to us. It's a different world there, even from here."

The former owners must have cultivated the land for flowers, the ultimate luxury crop. Trees still bore vines with flowering white and yellow orchids. Others, jasmine, different white conical buds on bushes, and some type of lily, grew in pockets on the overgrown paths. Bright, splashy leaves jutted up from the ground. Late-day sun glinted through crevices in trees, palm ferns, and things slightly above me. Rosemary and Turk came out and we yelled for them. Rosemary and her damn satisfied smile; I envied her wild-woman look as she sought to brush hair, reapply lipstick, and pat down the creases in her capris.

Subtlety failed us upon our return. Instead of getting off on a side street, we drove down most of the main drag—too far. Lee, Dirk, Stanley, and Ross spotted us as we got out and kissed our entertainers goodbye. Stanley and Ross and Lee would handle it O.K., but Dirk . . . Anyone who wears a Confederate hat down the main drag in Nassau doesn't keep his mouth shut for anything and Dirk, who had never fondled anything softer than a 1962 Impala, would run his mouth like a custom engine in a chicken race.

"Oh, come on, Selma Anne, we can fit one more in."

"Man, you think ah'm goin down as queer at the tender age of eighteen, y'all crazy. Oh all raght, give me room, girls, give me room."

The five of us had piled into the stall shower, each holding on to a bar of scented soap, each with a flowered shower cap covering her hair; five bodies, all reasonably slim, daily shaved and plucked, five different shades and textures of pubic hair scrunched up against one another, and all of us pretending propriety in the three-by-five shower stall, soaping down before the dinner buzz.

"How we gonna cover this up? Jesus, Dirk's the biggest flat-head rebel in the class—he's still fightin the war."

"Ah know, Cindy, ah know. Look, maybe if we act real friendly, you know, sort of play up to him and everything. Maybe he'll keep his mouth shut. Hey, Bubbles, Dirk got a crush on you; maybe y'all can do something in the line of duty."

"Sheeit, whad ah haf to do, feel the grunge's little dork?"

"If he has one."

"Gimme that towel, Shylah."

"Catch."

"Hey y'all, ah went to that cosmetic store and cleaned up. Wanna try some new junk?"

"Hand me the mascara wand, will you?"

"Whose high heels?"

Saturday night was dress-up. The captain's reception and dance after dinner. Back on with the stockings and merry widows, my green and black satin sheath, upswept hair; the works. Now, if Dirk'd keep quiet, we'd survive.

"Ah maght have known, nigger-lover bitch. S'pose you talked Rosemary into it, huh? You would. Man, she just dumb, but y'all need to have your ass kicked, girl. Always did say you was the queerest damn chick ah ever saw. Ooh, you wait."

"Let me go, Dirk; come on, that hurts. I want to get back to the dance. If you want to mouth off, you go ahead and do it, but do me the favor of keeping your hands off me. Leave me alone, asshole."

"Whore."

"How the hell would you know?"

"Ah heard enough about you . . ."

"Yeah, I'll bet—straight from your big mouth. You're a pig, you know that?"

Shaking him off like the tarantula he was, I walked back into the main room, threw back the old shoulder blades, and appropriately widened my mascaraed eyes.

"Absolutely ravishing, Shylah. Come dance with a decrepit old man and make his evening."

"I'd love to, Alexander."

There's nothing like Britain's answer to César Romero to move a girl around a dance floor in the most obtrusive and graceful manner possible. Alexander had the knack of dancing for both of us, the ultimate in gallantry—to make a moving swan out of a wallowing water buffalo. I looked good. Marvelous to be this glamorous, this ultimately chic and devastating, even when you weren't. I'd dance the redneck creep's expletives out of my head. A ship's officer, I think he was the purser, cut in, and after that a portly gentleman from Miami, and after that another officer.

By the third dance with the sixth partner, I had had enough of fox-trots and gorgeousness; my feet were tired. I excused myself from the Dade County Junior College blond and hit the buffet of champagne, rum, and snacks. Massive attention was debilitating—I wasn't used to it. Rosemary eyed me and we met over at the side for a short talk.

"Mah mah, you being Miz America tonight. Listen, ah saw creep-head pull you out on deck. What happened, Shy? Ah've been gettin it from the boys. Holy God, we're in trouble, ah know we are."

"Relax, Roseberries. What's to worry about? You'll slough it off, I know you will; if it comes to a lot of shit, you can just say that Dirk was trying to get at you and thought up this story cause you didn't want to put out. Anyhow, you're a tried-and-true conch. They'll dump on the obvious source, ME. Right? What the hell do you have to worry about?"

"Yah, but ah want to see him again tonight, Shy. Ah want to see him again."

"So go ahead. What's the future of it though? You can't see him in Lime, that's for sure."

"Ah don't know—ah'm crazy about him, you know. If ah lived in the islands . . . Look, Shylah, things are different heah. Ah'm not the type to make waves. Maybe ah can move here after graduation; maybe he'll send money for me to come, you know, for me to come. He makes more doing this and other stuff than a lot of the guys on our island."

"O.K., it's your night; if you feel that way, then I guess it's worth it. But, Rosemary, I'm with myself tonight. Not Timsy or anybody. I'm with myself."

A limbo contest announced by the bandleader drew a line of passengers. I got this notion I wanted to try. Why not? Two stewards held the bar high while the sick and the aged got the once-around. Eliminations, those who fell or hit the steel bar, ran generationally, with a few exceptions.

I won. All those cheerleading back bends must have done it. I went under, my legs spread and folded like a lawn chair, making a wide V from knees to crotch, feet up, head back, so my hair grazed the floor; my mouth open, I thought I'd be swallowing that bar. I won. For the first time I won.

"Ladies and gentlemen, Miss Shylah Dale. A great limbo champion, 1963, for the *Bahama Star*, and a beautiful girl. Shylah, a silver trophy and one hundred dollars. Let's hear it for Shylah Dale, ladies and gentlemen."

One hundred dollars meant I could get new materials, pastels, a set of oils, brushes, and a new formal for the prom. Rich.

"Shylah, ah've never seen you lahk this."

"Me too, you were amazing."

"Wowee."

"Yes, surprised me too. I've never done anything like this."

The captain, sort of an aging Tyrone Power, oiled up to congratulate me; even my skeptical teachers were closing in—they must not have heard the interracial news.

"Miss Dale, what a pleasure. Congratulations. I think that's the lowest the bar has been on a passenger in a long time. Won't you join us at my table? You'll perk it up, I assure you."

"Sure, yessir, I'd love to."

"Mr. St.-Remie, Mrs. St.-Remie, Mr. Harley—oh, of course, you know each other—you're a Ginger Rogers as well. My first officer, Reeveson, Mrs. Blumberg, and Mr. and Mrs. Papados, all the way from Athens—this is Miss Shylah Dale, this year's winner and a most attractive addition to the cup."

"What can we get you, Miss Dale?" Reeveson had manicured fingernails, oh God.

"Uh, champagne, if it's not too much trouble."

"An appropriate drink. Ralph, bring a bottle of the Veuve Clicquot for the young lady."

"Shylah darling, do let's dance again, shall we?"

"Oh yeah, sure, Alexander, if you can stand my dancing on your feet again."

"Isn't she an absolute dear? So modest. Come."

Gee, I was a star. Well, maybe not. But for one night, what the hell. I couldn't go wrong.

★

"So long, Timsy, I wish you luck in med school and everything. It was, uh, O.K. between us despite everything. Lovely."

"Maybe we see each other again someday. You come to Ja-MAYY-ca. You ahnd I . . . twas a pleasure. Shylah, you make dis mahn happy. You hurry, grow up, girl."

"Yes, I'll hurry."

The rain spattered my face as we docked. Rosemary wept for Turk. It was that kind of a trip. Miami in its architectural fantasy never looked so dismal, garish, and godawful.

11

"If it wasn't for graduation coming up, I'd suspend you, Shylah. What the hell you think y'all doing? You get out of here, y'all can marry a nigger boy if that's what you want—ah suggest you go back Nawth to do it; ain't no decent colored person down here who don't know their place. Jesus. You get a girl, impressionable, lahk Rosemary, in on your schemes. You know what her daddy's gonna do he find out about this— Y'all don't think, Shylah, you just don't think. Anybody else, ah'd say a senior is too old for the paddle, but with you it still talks, don't it, Shylah? Bend your butt over here, girl."

I bent over and let the principal resort to his ten whacks against my ass. This was supposed to leave me appropriately shamed. Though it stung, I had little reaction to this outrage one way or the other. Under the circumstances, I was getting off easy. In less than three weeks the class of '63 would graduate. I called it a godsend the old cracker didn't suspend me now, perversely compassionate that he was burning the seat of my pants. It was worth it, Conway's whacking away; it was worth it.

"O.K., ah don't want to hear one more word about your deportment before graduation day, is that understood, Shylah? It's a damn miracle we managed y'all this long. Now get the hell back to your homeroom, girl."

The marine-radio broadcast the stock-market closing prices as I lugged my suitcase and gifts back to the Florida room.

"Look, Daddy, the baby's back. Oh mah God, look at all the marvelous gifties."

"Hold it, Alice, let me find out the rest of the averages. Market's down."

"Hi, Alice. Got you a bottle of Shalimar. Hi, Daddy, here . . ."

I handed over the straw case of five duty-free bottles. Daddy waved and shut off the radio when the last of the prices had been read out.

"Ooh, y'all been out on the beach a little, haven't you, Shylah? Why, you're even darker. In'it attractive?"

"Yes, we spent some time swimming and stuff. Right now I could use a couple of nights' straight sleep."

"You know what we're gonna do, Shy, we're all goin to the inn for dinner. And guess who's comin with us, guess who's back?"

"No, don't tell me."

"Uncle Bobby Jay. Back from California. And divorced, a real quickie, from that starlet. Anyhow, as a special treat, he's taking us all out. Isn't that lovely? Just lahk two years ago."

"Terrific. Great—can't wait to see him."

I unpacked and threw clothes into the hamper. The shower washed away any remaining salt from the ocean spray. Three weeks till graduation; next week the prom, dinners, and banquets; white power in the school and Uncle Bobby Jay a free man and looming over the next dinner go-round. A nap now, just a little one. Two hours, that's all I asked till the son-of-a-bitch got to paw me hello.

"Why, Corky, Princess is all grown up. Look at that, a young lady."

"Howdy, Uncle Bobby Jay, long time no see." He looked ter-

2 0 0

rible—paunchy, and with that alcoholic skin beginning to show. Once again marriage must not have taken to him.

In his decrepit state, Uncle Bobby Jay had become unusually courtly. He did not interrupt at dinner; he flattered Alice, joked with Daddy, and spoke almost deferentially to me. Maybe the last one, the starlet, taught him humility; maybe that was it. Though I was tired, it was for once an almost painless dinner out. Even Daddy kept a low, less caustic profile. On the way back to the parking lot Bobby Jay blew it—made his move. I should've known he'd keep that two-year erection.

"How 'bout ridin in mah car, Princess? Been a long time. Ah'd lahk to talk to you, please, ah really would. C'mon, ah'm not going to attack you or anything. Please."

"Oh Christ, no, I'm tired. All I want to do is get some sleep. Another time, Bobby Jay."

"Hey, Bobby Jay, how 'bout lettin baby sit next to you in that new Starfire. Wouldn't y'all lahk that, Shylah? Got to do a little talkin with your father."

God, her timing knocked me out—Alice never missed.

"Yes, all right, I'll see you back at the house." What the hell, let's see, he wouldn't have enough time for sexual athletics, not with them waiting back at the house, or maybe it didn't matter. I supposed Alice knew. She wasn't dumb. She just acted like it.

"Ah'll take her for a spin, Corky. We'll see you in an hour or so."

"O.K., Bobby boy. Don't y'all go running the bridges down in that thing."

We drove south a bit, not far, off the highway and down one of the old roads that led to the beach. Bobby Jay cut the engine at its end, like a parking sophomore.

"Shylah, we never did get much chance to talk, you see, about that night. And then y'all took off for boarding school. That's why ah had to talk to you 'bout that night. You left cause of that, didn't you? You left cause of me. Look, ah know ah forced mahself on you, all along as well. Ah thought maybe in a few years . . . Hell, ah don't know why ah married that Hollywood bitch; ah hate those fucking whores, excuse mah French.

Shylah, you're eighteen now, you're grown up, right? Ah did mean what ah said. No man wants to be rejected, especially, well, you know, a lot of girls would lahk to get me—but ah think ah sort of knew you just put up with me . . . Good Lord, ah don't know what ah'm sayin any more. Lahk with that girl— we're divorced, it's final; maybe she was a little lahk you. And don't think ah didn't pay through the damn nose. Ah'm forty-one, that's pretty ancient to you; to me, well, ah don't lahk to admit this, but ah still don't have, you know, a home, lahk kids—a family. Ah'd lahk to have kids with someone decent. Would you want to get married, Shylah? We could go any-where, you know, travel a while before you started havin chil-dren. Shylah, ah swear to God, ah love you."

"NO. I don't like you that way. Besides, I don't want to stay and marry and have your kids. Jesus, Bobby Jay, you just got back; how can you ask me this? I don't believe it."

"Aw, Princess, don't give it up. We'll go somewhere else if you want. Ah know you and your daddy aren't on the best of terms. Pissed me off the way he was toward you sometimes."

"So why didn't you do something about it, bozo? Why? I didn't see any evidence of your protection."

"Ah didn't want anything to get in the way of mah seeing you. Ah figured he wanted me to marry you and, uh, keep them, ah s'pose. He kept his virgin lahk a full deck of aces, y'all see."

"Yes, well, we can forget about that virgin business, can't we, Bobby Jay? Look, I've got another three weeks to go and then I'm going back east. You'll find a nice girl, for Christsake. My graduating class is full of sexy, nubile, nice girls who would cream their jeans at settling down with you. Come on, let's go back, O.K.? No, don't, don't do that, don't touch me. Stop it, prick— Bastard, you just have to have it your way, don't you? Well, drive that big machine of yours back alone then. I'd rather walk. Go on, leave me alone."

I was too old for this jumping-out-of-cars shit. It made no dif-ference whatever what I said. He heard nothing. His thoughts, his outings, his needs—what a sad way to live. I sprinted to the highway, hearing Bobby Jay back the car out of the road, turn, and squeal out. I didn't even hate him now, guessed he had had a rough time of it, and if he really did have a crush on me and I didn't like him—painful for him; it was pain. I understood pain. But the pig had the power and all I wanted then was to get a little fucking sleep.

"Get in the car."

"No, I want to walk. It's not that far."

"Get in this fucking car, goddamnit."

"I said no, let me walk. Ow, stop it."

He had gotten out, run after me, gripped my arm, opened the passenger door, and thrown me in.

"Now, y'all listen, you arrogant little bitch. You coming home with me. Ah don't want your parents thinkin ah let you alone on the highway, for Christsake. Y'all some dumb snatch, you know that; your daddy maght have a point in that. Don't you think ah don't know you got bad habits, girl? You some asshole, ah'll tell you. Yah, you go nawth, that's where you belong. Ah do suggest you stay there this time, heah? Answer me."

"I hear you. Holy shit, what the hell is going on in the yard? Look at that."

Alice had a bucket in her hand, while Daddy was pulling up something from the grass.

"What the hell . . ." We parked and walked over.

"What's goin on, Alice?"

"Uh . . ."

"Your ass, that's what. You know what we found here when we got back, what was blazing lahk the last judgment, Shylah, you know what, huh? Y'all ought to, a damn cross; you heard me, some of your cohorts. What did you do in Nassau, sister? Did y'all get yourself some black buck? Did you run with them, Shylah? Oh, you bitch. God, you stupid bitch."

"Now, Corky, ah'm sure it's just some reactionary . . ."

"Shut up. Be glad you're leavin, sister. Now that you've sufficiently ruined mah name. Aren't you smart, huh? Now get your fat ass to bed. Ah don't want to lose mah temper."

In bed I daydreamed of strength, the kind that would bring me to Dirk under the smoking tree, with the class there and underclassmen watching, to smash into him with my fists. To use their tactics and to use them better, always superbly feminine, to demolish him with an elegant left to the jaw, to shame him. THAT would have ended the matter simply. Violence or physical force counted for a lot around here. They'd respect that; they'd shut up and defer. God, Shylah, hopeless. Luanne. I wished Luanne had been on that trip, Luanne could have handled it; Luanne knew how to coddle, to take care of things, even in the company of pigs. But all that went into Loosie now, went into ironing her little dresses and children's aspirin and making the barrette stay in her fine baby hair. Luanne the Madonna; for all the brawling mothers on Lime that ever raised a hand to their kids, Luanne stood as the young example of peace.

Luanne. Who accepted and endured, who would be here when I was not and when I returned, Luanne, who kept the nest like a feudal fortress. Her aspirations went as far as the length of her arms. A piece of the island, Luanne.

★

The group took off to a dress outlet in Miami for our prom gowns. The last of mutual shopping ventures before graduation; we had convinced old Conway to let us out at noon on Wednesday for personal needs, taking Rosemary's Impala and Cindy's black bomb for the 120-mile trip. Lee and Scottie followed with the other guys as a kind of hamburger-buying backup, also with the excuse of renting white-coat tuxedos. Scottie totaled his custom Ford on the way back at Hangman's Curve right off Jewfish Creek, but the boys were O.K. and the rented tuxes survived.

No one did anything these days except tend to personal appearances and the business of invitations. David and I doubled with Selma Anne and Lee for the prom. Her circular eggishness was even more apparent in pink-tulle strapless formal, the old kind—shades of Shirley Temple, I thought. I kept to white, this time white crepe, plain and straight, with long gloves and David's roses worn in my lacquer-frozen, pouffy hair. Upon our insistence, we were the first graduating class to hold its prom away from school, at the inn, with imported DJ special band from Miami instead of Key West.

"Well, gang, the last of the chaperoned-shindigs-drinks-under-the-tables, and Jesus, even Crabs took a bath, ah'll be damned. Ah can't believe mah single days are numbered."

"Oh man, ah hate to see it end. We've been the best. Jesus. Why don't we all do something, you know, on our own, a special thing? Just seniors, not even boy friends or anything."

"How about Peacock Island? We could take off after graduation ceremonies. Like we'd meet at the marina afterward. Graduation's at eleven; we'll be off by twelve-thirty."

"Shylah, that's a great ahdea. Hey, y'all, we haven't been out there since the eleventh-grade party, 'member. Look, let's see, there're thirty of us; that's eight boats plus all the food and stuff. Whyn't you guys take care of getting the boats and gassing them, and we'll figure out the food; oh, and someone can be put in charge of booze— Hey, Rosie . . ."

"Yah, O.K., mah permanent assignment through life. Case of what, Myers or Bacardi?"

"Make it Myers this time, we'll make up some kind of base for mixin besides Coke. Y'all want Cuban sandwiches, that O.K., and, uh, fried chicken and we can do a bake thing for cookies. Shylah, y'all wanna bake some coconut supremes?"

"Do I have a choice, Cindy? Sure, O.K."

"Lawdy, Lawdy, the last bash. Shylah, we gonna send you off lahk we found you, out of yoh mind and under the weather."

"O.K., Stanley, long as you all put me on that plane, you'll get your coconut supremes. Wanna little diagram of where you're going to get them?"

"Let's dance, Moose. C'mon, Lettice has deserted for the bathroom."

Stanley still maintained his status as world's clumsiest dancer, which was O.K. by me. We box-stepped around the floor.

"Ah hate to see you go, Shylah. If you hadn't left the first time . . . Ah didn't think ah'd ever see you again or ah would've . . ."

"Yeah, I know. It's O.K. I missed you though, you know that."

"We're the best, Moose, it's just nice knowing that. Stay, Shylah, please. Would you stay if Lettice wasn't around? We haven't been getting along for months. If it wasn't for the prom, you know, it wouldn't be right to break off with the prom and everything, but we haven't really been close in a while. Can I see you, you know, when we get a chance, maybe after gradua- tion; it'll be just our class. Come in my boat, O.K? We'll be together lahk before. O.K., Shylah?"

"Absolutely. Next Wednesday's our day. Oh oh, here comes David with his cutting-in look."

"Come on, Shylah, let's show the kiddies how to dance." David swirled, twirled, dipped, and almost flipped me in imita- tion-bandstand style, the braggart. But Stanley's movements were my own. I never cared that much for my steady date, whom Daddy and Alice found so acceptable. Now I saw that not only was I not particularly interested in him but that I had always found him to be variations of a flapping-roaring-stinking asshole.

I watched Stanley talking at the table. If I saw him at age sixty it would be the same. That familiarity—it didn't even de- pend on closeness. I just knew him. He and this island and Luanne.

★

"Daddy, aren't you coming?"

"Alice going for both of us, I got myself some business here."

"You know Daddy, baby, he doesn't go to these official things—it's just his way."

"But, Jesus, it's my graduation. Can't he make an exception?"

"Now come on, sugar, he'll be there in spirit."

"His spirit can go to hell. Aw shit, let's go, Alice. Please. I've got to get out of this house."

Alice and I, the cookies, a fried chicken, my graduating cap and gown, and a pair of white heels took off for Palm View. From the glove compartment Alice produced some tissue for my eyes and nose. Fathers came to graduations, like to wed- dings, but mine stayed home with the bourbon and some anon- ymous appointment. Bullshit.

I threw the cookies and chicken in Stanley's jalopy when we

2 0 6

arrived; Alice held the cap and gown and white heels. We proceeded to the home ec room, where the rest of the girls were in stages of getting ready. Our women teachers were there, Miz Larraine weeping as she pressed last-minute pleats into the robes, mothers clacking away at the joy of this auspicious occasion, fathers' voices in the corridor waiting for their daughters or going off to the civics room to help their sons dress. Enough bittersweet in the air to make a crocodile pick flowers. Selma Anne, Bubbles, Rosemary, Cindy, and I, along with our mothers and junior attendants, exchanged presents and flowers before lining up and joining the double line of boys walking the outdoor corridor to the cafetorium which was coral-lined. And there we were, one more time around at the double doors and the school band as godawful as ever, grinding their way through the opening bars of "Pomp and Circumstance" and all of us doing that practiced step-pause out of sync. Stanley and I switched around so that we'd follow one another up on that wooden platform, receiving our scrolled degrees, taking the tassel, and changing sides, so wedding-like, and Stanley and I holding hands after, listening to the closing prayer, holding hands, and his whispering, "Moose, you and me made it, huh?"

We filed out, while motherly sob inhalations were heard and the audience stood in respect for what would be, for most of us, a one-time graduation. The band broke it all up with a painful rendition of the "Triumphal March from *Aïda*." Even Conway held his hand in front of his mouth to hide his laughter. Over. Graduated, purified, redeemed momentarily, I acquiesced to mothers kissing wet cheeks, classmates hugging, and teachers hand-shaking.

"I'll see you tonight, Alice. Listen, thanks for coming, for everything."

"O.K., lamb, y'all have a nahce time at your picnic. Ah'm sure proud of you."

"Thanks, I wish my father felt that way."

The entire female half of the class broke out in a spontaneous display of competitive athletics by foot-racing each other back to the home ec room, removing robes in flight, changing upon arrival into bathing suits, shorts, and tops. We chanted, "We are free in '63," grabbing gear and walking out to the student parking lot. I looked back at the school. It would be due for a change soon. It couldn't stay that backwoodsy and survive. But then neither could I.

"Got everything, Moose?"
"Yup, oh no, I didn't bring any beach blankets."
"Ah figured you'd forget; ah've got that big old thing in the back. O.K., lez go."
The twenty cars bearing thirty young members of society, having graduated and not had a drink all morning, rode the few miles down Highway 1 to the bridge road to Lime, left to the pink-stucco marina and the eight boats we had docked there. Bubbles, Lee, and I stayed with Stanley.
Peacock Island, uninhabited, half-mile long and three-quarters-mile wide, ten miles out. Called Peacock because of some Spanish galleon carrying a load of the birds for a blood-thirsty governor-general in Cuba who needed them for his hat and for the ladies' evening attire; anyhow, so the story goes. Supposedly it wrecked on a reef and the birds walked the flats to the island. Two centuries later, Portuguese fishermen set anchor there and found the island overrun by a fish-eating peacock colony which was justifiably upset at human intrusion and, according to legend, pecked a fisherman to death. Later, between the early settlers on the Keys and a few capitalistic Indians, the peacock population succumbed to mass plucking between 1890 and 1925, and that was the end of that. Still, Peacock kept its historical credentials by offering the remains of two homesteads, one of white settlers wiped out by Indians and one of Indians wiped out by white settlers. Moreover, the island was lush with flowers, cactus, prickly pear, coconut, papaya, sapodilla, and a scorpion population brought over on the backs of the Everglades settlers and Keys colonists.
Behind our boat a couple of porpoises followed at a little distance, flirting for fish, clearing the water in their leaps, smiling as if they had just graduated as well. A stingray skimmed past, giant, like a small airboat riding atop the water. I had taken off my shorts and top, under which I wore my first, newly pur-

chased, white French bikini. Bubbles looked amazed at my flesh.

"Why, Brigitte Bardot, ah wouldn't have known y'all."

"Glad you approve."

"Well, ah approve," said Stanley, who swerved the boat to indicate temporary loss of mind. Once out the channel to full ocean, it got a little rougher, the short end of a northeastern squall, then sunshine again all the way to Peacock. I noticed a peculiar thing about the island as we came within sight of it—there was nothing else, no other islands or even a large sandbar, nearby, like a mirage, like a cartoon of itself, solo, alone with miles of horizon. And because it sat there without another thing to compete with, each tree or driftwood shape, as soon as it was visible, became startlingly clear. A kind of ghost island.

"Hey, Stan Bear, give me that coconut slicer, will you? Let's go out and get some of this fruit for the rum." Stanley and I took over official foraging for rum garnishings, slicing coconuts, putting the juice in a jar, and extracting and cutting up the meat, taking the scarlet prickly pear insides and mashing them with the juice, cutting up papaya. When we had gathered enough for a legion's tutti-fruitti ration, I leaned against a hurricane-sagged granddaddy palm, in the special pocket they make to endure a storm, and Stanley fit to me and the pocket, and I realized with my tongue in his mouth and my hands on his warm chino-covered buns that he had grown taller—out of proportion to me—so that it was different now: we no longer fit as evenly, I had to tilt back slightly from the waist to meet his mouth. His feet were bigger and his skin had cleared up. We weren't kids any more, even though we never thought we were anyway, but now the choice had been taken away . . . and to know it like a light in the middle of clinching.

"I need a drink. I just realized we've matured like some fucking bottle of sour-mash whiskey."

"One of your Nawthern words, Shy Moose. Yah, ah know, ah was thinkin that too; ah'm so much, you know, bigger now."

"And you've lost your baby fat, Stanley. I'm holding muscles on your ass instead of water wings."

"Yuh muthah, Mae West. You've lost your baby fat too. Watch

2 0 9

it, girl, you're going to bring me to the point of sexual asphalt."

"Assault, asshole, assault. Oh Bear, you're just so comfortable. I know it sounds funny to say it that way. Comfortable—like everything fits. Oh oh, we better get back to the group gropers with the stuff. I forgot."

"Let's come back here after we bring the stuff, O.K.?"

"O.K., sure."

"Why, there they ahh, we was afraid to come get you two. Lovebirds again? How absolutely queer, and at the end of the whole shebang. O.K., bring the gunk so we can get down to a little serious mixin here. Hey, put on the radio, Grasser. Ooh, ah love those Beach Boys; too bad we can't really surf down here. Ah guess that's mostly in California."

"Naw, they surf off Cocoa Beach, not very good though. Ooh, that's some drink."

All of us plopped down on assorted beach blankets, thirty kids, one island, eating fried chicken between gulps of makeshift zombies, lying on our backs, getting roasted, giggling, rolling over on each other, spilling drinks and chicken bones.

"Hey, y'all, we oughta top off the occasion with a class orgy. After all, we ain't never had one of those."

"Shut up, Grasser."

"Ah'm serious, who the hell's to know? Ain't nobody here but the graduation class of '63, so you can screw your reputation, Cindy."

"Hey, you know, Grasser, you're raght."

"That's the craziest thing ah've evah heard. You're serious, aren't you? Give me another one of them zombies, then ah'll give it some thought." Bubbles bubbled with hysterics—her capacity for alcohol had always been limited to a couple of sniffs, though she thought in terms of gallons. A certain alcoholism socially contracted probably endeared us even more to one another, an acceptance factor, like dueling scars or nose jobs or circle pins or Shetland sweaters or belonging to a country club, depending on what values were esteemed. I saw going East to college as one long drying-out period.

"Oh, come on, you're kidding. Orgy?"

"What do y'all have to lose, Shylah? There's only those Band-Aids you're wearin to take off."

"Listen to King Farouk here. O.K., Dirk, we can hardly wait to view your weenie. Quick, girls, the magnifying glass."

"Listen, boobies, y'all askin for a test run."

"Jesus, y'all sound lahk a bunch of screwin elephants."

"You would know, Stanley, you would know."

The idea of an actual orgy—absurd as it was and a joke in the beginning, made for the continuation of banter, all of us giving lip at once—scared and intrigued us. After all, we were here on a deserted island, high enough on our graduation, the makeshift zombies, and the surroundings to pop, warm and sticky from the sun, some of us leaving for places unknown. Nothing would remain of this except what we filled the moment with. Stanley and I looked at each other in disbelief. We'd never actually made love. This was hardly the situation we had planned for a first time. The rum was going quickly. Amazing how the mind works as group reflex. Orgy! God, quick, a drink, just a little one; well, just a little one more, not too much, a little nerve.

"Well, look, y'all, first we gotta take off our bathing suits."

"You suggested this thing, Grasser, so you first."

"Naw, we're gonna do this fair—first off we gotta swear nobody's ever gonna know, on pain of being kicked in the balls or, uh, or the snatch. O.K.?"

"O.K.!"

"Now, we gotta have a signal that'll mean all of us take off our suits at once, so nobody stands out, raght, and if anybody thinks they aren't goin to, then they get, uh—what do they get—hmm, ah know—they get stripped and tickled and slapped on the ass by the rest of us. O.K.?"

"O.K.!"

"So what's the signal goin to be, you guys?"

"Ah got it. Look, we take this glass jar, raght; now we dig a hole in the sand about here. See now, put it in so the lip just sticks up. O.K., tide's comin in. When that jar overflows, y'all see it clear? O.K., when that jar overflows, then we gotta take off our clothes together. It'll take awhile, so we can have another drink and watch it."

"Why, Roseberries, ah'm surprised . . ."

"Oh screw it, we haven't got anything to lose really, raght?"

"Yah, ah guess."

"O.K., y'all?"

"*O.K.!*"

The ladle and the paper cups flew around, another three fifths of Myers sunk into the spaghetti pot holding the ice and Zombie mix. Shore water had already begun to just kiss the lip of the jar. I looked around at my classmates to find them looking back. The two-thirty sun turned the world at beach level sort of baby pink. Normally we would have all taken to the water. It was just too goddamn hot to stay solid on a beach at this hour; yet for some reason—group paralysis—we sat glued to some jar that when overflowing would transform even old Shirl, the class Holy Roller—now a somewhat drunk Holy Roller—into a Roman siren. Admittedly we lounged there in unique frames of mind, but I couldn't believe that not one of us, EVEN Shirl, did anything to stop it. And Crabs, who was known and loved by every stray animal in Lime for the aroma that started at armpit level and worked its way up to a case of rotting-teeth halitosis that would have dwarfed the Green Giant— We had always been a hang-loose, relatively laissez-faire class, but an egalitarian, all-men-are-our-brothers class, never. I didn't say a word. And Crabs'd be screwing that paragon of beauty, Bubbles, who was engaged even. I wondered if the girls would make love to the girls and the boys. Oh purple shades of queerness, the South just moved to the Left Bank. I was terrified.

The jar had caught the third go-round of tide. Five of us threw our eyes back and forth to one another, a breeze picked up, Lee reached for the ladle in the zombie pot. Cooking under the now three o'clock sun, thirty sweaty piggies gleamed on their sand spit. Now water spread honey-like, spilling over the lip, making a surrounding dark circle on the sand. The class of '63, honor-bound and in a scramble, sat naked. Our first unified action and our last.

"Ah can't stand it any more. NOw what?"

"It was your ahdea, Grasser, y'all can make the first move."

"Sheeiit."

"Last one in's a queer—"

Sweat-sogged torsos flew to hit the first pocket of deep-enough water, four hundred feet out. Rosemary's outburst had saved us from heat prostration and fates worse than death. We made up for that hour of immobility, splashing and dunking, diving the ten feet or so, racing the flats, throwing sprays of water into the air and on the backs of those nearest. Stanley and I looked at each other in unfathomable relief. From silence we had gone to outbursts of laughter that would have embarrassed hyenas.

"Well, ah'll be goddamned, ah never seen so many naked crackers in mah life."

"Wahoo, wahoo, wahoo; hey, Bubbles, you're about to be dunked."

"Y'all get away from me, Rosie, ROSIE, AIEEEE . . . all raght, muthah, you gonna get it."

Crabs lay floating on his back, imitating a whale blowing water. Selma Anne bit Dirk's ankle under water, so Dirk pushed her to the beach and spanked her. Rosemary had hiccups from laughing. So much for an orgy.

An hour later, most lay on the pushed-together blankets, gasping for air, some asleep—all having wrapped towels around the revelations.

"Shylah, let's take off. Get the blanket."

We moved quickly then, grabbing what was needed for the lovers' retreat from between the sprawled forms of fellow nudists. A path led us away from the beach and toward the center of the island, where short prickly brush jutted from between coral rock and low-lying bush trees and palms formed a natural roof. An old campfire provided us with enough clearing to lay the blanket down, our bodies following.

"Hungry?"

"Yes, as a matter of fact. What did you bring, Stanley?"

"Last of the Cuban sandwiches. Here, we'll share it. God-damn, ah lahk to exhausted myself in that water. That was close, huh? You think we woulda actually gone through with it?"

"No. Well, for a moment, maybe. I don't think I could have done it, not with all those guys. Jesus, for one thing, most of them—well, you know, I've known them for so long. They're like brothers, sort of—big pains in the ass— I mean, it would have been incest, sort of. You know what I mean? And besides, we, uh, you and I, wanted to be together. It was crazy. Rosemary, God bless her for daring us into the water. A perfectly timed out."

"Water felt great, ah about frazzled under the sun by the time we got in. Mah stomach aches from laughin."

"My ribs do . . . Ah, what are you going to do now, Stanley, I mean, now that we're out?"

"Guide. Ah'm mate now, and well, ah'm well enough known and stuff now, I can start takin people out. Maght be hard gettin started. Ah can always pump gas for Mr. Floyd at the Basin."

"You ever want to travel?"

"Ah don't know. Scares me, sort of, you know. Ah never seen snow even, stuff lahk that. That'd be nahce. Gonna get drafted sooner or later; ah maght as well join up sometime in the next few years. Maybe travel then. Who knows? Ooh Moosie, your middle is sunburned, you know that? God, feel that heat."

"Oh yes, I guess I sort of am. Think we'll remember this day, Stanley, when we're sexless and senile?"

"You'll never be sexless and, uh, whatever you said. Ah wish you were gonna stay, Shylah."

"I'll come back, Stanley; nobody ever really leaves this place. That's just the way it is. But for now there isn't what I want here. I've got to go away to get it."

"Get what, for Christsake?"

"It. I don't know, education, different things."

"Well, hell, ah'm just a conch, but doesn't make sense to me that it's much better any place else."

"That's not the point. I know that. I know. This is in a way the best. I don't know, I sort of want to do something."

"You always were thinkin of things all the time. Me, ah guess ah just never thought the things you think. Y'all just don't settle, do yah, Shylah? In one place?—you gotta be in another, girl. You gonna miss this place when it gets real cold up Nawth."

"I don't want to talk about it any more, please. I'm leaving so soon, I don't want to think about it right now."

The last of the bulky sandwich having disappeared, wiping grease on the towels wrapped around us, we lay, side touching side, to look up at sea gulls, cooling late-afternoon clouds newly sprung with the breeze. The straight dark Indian hair, still bowl-cut-looking, with the straight ends standing away from the base of his neck—I put my hand there again, to separate the thick clumps with my fingers. Saline taste around cheeks and ears—more pungent there, and bumpiness of neck and slick, full mouth, mouth that always kissed as a question before rummaging mine like picking through food, then full and open, thick and silent with tongues, with the rest of his body following, becoming like that tongue. Slick, the way dolphins roll over one another, showing off. We moved randomly, our towels pulled open and discarded. Immensely awkward and pleasing, playful, attentive— I arched my back while he slid hands to the spine and lifted until my cheeks rested in his hands like stones. He moved on me and down, kissing my nipples, biting softly, then shaking his hair over my stomach, where the belly button took his lips. My dolphin. My dolphin. I'm hard and shaking. He kisses me there—there at the beginning of slit, runs his tongue down and back, licks me, still holding the rocks of my ass, still swaying his hips and legs on my knees and calves, where I move them to touch his penis, feel under, bringing my knee up slightly, the balls tighten against his skin; reach down, but it's too far to touch. I turn around and turn his body to the side and lick it all over—lick his penis, working down, tasting sweat and that oil under his balls.

"Shylah, can we . . . ah'm gonna come."

"Yes, please, I just finished my period, don't stop, Stanley; for once it's all fine."

I had turned around, side to side again, kissing. We tried to get into one another that way. I moved my leg up and bent like a dancer, and he held his prick to enter, but he kept missing me, the hole, until he fitted—mounted—and I had my hands flat on his ass and his were on my waist. I pushed and it stuck for a second, then went in, up, far up and in, my legs now crossing over my hands over his ass. He shoved one hand down between us and felt me there, like the way he had given me pleasure three years before, three years and short-term virgin. Pushed there at the top between my legs with his prick, and I gripped it, tightened the stinging muscle inside me, and let go and gripped again, until both the top thing and the inside thing made me come, and the flutter came of its own, sucking Stanley within me. He pushed once more and I felt the spasm, his flutter after mine, then relaxing. And we fell back, bodies glistening and soft from contact; lay there watching the sun beginning to glow pinker in the declining day.

"You know what?"

"What, Stanley?"

"In a way ah'm glad we're not the, uh, you know, the first with one another. Ah don't mean to be disrespectful but it was hell, you know, when Lettice and I started. Just that we know what we're doin. No, it's that, it's that it'll always be best with us."

"Yes, I think so. Besides, remember, you made me come first, even before now, before we ever had intercourse. When we'd pet for hours, you know. And that's part of it, isn't it? That's the most important thing, the closeness and the coming."

"So maybe in a way we're first with each other, cause of, uh, coming. Moosie, ah'll never stop lovin you. Ah don't care if you marry Ray Charles or go to the moon."

"Yes, I know. I feel the same way. It's one of the few things I know about myself; that is, that I love you. Don't leave me, Stanley, even if we can't see each other for years, no matter what, be with me. Because I'll—God, I swear it—I'll always be for you."

"Love you, Shylah."

BOOK TWO

1968–1969

He took his vorpal sword in hand;
   Long time the manxome foe he sought—
So rested he by the Tumtum tree,
    And stood awhile in thought.

And, as in uffish thought he stood,
   The Jabberwock, with eyes of flame,
Came whiffling through the tulgey wood,
    And burbled as it came!

One, two! One, two! And through and through
   The vorpal blade went snicker-snack!
He left it dead, and with its head
    He went galumphing back.

12

"Cocksucker! Goddamn you, Larry. My first group show in a decent gallery and you can't be bothered. What's the matter, am I losing my appeal now that I've finally graduated from the ingenue? Listen, I've sat through dinners with those assholes staring at my tits while you hustled sales, never saying a word. God. When YOU have a show, Shy's got to be there, sooo charming, Mrs. Karp, cunt consort. Why? Why. We're married, I thought that meant partnership—what does it mean, Larry, that I have to be your front girl? I hate this—I hate this life. It's a kind of whoring. When we were in Provincetown, in the beginning . . . Oh God, why go over it again? I guess we used to be supportive to each other, that's what I'm trying to say. Look, I did learn a great deal from you, but now, *finally*, at my first chance to have others see my work in a big way, you won't come. Look, I don't care about all that star bullshit. You're still the star. All I care about is having my husband with me at my first show—even if it is just a group show."

"Uh huh, well, look, I said I'd show at the party after. I thought you'd be better off . . ."

"Better off. You're my husband, schmuck. I don't care if you're de Kooning, life is not all auspicious political moves.

2 1 9

Sometimes it means you to me. I'm twenty-three years old, I'm having an exhibition of my work, I want you there. It MEANS something."

"I'm sorry. I've already made other arrangements for the time. Look, dear, how about we go out to Max's? I'm starved, we can talk about it over dinner. There's a party at Stacey Rose's loft tonight. You'd like to go, you know you would."

"Yes, no, I don't know. No, not tonight, you go on. I want to stretch these new canvases."

"Do it tomorrow. I'll be meeting Scarpelli then, you'll have most of the day."

"Fine, while you're with the dealer, I get to play at whatever I want. No, look, you go on. Seriously, I've got this work to do. I'd like to get them out of the way tonight."

"What do you mean, YOU'VE got work to do? Shylah, you know what you've become? A niggardly pain in the ass."

"Good night, Larry."

The two-floor-connecting loft space we shared held an uneasy silence whenever Larry left that way . . . like a basketball court after a losing game. I had never felt a claim to this space. Really, it was his, the sense of it was his, and I felt sometimes as if I had rented rooms in a motel. We had talked about buying a place together, even talked about doing some of the design and building of a house—it kept us occupied with plans for the first year of marriage, but neither of us made a move beyond conversation—the commitment, the amount of time spent away from painting. We remained here.

I had forgotten the mail, which lay on the kitchen table, where Larry's assistant placed it every morning. How could I do that? How could I forget the mail? I looked forward to it— perhaps a letter from Luanne or Selma Anne or a friend in Provincetown.

I picked up my feet and slid.

New turds dropped on the accommodating *New York Times*. I had forgotten our only child, Aardvark, glowering at me from under the sink. Five and a half months' worth of living shit, our champion-sired English springer tied no silver-plated bows around his droppings.

"Hello, Aardvark, y'old fool. No, good doggy, right on the paper. Very good. Just that I forgot the whole fucking place is your personal toilet. Good boy, here, have a dog Yummy, and another."

I took off my boots and dropped them absentmindedly in the sink. They'd do there for a while. And put down fresh paper—the gallery section, as it turned out.

Then the letters, tri-folded announcements of downtown openings, Con Ed bills, a letter from Luanne. Luanne, good.

Dear Shylah,

When are you all coming down to visit? I've got tons to tell you. First off, you'll have to excuse me for not writing. I got remarried. Wish you could have been there to be matron of honor. Jack Curry, you remember him, class of '60—has his own plumbing business now. Loosie's devoted to her new step-daddy. Haven't seen Harry in a year or so, not even for her. He's living in Key West. Hear he got himself a Cuban girl friend and they're both drinking too much. I guess you heard from me before about it. Thanks again by the way for the money. I didn't know what I was going to do and you really saved our skins. Finally Sheriff Carter had me take out a peace bond on him. Anyhow, I hope he finds happiness now.

How are you? I can't believe it's 5 years now. Please come down and stay with us. I always think of you. Guess things are pretty exciting in New York. Are you drawing much? Guess whose back from Nam? Stanley. He married this Vietnamese girl we all call Soy Sauce. (I can't pronounce her name, Soyee or something.) He's got a limp now from shrapnel in his leg. Asked me about you of course. Everybody does. Are you happy? Larry sounds like just your kinda guy, real smart and a little older. I see your dad and Alice once in a while. Guess you all aren't much in touch. Write soon and stay well.

All my luv,
Luanne

Hmm, Luanne. She had enclosed a snapshot of the three of them, taken at the wedding—her hair in a horrendous bubble,

Loosie in a pinafore, and Jack Curry in a ruffled evening shirt. Christ, they looked clean and all-American and posed. I poured out a glass of bourbon and mentally drank to her eyes, which still, despite gloss of photograph and silver eyeshadow, compelled.

The letter saved me from indulging again in despondency, a mood I drew upon with more and more frequency. No longer playful about frustration, I took it on with all the aspects of an armored tank. I'd write her back—now. I went for the paper in the desk, a felt-tip pen that filled out my nervous scrawl, and returned to the kitchen and the bourbon.

Dear Luanne,

Congratulations! Though sorry to hear that Harry's in such bad shape. It's great to know you and Loosie have Jack around, I remember him as always being very together and responsible. God, has it been five years! That's more than the time I lived on Lime. I will try and get down soon, to see you and the gang.

As for me, well, pretty much the same. I've got my first group show coming up next week. What I do now is only vaguely like the drawing you are familiar with. I work on large canvases, abstract patterns, but the colors are somewhat the same.

New York is exciting—theaters and glamour and food. It's another kind of island living entirely—yet it is an island—encapsulated and in this case made out of concrete. Larry and I celebrated our fourth wedding anniversary this past September. It happened that his retrospective (that's collected work from an older artist) opened in Boston around the same time, so there we were. It was pleasant enough; we got away to Provincetown for a couple of days, which is where the whole thing started.

Would you do me a favor, Luanne, please? Call up Stanley or, if you see him—tell him, *Shylah sends her love and congratulations—so you finally got to see a little of the world and brought some of it back with you.* Tell him that exactly, O.K.?

I'll write soon and you do the same— Best love and hello to everybody, kiss Loosie for me.

Shylah

Jesus, five years, why'd I keep thinking three? Back, I'd think back, bourbon and nostalgia. Sometimes just to be maudlin could be entertaining.

The end of freshman year at Radcliffe. Why the hell'd I go there anyway? Because I got in, because it was smart, full of smart people coming from different worlds. I swore I'd never go back—why a liberal-arts college anyway! I barely passed. Cliffies studied, ground themselves into Widener Library stacks, worked well under pressure, made grades. I had no time to paint; I had wanted to be there in Cambridge with the best-minds-of-our-generation schmalz, and all I did was suffer books on art history. They said it would be a grind the first year, I lacked solid educational background; they said my SAT's got me in, while I figured it was the regional quota system working—they got one from the Keys. My trust fund from Mummy's estate paid tuition and keep, summer was my responsibility, old what's-his-name said austerely, rising to his full J. Press-suited five foot four in my initial lecture on future monies. He thought Radcliffe too intellectual anyway—either go to Briarcliff or learn to take shorthand—but, well, I'd do what I wanted anyway, he said, a young lady now, he said, and sought out the ceiling with his eyes. But the summer—the summer was my business financially.

And Fernanda, dorm sister, fellow freshman, arty and haughty and terribly adept at the last-minute cram, suggested in her ennui'ish way we invade Mama's house in old P-town for the summer. Easy. I could waitress at her friend's restaurant, she said—the Whale's Whistle—I could use the extra VW they kept up there. And Mama, Mama was in Germany with the Toad King, as she referred to Mama's husband, new stepfather number two, the Prince. The perfect marriage of American money and the Prussian aristocracy—neither would last through another war. Fernanda the poet—Fernanda said these things so well.

Fernanda's house in Truro, the town adjoining Provincetown, had a kind of Frank-Lloyd-Wright-gone-gross-and-undirectional quality to it. Wood and glass surrounded by pine trees, it flung itself into as many extensions as there were rooms, so that in order to get anywhere one had to face the inevitable corridor to another corridor to another, and a few stairs here and there. Five or so demi-split levels' worth.

Mama collected paintings—contemporary work—but unlike

the Corcoran or Whitney, she hung everything she bought, any-where and without thought to color or neighboring textures. The four bathrooms existed for the hanging of prints, smaller Kulicke-framed Lichtensteins, Picassos, Oldenburgs, Riverses, thrown on the walls side by side or at angles to one another. At first I found staring at Olitski and Dubuffet while trying to push shit a little constipating or just irritating. It went counter to the Introduction to Contemporary Art class I had taken.

But it was easy to grow like the house grew, blasé and arro-gant about it all. I had begun trying canvases using acrylics, for which they had a suitable workroom. I couldn't complain. Fer-nanda wrote poems and I painted. Though I wished I enjoyed her more. How can you enjoy someone who is always on the brink of dropping dead from boredom? I guessed she felt apart and lonely—packing all that contemptuous hyperbole. She liked me though. That I couldn't understand. I was neither that erudite nor that culturally developed. My taste, as she once said, came from my asshole.

I worked the Whale's Whistle Fridays, Saturdays, and Sun-days on the lunch shift, the older Peck & Peck trade who drank Manhattans and old-fashioneds and picked at king crab legs. The place was usually packed and there were always good tips, the work made easy by an abundance of sixteen-year-old bus-boys. We wore godawful mid-calf, imitation whalers' wives' uniforms with white flounce caps pinned to stay center. I smiled at the customers and the customers smiled at me. Averaged seventy-five dollars for twelve hours' work a week. I was flush.

That first month, gushing freedom, was the best. I walked through June in a maniacal daze of well-being. I had begun learning color, learning it on canvas by building and positioning paint in varying sized swatches. Freed from sketching anatomi-cal nudes and crumpled paper, never to return to girls' heads in pastel on velvet, I deified what had been so hastily learned in theory and the contemporary New York School associated with it. Star-struck with modern art. And afternoons. Afternoons I took off and went to the dunes, usually alone—Fernanda hated the beach—and swam and sunbathed and read science fiction

and books on art criticism. Even in high summer the long expanse of beach was never overcrowded—there was always the
possibility of solitude. And unlike the lush, slow tropics, New
England's finest beaches had an austerity and difficulty about
them—the ocean always cold, hard to swim in its roughness, the
constant beating of sand with wave sound and the hills of
wheat-colored dunes enlarging everything, giving a sense of
size to all that yardage of texture. After a year of insides—buildings, books—I began using muscles again, trudging the dunes
and surf-swimming. The first sun streaks came back again in my
hair, I lost weight, and my skin deepened from red to very tan. I
had never looked or thought so well of myself.

Fernanda took me to summer parties—the hard core of returning college kids, most similar to her, only less intelligent, less
rich, or less attractive. She dated the local males, slept with one
of them, but was otherwise pretty much disinterested. Or so she
explained . . . everything breaking down to a kind of convenience. Which gave her that irresistible quality of pedestalism.
She smoked pot before she went to these functions, hating the
booze they offered. I could never get into it, not then, preferring the social hit of rum to the more reflective aspects of marijuana. She didn't push. She never pushed about anything. We
got on, Fernanda and I. For some reason, I suppose it was that
for the first time I needed little that wasn't provided or that I
couldn't get on my own—I had no interest in the jocks from
Dartmouth or the local beach boys. Privacy made love to me,
the hot vague days, the morning concentration, the pleasure of
new paints—and nobody asking for explanations. And I had this
sensual, queenly feeling, which didn't extend very far or cotton
to the locals. Bitch.

I met Larry Karp at the only party Fernanda got up rather
than high for. It was one of those special invite-do's, thrown by
arty neighbors, and for once there would be enough summering
poets, authors, and artists around to saturate Fernanda with
noble thoughts. One poet in particular, Kathryn something or
other, she knew would be there. Fernanda worshipped her,
which in itself or, rather, in Fernanda, was hard to take. She had
come to Harvard once for a month's residency. We had both

gone to a reading, and while I explored the different positions of my own weight-shifting and facial placement, Fernanda hung on the poems about her attempted suicide. The party meant all of this to Fernanda, the grownup art world of pathos and tragedy. God, she almost radiated, and even drank champagne, cracking her mother's best Dom Pérignon supply, while dressing.

Names. Everything became a Name—people weren't actually people, they were their names—disjointed little animal symbols that huddled together and became worlds unto themselves. Larry Karp stood just a tad lower than top drawer in the name department, stood there with the others, handsome as a mad Russian wolfhound, when I entered the hostess's living room. God, to think of it, Larry, the warm-fleshed piece of art, the half-lidded look to me, the smile. It was more or less instantaneous. He needed a girl—one of those lugubrious, indefinable lover/ingenue attachments that Names needed to play in their moat or to be shown with, raised and flying, on feudal occasions. I needed a lover/teacher/bestower of gifts and all good things, and a daddy. We didn't think that way though. One could not fall or dissolve in love and think those things. It's just that those things surrounded us, the business of our habits. In the beginning we were exquisite. Yes, I think so, tenderly exquisite. We did not sleep together immediately—it had time to build—and he saw other women, a few in their late twenties or early thirties—the life of the newly divorced male. When we met in those days, it was to beach a little and swim, maybe have an early supper out before the crush. Or sometimes I'd go over to his place or he'd come to the house and we'd talk about and look at paintings. He was helpful—not just full of opinions but knew and could explain simply what a color or texture would do, things like that—and he loved his work. Not like me, not like a crush on art—like a grandfather, more like a grandfather.

At first it was just that way, about art. I think he struggled with reticence about my age, enough to keep us pretty much to ourselves. He'd take the other women to the dinners and bashes thrown around town. That was at first. At the close of July we were making furtive, half-drunken love on his Mexican rug, and then our privacy ended. The reticence discarded, we were lovers, and to Larry it could best be brought out in a social atmosphere. I moved into his Edwardian rented house, causing Fernanda to drop me flat out. I couldn't blame her.

We partied and dined. In early September we married, not the wedding kind, the elopement J.P. kind. We stayed on past the season, both of us painting, me taking instruction devotedly from Larry, quiet again. I became unbearably domestic, launching four-course French meals—he told me what dishes to prepare, which wines were O.K. I drank martinis before dinner. We made imaginative love at night and quiet love each morning. And walked and talked and, once on the beach, listened to silence. I began taking on his mannerisms, his speech inflections, his taste, even his anger. I found myself becoming critical when he would become critical. In mid-October we returned home, his New York City home, and I started at Cooper Union as a painting major—and quit—and went back again. It was the old school thing, a problem of institutions, but I stuck it out, easier in the married state—a counterinstitution—and I worked, I worked all the time.

But somewhere between art and bedroom the marriage ceased being a marriage; its domestic side ended and it became something else—a heterosexual social function. A hard anger began. Began and built, and became a reason for more work and getting through a day. I didn't even know it for certain, couldn't name it right off. Like an itch. There was all the bubble gum of his life I was stuck in—his friends, soirees, retrospectives, parties. I felt like an addict who hated heroin, needful and disconnected.

I poured myself another glass of the bourbon. I really shouldn't. The bouts with my cystitis were getting worse; the doctor said it came from drinking, nervous tension, and caffeine. If I drank ten cups of coffee in the morning, I had to balance it out in alcohol in the evening. Anything to suck on, the boozy tit. I wished I wouldn't think this way. God, don't. Only everything, even this space, the bums outside on Fourteenth Street, the fag art dealer at dinner last night who spoke French in front of me to Larry and the others, some subtlety between

the osso buco and the endive. Lonely—lonely. The woman who
had been so terribly warm, the one I counted as friend, a young
sculptor living alone who wanted so much to meet Larry Karp.
Ended last month. Some friendship. I had invited her for one of
his dinners, or our dinners, but they were really his. That's
what she wanted, to be invited. So much for friendship. Larry's
new luncheon date these days. Best of luck, Meredith, you can
drown in it. It's not the first time.

Despite my first official exhibition and everything, I hadn't
done work I thought good in a while. But then Larry thought it
was getting better, more acceptably subtle—classier use of
color. Jesus, Shylah, you should have let him go after the first
year. You should have let go—you should have. Hate that word
"should." Hate this city. Hate this series of canvases, hate the
shape—hate French-spouting faggots—hate women sucking up
to me—But no, no, no, can't hate Larry, Larry of the summer—
non-violent Larry—discrepant divine. No, not now; I'd wait
until after the show—don't want to think that way now. My fault
anyway, lousy lay—never liked it now—said it made me weep.
Larry said I was full of shit, frigid—not then, not that summer;
I'd do anything then. Fat, bloat fat, like whale, Shylah-go-on-a-
diet, don't-drink-Shylah, can't-drink. Go stretch the new frames
like you said you were going to, go stretch them. Aw please,
Larry, I'm sorry, I just don't feel like hanging out at Max's, don't
wanna nother party—you could have stayed with me. No, glad
you didn't—makes it work—that's real high-fucking-class
estrangement—you and me in a room.

"Aw fuck. Aardvark, don't be crazy on me; see, I'm not crying
any more, Shylah's fine. Mouse. MOUSE. Go get your mouse,
Varker, go get mouse. And I'll throw it, O.K.? There, good dog.
Go get it, boy, go get it. VERY good, yes. Wanna curl up with
Shy, huh? Wanna go to sleep on the bed with Shy? C'mon, you
can get on the bed. Old Larry's out screwing around, c'mon,
c'mon. Fuck the frames, I'll do them later. Just a little bourbon
for the bedside. What's that Tom Lehrer song, hmm, oh . . .
—'Hearts full of Joy / Hearts full of truth / Six parts gin to one
part vermouth.' "

"Hey, man, what the fuck is this! Get off the bed, pisshead, get off MY bed. What you do, Shylah, invite him on again? Oh Christ, you're terrific, you know that, just terrific. What—you like to stay here alone so you can get in bed with the dog? Shylah, you are fucked up, let me tell you. And I thought you had all this work to do."

"I thought I'd just lie down for a while, you know, then do them later. I thought . . . God, what time is . . . three o'clock! Thought you'd be back early."

"I got hung up. Uh, some old friends back from Paris. Good dope. Wanna fuck?"

"No."

"Hmm, your ass is getting monumental. Look at that."

"Don't, Larry, give me back the sheet. Goddamnit."

"Why don't you lose ten pounds? Do wonders for your sexual capacity, I should think."

"Yeah, O.K. Larry, could you just hold me for a minute? I'm cold, could you hold me?"

"Cold! Hey, baby, it's 85 degrees in here. Wait a minute, let me undress first and get in."

"No, now, just for a second. No, don't do that, Larry, don't, I hate it when you push my arms away."

"Aw shit, wait a moment, will you? There, hmm, come here, hmm, feel that."

"I'm not into it, I just wanted you to hold me. Stop it."

"Go to sleep then, kid. No one's gonna give a shit or rape you tonight. Not with that much bourbon in your snoot. God."

★

The Gallery Soixante-neuf, obnoxious as its name was, had a certain demimonde good reputation about it. The large down-town space showed supposedly "new, far-out" talent. Part of the function, however, was to provide shock value to patrons, a strong reason to buy and establish taste if you were filthy rich, so the more violent or erotic the material the better.

Guy Binet, so utterly soigné as to undermine human functions, had seen my work, partly, I knew, out of deference to Larry, but he could hardly avoid it. My recent canvas, which hung on the dining area's wall, was a brazen seven feet of color. As proprietor of Soixante-neuf, he had the necessary credentials to appear at our table for "business dinner," as we called it.

"But, Shylah, zees ees charming, really, you have such delicacy in your choice of color, charming." And I spoke a little to Guy about the painting, flattered off my ass, as I dished out the cassoulet for the other guests. He had called later to see my studio and then to ask would I care to participate in his show of six young lady painters, and I jumped at it of course. Then, remembering other openings at the gallery, the materials including chicken blood and sweetbreads, the sponge-cake penis, the realistic car accident featuring mass decapitations, the black/brown canvas entitled "Elephant Shitting"—I wondered if my work was not a little inappropriate and old-fashioned.

Larry's assistant, Paul, helped me with the canvases, taking them and me over to the gallery in his van. I was to show two of my larger recent ones, the ones I wasn't sure of, plus keeping with Guy prints and the few drawings I'd done, the kind of thing he could sell.

"Yes, over there, Paul. I think. Wait a minute, I'll check with Guy."

"Ah, Shylah, merveilleux. Right over to ze left there. I sink zat space is good to your work, don't you? Right on ze angle."

"Yes, O.K., fine, just leave them there. Thanks, Paul."

"Sure. You all set? I've got to split. Larry wants to . . ."

"Yes, all set. See you later on."

Morning is closed shop for Soixante-neuf except for setting up. Most of the show was already hung for the opening that night. Sunday. Two hours of pissing around, putting my paintings up, switching the two around. Guy suggested lunch at Benito's, a short walk in the March early thaw to Little Italy. Zuppa di pesce and a bottle of Soave. I ate because I was scared.

"Are you feeling good about your first group show, Shylah?"

"Nervous, I guess."

"Ah, but you'll have Larry to hang on to. Zis ees really easy.

And you are, you know, ze loveliest of ze artists, zis ees true, yes?"

"No. Larry's not coming and, no, I am not so lovely these days. Listen, do you really think the space is . . ."

"He isn't coming? But I thought . . ."

"No, he has, uh, some emergency, you know, and, uh, well, something came up, that's all. He'll try and make the party after."

"Sheet."

"Well, you know, he thinks, probably rightly so, that his presence and everything—well, you understand. It's my first go-round and we think it's better that I'm by myself."

"Of course I assumed zat he would be there."

"So what the fuck's the difference whether he comes or not?"

"I told zeeze people he would be there. Sheet. Shylah, you ask Larry to come. Zis ees peculiar he doesn't come to your opening."

"I have to go, Guy. How much on the check?"

"No, eet's my pleasure, please. You tell Larry eet's only right he come."

I decided to walk the mile or so back to our place rather than cab it. Larry would be there. Larry would draw me a bath, sit on the toilet, and talk to me.

"Hi, love, how'd it go? Get your paintings up?"

"Uh huh. Christ, that Binet is such an opportunist, Larry. I thought he was going to cancel out when I told him you weren't going to make it."

"Oh, so you're finally catching on. Example always helps. Can I get you a drink?"

"Uh no, I want to be fresh for this—make yourself one and come talk to me while I take a bath. Please."

"Of course, angel."

Larry's concession to my needs, when we renovated the second loft, drilling a hole between the two floors for a staircase, was a sunken tub large enough for two, with a Grow lamp tropical jungle off to the side. Though we rarely bathed together

2 3 1

any more, I still enjoyed the extra space. I shed my jeans and T-shirt, throwing them into the overflowing hamper, checked in the mirror the new underarm hair growth I hadn't quite gotten used to. Into the running hot water I shoveled out a load of blue bath-oil beads, which turned the water aqua—sort of plastic Caribbean—to go with the flora, then settled in under the steam.

"Jesus, how can you stand water that hot? Fucking freaky. Look at your hand, it's all red."

"Hmm, cause it relaxes me. Why don't you come in, Larry?"

"Not with the family jewels. Here, I'll wash your back instead . . . there."

"What time'll you be there tonight, I mean after, at the Schneigals'? Please come early, I don't want to stay long; then maybe after we could go out, just us. I'm kind of crazy with this nervousness."

"I don't know. Nine. Maybe ten. It depends."

"I'll be faint by ten. Look, just this once, let's tend to my business. Nine, can you be there by nine?"

"Shylah, stop being a baby, you'll make out by yourself. Good Lord."

"It's not that. Is that what being a baby is . . . Shit, I'm not going over this again. Listen, I can understand your not coming to the show—all things being unequal and so on—but after, you know, when I come back from the whole opening thing, I want to share it with you. I don't know, Larry, it makes sense to me. I'm sorry. I think you're being an absolute bastard. Don't come at all."

"You know, Shylah, you're becoming very hard. Makes me less than interested. Who wants your ball-breaking? Puts me off. You're losing that softness you had when I met you, that dreaminess—I guess tenderness, like in the morning cooking breakfast."

"Larry, for Christsake. Please, not that again. Let me grow, will you? Whatsah mattah, pumpkin, you losing status? Don't you think my, uh, entrance into the art world is a good thing? How long could you carry around the burden of Big Daddy anyway? Sort of makes the marriage more equal . . ."

"Bullshit."

"Oh, bullshit to you."

★

The gallery was already crowded when I arrived. Mostly it was our friends, other young painters, and maybe a quarter of it other dealers and potential buyers. Fernanda had come and we greeted one another semiformally. She had forgiven me after my marriage, had come to New York full of poems and invitations after graduating. We saw one another once in a while, "luncheon dates," as was the way, and occasional dinner parties. She had sustained one breakdown already for which she was now recuperating with a four-day-a-week therapist and stabilizing drugs. Fernanda's beauty had burgeoned like an atomic blast, her tall litheness and that thick road of hair she wore loose to her ass. She had become the natural master of high-cheeked, non-being stares. For all that ethereal grace, she still wallowed in boredom like the clumsiest of water beasts.

"So your first, uh, thing, Shylah. Thought I'd drop by. Who is that asshole who runs this gallery? I thought he'd drool on my boots. Ooh, God."

"Yes, I know what you mean. Guy Binet. Actually, it isn't so bad. A lot of those people are that way. In a sense it's easier with him just because he's so obvious, you know, out front with that dreadful hungry-wolf way about him. And he's good about new talent. This gallery is pretty experimental."

"Baloney. What's experimental about tits and ass? Have you noticed a certain incongruity between your work and the rest . . ."

"Yes, it seemed a little peculiar. So O.K., who's kidding whom?"

"You know, I think he's a coke freak—acts that way—there's the hardness, that stare."

"Maybe. Oh, hi, nice to see you, Beryl, John, thank you. Yes, he's fine. No, couldn't make it. Well, maybe at the party after. Good to see you."

The conversations had begun and I took off so they'd at least be in the shadow of my work. Guy moved over toward me—I looked for the coke stare Fernanda had talked about—she had a point. Also slightly fey in his Meladondri suit and scarf tied drunk-cowboy style. Oh hell, who cared if Fernanda had a point?

"Shylah—isn't she marvelous— Come, I want you to meet the Galoons. Mrs. Galoon, Elaine, expressed interest in your South II. Hurry; come, my sweet."

The Galoons expressed their interest in the earnest, sincere, profound-way-about-art that simply defied comment. They both looked like survivors of an attack by Emilio Pucci: pink, black, violet, plum, and crimson run amuck. I did try to look as preoccupied in theory, as casual and monosyllabic in reply—imitation. Imitation. They were pleasant enough, were experienced with openings, were experienced with talking to young artists. I sunk into myself. Scary, this public life. A short chitchat with them hastened my exit to the subtler joys of the party after.

The Schneigals had a townhouse in the West Village, one of those narrow four-flights-of-modern-furniture buildings. I liked them. They had about them this spatial quality—expansive and relaxing. Whit, as she was called—maybe fifty, solid, attractive, and smart, not in the factual sense but in the common-sense sense—and I had been friendly for over a year now. Boyd was O.K. too, not so sensitive, but funny. Larry and I had had this reciprocal dinner thing going with them, and the four of us entertained one another.

"Hey, Shylah, how's it going? You look a little done in."

"Oh, I am a little, I guess."

"Where's Larry? Whoops, I shouldn't ask, should I . . ."

"I don't know, Whit, beats the shit out of me."

"Here, can I get you a joint? Oh, that's right, wait a minute— George, may I have a large bourbon on the rocks . . . there you go. Hey, it went very well; you got a terrific number of people in the old greaser's gallery. I liked your South I and II."

"I might have a buyer on II, the Galoons . . ."

"Terrific . . . except that they buy everything. Oh hell, that's great. Shylah, have you met Coward and Chris Matricof . . ."

I made a quick exit to the john, carrying my drink and cigarettes with me. Locking the door, I sat down on the rabbit-fur toilet cover for a little relaxation. That first hit of whiskey mellowed me, took a little of the manic feeling away. It seemed to be going O.K., I had that removal thing coming on again—I found it difficult talking with people, making words for conversations that would be mutually forgotten in ten or fifteen minutes. Perhaps there would be an exception this time though, myself and without the gloss of Larry—with a little more bourbon maybe I could fake it. I chased my yawn with the liquor and muscled up to go out to the swells.

"Shylah, we got a problem."

"What's the matter, Whit?" It was going on ten—I was getting ready to leave.

"Larry's here. He's in one of those, you know, those crazy things he gets into when he's really blasted. Would you mind taking him home? He just poured a drink down the editor of *Art American*'s dress, and I don't think that's the end of it."

"You know, tonight I'd most expressly like to say no, I really would. Sure, O.K., I'll get him home, was leaving anyway."

"It's a shame, Shylah, I understand that. You really could have used his support. I think it's that he's freaked out with your success, don't you agree? He'll adjust."

"Maybe, and then maybe I won't. Good night, Whit. I'll call you. Thanks for all of this."

Usually I didn't mind Larry's once-a-month obnoxiousness—he was easy enough to pour into a cab—but tonight . . . What a motherfucker to do this tonight. He knew I'd wait for him and starve as well. Back in our loft there was nothing to eat except eggs. Eggs were not what I had in mind. So for once I dumped drunk Larry at our doorstep, got back into the cab, and continued on to Max's, not exactly appropriate, me-on-my-solo-own, after all the festivities, but I needed a big dinner and I could charge there.

"Shylah, Jesus, what are you doing alone tonight? You just opened."

"Hi, Paul, sit down. Have you eaten?"

"No, can I join you?"

"Please. Oh, I was starved and, uh, Larry's exhausted, so I thought I'd have a leisurely dinner here."

"Uh huh, right. You know, I thought your paintings looked great up there. Really. As far as I was concerned, the show was yours."

"You really thought so, huh? Well, thanks, Paul, and thanks again for helping me move them over to the gallery. Guess Larry keeps you hopping during the week."

"Well, it comes and goes. He, uh, he hasn't been spending that much time in his studio lately. Uh, Shylah, maybe you'd like to see my work; you know my loft's right around the corner."

"Sure, Paul, but just because he's fucking around doesn't mean I am. I'd like to see your work—not tonight though, I'm glutted. Oh shit. I'm sorry, really. Didn't mean to come down so hard. Just that it's been heavy all evening."

"So I guessed. But I really wasn't hitting on you— What I meant was, I hope you do drop by sometime to see my sculpture. Anyhow, feel like working out after dinner? There's a group playing upstairs, they're pretty good."

"Oh sure, why not. That's a good idea."

The Popsicle Insomniacs in full decibel sound system were enough to make a school for the deaf stand up and salute. To drown in music one must be overwhelmed. I was dead drunk by our second dance and overwhelmed.

"Noooo, don't wanna go home, Paul. I've got all this energy."

"Shylah, I don't think I can dance any more. You don't look too well."

"Waitress, can I have another double Jack Daniel's on the rocks?"

"Oh, Shylah, come on, that stuff is awful. Get stoned or something, but don't drink that shit."

"One more, Paul, one more; then maybe I'll be able to sleep . . ."

★

"Ooh, ow, God. What did I do?"

"You passed out at Max's. You're at my place."

"Bathroom, where is it . . . sick."

"Here, come on, I've got you, right in there."

"Feel a little better now?"

"Feel a lot lighter. I guess I won a prize, huh, Paul?"

"I'd say your liquor bill at Max's went up by about twenty bucks. It's O.K. I just think it's rotten that on that particular night you had to be so unhappy. You did a lot of talking, Shylah, and you practically held a half-Nelson on me when I got you here and tried to get you a glass of water."

"Don't tell me. Did I rape you or did you me?"

"The only thing that got raped was that pillow. Look at the way you're holding it."

"Jesus, I'm a mess, aren't I? Shylah, stop crying, stop it. You didn't ask for this, did you, Paul?"

"No, go ahead, only me and the walls. Aw, Shylah, God, you're so talented and decent. Here's some Kleenex; it's O.K., let it out."

"Can I take a shower? I feel so grubby— Would you mind if I stayed with you for a while? I don't want to go back to his . . . to our place. What time is it anyway?"

"Seven-thirty, and yes. I'll make a pot of tea. You should take a couple of vitamin C."

"God, you mean . . . . I thought it was still night."

The shower I stayed under, steaming and turning the skin rose, brought me into focus again. What it was that got me now, I didn't like to admit to myself. I had to get out of this thing. It wasn't a marriage, it wasn't a love affair; it was financial dependence. My inheritance had dwindled to a thousand dollars or so. I'd been running with Larry so long now and there still remained that frustrated love for him that had been born and died after the first year. I didn't know if I could bury the corpse. Our Provincetown summer had been so much, first flight, and now there remained a last feeling of whatever that perfection was.

What do I do? Get a lawyer, right? Do I want alimony? I'd have to get a job if I didn't get some sort of support from him. My studio was a part of our loft, but it was his loft, wasn't it? I'd be the one to move out, I knew that. Yes, I wanted support. I didn't want to rip him off, but I wanted support for a while. I wanted some of the rich art lucre. I'd earned it, I'd earned another summer on the Cape. Oh Christ, Larry, I don't want to let go. And this heat; I can't fuck you the way you are, but I'm so hungry for it all the time. And I'm so tired of doing it to myself, tired of it.

"Hey, my shitty old kimono never had such class. How do you feel?"

"Much better. Oh, tea, great."

"How about some breakfast? Could you handle it? I make a spectacular omelette aux fines herbes—meaning oregano, really."

"Yes. I'll look around while you cook, O.K.? There's a certain six-foot object over there that needs closer inspection. Hey, I like this—uh—what's the material, car parts?"

"Yup, I weld scrap materials together, then use a metallic paint over them. I've been doing this for a while. It's nothing new, of course, material-wise, but what I'm trying to do is give them a soft edge, you know, an almost romantic cast to them. Kind of passion but hard but soft. Do you understand?"

"I understand it better when you don't talk about it."

"Come on, Shylah, your omelette is tempting my roaches."

"Wow, delicious. Hey, did you get any sleep last night, with all your administering?"

"Sure, uh, I don't have a couch so I slept beside you. Once you'd stopped talking in your sleep, you didn't move. You curl when you sleep like a little kid; that's what you looked like."

"God, don't say that. I could sleep another ten hours."

"Go ahead. I don't have to work or anything. I know you're doing a lot of thinking; I mean, you look like you are, anyhow. Stay here."

"What's the . . . I mean, how come you're being so great, Paul? You've barely said two words to me in the past."

"I like you, Shylah. I have for a while. Larry's a great artist and all that, I mean, well, you know, he is in his way one of the best—teacher as well. I like being around him for that matter. But it's a lousy scene for you, it just is. You know, it's been going on for a while. I mean, you're special; it bugs me to see you put down like that. Man, that time you all had that dinner, you know, it was when I was first working for Larry, and I went over and told him how much I liked you and that I thought the painting in the dining area was pretty good. Put him right up the fucking wall. What kind of reaction is that about someone you supposedly love? It's bullshit. I don't know, it's none of my business. Maybe things'll get better for you. I just—oh, never mind. Jesus, you really cry a lot."

"Would you, uh, would you just hold me for a minute? Just, I need . . ."

"Yes, yes, I'll hold you. God."

So warm, I wanted him then. Someone my age, less complex, I wanted that touch, I wanted him to give it to me, wanted to give tenderness to somebody that way again.

"Shylah, don't start that if you aren't serious about it. I'm no celibate and I'm no Dr. Kildare either."

"Please."

I had nothing on but the kimono and he wore only jeans. Lying back on the bed, it felt so good, and warm. Paul had more physical warmth than Larry with his wiry body. There was more to his physique, a certain suppleness. And Paul wasn't accomplished. I had grown tired of Larry's programmed fucking calisthenics. Paul was still finding out, and his hands, calluses and all—I liked it. I liked the roughness over me—over my breasts; funny I knew more about it than he did, I liked that too for a change. I liked having that assurance. I'd make it good for him.

His cock was bigger than Larry's and younger—the skin smoother—the hair surrounding it softer. When I went down on him, when I gave him head, it occurred to me I had let myself do what I wouldn't do for Larry, not after the first year. Not when everything became crazy. Paul moaned and pulled me from there and wanted to put it inside. I slid my body over his, still fresh from the shower, put my hand back to it, and held it long enough to squat over and lodge it in my cunt. He came almost right away, before I had had much pleasure, but it was O.K., it was O.K. I got off watching him. And he wanted to play again—he had all that going for him.

"Shylah, you're fantastic, I want more and more and . . ."

"More and more and I like adultery with you. Oh yessss, kiss me there, yes, do it, c'mon, do it. Hmm."

I panted so loud he stopped—I scared him—so I had to tell him it was O.K. I was really loving it, which made him feel like the stud he so organically was, and he went back down and then, when I was coming, he entered me again from the top and fucked me until he came again and my head lay over the edge of the bed and I felt like I'd won some sort of Olympic game.

"Oh goddamnit, Paul, do you know what you are, the ultimate sanctuary. I'm actually feeling, with this hangover and all, better than I have for an age."

"Want to take the day off, Shy, want to just screw around? We could, you know, do something; hey, how about going over to Brooklyn? We could walk around Prospect Park, go to the museum, maybe go down to the Heights and eat some Middle Eastern stuff. It's been pretty mild out; I've got a couple of bikes, we could trek over the old Brooklyn Bridge."

"Yes, I'd love to trek over the old Brooklyn Bridge. Just you and me, kid, and the spirit of old Walt limping across. May I borrow a sweater?"

"You can borrow me and the sweater."

"You're on."

★

"Where the fuck have you been? Man, you are something. And what about your dog, huh, who's goin to clean up after your dog?"

"I understand Aardvark to be equally ours. I have in the past done about 50 percent over my share; I'd say my conscience is clear. And you can go fuck yourself, dear heart."

"Hey, man, you come home—it's five-thirty, you know, we're supposed to go over to Conrad's— You don't even phone . . ."

"Leave me alone. You go to Conrad's."

"Hey, you know, you can be replaced."

"I assumed I already had been. What difference does it make?"

"No, don't go off to the bathroom. For God's sake, I want to talk about this, Shylah."

"Funny, it's usually the other way around. I don't want to talk about it."

Walking into the bathroom, MY bathroom, taking the can and giving the spider plant some water, I peeled off clothes, letting them stand in puddles on the tile, drew the bath with the blue in it, plopped in, and settled down with a back issue of *East Village Other*, getting it wet around the edges. Aardvark sat at the tub side, so I could pet him and read at the same time.

"Where were you, Shylah? Answer me."

"When I dumped you here, I took off for Max's—remember, we were going to have a quiet dinner together. So anyhow, I went and ate."

"Who'd you spend the night with?"

"I stayed out, we closed Max's. The Popsicle Insomniacs jammed after. You know, I hung out. Like yourself, Larry, like yourself."

"Hey, Shylah, I've known you going on five years and you don't hang out until five-thirty the next afternoon. You can't stand hanging out!"

"Look, all I know is that right now I can't stand you. Get out of here, Larry, just go. I wouldn't become you at Conrad's, that's for sure."

"What the hell is wrong, Shylah? I don't understand what this is about."

"I know you don't understand, Larry. I honestly believe you."

"Look, uh, we've both been under a lot of tension. Why don't we get away, huh? How'd you like to spend a week or so in Al-munécar, like we used to. We should really get away from all this. You'd feel a lot better in the sun."

"No, I can't."

"What do you mean YOU can't? You don't want things resolved between us?"

"No, I don't. I don't think I do want things resolved between us any more, at least not the way you mean it. Hey, look, you've been fucking around now for two years, nothing big, mind you, just enough to assert your total independence from marriage. Now I'm fed up, not so much with that as with the fact you find it so necessary to your ego to put me down. That's bullshit—you make me into a post-facto masochist—an alcoholic one too."

"You love me, Shylah, I know you do."

"Sure I do, so what?"

"But I love you, you know, I'll always love you. Be reasonable, you're so possessive."

"Bullshit."

"Aw, baby, look, I'm sorry about last night. I just tied one on, that's all. Nothing new. Come on, let me get in the tub with you."

"No, absolutely not. And I know you're sorry about last night. Larry, I want to finish it. You know, split up, make some other arrangement; this isn't working out and you can't be that dense not to know it. After all, you complain I won't fuck you, I complain you don't take care of my needs. We're a mess. Even Aardvark's neurotic. Look at that, he's shaking again."

"Goddamn you, Shylah. I can't deal with you when you get bitchy like this. You're right, you wouldn't become me at Conrad's. I'll see you later, early tonight, I promise."

Larry went downstairs to his study, for that martini in silence before his dinner engagement. The water oiled and caressed my neck. Wasn't that the way it was? I tell him I want to split up and he brushes the words off with the kind of gesture men make when a woman's menstruating. But for the first time I didn't get uptight or frustrated about it. I didn't know how; it terrified me to think, but I wanted out. I wanted my own place. I wanted to be alone and without all this. It wasn't worth it.

My skin had begun to pucker and get ridgy with softness. The palms, the miniature orange tree Larry had given me for Christmas, the gardenia and coleus—my treasures put me of a mind to call Lime, to call Luanne; she'd like that. Maybe Daddy and Alice too. No, no, I couldn't. God, tired.

"Oh Varkie, what the hell am I going to do with you, huh? You're so fantastic. You deserve a better fate than two neurotic horrible married artists. Any stable animal would be housebroken by now. You're still cocking your leg at the stretchers.

Wanna play mouse? Where's your mouse, Aardvark, where's your mouse? Mousie, mousie."

Guilt, the dog gave me that. What the hell business did I have having a dog in this city with us? I got dressed and found the training leash. Undoubtedly my spouse had not taken him out.

"Eh, linda, ay qué Liiinda, chi, chi, chi."

"Hey, nice, beautiful; hey, Miss America, brush yoh hair."

Fourteenth Street at dusk was a giant walking hard-on, all colors, creeds, and horns. I never got used to it. Never. For that I had only avoidance. Even the old bum, who bled and pissed and shat and cried and drank and laughed on the stoop before our door—I couldn't deal with it. I used to give him money, which infuriated Larry when he found out. And he was right. Or partially right. If a bum had money, he'd get rolled before he could saturate himself in enough cheap sauterne. Then for a while I'd give him sandwiches, shit like that, until I saw him trying to sell the stuff to another guy for a drink. Bums who hit Fourteenth or the Bowery were last-stage terminal. The ones I had spoken to mostly came here from elsewhere, many from Kentucky; many had been involved with animals, horses mostly, though some had dogs. Country men. What does one do when a suicide runs his course in front of the passing world? Nothing. One does nothing. One stops being self-righteous. Right? Shut up, Shylah, stop it.

"Oh good, good dog, nice big dump right in the street."

Inside again, I fed Aardvark, passed up a drink for a beer— good solid carbohydrates supposed to be good for hangovers— and more vitamin C. I finished reading *East Village Other*, which was saying something about my reading endurance, and lay on the bed with the phone. Luanne, oh Luanne.

"Hello, uh, is Luanne there? . . . Hey, Luanne, it's Shylah, thought I'd call."

"Shylah. Mah Lawd, Shylah. When y'all comin down? It's good to hear your voice. You all raght?"

"So so. What's new; tell me about yourself and the Keys."

"Well, Jack and me and Loosie are doin O.K., ah moved, Shy, we're down by Turtle Beach now . . . yeah, same phone . . . oh, ah just got your letter and called Stanley. You got him all excited. Selma Anne's 'bout ready to drop her third nuisance upon the world. She and Beau aren't doin too good together these days. Bubbles and Ralphie are doin O.K.; she's turned into the perfect mother; she better be, she got four—we tried to talk her into gettin her tubes tied. Rosemary's wild as ever—no kids—and Cindy left, y'all know that? She a lieutenant or something in the Waves. Oh God, I forgot, Dirk got himself killed about six months ago; he and some guys from Key West were out ridin around, you know, drunk and everything—man, they tried to pass on Bahia Honda Bridge on the really high part—goin seventy—eight people, two cars demolished. It was a mess. Ah heard the sirens goin for an hour. They had to shut off the bridge, wreckage and bodies—you know, pieces of bodies all over the place, one car stuck in the side of the bridge around the rail. Sheriff says it was the worst-lookin accident we've had in the lower Keys yet. Real hard for his mom and dad, ah know. Dirk was the only boy. Otherwise, we been doin some partying on Peacock lately, takin the kids and stuff for the day. Everybody wonders when y'all comin down, Shylah; it's goin to be one big party, ah'll tell yah that much. Oh, guess what, y'all fall off your chair. Palm View got itself integrated last year. Ah lahk ta died; they got ten of them now, clear through, even first grade. Guess you win your bet, Shy. Hey, what's with you? Is that Larry mean to you? Nuthin lahk that, ah hope."

"Well, not in the usual sense. I mean, he doesn't hit me or withhold things. He's really quite generous in some ways."

"Well, what the hell's the matter, girl? Honeymoon doesn't last forever, y'all know."

"Yes, you're so right. It's hard to explain. I'm feeling a little powerless and frustrated. It's his world."

"Ah don't know if ah understand what you mean, Shylah. Lahk he puts you down?"

"In a way, very much so. Oh, it's O.K., probably will work itself out. I just wanted to call."

"Well, y'all get your ass in gear and come down; we'll cheer you up."

"Oh, I feel good, really. Sure, I'll be down one of these days.

Hard to just pick up and go. Look, give my love to everyone, hi to Loosie, and mostly love to you. O.K. I'll stay in touch."

I hung up and rolled over on the bed, and then realized that I had been trembling. Trembling because I hadn't voiced my discontent over our marriage before. This was the first time, if only in dribbles. The thought of its logical end—leaving Larry—terrified me. Like leaving earth or something. He had been my ground, essentially making all the decisions, instructing, paying the bills, bestower of love when he was so inclined. If it was love. Did we love? Yes, I guess we loved, whatever the hell that means. Differently. We loved differently. Larry loved on plane A and I loved on plane B. Maybe A and B had been AB and AB when we met, that summer we met. Oh Jesus, I didn't know how to leave, I didn't know how. What the hell comes of leaving your ground? Mostly the business of it scared me, some yawning void that spoke in incomprehensible terms. There was no talking about it; I couldn't talk to him. He didn't connect to it, he put it down as bitchiness. So what do I do? Start packing? What DOES one do, go to a hotel? Get a lawyer first. Fernanda. Maybe I could stay for a while with her. I'd call. She had an absolute corner on independence; she'd know. Aardvark had curled up over the phone, growling now as I placed him elsewhere.

"Hi, Fernanda. It's Shylah. Oh O.K., show went well and everything. I'm glad you came, though we didn't have much chance to talk."

"What's happening in your life, Shylah? You looked terrible at your opening. I figured you aren't as optimistic as you used to be."

"Well, not exactly. I'm, I guess, optimistic, but even fools can be miserable, right. Right? Fernanda, I, uh, I've decided to split, you know, leave Larry. I know, I know, I've been out of touch. I figure I've been out of touch for three years. Anyhow, it occurs to me that I really am unprepared for this sudden independence. I just don't know anything. What I wanted to ask you among other things is do you know the name of a lawyer?"

"God, you don't waste any time. Sure I do. Tom Feldstein,

MU 7–2853. I've got it memorized. It's his office, I mean, you can't reach him until tomorrow morning. He doesn't beat you or anything?"

"No, it's not that kind of thing."

"Come stay with me for a while. I have a hell of a lot of space. You can choose between two bedrooms. I mean, it might do you good for a couple of weeks to have a place to crash. I'm no pro about marriage—the thought of it nauseates me—but I'll help however I can."

"I don't know, Fern, I got a problem in that we have this puppy, Aardvark, and if I don't care for him, he'll go unattended, if you know what I mean."

"So bring the dog. I assume he doesn't eat piranha fish. Those are my little babies."

"Christ, you mean the South American compulsive eaters? No. I thought it was the other way around."

"I have only a few in the tank. I feed them my relatives. Seriously, grab your shit and Aardvark. God, whatever possessed you to name a . . . Well, anyway, grab everything and take a taxi. I assume the old man is out of the loft now. So do it, Shylah."

"Yes, uh, O.K., I will. I will do it. I'll be there as soon as I can. Yes, I have the address. Ciao."

Logical. To just leave. Isn't that the first thing? To leave. I did tell Larry I wanted a divorce; he passed it off. What else is there to say? Traveler's checks, bank checks, cash, clothes, toothbrush, daily journal, brush, cigarettes thrown into a leather traveling bag, and the dog, dog food and water bowl in my satchel. Fifteen minutes passed. God, you can leave someone in just fifteen minutes? I started to write a note—I had always written notes to Larry, where I'd be and telephone number. A matter of habit. I tore up the paper. I had already said it. If I didn't leave a note and he didn't know where I was, maybe then it would be clearer; drive it into him by silence. My hands felt oily, though I was shivering. One look around the loft. Did I remember everything? Nothing. Nothing to get nostalgic about.

Fernanda lived in rich squalor. Her apartment on Riverside Drive, in one of the older buildings there, sprawled around corners into large, high-ceilinged rooms, eight of them by my count. There had been no attempt at interior decorating or cleaning. Fernanda belonged to the pillow school—she could have bought up Design Research and Bloomingdale's blindfolded. The living room had one sawed-off table, Japanese-style, an early painting of mine on the wall, and all those bright, cheery pillows. The kitchen established her philosophical modus operandi—a juicer, a nut grinder, a blender, a shelf full of vitamins, a shelf full of vegetable cookbooks, and, in the bin, a four-year supply of fresh Chinese cabbage. My room, as Fernanda designated it, contained a mattress, one writer's desk and chair, and copies of the Bhagavad Gita and *Mad* magazine. Candles were everywhere, vying for space with the accumulations of dust. Only then did I feel a pang—seeing the harsh, paint-chipped room—a pang for the lushness of my thinking room, the john with its jungle and sunken tub.

"Want to smoke a little, Shylah?"

"Uh uh."

"Oh, I forgot. How about wine, or I have some brandy?"

"No, uh, no thanks, I've been drinking too much anyway."

"I've got some mu tea I made today."

"Mu tea's fine. Fernanda, you lead a healthy life. Am I so decadent then?"

"Nope. You aren't decadent, Shylah. That's one thing I'll say about you. You may be surrounded by it, but you're about as decadent as a tree frog."

"Oh shit, I don't know. How did I ever get to this, huh?"

"You married it. I wonder how you stuck it this long. You're much too egomaniacal and basically sound to be an artist's wife, especially since you're an artist yourself. Know what I mean?"

"I'm finding out. I guess I hung on because we were so good together at first, those first few months."

"Larry struck me as a person who gets off by annihilating women."

"Aw, c'mon, you sound like a fucking textbook. What the hell does that mean?"

"That he hates women, you know, so he gets around it by making them as doll-like as possible. I knew Larry from summers I spent in Truro when I was still in high school. He even went out with my mother for a while. Yup, you didn't know THAT, did you? He's a very intelligent, charming guy, Shylah, but he's too armored for any real feelings to come through. I think he even had a thing for me when he was sleeping with Mother."

"Yes, but everybody has a THING for you, Fernie, and it's sure to bring out your disdain."

"Maybe, but still, on the sliding scale of things, I don't know, I guess I just feel contempt for that kind of phony paternalism. But genius I guess he is, at least in one respect. Anyhow, what are you going to do, call Tom? See if he's free to see you tomorrow. At least you'll find out something about economics and marriage. You never COULD count, Shylah."

"Yes, I guess that's the first thing. Right now, I seem to be having a physical reaction to all this—I'm sweating and cold at the same time. Zombie-like."

"But you made the decision. And that should put you in a pretty powerful frame of mind."

"It does. I'm scared shitless and I want my mama. Goddamn her."

13

"Merry Christmas."

"Merry Christmas, Shylah. Come in, come in, you must be freezing."

"You couldn't have picked shittier weather, Zoe. Rick, God, so long since I've seen you both. We finally got our Christmas back together after—what has it been?—eleven years, I guess."

"Zoe says you're living alone now—that true?"

"Yes, true."

"So who's taking care of you now?"

"I'm taking care of myself, Rick, just as you are."

"Hmm. Not exactly a parallel situation. Have you heard from Dad?"

"No. Not for years, and you, Rick? Zoe? You heard from Dad?"

"Uh uh, once in a while a note from Alice, got a Christmas card."

"Nice fucked-up family we have. Oh Zoe, you've got the same bulbs on the tree. You kept them all this time. Are we having a traditional Christmas Eve then, with all the trimmings?"

"Forget it, Shylah. Why dredge it up after so long? We'll just make this a reunion of sorts. So if nobody's taking care of you these days, what are you doing to make money?"

"I get some from Larry under the terms of the separation, some—a little left from the trust. Hopefully I'll be able to get some sort of teaching job."

"Perhaps you'll get back together again, so that won't be a problem. Although he never struck me as the type for you to permanently settle down with."

"I guess maybe I don't want to SETTLE any more—it's so, uh, unsettling, in my case. Besides, we won't get back. Let's talk about something else, like you, for instance, Rick. How's your writing coming?"

"Oh, I stopped, let's say, for a while. I've been accepted into a doctoral program at Columbia. You know, you might think about going back and getting your master's."

"In painting? Never."

"It'll make things easier for you."

"Never. I'm no art academician."

"You'll have a hard time without advanced degrees."

"Terrific. I'll have a hard time without a husband and without a master's. So I'll have a hard time."

"Jesus Christ, you really like to make things hard on yourself—you're damn maniacal about it."

"Hey, Rick, leave me alone about it, O.K.? Please, this is Christmas. Let's talk about food or go sledding, or anything. I mean, look, we're all together again—that's the main thing, isn't it?"

★

Brothers. And brotherly carping and rejection—a low blow to the matriarchal groin. I had kept this wild dream throughout parental siege and into heterosexual feuding that somehow my "brothers" would come through, that this was the ultimate trilogy—straight out of Bibleland. Only it didn't work that way—I wanted it to work and it didn't.

Nine months out of marriage—what now? I drove Fernanda's VW down the Connecticut Thruway as if my brothers were lying under the tires. Cold cocksuckers—all of whom I loved maniacally, desperately dreaming I could somehow amputate that love and live well without it. It had been O.K., pretty good in fact, at first, after I left Larry. I'd rented a loft, spent time fixing it up, kept frantically busy—then entombed myself in the effort—worked. Worked constantly. And the paintings. Large and frightening. I could taste the hate. Nothing worked that wasn't severed or surreal. Red—I used four shades of red almost exclusively. Large, thick swatches of it. Red Fortress I, Red Fortress II, Red Fortress III. I had lost my sense of humor.

And then this idea of seeing my loving brothers—it had been something looked forward to—after years, something new from an old bond—what a waste, Shylah. Why not just give up? You failed, you're miserable, Shylah; there's no foundation to stand on. Maybe Larry. Maybe I won't ever have what is my own to have. I had missed the habit of him. I had stayed away long enough. I would call. I would call after New Year's. Then maybe I could get a little fucking sleep. Jesus help me.

★

January 1969. I had given up. I had phoned Larry and asked him for dinner Friday. So much for nine months of conspicuous absence. I wanted husband.

Shopping for food for him gave me a contact high. I walked down to Little Italy, to the vegetable store, fondling the eggplants, picking out two unbruised, slick purple ones for a moussaka, and a pound of hand-chosen mushrooms, only the pure whites, and pomodori. Then the bread lady—we exchanged greetings; where had I been? she said. And the liquor store a, fifth of Tanqueray, dry vermouth, two bottles of Fleurie—God, the prices had gone up—and a bottle of Strega. And oh, cheese, to the cheese store on Eighth—to buy some nice sickly runny pus-y delicious Brie—and over to Christopher Street for a pound of espresso, watch them grind it. The day almost shined.

"This is quite a spread, darling. You might make a good cook yet."

"Yes, I might. Want some more cheese?"

"Why not. You've lost weight, Shylah, you look very good."

"Well, I don't eat out so much. That's part of it."

"I've missed you, you know that, don't you, you know I miss you. I was over at Boyd and Whit's house and they asked about you. What's happening? You just sort of dropped out. Nobody's really seen you around much."

"I guess not. Most of those people were more a part of your life than mine. I guess it's only right. I mean, you know, they were your friends, I really didn't have much chance to develop my own. The age discrepancy between us, I guess. Would you like a little more Strega?"

"Please. Why don't we go over to the couch and drink it? This table confines me."

"Hmmmm, Shylah"— We were kissing then, very cuddly—on the couch with all that Strega— Holding him, I reacquainted myself with the odd combination of muscles and skin that made up his body. "Come back, babe, come back. This is bullshit. I know you're miserable—look at this place—you're out of it, Shylah—come home with me."

"What about you, Larry? Are you miserable without me? You keep telling me what I need. What do you need?"

"Oh man, you're so hostile again. What has that got to do with it? I want you to come back. Isn't that enough? When it's good with us, it's superb. Isn't that enough?"

On the mattress I made love as if there were a sheet of cardboard between us. Maybe it would take time to feel again. He had a point. I WAS out of it. I did love him. Logical. Going back, doing all that—sane, logical— Oh Larry, hold me. Why are you holding me? I'm not feeling held. I'm not really holding you. Holding. Holding power. Oh God, the ceiling's so fucking filthy.

"Hmm, Shylah, nice. Nice to fuck again, yes?"

"Yes. Yes, nice. Very nice, Larry."

"Listen, I told Scarpelli we'd drop by later on. He's throwing Nash a little party. Small, you know, just a bunch of us. Why don't we get dressed and hail a cab? Come on, babe, a lot of old friends."

"Christ, I thought we'd just kind of have the evening to ourselves. Get to know one another again."

"You can't just hole up like this. Part of getting out of your-self, Shylah, is seeing other people. Really."

"Of course, you're right. O.K., we'll go. We'll go, Larry."

Maybe he was right was what I was thinking as Larry and I entered the overflowing townhouse to haute culture. A "bunch" in art-ese meant, in nice round sums, like a hundred maybe. That was a bunch.

"Why hello, dear, so nice to see you again."

"Hi, Scarpelli."

"Larry, glad to see you in town. You look absolutely edible, Shylah, lost weight, very skinny, how de rigueur. Still paint-ing?"

"Yeah." (Break your ass, why don't you?)

"Larry, I want you to meet Hinden Beam. He's the curator of the new Modernica Museum in Berlin. Have you been follow-ing all that buildup in the *Times*?"

Larry wandered off with Scarpelli while I wandered to the bar, passing a dozen or so faces I had dined with, who had kissed my cheek, who had brought the hostess flowers—faces I smiled at and began to greet, only to realize they did not re-member me— Shylah, why don't you learn? But Whit was there at the bar. I'd have someone to talk to—I wanted to see Whit. Had thought about her.

"Hey, Whit, it's great to see you. You're so tan. Have you been down in the islands?"

"Why, Shylah, hello. Yes, Curaçao actually, we just got back. You and Larry back together?"

"No, just hanging out for the evening."

"Oh wellll, you know how it is, keep in there plugging. He'll unbend."

"What? Well, that's not exactly my perspective, I . . ."

"Oh God, Boyd's hailing me, I think I better get over there. Excuse me, Shylah, nice seeing you again. You look great, lost weight. You'll have to drop by one of these days."

Don't cry, schmuck—don't you dare get tight-throated— maybe I just saw things a little differently, that's all— God, Larry, let's go. Shylah, don't go into the upholstery—live it up—be for the masses. What masses? The hounds of art? Suck. Oh God, can I just walk out? Can I do that?

"Hullo, what are you doing standing there like a stone? Is it true pretty girls are really profound? I'm Ken Ratcliffe; what's your name?"

"Shylah Dale, and your question isn't worth answering."

"You're probably right. Hey, you're Larry Karp's, uh . . ."

"Yes, we've been 'uhs' for four years now."

"Oh dear, you are touchy. I didn't mean to tread or anything. Are you also an artist?"

"Yes, and yourself?"

"Nope, I write books."

"What kind of books? Oh, wait a minute, you wrote *A Last Move to Exit*. I read it, both Larry and I, that is. Oh man, that part when she's dying and the turkey gets loose in the bedroom. You had me there. I was feeling guilty about laughing with her so consumptive and all, and guilty about taking it too seriously. I really like the way you write. Pain with humor."

"I like it too. I got, I think, the most out of that particular passage. I'm also glad you enjoyed it, Shylah. You're pretty perceptive for an old stone face."

"Come on, you can do better than that."

"I'd like too. Permit me to ask, I understood that you and uh—your husband—are separated. I mean, I'd like to ask you out to dinner if that's possible. Is that possible?"

"Yes, it's possible, and yes, I am separated, though I don't see that it makes much difference. Larry's a great proponent of the civilized code of free access. I'm just kidding. Are you married?"

"Divorced, just last week, as a matter of record. Ten years, two kids, two dogs, one house, three cars, if you include the van, one apartment, and a pure-bred, best-of-breed Abyssinian with mange."

"Should I congratulate you?"

"I don't really know yet. Try it and we'll see how it feels."

"Congratulations."

"No, I guess not. It appears you can't really effectively get congratulated for participation in the funeral. Anyhow, I'm sort of getting settled in now. You know, you're very funny, Shylah. Why so glum?"

"Am I glum? Oh fuck, I'm trying to be unglum. I guess the atmosphere, present company excepted, is a little beyond me. A little like being a pet Lhasa apso in Dalai Lama land."

"Well, that I don't believe—aside from my aversion to Lhasa apsos. I'm a little out of it too. Most of this decorative gathering is in some way or other buying or selling. I'm like you—nice to have around but nonessential, if you will. Scarpelli, I've known and bought paintings from—nothing amazing, but once in a great while I buy and we have a sort of friendship. I take it you're with Larry this evening or I'd suggest we have a drink together elsewhere and match jokes."

"With him? How is somebody with somebody? Yes, no—I guess we are. We had a kind of rapprochement dinner and this was his idea for me getting out of myself. Do I look sufficiently external? So I guess we'll have to postpone our privacy."

"Are you in the book?"

"Which book?"

"The phone book, or is there a Directory of Caustic Young Women Artists I have been denied subscription to?"

"Well, there's always the World Almanac, Ripley's Believe It or Not or . . ."

"Shylah, stop hiding. What the fuck's your phone number? I'm not a producer for vaudeville."

"O.K., wait, just let me write it down."

"Thanks. Look, I'll call you late tomorrow morning. O.K.? Hey, you're about to be summoned by your Wandering Jew. I hope you noticed he has been eyeing us with a certain amount of petulance. I think I'll go pay my respects to Scarpelli. See you soon, Shylah, be of good cheer."

Ken shuffled out and over to a group that included the host while Larry shuffled over to where I stood feeling better because I liked funny men.

"You ready to go? I didn't want to interrupt."

"I don't know why not, I mean, why you didn't interrupt."

"Hoo hoo, so the old lecher got to you, huh?"

"He didn't strike me as unusually high on the pendulum swing of lechery. You know, we BOTH dug his book."

"Oh, he's a good, facile writer, maybe a little lightweight, but funny, accessible."

"Oh no, Larry, you old bitch, who's to know. If Proust were alive today he might well be writing copy for *Mad* magazine. Anyhow, you're through, I mean with all this healthy 'getting out.' You know, I can't honestly say I'm feeling all that goddamn replenished. So yes, let's go."

"Hmm, you can take a nice bath in that herbarium of yours. It's been rather neglected of late."

"No, not tonight. I, uh, I think I'll stay at my loft. Got work to do and stuff."

"What? What is this?—you got something going afterward—not your new writer friend, by chance?"

"No. Look, you drag me here for my own good, you say, and then—shit, what's the use? No, I don't want to sleep without you. O.K., Larry, we'll spend the night together, but not at your place, at mine. Come stay with me at mine. That way I'll start work early, and I'll make you breakfast."

"Oh man, what is this, my place, your place? We'll stay at mine; it's bigger, and it's . . ."

"No. I want us to stay at mine, Larry. It's my, uh, my home now. It means something."

"I don't want to stay at YOUR place. You know you REALLY are nuts. Is this your new independent-woman, ballbreaker phase?"

"No, please, I just—just want you to be with me, please, Larry."

"You're impossible. Fuck you. Come on, let's say good night to Scarpelli and get out of here. We can discuss this further in the cab."

If I could stop thinking. The bed was too large. I'd get rid of it tomorrow and buy a single mattress. Maybe a glass of gin, if I warmed it up; if I could sleep— Larry, if you love me so much, how come you couldn't have stayed here? Why don't you do what I want, once? Just for a little fucking sleep? Fire under the saucepan of gin. Don't boil, it takes the alcohol, just warm it. In the glass beer stein, that ought to do it. Don't cry, Shylah, don't cry, you'll get to sleep. Maybe get Dr. Simik prescribe some sleeping pills—oh God, I hate drugs—maybe just to get you to sleep for a while—till you get regulated—gotta get up early tomorrow. Jesus, let me sleep.

★

"Hullo."

"Hello, is this Shylah? Hi, this is Ken, your fellow comrade of last night."

"Hmm, what time is it?"

"Nine-thirty. I called early because I figured you wanted to get up but wouldn't. Was I right?"

"Oh God, right."

"How about lunching with me? I've been possessed by Julia Child. Stayed up last night reading her cookbook. How about coming up to my place around one? You'll be my first official guest. Please, I'm all excited about cooking us this gourmet lunch."

"Yes, I guess you are. Sure, why not. Can I bring anything? Where do you live?"

"Park Terrace Arms, Central Park West; take a taxi, I'll reimburse you. No, for Christsake, don't bring anything; well, you could bring some photographs of your work if you like. You're in for a culinary treat; I guarantee a crust on everything."

"Is it O.K. if I bring my dog, Aardvark, he's very friendly, I might walk him in the park a little."

"As long as he isn't a gourmet. See you then."

My head hurt from last night's stein of gin. I made some instant coffee in the saucepan and glared at the unwashed dishes from my romantic little dinner for two. I considered throwing them into a plastic garbage bag. I did throw them into a plastic garbage bag. Went and sat down before the demonic red canvas resting on its wall bed of fat nails. Picked up a copy of last week's *Voice* resting on the work table—an article on Louise

2 5 7

Cielli starting a women's interart union. Interesting. Oh, come on, Shylah, you can't work in groups. All that torturous rhetoric. So what's come of this solitude? A desire for large doses of gin and maybe Seconal. Maybe I'll go to that thing I saw posted. I'd never go. I'd forget about it. I took the fattest of the three brushes lying in the turp and rinsed it out. Let's see what I could do with a vertical stroke for a change.

★

"Look, Shylah. I just don't want to get involved. You're very lovely, feminine, all that sort of thing, but I just don't want that closeness."

"Involved! We're lying naked side by side, your cock asleep in a puddle on my right thigh—you don't call that involved? I mean, even if we didn't work out together in the future, weren't we just INVOLVED? I don't know, maybe I'm missing something. We had this great lunch together, and we were laughing with each other and walking the dog and you were talking about going out to East Hampton, we'd go spend the day out there, and God, wasn't it great to feel so alive again and I'm feeling good and we come back here, make love for four hours, I'm feeling warm and all sloe-eyed and you were just snoring into my armpit ten minutes ago—and you don't want to get IN-VOLVED?"

"Look, honey, you're very young. You'd think differently if you'd just come out of ten years of concentrated involvement."

"Well, I managed to come out of four years of involvement, and with our age differences I'd say we work out pretty even ratio-wise. Oh shit, O.K. No, it's not O.K., you've got me really liking you and now you just turn off. What would have happened if I had been less honest about it, wouldn't sleep with you, kept you coming around, hungry? Jesus, would you ever want to become INVOLVED! I thought we were beyond that crap. I'm too accessible, I know. You don't want me cause you got me. What about ME? Why is everything so fucking preordained?"

"Well, we'll see each other; I didn't mean we wouldn't see

each other. It's so, uh, good with us, I mean, you enjoyed sex, right? We communicate well . . . Shylah, come on, where are you going? Hey, come on, how about having lunch next week? Shylah! Are you just rushing off without saying goodbye?"

It had begun to drizzle. A January rain, too warm to be sleet, too cold to be comfortable. My peacoat, no hat or gloves—bitter. Aardvark and I cut across Fifty-ninth, then took Fifth Avenue down. Nine o'clock, the avenue was relatively quiet at this hour. Some evening dresses and tuxedos seen dashing out of cabs and limos into the various hotels that lined Fifth, a few lonely-looking, plastic-flowered buggies with decrepit horses and bundled drivers near the Plaza. I wanted my mother from Fifty-ninth to south of Houston Street, wanted her for the duration of the hour and a half walk. Aardvark loved it all the way.

I thought of Paul—no, not Paul, too close to Larry's life, too much chaos. But I couldn't stay home tonight. I sat on the bed, Aardvark asleep on his army blanket next to me. I reread Koestler's *The Act of Creation*, page 360, four or five times and yet I had read nothing. Christ, for a little sleep. No more gin. I couldn't stand the Strega. Midnight already. Varkie fed and dreaming from his exertion on the pavement.

Orlofsky's, the neighborhood gin joint for artists, stood at my corner. I waded through the three-deep crowd at the bar to order my double bourbon and a draft.

"Hey, Shylah, where the hell you been? God, you just kind of disappeared."

"How you doing, Frank? Joe, you let your hair grow. Yes, I've been working."

"How are things?"

"Oh, great, productive, really good."

"You go to the Orson opening last week? Thought I'd see you there."

"No, didn't get a chance."

"Seeing much of Larry?"

"Uh no, not much, saw him last night though. He's the same. What's with you these days, Joe?"

"Oh, I'm doing a show couple weeks from now—using video. It's a group thing at the Sonerson. Just bought a loft on Prince Street. I'm ass-deep in plywood."

"How's Mary?"

"She split for New Mexico. To find herself, she says. Anyhow, we weren't really making it for a while."

"Doesn't seem to be the season for making it."

"So I see. You're really on your own then, Shylah?"

"Yes, I guess I am."

"Want to drop by my place and smoke some great Colombian dope? I just bought an ounce."

"Yes, sure, in an hour or so."

By an hour later the liquor I had consumed had only made me frantic. No, I still couldn't sleep. Maybe the dope at Joe's would make me sleep. Anything. And it was practically next door. Practically.

"Hey, Shylah, you don't look so good. What's the matter, not getting anything off the grass?"

"No, I'm kind of tense. The grass seems to be making it worse. See, I have this wretched insomnia. It's been going on now for weeks. I've got to call my doctor and get some Seconal or something."

"I've got a whole bottle. Save your bread. I never use it."

"You got any bourbon here, Joe? Don't think I want to smoke any more of this shit."

"Yes, in the cupboard there. But I wouldn't be mixing the reds with booze, O.K.?"

"Sure, I just feel like a drink."

"Want to stay here for the night? Might help you sleep if you're not around your paintings. Besides having someone next to you . . ."

"Sure, stay with you, good idea."

In bed, Joe pounding me between my legs, I played with the idea of what blood looks like spurting from an artery, what it would be like to stab him in the back and watch all the liquid leap up. Would it leap up? To feel his body leap up with it, then sag full weight upon me. Would he come then? Or would he just sort of fall out of me? I started to cry. Why should I hurt him? I liked him; hadn't he been a sweet buddy of mine? Why couldn't I get that kind of pleasure any more? He probably doesn't think very much. He'll roll over now—see, he rolled over, he'll fall asleep—it'll be a fine-deep-relaxed-cozy sleep for him—yes, baby, go to sleep. Head's spinning, can't sleep, you go to sleep. Mummy, put me to sleep.

Pills. Ho ho. Gotta get some sleep. Go sit at kitchen table and take them. Don't, can't relax with him here, with me here, want to go home. Want to go see Daddy. Daddy, Daddy. Please talk to me. Please talk to me.

Hey, they're red, they're red—red like the plus-red base, good solid red. Power red—lipstick red. So fantastic red—ought to write the drug company about that. Larry, why have I grown down instead of up? I don't have anything left. Haze. There's only haze. Even the red can't cut the haze. Help me. Help me. And glitter. Broken Coke bottles. My eyes full of broken glass. Baby, baby, baby, I want a baby. I want, goddamnit, you let me sleep. Please, God, please, sleep.

★

"Is this your first attempt at suicide, Mrs. Karp?"

"No! I mean, I wasn't attempting suicide. Oh Jesus, where am I? Oh, feel so sick, just trying to sleep, name isn't Karp, it's Dale. Shylah Dale. Leave me alone, will you. Please leave me alone. What did you do to me, what's this shit coming out of my arms? Let me out of here, I'm not sick. Please, I want to go home."

"You're very sick. Relax, don't try to move so much. That's an IV you're on. Now, let me explain, you'll feel better. You're at Beth Israel. I'm Dr. Kaufman, the resident psychiatrist here, and I've known your friend Fernanda for years. She called me when you were brought in. Your husband and she are very concerned about you. You see, you've been in intensive care for the past two days. Under the circumstances you were quite lucky. You overdosed on Seconal, coupled with the alcohol built up in your system; you came very close to not making it. Do you understand?"

"Yes, yes, I understand."

"Aside from that, you have a renal dysfunction; that means your kidneys are not working properly, and you have hepatitis. You'll be O.K. if you want to be, but it's going to take some doing on your part. Do I make myself clear?"

"Go fuck yourself."

"That's not going to do you any good."

"Oh please, Doctor. I feel lousy, O.K.?"

"You're going to feel a hell of a lot worse before you get better. All that torment going on in your head has debilitated your body as well. Alcohol's out, Shylah, if you want to survive. Your body can't handle the kind of abuse you've been giving it. See, it's like a card house tumbling—it's not just your head; it's your liver, your kidneys, you're anemic as well. That's one of the reasons you're cold all the time."

"WHEN can I go home, or wherever? When do I get out of here? I'm essentially O.K. now, right? I mean, if I follow your instructions. I can't stand hospitals, you see, they depress me."

"You must have been very deeply depressed to get here in the first place. Maybe two weeks here, until your blood tests come out clean. But you'd go back to the same thing, wouldn't you? That was pretty awful, don't you think?"

"Yes, I guess so. Don't really want to go back."

"Well, there are alternatives. You have to want to go, nobody'll commit you, but there's an excellent program going at Longview. It's out on the island, Long Island, I mean. But you have to commit yourself to it, sign yourself in. Basically, there'll be a therapist to work with you, group therapy as well; you live there but can get privileges for weekends or afternoons, that is, if the staff feel you can handle it. It's a respite really, so you can work on the problems and resolve them. There are a number of creative peop—"

"Yes, I've heard about it, of course—sort of a boarding school for well-oiled, gifted psychopaths. You think my separated husband is going to pay for this respite? I think he prefers the south of Spain."

"Yes, he's willing. I know you've been separated for some time. Perhaps his motivations in the marriage were wrong, but I think he wishes you well, to get well first. Certainly he can afford this. You see, your friend—the young man you were with—called him from here when he brought you in. And I think after he got here he called Fernanda. Perhaps he knew you'd need a friend more than an estranged husband. You're very lucky, Shylah. A hell of a lot of people pass through here with nothing and nobody. Be glad about some things . . . I have other patients to see now. Your friend Fernanda's here. Also, Dr. Freid will be by in a couple of hours. As I say, first you've got to get physically healthy again. It's really a question of attitude. Do you want to get well?"

"Yes. I don't know. Yes, I want to get well. I don't want to go back to the way I was before. Thanks. Doctor, can I see Fernanda? I want to see her."

"Hi, Fernanda."

"Hello, asshole. Can't you give a friend a call when you're up to self-destruct?"

"Yes, if I had known. What's in the paper bag?"

"Recent copies of *Analog* and *Fantasy.* I remembered from the old days you were a fan of sci-fi. Also a copy of the Bhagavad Gita, some underwear, and your toothbrush. I used your neighbor's keys, the ones you gave her. So how do you feel, Camille?"

"Horrible, I don't want to be left alone. Fernanda, you've got to believe me, I wouldn't try to . . . not on purpose. I was just trying to sleep, really. I couldn't sleep."

"You're not an idiot, Shylah, twelve Seconal on top of a lot of bourbon—that's a permanent sleep. You've been hiding again, really, since the separation."

"I don't know what it is—I can't get anything on right. I had hoped Larry would have, you know, changed—changed so we could get back together again, but he doesn't see things the way I see them— Well, you know, you said it yourself, I feel like he's sort of annihilating me. I can't be close to anyone."

"You have to get close to yourself first. I'm no shining example of mental health, but that's one thing I learned in the funny farm. You've got your work, Shy, you know that. That's more than I can say for a lot of women who go off the deep end."

"I don't get anything from it any more except hate."

"What about your father or your brothers?"

"God, my father. Haven't thought about him much for a while. He doesn't give a shit about me, Fernanda—don't think he was ever much into having a daughter, miserable cocksucker that he is. And my brothers have their own lives. I saw them over Christmas and all I got was the question 'Who's going to take care of Shylah, poor Shylah?' bullshit. Have you got a cigarette on you?"

"Here, take the pack. I thought it was pretty courageous leaving Larry, but instead of really getting, you know, constructive help, like friends, networks of things, you wanted to take it all on alone."

"But that's not altogether true. I don't have things—groups and friends my own age and interest level—you're my one and only close one in New York. I don't know how to ask that way—seemed easier just to do it on my own."

"Well, now you know it isn't. But you've got a lot going for you. You're much more alive, you know, you enjoy the things around you more than, say, I do. Like remember up in Provincetown? You were the one who got such a kick out of just being there."

"Yes, I remember. That was such a marvelous summer for me. For one thing, I looked so damn good, all that sun and the first real painting I'd done and being away from school. God, I was a proud bitch, huh?"

"That's O.K., you did look and act up, while I was totally morose all the time. Now I'm a little less morose and you're the one who's down. Look, I don't usually give advice, but take the time, Shylah, you've got to. Go to Longview, get your head in a different place; you know, become. Since Larry's willing to spring for it—the s.o.b. ought to spring for it—use that time well."

"Well, I'm here for two weeks at any rate, plugged in. Oh God, I've got to piss. Now what?"

"No sweat, they keep the bedpan in the bottom drawer. Here, lift up—I've been this route before."

"Oooh, ahhh, ouch. I'm really sick, huh? Feels like I'm pissing switchblades."

"Hello, Mrs. Karp, how are you feeling? I want that urine for testing."

"It's all yours, nurse. How long do I have to have this thing in my arm?"

"When the doctor comes and checks on you, he'll probably order it removed. Then you can try and have some supper—I'll get the dietician up to find out what you'd like."

"I'd like a Bloody Mary."

"Oh, come on now. We wouldn't really want that. Worst thing in the world, honey."

"Not with Tabasco and Worcestershire, it isn't, uh, honey. Bye."

"Shylah, I can tell by your outrageous bitchiness, you're on the mend."

"God, Fernanda, nurses. Oh Jesus, what a curse. To wake up locked between the pages of a Frank Slaughter novel."

"Shut up and bend your head to the till for once. She may sound like Juicy Fruit, but she knows what she's doing."

"I, uh, I feel like I'm going to be . . ."

I was too weak to do much moving, so when the gagging started, I just barely moved my head to the side. Bile—ugh, what a taste—choking me. Fernanda went out into the corridor and called back the nurse, who held me so that I could bring the stuff up. Fernanda held a kidney-shaped pan.

"Nurse, can I have something to sleep? I'm pretty weak."

"No, not until Doctor orders it. See, Mrs. Karp, you have to stay awake for a time anyway, you could choke while you're vomiting."

"I feel so rotten, when's the doctor coming?"

"Oh, an hour or so. Would you like to try a little Coca-Cola?"

"Yes, please, Coke, thank you."

"Larry's here, Shy. I—uh—it was pretty hard to keep him away. I'll hang around while he's here."

"Yes, would you?"

"Shylah, look, I bought out the store for tropical growth."

"Oh, a gardenia bush; bring it over here. Let me smell it. You know how I love the smell. No, don't pick it, they die so quickly, bruise, you know; just bring the whole thing over. Thanks."

"Why didn't you tell me you were feeling THIS bad? I knew you were acting very peculiar, but Jesus . . ."

"I tried, Larry. But you wanted everything your way. I wanted it to be a little more equal. I wanted to do it, to—you know, exist myself."

"Well, you've done a piss-poor job of it, babe."

"Oh, please, don't. Don't. I don't have anything to fight you off with; please, Fernanda, don't let . . ."

"Hey, Larry, we agreed you wouldn't do a number. Right?"

"Well, what the fuck am I supposed to do? What do you want of me? I don't understand."

"Yes, that's part of the problem, isn't it? Men don't . . ."

"Don't give me that cunty bullshit of yours, Fernanda. It's not an either/or . . ."

"Here you go, Mrs. Karp, some nice Coca-Cola. Just take the straw and—that's right. One of you want to hold this while she drinks? I have another call . . ."

"I will. There you go, babe. You know, after you rest up at Longview, if you feel up to it, we could get away from it all; you'd like that. Where nobody knows either one of us. Wouldn't that be—whoops, you dribbled— Got a tissue, Fernanda?"

"Here."

"Please, Larry, I can't think right now. I guess I want time to think. I mean, I'm not up to making plans or talking much."

★

Two weeks passed with a number of needles and pills, bedpans and massages.

I got into it; I mean, I liked being taken care of. Since I couldn't paint, I read everything I could find. And I had a room-mate now. A woman, Liza, of indeterminate years—maybe thirty-eight, maybe fifty-eight—whose hair was only wisps

through which I could see the size and shape of the skull, who
was blind in one eye, whose body had deteriorated from cancer
and massive doses of cobalt to the point where she had lost the
ability to walk.

Liza had four sisters, two female cousins, and one seventy-
odd-years mother, who was the sturdiest of the sturdy bunch.
The women came and stayed, bringing Lebanese food in chafing dishes, bars of chocolate and Turkish delight, wigs, cosmetics, perfume. They sat and talked and read the paper aloud,
plumped pillows, brought bedpans, gave sponge baths. And
Liza was not enough for them as long as I lay in the room. Now
they had another to comfort as well, a young one too.

I felt guilty at first, felt they were wasting their maternal gifts,
these women, while Liza died a day at a time in her shriveled
body shell. Sometimes she'd talk, ask how I was feeling and say
what a pleasure it was to have such a nice roommate and being
a painter must be exciting and she missed her job at the insurance company where she'd worked for twenty-five years and the
doctor had told her the cobalt treatments would help but they
didn't. Her voice and one good eye would sparkle while her
body daily fell apart—noticeably from one morning to the
next—until the single hospital bed appeared as if it contained
only a doll propped up between the covers.

During the day she'd chatter and tell jokes, ask questions,
bitch back and forth with her sisters about her condition, as if
her condition didn't exist or as if it was just a question of finding the right medication or treatment. Then, at night, asleep,
she'd moan and call out for things, for something to stop the
pain that brutalized her. And a nurse would appear dispensing
painkillers, sleeping pills. And the next day the conclave of
women arriving at noon . . .

"Shylah, I brought you nice kibbe kufta. Come, I sponge you
off a little and you eat some of this. That hospital food no good.
Arani, you help me with her."

"Yah, Mama."

And then there'd be this chorus of voices in Arabic dialect,
giving advice and helping out so Mama could lift herself to
bathe my back. Then they'd bring out the paper plate, bring the

swinging table over, and I'd nibble at the food I would have wolfed down if I could.

"Liza, what is it?"

"Have to go to the bathroom. Wish I could get up."

"You have to move bowels? We pull the curtain. Here, I help you." Another explosion of Arabic from the women as they positioned the shell of Liza, these hefty, superb testimonials to Lebanese cuisine and motherhood.

"Where your mother, Shylah? I don't see your family. Not good. Are they out of the state?"

"Yes, scattered, you know."

"You should gain some weight. Eat, eat, is good, yes?"

"Oh yes, delicious. Oh, I'm not skinny or anything."

"You got to get strength back. Such a young girl. You got a husband?"

"Yes. Uh huh."

"Well, you got to get your strength back for that." The women dissolved in laughter at the remark by Mama. And I faked it, due to marital circumstances and because I enjoyed them all completely. These women. Oh women.

★

It was Fernanda who took me out of the hospital after my release, helped me pack back at my loft. And Aardvark—Larry was caring for the dog while I interred myself. Which worried me.

"Fernanda, I'm worried about the dog. Do you mind? I'd like to just see him before I go. It's not that far out of the way. I want to establish . . . see if Larry's taking care of him. He's been pretty neglectful in the past."

"Yes, all right. But don't get into a heavy discussion with him, O.K.? I don't think it's particularly wise for you to see one another right now. You don't have any defenses from that bastard."

"Oh Aardvark, oh Varkie. Good boy, that's a good boy. Have you got water, huh, have you got food? Larry, you, uh, you can

2 6 8

take care of him; you WILL take care of him, won't you? Please, tell me if you, ah, you know, if you would rather not or anything. He has to be loved a lot besides being given food and water."

"Yes, for Christsake, I told Paul, you remember Paul, my assistant, to double-check every day and make sure the dog's O.K. and walked and petted. He'll be fine. Man, I think I may start taking the beast with me to the bars, he'll get a lot of attention there. He's not sleeping on my fucking bed though, Shylah. That's bullshit."

"O.K., but here's his blanket; let's put it in a spot on the floor he can call his own; he'll want to be near you. I'll just put it here at the foot of the bed, O.K.?"

"Sure, O.K., anything. I'll come visit you as soon as they let me. You tell me if you need anything, Shylah."

"Just to take care of the dog. You do promise . . ."

"Yes, Jesus, I promise. My God, Shylah, he's a fucking dog, not a Chinese emperor. Oh shit, don't cry over the dog."

"I'm not really, I'm fine, just worried, that's all. Fernanda, we better get going, I, uh . . ."

"Oh now, stay for a moment. Have a drink or, whoops, how about a Coke? Maybe some tea?"

"No, Larry, I have to go. It's pretty tiring the first day. I guess I'll see you. So long."

"You're going to be fine, babe. I just know you're going to be terrific again."

14

Longview, with its all-encompassing stone wall, was the kind of once-a-great-mansion where a person has to drive awhile through richly appointed acreage before being allowed to view its majesty. In this case, the 1880-ish stone manor house had been eclipsed by recent architectural extensions that gave it, at best, an incongruous and blatantly medicinal look. There was something about positioning ranch-designed blond wood next to gray rock that destroyed everything the gray rock had intended.

"Jesus, Fernanda, I must be someone else going through these motions. This place, look at it. It's all F. Scott Fitzgerald. I don't know, I don't know."

"Come on, buck up. It's really pretty relaxed. Look, I'll park and go in with you, stay with you while you fill out the forms. Nothing to it, Shylah."

"Easy, huh?"

Admission for the emotionally disturbed but lucid took an arduous two hours. Next time I'd play it safe and go in with catatonia. Next time, they wouldn't ask. I filled out papers, got examined—the fuckers—even for lice. No louse could afford it. And talk: I talked and was explained to—how we would work it. All very low-key in sumptuous surroundings. At the end of an overworked rainbow—a lunatic asylum.

Longview operated on a caste system in reverse. We women who functioned more or less, where it wasn't a question of catheters and padded cells, lived in a wing on the first floor. We were the "voluntaries," thirty-odd strong in our section and most of us premenopausal. There were no bars or locks; I saw no women running around throwing shit or anything. Dormlike, right down to the soft radio sounds and the TV in the living room. They took me to my bedroom, large enough to hold bed, bureau, table, chair, with four footsteps to go. A four-hundred-dollar-a-week nun's cell.

I unpacked. Some of the inmates (but I guess we don't call them that) came in, friendly, introduced themselves. Why was everything so sane, polite? I wanted external proof of insanity, a little writhing, a hissy fit, anything. The women were solicitous—they assumed I was out of it. That was normal, wasn't it? To be out of it the first day. God, I had forgotten to say goodbye to Fernanda; oh Shylah, what's wrong? I lay down. My appointment to meet my therapist was not until five. The women left. I had an hour. The freshly painted white ceiling served as a shroud for concentration. So fucking tired.

★

"Hi, I'm Pat, Shylah. We're all pretty much on a first-name basis here. I'm one of the wing staff—means I work with the outpatient groups. Your appointment is with Dr. Saint. She'll be your permanent therapist while you're here. Are you ready, dear?"

"If everyone's on a first-name basis, how come she's called doctor?"

"You can work out what you call her in a minute. I'll show you the way to her office."

"Thank you. You do that."

If Freud had lived and dressed up in drag, the age and bearing would be just about accurate for Dr. Saint. She might have counseled Lysistrata.

"Oh yes, Mrs. Karp, or let's see down here . . . Miss Dale?"

"Dale."

"Good, sit down, I'm Dr. Saint. Oh damnit, I've got to organize this desk, all my papers are coffee-stained. Just a moment, ah there. Well, Miss Dale, you've been through quite an ordeal—just perusing here—liver, kidneys—physical then as well as emotional. If you so choose, I'll be working with you individually at first on a four-day-a-week basis as well as twice-a-week group therapy. Perhaps you have some questions you'd like to ask this first session?"

"What determines when I go home?"

"Well, of course your feelings about it and my recommendations. Since you've voluntarily signed yourself into our outpatient section, certain freedoms are assured you to begin with. You understand that at first we have the patients stay within the grounds, just for a few weeks; then you may sign out for movies in town or weekends at approved places. It's not a big-sister routine, I assure you. We limit your outside movements at first only, unless something extraordinary occurs. Mainly because these are new surroundings; there's initial trauma—it's an adjustment."

"Yes, I guess it is. I'd like to do some work—anything—maybe sketches, maybe paint. Do you have any facilities here?"

"Yes, I see. We don't have a professional setup, but we do have some,materials and a large work space. As you know, there are a number of painters here. How do you feel about painting these days?"

"God, right now? Uh, I don't know. Dead, I guess. No, that's not right. I was pretty much caught up with, uh, work—yes, I guess I worked my ass off after my marriage split up, until I, uh, I wound up in the hospital. Something—hateful, I guess, just before—uh—I mean, the paintings were hateful."

"How is that?"

"Well, it's just that . . . well, the form and stuff—I don't know—big reds, swatches, fire. Like a stabbing in color. Like blood, like blood on a glass shard?"

"Glass shard?"

"Yeah, you know . . . something sharp and broken—at least that's the way I've always—uh, well—I guess I was pretty angry. Furious—right, I was furious . . . and the feeling—like it started some time ago—is pretty much the same. Glass pieces, bright color, fast-moving—frustrated—something of . . . Look, uh, Doctor, I don't think I can—O.K., O.K.—something like being tied up all the time. But you see, I had this insomnia, it was ridiculous; no matter how much I drank, I couldn't make it stop—I couldn't sleep. That's why I accidentally took too many Seconals."

"Why do you think you took so many?"

"I don't know, who knows—I was in a hurry, I was running to sleep. I wanted to sleep. You know—I just couldn't stand it. And then this guy I picked up and fucked. I don't know, it's hard to say. I was just so pissed off and drunk and couldn't sleep."

"Can you describe your insomnia?"

"How can you describe nothing? Insomnia is nothing. Lack."

"Does it have a color, as with your anger in the paintings? Does 'nothing' to you have a color?"

"Yes, gray, I guess; nothing is gray. Sleep, on the other hand, is maybe green, no blue-green, Caribbean Sea–blue. Jesus, but that gray . . . Tell me, are you going to give me something when I can't sleep?"

"We hope you'll be able to sleep without anything, that's the point. I have recommended, however, that you be put on some physical therapy. This will build you up in general besides relaxing you. We do yoga here; have you tried it? Not just the exercises or more athletic asanas but ways to relax the thoughts as well. And something I think you'll like—a swimming pool in the basement. You can swim an hour a day. Also, we have special attachments for baths that . . ."

"Oh, I love baths."

". . . that swirl the waters around—excellent for muscle relaxing. How do you feel now?"

"Well, the baths are a plus."

"Why do you think you like bathing so much?"

"Who knows—the warm water, I guess. Gentle, soft, a liquid blanket. Hey, I didn't see that. A cat. Is that your cat? Gee, she's fantastic-looking—nice and tubby too—a calico. I have this dog, a springer puppy, Aardvark, that's why, you see, it couldn't have been on purpose, the pills, because I had this dog at home I had to take care of."

"You feel that you would not knowingly harm yourself because of the dog?"

"Yes, makes sense, doesn't it? See, he's mine and my separated husband's, but Larry's so goddamn sloppy about caring for others, well, in terms of, you know, nurturing them. My God, now I just realized what's so peculiar about all of this. You're talking to me. When I was in boarding school, I had a psychiatrist who said nothing. Godawful really. I kept making up the tragic to keep her happy. I felt guilty."

"Guilty. How did that guilt feel?"

"Hmm. How does any fucking guilt feel, for heaven's sake? Well, uh, let's see, umm, you know, when people, especially men, do this a lot, when they give you that cold, stony silence—well, you feel you have to apologize for being alive, that you're somehow lesser."

"Can you say that in the first person? I. Could you try that?"

"Well, it's kind of, uh, embarrassing saying, 'I,' well, shit, you know."

"Sometimes we hide behind the third person. The feelings come closer when we use the first person."

"Oh, O.K. Well, I sort of felt like, uh, shit. But it comes and goes. Sometimes I feel very masterful, you know, when the pressure's off, but that doesn't last very long."

"Can you think of other people who gave you that cold, stony silence? You talk about your former therapist—otherwise, men usually more than women?"

"Uh, let's see. My friend Fernanda is that way sometimes, Larry's that way sometimes, umm . . ."

"Before Larry and Fernanda?"

"Well, my brothers to some extent and, uh, Daddy. Daddy didn't talk to me much. Except to disapprove or give an order or challenge me some way. Yes, my father was really that way. I mean, it's not that he didn't say anything to me, it's just, I guess, that he never, you know, communicated."

"Why do you think he didn't communicate with you?"

"He hated me. I mean, I wasn't, you know, the sweet ladylike little drip he wanted. I think he thought I was a whore. A whore from the cradle. My father thinks most women are whores."

"What about your mother? Did he think your mother was a whore?"

"I, uh, well, you know, see, she died when I was thirteen or fourteen, and they were divorced when I was eight or so. He kicked her around a lot, I mean, used to hit her and everything. And the drinking—God, they both drank so much. I grew up thinking that that was the way adults lived, that was the norm. What a mess. Once, I remember—there was a time I thought it was up to me to protect her. I remember her weeping—broken ribs—and then the hospital—the whole shebang—what they passed off as a bad fall. You see, she didn't help herself and I . . . Anyhow, what was the question? Oh, that's right, did he think she was a whore? Sorry, I got sidetracked. I don't know; maybe. She was conservative to the extreme, like she wore tweeds all the time, and wore them a size too large, that kind of thing—but there was this one kelly-green velvet evening suit she had. I loved it, the bright color, green; I even wore green when I got married. She didn't look dowdy for once. I remember she loved it too, but Daddy wouldn't let her wear it. Said she looked whorish. I remember that. He said she looked that way. The suit got hung in the walk-in closet with things that were never worn. She put it in one of those plastic bags and hung it there. I used to go there and look at it when they were out and . . . and . . ."

"I'm sorry, I see our time together is up. We'll talk about this some more tomorrow at five, Miss Dale. The coordinator will show you the ropes this evening."

"Just like that, I can turn it on and then off?"

"Just like that; it's necessary, you'll see."

"Jesus."

Pat took me back to the living room in the wing, where the women were hanging around waiting for the supper bell. I had the feeling while we walked that I had somehow been had. That right in the middle of my personal confessions I had gotten the boot—I fantasized slitting my wrists in one of these sessions and the old girl getting out the sutures and gauze and tape while I'm spurting all this blood all over the linoleum floor and she's just getting into saving my life, then she glances over at the clock and says, "Oh, Miss Dale, I see our time is up, we'll see you tomorrow." You bet she will, tomorrow, a bloodless corpse decomposing on her rug—oh, cut the crap, Shylah.

★

"Hi, Shylah, welcome to the farm. I'm Sally Mathiesson. Cigarette?"

"No, I've got some, thanks."

"I mean, can you spare one? I just ran out."

"Oh sure, here."

"The other women don't like me because I'm always bumming cigarettes."

"Oh—uh—hmm—well, why don't you buy some, or get somebody to buy you some?"

"Well, sometimes I do. But I always forget. Who's your shrink?"

"Dr., uh, Dr. Saint is . . ."

"Mine too; she's crazier than we are, you know. I've never seen anyone more eccentric. Don't think she's ever been laid except maybe by that fat pussy of hers."

"What?"

"The cat. That goddamn cat. She knows I hate that cat. She puts it out now when I'm around, after I threatened it with a little catnip dipped in prussic acid."

"Yes, I guess you do hate that cat."

"Hi, Sally, I see you're getting to know Shylah here."

"She's nice, Pat. See, she gave me a cigarette. That's good for openers."

"All you have to do is buy them, you know that. O.K., there goes the dinner bell. Shylah, I'll show you where you'll be sitting from now on. We keep a particular place for each person for dietary reasons."

"What does that mean? I can't sit with the people on low-salt diets, or what?"

"No, hardly. You just sit in the same chair. Your diet, for instance, allows no coffee or tea, vinegar, spaghetti sauce, things

2 7 6

like that. Otherwise it's pretty normal. You'll probably be having that in a while anyway, once you stabilize, your kidneys, that is. Also, you're getting what we call a vitamin supplement with your meals—it's like a milk shake. Shylah, you're going to get so healthy it'll be like holing up at Jack LaLanne's."

"Am I getting any medication to sleep tonight?"

"No, your diet's the best medication of all."

"Oh Jesus, maybe you're right, maybe I can eat my way into a coma."

I assumed there were several dining areas around the old homestead that imitated this one for size and sterility. We did not eat with the men patients; it was just us, just the thirty or so of us vaginal lepers. The tables held eight, I think there were four or five of them. The once-elegant room must have had at least one crystal chandelier and probably a lot of paintings, second-rate imitation Gainsboroughs and maybe some of the Hudson River School. Now it was, of course, white, and the chandelier—yes, I could see the remains of a socket, nipple-looking think in the ceiling—had been replaced by those hanging, long, tubular lights. The fireplace remained, huge and immaculate in its stone façade, without so much as a cinder to make it more homey.

We ate institutional-riche. They gave me steak, roast potatoes, carrots, peas, a roll, and a chocolate-milk fortified special. It occurred to me that if I ever got it together I'd be too fat to do much about my mental health, except ponder it over a box of potato chips.

"The first day's a real mind-fucker, don't you think, Shylah? At least it was for me. I'm Nalani Bunting, glad to know you."

"Hi. Confusing mostly. Have you been here for a long time?"

"No, not long. A week. It's my second go-round here. It's either this or the Canary Islands. My crutch."

"You like being here, then?"

"No, not that exactly. I mean, I don't want to become a habitué. I have a hard time keeping myself even in the big world. This last book I finished and then coming out, well, sort of overcame me—I freaked out."

"Your book coming out or . . ."

"No, I mean women. I'm gay, or sort of gay. Don't like men

much any more, and intellectually, you know, as a writer, I can't relate to the whole thing of standards. Shit like that. I found myself involved with women, you know, uh, loving them, but then women are impossible in a different way. We're all drowning."

"Oh sorry, I didn't mean to be naïve. I see. It's just that I can't stop the chemistry I have for men—you know, the rougher skin and cocks—I hate the double bind. I think that's what got me here— I wish we were all a little more humane and not so specialized sexually."

"You're dreaming."

"No, I don't think so. I've met men who I thought had those qualities, or what I see as those qualities, tenderness—tenderness, you know, womanly in a way—but it's intolerable. The attraction's for exactly that coldness that I guard against—that, my friend Fernanda calls it, annihilating quality—let's see, what would be a word for it?—declitorate—men are declitorators—know what I mean? Anyhow, it's a lot different saying it to you and dealing with it within myself. Blows my head apart, Nalani. Nalani! What a great name, hmm, it's so tropical."

"My mother was strictly a Teutonic that never forgave herself for being Teutonic. So she named me something exotic, thinking I'd grow up to be a Polynesian or something."

"Hmm, so what do you write, tracts on growing orchids?"

"Well, children's stories mostly, and I'm sick of it. I mean, I really want to write a novel, but I get these things published and it's a way of avoiding myself. But this last story—it's about a little girl who runs away from home and discovers a magic sequoia; inside of it there's a fairy world—sort of 'The Tinder Box' and *Alice* and *The Wizard of Oz,* only I make it contemporary—anyhow, I found I was writing about myself and it just became surreal and horrible. And then this woman I was living with . . . Anyhow, I make money from kids' books which I don't need really— Mother's loaded—in many ways. I told her I thought I was a Lesbian and she didn't exactly embrace it, you might say."

"Yes, but God, what an act of courage telling her that. How old are you anyway?"

"Thirty-seven. I know. I look younger. Mother's only fifty-five, which gives you some idea of her orientation toward goals and stuff. She functions quite well in her idiotic duplicity. Her feeling is that a woman gets married first and establishes security and then takes the reins—you know how that works—you just sort of preside over husband and world because you're protected by the institution and therefore freed by it. Jesus, I don't think she even likes my father."

The other women at the table had been listening to this exchange—anything new to pass time—and now took occasion to join in except for one at the far end who sat morose and silent, pecking at her plate with a fork.

"Yeah, it's just like you say. I've three kids, and wouldn't you think that son-of-a-bitch would take over once in a while? The only time he got into home life is when he wanted some kooz."

"Kooz?"

"Pussy. Then I got involved with the guru, got some enlightenment, well, a little, and I was feeling blessed and holy and that bastard husband of mine starts legal action that I'm an unfit mother. Because HE won't take care of the kids even for once. I don't want any of it. I'm tired of being used."

"But what *about* your kids?"

"Well, it doesn't matter. He's got THEM against me too."

"You don't like your kids though, do you?"

"I don't know any more, they're just like him—they suck up everything. Things were going better with Guru Gawa and this program he started—Light of the Blessed. I even took the kids and gave them these special baths, but my husband stopped it. Said I was giving them acid. Can you believe it? Shows you how much he knows about spiritual abstinence. Fuck him."

"Have you been here long—what is your name again?"

"Kathy, Guru says time is only a measure of growth, so I'd say I've been here about two-feet worth."

"She's been here for a year in human terms."

"Oh."

★

Lights-out was at ten. The middle of the afternoon in my head. After dinner, Nalani and I played a little Ping-Pong, something

I had no knack for, but she did. The women, for the most part, seemed on the gloom side of motley, more like Kathy than Nalani, who had something, some fire. In a way, except for the depression, I didn't see any of them, even Sally or Kathy, as being particularly unhinged, so what if she was into her guru and didn't dig her kids and expressed paranoia about her husband. If it was paranoia. I could see him as being controlling and piggish—maybe it was his standards ultimately that brought her here. Just seemed so confusing—the lack of definitions. Christ, sleep. Shylah, go to sleep, make yourself sleep. Ten o'clock, God: the bed's too small. I want to do something. I want to do something.

I wanted a drink. My mind raced again. I hated it when my mind raced. Some mechanism in there wouldn't shut off. I thought about Daddy. Hadn't seen them for over two years, just a couple of letters and calls since then. They'd never know about this—I could see the look of shame if he knew his daughter was lodged in a home for loonies. But I missed him now, a part about him, the way he'd be when he told jokes, entertained, the charisma, his laugh, the magic in his laughter. I missed that.

Please, let me sleep. Dear God, I want to sleep. When I was a kid I wanted to be a missionary. Saying "Dear God" to myself reminded me—raunchy little Episcopalian. Stop thinking, Shylah. Don't think about anything. Nothing. What's nothing? Nothing's being inside something. Something gray. A hand. Being in nothing's fist. I didn't want to be squashed. I don't want to be in nothing's fist. Wonder about Stanley; what about Stanley? We had that closeness, didn't matter whom he married. Wonder what he's like married. Wonder if he's a guide like he said. Jesus, maybe they'd give me something after all. Please. Maybe I could start doing some preliminary sketches for a new series—Bedrock I, Bedrock II—stop it, Shylah. This is crazy, it's starting again.

I threw my bathrobe over my shoulders and walked out into the corridor.

"Excuse me, I don't seem to be able to sleep at all. Could you give me something to sleep?"

"Well, try. Just relax. You just relax. You'll drift off."

"No, I won't. Please. I can't stand it. Just, you know, a shot or something to make me sleep."

"You aren't on the medication list, Shylah. Go back and try, O.K., just try."

Cunt. Try, just try! To attempt to attain nothingness. I tried. I counted. I prayed. I masturbated twice. I wouldn't let myself run mind-movies; I'd interrupt them. I couldn't do it. Maybe I had lost the knack. I must have sleep amnesia. I'd forgotten—on and on and fucking on.

"Please, I'm exhausted. It's after two. Please do something."

"Hmm, you do seem to need a little push. Tell you what, how about a nice hot bath and we'll put one of the whirlpool machines in it. That will help, I think, Shylah."

"Oh yes, a bath, please. That'd be great."

The second night attendant took me to the bathing room, the one where they kept the whirlpool what-cha-mah-jiggies. She ran the water deep in the old-fashioned tub, then stuck the machine in. I sat in the water while she put on some kind of sheet that fitted over the tub up to my neck; I assumed it was there to keep the steam in. Hot, but not too hot. Delicious. She sat in the chair next to me, occasionally adjusting things. Christ, could that woman smile. Every time I looked at her she smiled. Downright embarrassing. Sitting naked in a covered tub being smiled at like that. Was I being paper-trained? Good girl.

★

"Good morning, Shylah. Guess you didn't hear the bell. Time for breakfast."

"Hey, I fell asleep. I don't remember falling asleep. I'm exhausted. May I, uh, may I sort of skip breakfast and sleep some more?"

"No, we keep a pretty tight schedule here."

"Oh, come now, bend a little. I only got around three hours."

"No."

"Leave me alone."

"Up you go. Come. You'll see, Shylah, if you get up now, you'll be tired tonight. It'll work in your favor."

"So would hemlock. O.K., I'm up, sort of . . ."

"You're cheating. You don't want me to beg you, that wouldn't be a very positive method, now, would it?"

"Oh, go ahead, beg, I want you to beg. Beg away."

"Up!"

Ken Kesey's Big Nurse in *Cuckoo's Nest* hardly fit this one's five-foot stature, but I saw resemblances. Her Napoleonic complex won out. I was docile, obedient, and tired. Coffee. I could do with a little coffee.

Breakfast. I had forgotten—no coffee. Everything I didn't want: soft-boiled eggs, those horrible fetal things, toast, orange juice—well, that was O.K.—countered by one of those godawful cruddy speckled milk shakes. I busied myself with picking caked sand from my eyelids and the corners of my eyes. I usually talked, getting used to new places and people. The noise annoyed me today. Chatterers—how could they talk so easily at the waking hour? I kept my eyes down and attempted sleep with them open.

At ten, I was scheduled for yoga, two hours of it, from lion to cobra asana, and then the one where you relax each little bit of your body a little at a time. Therapeutic yoga. Good idea. My muscles ached. I did need exercise. Lunch was some subcutaneous-looking pork chop dish. I wasn't hungry. The staff woman at my table let me get away with not eating if I drank my crud cocktail. If I pretended it was a Mai Tai it still tasted like shit. After lunch, praise God, we were on our own for a couple of hours. I wasn't scheduled to swim until three.

The crafts room was connected to the library. I surmised it had been either a music or a billiard room in its day. Large, but not that large, with bay windows looking out on the lawn. The floor had been recently laid with some kind of cork squares. I looked around. There were several easels, a sewing machine, a basketful of material scraps, leather stuff, punchers, one table full of assorted paints, rags, chalk, and a rack of prestretched canvases, the kind you'd buy from an art-supply store. They must have paid Grumbacher a person-to-person call once a month and ordered indiscriminately. Who needs manila paper? I looked around for a sketch pad and finally found one that hadn't been completely covered. I picked through the glassful of pencils until I found a reasonably together number-one pencil and sat in the window seat. Think of all the starving Puerto Ricans in Nueva York, Shylah. What happens if some young woman freaks out in Spanish Harlem? You think she gets this action of window seats and once-upon-a-time ex-billiard rooms and whirlpool baths? I didn't know. I guess if you're having it rough you go to the priest, who tells you to have a baby or get married or join a nunnery or be pious or go to confession. Some such thing. While their husbands and daddies are out on the street going "chi-chi-chi" to everything with a womb. I played with the pencil on paper now—don't start thinking about how much you don't deserve this, Shylah, and the downtrodden Puerto Rican women; wait until you can do something—blocking shapes on the page, fitting hard-edge rectangular shapes with icicles and waves to see if there was a way to bring them together.

A woman at the easel had begun weeping over her painting. Pat took her out. She didn't protest though—I think she wanted to be removed from whatever sat upon the easel ledge. I went over for a look. Sweet Jesus. No wonder she wept. Grotesque birds all over the place. Sort of Magritte out of control. Frightening, sort of terrific in a way, had she a little more technique to go along with it. That was it for my rectangles and waves for the day. What a vision—woman, are you in hell. I suffered from looking.

The swimming pool wasn't all that big. Ten of us in tank suits, our hair under white bathing caps—a regulation I deplored; the rubber around my skull made me vaguely claustrophobic. We took turns diving, little chicken dives off the low board. My old adoration of indoor pools returned full force. There's always that reflection of waves on walls, then the water echo and wetness everywhere, on the tiles, the air thick and misty. A certain surrealism takes over, voices become two-dimensional, the room appears to be constantly moving with wave movements mirrored on three sides. A bit weird, a kind of goldfish-bowl effect, but I liked it—felt at home in it, swimming inside a room.

I swam hard—long, defined breast strokes—swam until they told us it was time to dress, Nalani sometimes alongside of me. I liked Nalani; there was a certain generosity in her craziness—like she'd never cheat waiters of large tips or women of love.

★

"Is your name really Saint? I mean, it's kind of ironic, you know, for the business you're in."

"Yes, it is actually Saint. My colleagues have kidded me about just that. Well, how do you feel after your first night and day at Longview, Miss Dale? I see you had a little trouble sleeping. Can you tell me about that?"

"What's to tell? I told you, I have insomnia. I just can't turn it off . . ."

"Turn it off?"

"Yes, the thoughts, things kept running through."

"You say running a lot. Do you feel that you're running?"

"I guess so. It's frightening me. It's like I'm some needle on a phonograph record and I can't reject; I keep playing on and on, over and over; I'm sick of the music, sick of thinking the same way. I hate it. God, I can't stand to think about it. Oh, hello, pussycat, come sit on my lap; yes, you can sit on my lap, good cat."

"Try and concentrate on being that music. What does it sound like?"

"I can't, because I'm not the music, I'm just the needle that makes the music go on unceasingly. Oh, I hate this, can't we talk about something else; it's difficult to concentrate."

"Well, try, just try."

"Shit, that's what everybody's programmed to say around here. TRY, JUST TRY. O.K., let's see. Oh no, I can't really. Please."

"Relax, let yourself get into it."

"Well, in a way, you see, my thoughts, the music, that is, are

2 8 4

exquisite. But I'm not really living it, I mean, it's unattainable, whatever it is—and I want to get off, I don't want this mind view; I don't want to see these things and not have them. It's obsessional. So I try not to think about it. I try to cut myself off when I think of different people or things, or even terror—I try and cut myself from that, uh, terror and I can't. I get wound tighter and the music or the things keep going on and on."

"Why do you say the music is exquisite when what you are thinking about is painful to you?"

"I don't know, it's a sugary feeling. In a sense there's this aura of loving about everything, sort of a sheen on all the dreams. I guess I desire a lot of what I think about. Like I desire Larry and I want Daddy to love me. But the only way that's going to happen is if they somehow change or I somehow change. I mean, I know I'm fucked up, but I keep thinking that really they're the ones that are, uh, wounded, you know what I mean, that it's their hang-ups, though they'd never say they are hang-ups, that makes me crazy. Because I love them, I guess. I don't want to love them. I certainly don't want to need them. I want them to need me. And besides, I also—I guess—hate them. I hate their wrongness. They want me to be something I'm not. An impossible doll. Mindless."

"Yet you say you want to turn off your mind for a while. Wouldn't that make you mindless?"

"In a way, yes. But see, I don't want to turn it off all the time. I want to be able to use that energy during the day, for constructive things, to be free to live. At night I want to use the thoughts for the business of sleep. But it doesn't work out that way any more."

"Why do you think it doesn't work out that way any more?"

"Oh God, how the fuck should I know? I don't know. No, it's, uh, it's that I'm not *me* any more; I have no 'me' or my ME is not in agreement. Like I'm fighting for it in a way, aren't I? When I split from Larry, it was ME that I was thinking about. Ego, if you will. A knowledge of myself, a self-esteem I had when I first met him in Provincetown."

"In Provincetown?"

"Yes, after my freshman year at college, I spent the summer

there with my friend Fernanda. She wrote poems and I painted. God, I had this even balance and sort of arrogance about me. Like I was really just finding out the possibilities in the medium, you know, painting, and in the mornings I'd work my ass off—loved it, loved painting—no more academic grind. God, I've balked at schools right down the line— Then in the afternoons I'd walk for miles up and down the dunes beach, getting tan—I was sure I had been possessed by the spirit of a panther—graceful— And Fernanda let me use their other car. I worked part-time at a hoity-toity-type restaurant which paid me more than enough to get paints, shit like that. Independence, you know, no hassles, summer. Christ, I was O.K."

"And did your husband, did Larry change that, did he influence you?"

"Oh Jesus, did he ever. In a sense, you see, that was part of it. He knows a lot about technique, about use of color; there's no doubt he's a terrific teacher. Though when I think about it, the stuff I learned from him of value was more mechanical than theoretical. I mean, he gave me all this garbage about what was right and what was wrong. Now I sort of think he was full of shit when he started throwing out his judgments. Art is subjective, right? All somebody can do is develop with skill and materials what they feel makes sense. Anyhow, toward the end, I knew he was seeing a number of other women—it hurt kind of—but like I knew it wasn't a big deal."

"What do you mean, it wasn't a big deal?"

"Well, see, I just couldn't get into fucking him. I couldn't stand it at the end. We'd be battling all the time, so how could I turn that off to fuck him? I slept and drank a lot. Then after I left I seemed to be O.K. for a short while. The decision to leave him at least gave me some self-assurance. But the loneliness sucked on me gradually. Finally I just stayed in my loft most of the time. I hid. Then the insomnia and desperation."

"Did you have trouble sleeping before you met Larry?"

"No, not that I remember, except, well, as a kid, when I'd be afraid, you know, when my father started being abusive on some toot, something like that. But not when I knew it was safe to sleep."

"Safe to sleep?"

"Yes, well, you know, Daddy's time to be rough or abusive came around a half hour before or after my bedtime. So sometimes I would be afraid. For my mother mostly—and sometimes for myself."

"Can you remember that feeling you had when your father was being abusive and you couldn't sleep, and can you relate it to now?"

"I, uh, I don't know. Let me think. Well, the shards, the colored broken glass. That, I, uh, oh yeah, I remember something . . . I was about seven, I think, in our summer home, I watched an electrical storm from our porch. I stared into the lightning that struck close to the lake nearby. I think I was blinded by it—yeah, I was—for several days, in fact. Funny how I remember so well—lying on my stomach on the bed with all these bursts of light. I don't know how that relates to my father really, except that I think I used to see the lights when I closed my eyes tight and tried to sleep, you know, when he was screaming at Mummy. It was crazy. When I got a little older and Mummy got divorced, I remember anger. Always being angry. Her boozing and me pouring her into bed or something—you know, trying to cope—and she'd get that droop about her, on her face, I mean. I'd freak out, I'd get absolutely beside myself with rage and start seeing it again. I'd yell at her, and one time, God, we got into a snit. She had me in a white rage—and I picked up a kitchen knife. She came for me and I grazed her forehead with it—just a little cut. I was absolutely disconsolate. I begged her to forgive me. It was just barely bleeding, but I ran and got the gauze and Mercurochrome and everything. I told her I loved her and couldn't imagine how I did such a thing. Christ, it tore me open—you know, the mother-kill thing. I never got that angry again. Never. Terrifies me even now to think of it."

"So you've never gotten beside yourself with anger since then?"

"Well, I get angry, of course, with people. I used to rail at Larry. But certainly not to that point. I still see the lights, the, uh, oh God, please, this is so depressing, can we stop, please can we stop."

"Our time is almost up, anyway, Miss Dale. You know, we

have group therapy tomorrow as well as your regular appointment. See you at two o'clock."

★

After dinner Nalani and I played a little Ping-Pong again. After this week they'd let me start trooping around the grounds, go into town, do things like that. The difficulty of staying inside twenty-four hours was beginning to tell. I wanted fresh air and the feeling of earth. The world sense.

Nalani and I had already established ourselves as buddies. The others were O.K. for the most part too, but this air of sexual frustration of women denied things, it made for constant cunty conversations. I supposed it was the same for males away from women, only it depressed me now. And Nalani's orientation seemed a little different. We could talk superficially about other things, maybe a little heavy on the intellectualization, but that was O.K. too.

They gave me the bath automatically that night. And I did sleep. Calmer now, I slept, and had a series of nightmares close to morning, nightmares about someone trying to kill me by pushing me off a building; one about my father, but I couldn't remember exactly what he was doing in it.

★

There was a certain sameness to everyday habit in this place; people went along the same route until some emotional event, some freak-out, upset the schedule a tiny bit, and then everything fell back into place again. At two I went with Pat to a small living room where the group met. Dr. Saint came in— without her kitty—as one of the "groupies" was old cat-hater Sally. There were seven of us. What the fuck am I doing here?

"Well now, ladies, I presume you all have met Miss Dale. What we do here mostly is just talk; I don't say that much. But we tell each other our feelings and sometimes find they're shared by all of us in one way or another."

"How's your rash, Myra?"

"Better, Nancy; you know, it goes away when I'm feeling

good. Crazy though, now I'm having trouble breathing. Anyhow, I spent the weekend with my lover—he didn't call me crazy once—so I feel better."

"I thought you hated him."

"Well, yes, that too. I mean, sometimes I hate him. It's just that he can be so insufferably boring and stupid about things. He picks up on things—now's he's into being Madison Avenue-mod. Christ, why don't I dump him—what an asshole—doesn't think for himself."

"Well, break it off."

"For what? I don't want the hassles."

"You got here out of hassles. Longview's protection—you can break off with him over the phone. So that gives you a clear field. I mean, take advantage of your craziness."

"I don't know. It's better than nothing sometimes."

"Then it's your problem, Myra. The guy sounds like a eunuch."

"Bullshit. He makes most of the decisions."

"Is he a good fuck?"

"Eh? Why do you ask that, Nancy?"

"Well, I'm always looking for that in a man. Most men just plug in. If the guy really makes love to me, I like it better."

"That's what my husband did, just plugged in. Until I got beyond that with Guru. I don't think it ever is supposed to work, except to have children. Well, I bred, I got that much from it."

"Kathy, you drive me crazy with Guru. Try masturbating."

"You know, I never even tried it until I was well into my twenties and married. The sisters used to say . . ."

"Score one for Catholic education."

"Shut up, Louise, you're just giving me that dyke talk; all the women are getting that way. Depresses me; I don't want to be a dyke. Sometimes I think that in twenty years everybody's going to be dykes."

"Half of everybody, Kathy."

"Why do you say half of everybody, Miss Ginzberg?"

"Well, women are half the population. Why not? I don't know—the subject is boring either way."

2 8 9

"Why boring?"

"Well, constantly talking about sex—men. I consider that boring. Don't you?"

"Not if it makes us feel better to talk about it. Men play a large part in living, no matter what our persuasions are. Perhaps we can shut ourselves out of some of it—but I think it would be very difficult to, say, pretend we only come from our mothers and not also recognize our fathers. How do you feel about that, Miss Dale?"

"I don't. I agree with Louise. I'm tired of hearing all this cunt verbiage."

"What would you like to talk about then?"

"Nothing."

"Well, aren't we the superior person. I think you're a snob. I felt it when I met you."

"Why? I gave you cigarettes. I didn't snub you, Sally."

"Because you and Nalani have a thing going, you think you're the only ones worth knowing—real upper upper."

"Oh, that's bullshit. I like her—that doesn't mean I don't like you."

I hated the group. Sally had seen through me. I thought they were superficial and narrow—all except Sally and Kathy— because I felt they were coming out with something, were direct. The others I saw as faces with incessant mouths. Well-bred neurotics. I had no compassion for their problems, short of telling one of them, Helga, that the frustrations she masked so well were lodged in the hundred pounds or more she needed to lose. When the therapy session ended, I vowed to tell Saint to take me out of this sow pen.

"Hey, listen, I'm not going back into that group again. I can't believe you had the bad judgment to put me there. It's hardly therapeutic, it's cuntal first grade."

"Why do you say that, Miss Dale?"

"Oh, come on, you can't expect me to share feelings with these women. My viewpoint is considerably different from theirs. I don't find their experiences relevant. You of all people ought to be aware of that."

"How is that? You're not saying why you feel this difference. Oh my, that damn ashtray keeps going over on the floor. Just a moment. There. Now, why, Miss Dale, do you feel that you can't have anything to share with the other women?"

"I heard you—you know exactly why."

"You tell me."

"Because it's not an equal situation. Because they're, uh, they're what scares me. They're sows. You put me in with a bunch of sows; not one of them DOES anything. Except talk about men, romance, fucking, that kind of twit. That's not where my needs lie. A good marriage or relationship is not my goal. I want to resolve that so I can get on with the business of surviving on my own. Not being some cretin attachment to some fucking daddy. For Christsake, Saint."

"Why do you say I of all people should think that?"

"Well, when you were, uh, young, you know, and studying in med school and doing specialized training, I'll bet you got a lot of shit for your efforts. You know, you wanted to be a psychiatrist. So who were YOUR models, God help you? Freud, Jung. They made you a freak by definition . . . said the ideal for a woman in mental health was childbearing, the logical creative assertion of the female—anima, anything you want to call it. I know you're no Freudian, you're eclectic, you use different techniques—but I figure you're older—that your training would come from all that. Am I right?"

"Yes, indeed, you're quite perceptive. It has been difficult and I do draw upon different sources. Why is it, I wonder, that you are so familiar with the field?"

"I don't KNOW that much, but anything that has to do with a kind of knowledge for change or understanding I'm interested in. But these women just want their Prince Charmings. What the fuck is this—an ovarian torture test?"

"You say THESE women. You feel estranged, contemptuous?"

"Oh God, is this really important? My needs are different, that's all."

"Can you give me one word that fits your feeling about them?"

"Disdain. I disdain them. Except Sally and Kathy. For them I feel more compassion. I don't want to disdain anybody. I'm ashamed of it."

"Why do you feel compassion toward Kathy and Sally and not any of the other women?"

"Because I see them as the true victims of all these pressures, of the sexual war, if you will. They're innocents, they have no armor. They want things, love, some kind of justice, but their own way, naïve, right? With Kathy—all that guru shit—what is it, an outlet for her severe sexual repression—the discipline—counterculture Catholicism. She gives herself so passionately to someone's trip—she doesn't mask her feelings about her kids—she says right out she doesn't want them."

"Do you see anything of yourself in Kathy?"

"Hardly."

"Well, try and think. What makes you feel sympathy for her? Relate it to yourself."

"I, uh, I can't— This is stupid— Maybe; I don't know. Her incapability, her, uh, her victimhood. She wants things her way, I guess because she wants things and she feels sort of removed."

"Do you feel removed?"

"Yes. I'm trapped inside myself. I'm different. I'm different from those women. Don't put me back there— Oh damnit, I don't want to cry. Please, I don't want to cry."

"Tissue?"

"I don't want to hear these things about women failing with men or hung up in that bind. I made my decision. I left. I don't want to hear about it."

"Why don't you want to hear about it? Can you tell me what about women talking about men and sex disturbs you?"

"It's so fruitless. I mean, if everything was perfect in the world, we'd all be sublimely mated, happy in love and work and play. Or maybe we'd be marvelously ascetic—and peace, solitude, would reign—no one would ever worry about getting together because no one *would want* to get together. But nothing works like that. We're raised in corn-meal–Rhett-Butler–Scarlett-O'Hara mush. Christ, what a suck."

"Then isn't it a process of finding out what is workable and real; what we really are about, Miss Dale?"

"For you, maybe, not for me. Not out there. I'd rather hide."

"Do you think the other women in the group are hiding?"

"Yes, no; I don't know. Maybe they are hiding. I guess there are some similarities."

"Well, we'll see you tomorrow in group."

★

I took walks now, sometimes with Nalani, sometimes by myself. The initial first few weeks had passed and with it my insomnia, the terror subsiding under the structure and safety of Longview. I felt better; without liquor my face appeared less flushed and swollen. I was eating right—the yoga and swimming built me up. I doodled on paper and read. The weather warmed up briefly so I scouted Longview's small gardens and walked its paths. I stopped minding group therapy, became a little more involved in it; actually, I found I liked being a travesty amid other travesties. I began to learn. Though what it was I was learning puzzled me. I had no definitions.

★

"Miss Dale, you know you're cleared for a weekend pass should you choose to take it. Your husband requested that you spend Saturday and Sunday with him. You see, you must be signed out into someone's care."

"Absolutely not. I don't want to see him. Please don't call him my husband; he's not my husband and I don't want to spend five minutes with him."

"Well, in any case, the weekend is yours to take. Would there be someone else? How about your friend Fernanda?"

"Yes, I could stay with Fernanda. I hate to ask her. You know, I hate to depend on her any more. Embarrasses me."

"Well, think about it and let me know."

Irritating to be so dependent upon others. The fact that Larry, whom I saw as enemy, paid for all this, that I felt beholden to him and yet did not want either the obligation or his presence, kept me wanting to remain hidden as long as possible. Then again Longview overwhelmed me with boredom sometimes. There was all that insulated sameness, and now that I felt on the mend, part of me wanted something on the outside. That, if anything, would propel me into leaving here—the fucking boredom of living only for my emotional improvement.

Boredom won. I needed to see the city again, to look over my loft, to walk and play with the dog. I'd burden Fernanda again; I'd learn to be a burden gracefully. She could take it. I'd be helping her, wouldn't I—compassion was food for the poet, wasn't it? Especially a rich poet.

"Hello, Fernanda, it's Shylah. I hate to ask you. I want to take a weekend—you know, someone has to pick me up and take the responsibility and all that. Don't let Larry know, O.K.? I don't want to be in his charge. You don't mind? Great. Yes, well, he's been calling and I've been avoiding talking to him. You do? Well, I do too. O.K., well, Friday night if you can swing it; I have to be back Sunday by ten. Terrific. Thanks, see you then."

15

The old factory buildings that lined Broadway south of Houston Street glistened. Early-morning rain had taken the last of the slush off ledges and sidewalks, freeing dog shit and car oil smells. New York at its ugliest, the dead of winter—I found it exquisite now, trudging the filth, breathing the noxious air, all the way to my loft. I had been impatient for this, for this walk, after staying the night at Fernanda's, sparring with insomnia again.

The crazy painter who dressed up D'Artagnon-fashion cum roller skates, accompanied by two borzoi hounds and vermilion feathers, passed by. We looked at each other and smiled, pleased but preoccupied. Now who's crazy, Shylah? To be bizarre yet functional, to create some artifact proving to future historians that we were not, in fact, all screwballs; that we were, in fact, a civilized culture. Hooray for us twit-heads.

I had forgotten about my mail. The box inside the broken wooden doors was crammed—mostly art supply bills, telephone—but a letter from Luanne, and one of those perfectly penned, blue-envelope, monogrammed-stationery letters that could only be from Alice. Alice! I climbed the three flights of stairs playing a game of don't-open-the-letters-till-you're-sitting-down-with-a-cup-of-tea-and-a-cigarette. Inside I opened a window in the kitchen area and caught myself looking for Aardvark. It must've been the rank smell. I'd have to find some way of seeing the dog without Larry around. I still had the keys—I'd figure out something.

The last canvas, larger than its preceding ones, still hung there—the slab of freshly butchered art—the reds too immediate now to look at. I took it down from its nail, placing the offense in a rack with my finished work. Other than the lack of dog and shock of painting, I enjoyed my devil's playroom again. Home. The thought came strong, the word "home"—it was my home. Rock collection, wineglasses, Chinese box, Mexican bedspread, mine—they were mine.

I put a Jacques Brel record on the stereo, turned the volume up, wandered around the loft turning lights on, picked up Aardvark's extra mouse and rubber bone that lay next to the bed. The kitchen still contained the half dozen dirty dishes outstanding from before—what-was-it—my illness? My attempted self-murder? My blowout? Bloody fucking mistake—that was all.

God, the letters, I had forgotten—how could I forget letters? I took my tea and fumbled in the leather bag for a cigarette. Luanne's letter, chatty, short, shorter than mine to her, said they were fine, when would I come down, and that my father had been in Key West Hospital but was back home. Less forty pounds, she said. I skipped the rest and opened my stepmother's note quickly. Why else would she write?

Dearest Baby,
Time flies, doesn't it? Hard to think you are now closing in on a ripe old 24. It's been too long since Daddy and I have seen you, and you know how much we miss you.
Bad news, angel. You know Daddy's drinking couldn't have continued as it was going. He collapsed last month and Uncle Bobby Jay and I somehow got him to Key West Hospital. One o'clock in the morning, no less. He's home now, and up and around, but the doctors feel that he's been living on borrowed time and is lucky to have pulled through. Of course, with the liquid he lost, he's down to 190 pounds and drinks Tab now instead of bourbon.
His liver seems to have stabilized, but, you understand, it's a

gradually deteriorating condition. Thank the Lord he's finally on the wagon. I see Luanne from time to time and she mentioned she had heard from you. Do call us, dearest, and let me know how you are, how you've been doing. Let's stay in touch.

All love,
Mother Alice

I read the letter over three times. Dated January 20, 1969. Three weeks ago. When Daddy was getting out I was going in. Jesus Christ, why now? Daddy, you don't really want to hear from daughter, at this stage, huh, do you? If you wanted your daughter, you could have scribbled on the back or on a postcard, or called information and found out my phone number, or called Larry. Oh damn, I forgot. The letter had been forwarded from Larry. I had been out of touch—how long this time? Then this bug about me—bug of curiosity. I tried to remember my father's handwriting and couldn't. When did he last pen anything to me? On a Christmas package, maybe. As a child. I wanted my father's handwriting. Just a word or two. Why couldn't he write me? Why couldn't he? What do I do now? Call them? Yes, I'd call them. Children always called parents, didn't they? Parents didn't call children. No, I didn't want that. They'd ask me why I didn't respond right away to the letter. I didn't want Daddy to know where I was. He'd laugh at me. A letter distance—I could handle that; I could say we were in Spain, give 'em a load of bull. They'd approve. But not now; I wouldn't answer it now.

I telephoned Fernanda and told her I'd be sleeping at my loft tonight, not to worry—yes, I'd be fine, there was so much to do—she could relax. Then I phoned Larry and got no answer— Daddy wasn't dying, Daddy was eternal— Of course no answer, he'd be going to galleries today. A good time to go see the dog. Then Guy. I called my dealer, thinking something might have come out of the show.

"Shylah dear, zees is marvelous. I've been waiting for your call. Yes, zay bought it, and some of your leetle prints I had around. Don't you worry, I heard you were, uh, under ze weazer. You just get well, chérie. Perhaps I see you tomorrow, yes? Good. À bientôt."

I had been sold. At least some work of mine—my first. The

old Continental greaser had done me a service and I was grateful.

I left then, hopping a cab on the Bowery. I assumed Larry would be out arting and drinking until at least seven. Plenty of time to be alone.

"Aardddddvark, hello, puppy dog; you're bigger, yes, you are, you're getting enormous. Thank God, they left you with water and food. Oh yes, good dog."

Well, he looked O.K., frisky, his coat freshly washed and clipped—Larry must have had him professionally groomed. I checked the cupboards—enough Alpo for a kennel. So Larry or at least somebody was caring for him. I took the leash off its hook.

"Hey, Varkie, I'll take you for a nice long walk. You'd like that—all the way to Washington Square Park, where you can cavort with eight million other dogs and eight million tons of shit. C'mon, c'mon."

We cut across Fourteenth Street and down University, past boutiques and gourmet delicatessens that caught the Fifth Avenue trade. Washington Square on a bright, soggy day was something of a cosmic subway stop. Animals and humans—the urbane, profane, canine, and insane—came here to rest and to play, to live, die, and mill around in the process. On a particular spot of earth, covered with local dogs, I unsnapped the leash and Aardvark went to shit, sniff, and play. A gang of N.Y.U. folk singers stood by the fountain, busting eardrums with "If I Had a Hammer," some bums were passing a bottle of muscatel around, sitting on park benches otherwise populated by lovers and the aged. I sat and smirked and smoked on the first contact high I'd had in a long time. Good to walk around with everybody else walking around. I ought to learn not to take things so seriously.

The last few blocks of walking him back exhausted me nicely. I could see taking a nap now; I'd sleep, something rarely accomplished in the afternoon, that is, if I were going to my loft instead of Larry's. Inside, I unleashed Varkie, changed the water in his pan, and looked for dog biscuits. Larry's unique key fumble, when he rummaged through the familiar jungle of keys on his ring, gave me warning. Some gesture from the past—I patted down my hair.

"Shylah! What's this? You're here; what, they let you out for the weekend after all? Terrific, babe."

"Well, uh, yes. See, I had to take care of some business. I thought it would be nice to take Aardvark out for a walk. Hope you don't mind."

"Mind? Shit no, I don't mind. Well, let's take a look at you. You know, Shylah, you look a hell of a lot better, really much better. How do you feel?"

"O.K. What's happening with you, Larry?"

"Oh, I was off to Cleveland for a few days—they opened a show of mine there. Hey, babe, why don't you join me for dinner? I was just going over to Stokeley's, I'm sure he'd love to see you."

"No."

"Well, I could cancel it. I know, I'm thoughtless. You don't really want to be around other people right now. We could go out, just the two of us. How about lobster and a movie? See, I can be considerate."

"I never doubted it. No."

"Well, at least a cup of tea or coffee, or I put in some Cokes. Want a Coke?"

"Oh, I don't know, Larry, I should really go— I, uh, well, O.K., a Coke, in the bottle's fine."

"Why didn't you tell me you were coming in? You know, I've been trying to get you out. I would have taken you, picked you up."

"Oh, for Christsake. Why, it's over. Larry, stop being nice to me. We're not going to make it, trust old Shylah to know. After I leave Longview, I want it finished. Please, Larry, let's not drag it out—no more of this separation shit—I want a quick, clean divorce. If I thought you were coming back before I left here, I wouldn't have come. Your life makes me sick. I want my own life. We've been through it before. Look, I better go."

"Wait, Shylah. I, uh, I'm not very good at giving, I mean, giving of myself, but could we start talking about what you want, for a change? I'd try, Shylah. I know you've been avoiding me. I know you still love me. Please, I need you. Hear that, Shylah? I really need you. It's just, I find it so hard to say that. We could try. I would try. You're still my little fish, Shylah, my own."

"Yeah, well, my mother used to say, 'You can't put a whale in a frying pan.' Well, maybe she didn't say it, but you get the point. No, Larry, can't you see? Maybe a year ago we could have salvaged something—no, actually, I don't think we could have—not ultimately. I need to be alone, or maybe not alone, but I need to build something on my own foundations, shaky as they are. Come on, give up. Who knows, maybe we can get together again sometime. Don't you see, I've never really had a chance to be out from under. It's always been someone or an institution. Oh hey, not to change the subject, but, you know Guy sold one of my paintings and some prints. Pretty neat, huh?"

"You bet. You're getting to be an old pro. That's what you want, isn't it? Guess I really fucked up for you that way. Look, why don't we go out for dinner and a movie? Just a celebration of your sale. No hassles. O.K.? Or, uh, maybe you have something planned—please, I'd like to, if you would."

"No hassles? Promise. O.K. No, I don't have anything planned, just sort of walking around."

"Great, I'll call Stokeley and cancel. Would you like to take a bath? Your blue bath goop is still there. The plants aren't doing too well though."

"Yes, O.K. God, they aren't doing well at all. Well, they're all Southern types—probably ganging up on you. All that unexpurgated Yankee karma. Have you got a copy of the paper? While I'm bathing I'll check out movies."

God, my bathtub. No wonder the plants weren't doing well. The tub, the floor, and their leaves were dusty from neglect. Larry had his own hard-pressure shower downstairs. Now it looked untouched, a mausoleum for a dead porpoise. I took a sponge and carefully dripped water on the leaves, then rinsed it and washed the bathtub before drawing the water and throwing in the bath beads.

Ah, what a soak, isn't it fantastic. One of the lasting pleasures. I opened the *Times* to the movie section and broke into "Anchors Aweigh"—the only words I knew were the title ones, so I just kept singing them over and over. If the bastard really wanted me back, he'd think twice about a woman who sang the words "Anchors Aweigh" over and over again in Ravel's *Bolero* revenge. Shylah, how nasty you can be. Uuh, all that slick water, hmm.

"Come on, Larry. Get out of here. We're not playing house any more. Didn't your mother tell you that you don't enter a woman's bath uninvited?"

"But you look so great in there. When'd you start singing 'Anchors Aweigh' eight thousand times over?— You could drive even the plants to a wilt. You're no Leontyne Price, you know."

"Maybe for my next series I'll have a tape of me singing *Salome* as a companion piece to the canvas."

"You and Andy Warhol. What are we seeing tonight?"

"Well, there's *I Love You, Alice B. Toklas,* or how about *Bonnie and Clyde?*"

"Jesus, you really want to see that shit? Look, there's a Japanese film festival; how about *Gate of Hell* or something?"

"No, please, no art flicks. I can't cut it."

"No. You're right, Shylah, something kinky. How about *Bonnie and Clyde?* Where's it playing?"

"Uptown, eight and ten-fifteen. What time is it now?"

"Seven. Let's do the later show. We can go to the Lobster House first. How's that?"

"Sure. Can I get in like this? No, silly, I mean dressed with my jeans and stuff . . . Larry, get out of here; come on, I don't want you looking at me naked."

"O.K. Come out soon though."

The Lobster House had always been one of my favorite joints in New York. It was strictly neo-Howard Johnson's, all turquoise waves painted around the walls and netting hanging from the ceiling, and lobster and crab tanks big enough for the Miami Seaquarium. The seafood was fresh, everything was à la carte, large plates of vegetables. Just my kind of debased eatery. And my appetite from the vitamin B_{12} shots was nothing short of barbarian. Larry, for once, tried to keep our conversation light, which meant, for both of us, inane—a feat to discuss Claes Oldenburg over a two-and-one-half-pound lobster. Not a bad idea, Oldenburg making lobsters, gigantic four-foot floor pieces out of soft plastic, something kids could dig in a museum, something they could climb on.

Larry and I sitting there—making superficial chat—it was O.K.

"Larry, I've got to get out of here. I can't stand this blood-and-guts stuff. Panascopic gore—watching for Bonnie or Clyde to shoot somebody else in the head so we can watch what comes out. Please . . ."

"Shh, lady, can you be quiet."

"I'm going out."

"Sure. O.K."

My lobster was sitting precariously in the upper regions of stomach. With another spray of bullets it would be in my throat. Larry followed me up the aisle, waiting in the lobby while I fled for the john.

"Are you O.K., Shylah?"

"Yes, false alarm. I just pissed for five minutes, that's all. Look, if you want to watch the rest of this, it's O.K. I'll wait out here."

"No. Let's go for espresso at the Roma. It's right in your neighborhood, we can get a cab on Lexington— You *really* reacted to all that garbage."

"Yes, I guess I did. Who wants to see people get blown to bits and those doing the killing on either side come out heroes? Forget it."

"We should have stuck with the Japanese film festival."

"So what's the difference between samurai slashes and bullet holes? Walt Disney, where are you when I need you?"

The cab took us downtown to the regions of Little Italy, walking distance from my loft—to the Roma, where we had gone on rare occasions in the past when craving sweet pastries. I ordered cannoli and hot chocolate—good for getting to sleep tonight.

So far Larry had held true to keeping the evening light. Unusual for him to maintain restraint. I distrusted it—enjoyed myself, but distrusted the enjoyment.

"Shylah, do you have any idea how long you'll be at Longview?"

"Uh, uh. A month or two, I suppose. A lot of the women in my section are very short-term. Look, I know you're paying an amazing amount of money to keep me there . . ."

"No, it's not that. My accountant just takes it off what I owe the government. I was wondering how, uh, you were doing, that's all."

"It's hard to tell. I feel much better. I'm sleeping—that's the major improvement. Why?"

"Well, the Tillichs have a house on one of the Greek islands, supposed to be pretty fantastic. They offered it to me—us, I mean—from April through the summer. I just remembered how much you loved Greece. I thought maybe . . ."

"No. You know that's not going to work, Larry. Don't ask, don't give me the sumptuous bait. When I get out, I guess I'll go job hunting—something I'm not very familiar with. Well, I can type."

"Oh, babe, what are you going to do? Get some typist's job at two bucks an hour. Come on. You don't know how to be poor."

"I'll give it a go, that's all. Maybe I'll come out of it, more, uh, well-rounded. Or if I'm really lucky, maybe I can get a teaching job."

"You finished with your hot chocolate? Let's go back to your loft."

"I'm tired, Larry. I think I just want to be alone."

"I'll walk you there anyway. Don't want you getting mugged—knowing how susceptible you are to movie violence."

"Yeah, O.K.—you win."

The waiter brought the bill and Larry paid—the machinations of payments—when was the last time the tab was pushed my way? Even Dutch treat with young male artists, I was always second to see the check and then it was their tabulations that decided how much I paid. No wonder I was lousy at math.

"Thanks, Larry, thanks for dinner. Sorry about the movie . . ."

"How about letting me come up for a minute to see your new work? I didn't really get a chance to look last time I was up—Remember, you had tucked the canvases into the rack? I ought to at least examine what you've been doing, you know, so if somebody asks . . ."

"I suppose you should. O.K., but not for long, it's after midnight. I'll show you this new series."

"Titled?"

"I don't know—maybe 'Blood Sun', maybe 'Menstrual Sun'—I like Sun something or other— Actually there's a pun in all this."

"Hmm."

I took the twelve canvases from against the wall, standing front to back. I had not had occasion to look at them myself since my illness; perhaps I did not want to look at them at all now.

"This was the first of the series. I started it about the time we split up. They get progressively larger in size. Mostly experimentation in the cause/effect of five shades of red with the main difference being in texture. See, like that was done with a roller—looks spattered, doesn't it? Then this with a large housepainter's brush and thick, smooth—you know. Then this is built-up and bunched fabric painted over and down. And so on."

"Jesus Christ, Shylah. They're good, really fine. Maybe a little sloppy at times but the best certainly you've done."

"It's hard for me to look at them. Terrifying, in fact. Do you mind, Larry, I don't think I want to continue this right now."

"What's this business over here, looks like icicles or an encephalograph. It's so exact compared to the rest of the painting."

"I reverted to a kind of surrealism there, outlining first and painting in, using a watercolor brush. Think glaciers in blood on an expanse."

"Hardly pop art, is it?"

"Hardly, Larry. Now, I've got to . . ."

"Oh poor little fish, oh Shylah, don't cry. Here, let me hold you; there, I . . ."

"NO. Get out of here. You're impossible, really sucked me in there, didn't you? Stop being Florence Nightingale. You're too fucking late, I don't want you to. Accept it, I can't stand you any more. I think you're a schmuck. And I'm not crying because I'm blue. I'm pissed off. You've got the worst fucking timing. Dump it on someone else, willya."

"Look, I'm not perfect. Nobody can be everything to everybody else."

"Sure, sure. I should be the one to say that. So I can't be your little fish any more. Even if you had me, you'd be screwing around, which would be O.K. if there was some honesty to it. But you, Larry, you get off on deceit; deceit gives you a false control. Mr. Cold Silence. So do it with somebody else that likes it. I don't buy your Mr. and Mrs. Right crap. Please go."

"I don't want to go. I pay for your bloody loft. Remember that. I pay for you, Shylah."

"You damn well ought to, for services rendered."

"When did YOU perform any services? You've been just about as fuckable as those paintings of yours."

"Tough shit."

Wham. I found myself on the wooden floor with my lip stung and gushing. I looked up at what had always been his detached, paternalistic face. The manner, the twisted mouth; I would not have recognized him if I hadn't known it was him. Larry had never been one for physical retaliation. His bullying had always been a mind bullying, a manipulation. Amazing. The human animal stepped forth. Now how to remove it from my loft?

"Bitch. O.K., cunt, you're going to find out what being a loser's all about. I want out. No more easy separation, Shylah, I'd like a divorce. Die on your own time, do it your way."

"I thought I was the one who had suggested divorce. You could use some lessons in losing yourself, Larry . . . Don't you hit me again."

"Christ, of all the crazy dykes in the world . . . you know what you're all about? You lack intelligence. Basic intelligence. You know, Shylah, you better get yourself another john, it's the only way you'll survive. Certainly not on your talent, honey."

He left with his twisted face, his new face—slamming the heavy metal door. Hatred, wasn't it? Frustration maybe. I sat cross-legged, still on the same spot of floor where he had pushed me, sat touching my lip with an exploratory finger, shocked. I hadn't been shocked in a long time. The feeling interested me. Because Larry had lost his control, I now had my freedom, or some assurance of a quick divorce. He had given up. He had shown himself. It would not be his way to try again, to go back on the embarrassment he'd feel later. I sort of liked him now, his sudden frailty making him perversely touching. In love there had never been that between us; there had never been a giving-in time—until maybe earlier today when he had said he needed me—I did think he made the effort, but humility was such an underdeveloped facet of Larry Karp. But the anger, that was more than developed. It bloomed like some atrocious tulip.

Now why did I feel so light? One of the blessed, oozing Grace, sitting with my fingers sticky in the congealed trickle of blood. Dear God, everything suddenly so clean and alive. I started laughing. Life with Larry passed through me and was put to rest. It would have made a plausible television movie. I lay on my back, sucking in air with the laughter. Hiccups, that was my legacy from the old fart, hiccups. I stood up and locked the door, drank some water, holding my nose, held my breath, and danced around my work space. Shylah, beware of future nostalgias; look at the burden they hang on you and the bore you become to others. I'd call Fernanda and wish her a good night, share my sudden and joyful humor with her. She could always use a little of that.

"Hello, Fernanda, it's Shylah. No, I'm O.K., well, a cut lip, oh nothing, never mind. Oh, I'm sorry, did I wake you up? I forgot about the time. No, I feel terrific. Absolutely, I'm not drunk, I've been drinking Coke and tea and hot chocolate all evening. No, I just wanted to say I'll see you tomorrow morning. Why don't we do something—I don't know, go to the zoo or something—maybe visit people— No, really, I'm absolutely fine. Oh, it's a long story, tell you tomorrow. Go back to sleep."

I hung up the phone and looked at my T-shirt—the blood had given it a tie-dye effect chest level. I took it off, along with jeans and boots, alternating holding my breath and drinking the water, then made my way to the shower. Water beating down upon my back, something I never used to like, now so delicious—I didn't even mind turning around under the spray. Before I had begrudged its hardness, had cheated in showers, allowing only the front of me to get doused, except for shampooing, where I stuck my head under like a warrior undergoing purification rites.

Sheets when the body is water-relaxed—hmm, God bless the person who invented sheets. Sheets were old friends. Who knew me better than my sheets? I fell into a smug, egotistical snooze.

★

"Hi, Fernanda, what? Did I get you out of bed?"

"Shylah! You said morning. That means noon. It's only nine-thirty. I'm still paraplegic at this hour."

"Oh, come on, get dressed. Do you good, Fernie. I'll make us mugs of your cure-all health-store tea. It's sixty degrees out. Sunny mild—I walked here, all the way from my loft; took me two hours."

"What's with you, Shylah? You want a Valium or something?"

"No, for Christsake, I just feel terrific. And spring under my athlete's feet, why not? Hey, I bought us a paper. We can paw through it. Ooh, you've got the *Voice*. While you dress, I'll check out what's going on."

"What are we doing by the way?"

"I'm not sure, that's why I'm checking the paper out."

I followed Fernanda into her room, scanned the paper while she flushed out jeans and shirt from the clothes pile overflowing her chair.

"Well, what movies are playing?"

"There's an ad for Women's Interart Coalition—says 'Discussion/Tactics,' three o'clock downtown with address. Let's go. Why not?"

"If it's such a great day, why waste it listening to a lot of ego-blowing rhetoric? You're kidding. You know politics on art is bullshit."

"So is going to the movies. And what have we got to lose, we can always leave, you know."

"Well, we could go to a book party, if we're that desperate. I got this thing from Kathryn. Her new book just came out."

"NO. Look, we've got plenty of time, Fernanda. Let's head

downtown to the Village anyway. The air's a bit too thin up here; we can have Sunday brunch somewhere."

"It's your day, Shylah. Are we walking it or do you think for the sake of my poor feet we can get a cab?"

"Come on, Fernie, you're gonna love it, I know you're gonna love it. Little exercise will be good for your appetite and your poetry."

"Nobody said long-distance walking was a prerequisite for verse form. O.K., coach."

Fernanda got into it despite her contempt—the sunny day, the walking. We window-shopped and talked, even raced one another from one block to the next. My boot soles wore down to tissue paper. By the time we hit Eighth Street, my feet ached and food had become an obsession. Looking into the window of one of the local West Village bistros, I encountered my lip. My ministrations of ice last night had not helped it much. Swollen. And stinging now. I hadn't realized how much it hurt. Nothing like going to some feminist art thing with a little battle scar.

We decided on the Harlequin Restaurant, one of those bar joints that offers brunch and a free drink on Sunday. I ordered steak, an omelette chasseur, grilled tomato, V-8 juice, toast, potatoes, and a double espresso. Fernanda ordered only slightly less. Our bearded waiter took it all down with disbelief.

"Shylah, I can't not ask you any longer. What happened to your lip?"

"I'll tell you, Fernanda, but I hardly believe it myself. Larry lost his temper and laid one on me. A beaut, isn't it?"

"I figured. Why don't you believe it?"

"See, it's this way. He sort of broke through—the first time in five years I've known him to lose control—you know, when he wasn't hiding behind that fucking veneer of his. Amazing to discover his joining the human race in an act of violence. I didn't even recognize him with that face of his all twisted and fiery. You know, it cheered me up. It actually cheered me up."

"You're a masochist."

"No, my dear, the other way around. Not now. I just don't

care. It cut the cord. I wanted to see Larry Karp. And after all this time I did 'see' him. See what I mean? He gave up. Big Larry could not handle something. I think it's hysterically funny. Jesus, the binds we put ourselves in. Well worth this banana lip I'm wearing around."

"He could have killed you."

"Let the son-of-a-bitch try. Let him try. I'd pulverize him with every Cuisinière skillet he bought to keep me in my place. Don't worry, Fernanda; I'm not worried one bit. It can't happen again. Poor baby, he'll be licking his wounds from here to China. You know what he said to me, cracks me up. He said, 'I want a divorce—die on your own time.' God, can you imagine? Coming out with something like that. HE wants a divorce. Who left who? We've been separated for a year and now HE wants a divorce. You remember how I wanted it to be finished right away and finally agreed to the separation under those Larry Karp tactics. Christ. Now HE makes this horrendous decision as if nothing had passed. Oh Fernanda, the whole thing, all that agony, just strikes me as ridiculous and funny. I mean, what can I do but laugh? It's been an education—I learned how not to take others seriously."

"He'll try and cut you off, Shylah. I think he wants revenge."

"Let him cut me off. Oh, I can get money from him. I'll talk to the lawyer tomorrow, I'll call him from Longview. I've got it worked out in my head anyway. I want him to continue to pay for my stay at the sanitarium and to make a cash settlement amounting to my spent inheritance. It won't really set him back much for long. He sells that in six months. And that'll be the end of it. No alimony—no hassles over furniture or things of that ilk."

"You're nuts. How are you going to paint, keep the loft, buy materials once the bread runs out?"

"Well, I've got some time to figure that out. See, Fernanda, I don't think I could stand looking at checks with his signature on them coming once a month in the mail. I want to be done with it."

"What about your dog?"

"That's the only battle really. He's not that interested in having Aardvark around, but he knows how much I care for him. So he might make a stink about keeping him, just to be mean. So he thinks he's winning."

"Well?"

"Well, so if he becomes intolerable about it, I'll have to give up the dog. That's all there is to it. I know, I know. Cruel, aren't I—my little pooch—Shylah's giving up her love toy. It's my survival; if it means sacrificing an overbred springer I happen to adore, then that's the way it's going to be. And if he knows I'll do that if need be, you can bet he'll hand over the dog. I mean, what's in it for him if he can't hit me over the head with it?"

"Shylah, you amaze me."

★

Over on lower Broadway a storefront had been set up to accommodate the coalition officially called Organization for Women of the Arts—OWA. Fernanda put on her million-dollar sneer as we entered.

Familiar faces. Lots of them. Surprise, surprise. Sort of timidly entering a meeting of Alcoholics Anonymous only to find your parents, your best friend, and your parish priest in the front row. Two of the women who had participated in my group show sat behind the podium. Fernanda recognized a couple of poets.

"My God, it's a little bit of old-home week, Shylah."

"I know, I know."

The meeting had been going on for some time; the space was crowded with maybe three hundred of us. Currently under discussion was an argument on unifying women to picket a museum which was denying access to young women artists. There was some talk about an antiwar demonstration mixed in with the equal-rights situation, as well as discrimination against black women and radical Lesbians in particular. That is, there appeared to be a factional breakdown among the women on issues. An older woman, black—Fernanda whispered, "Poet"—walked over to the podium, requested and got the floor.

"Uh, sisters. We seem to be getting bogged down here. We have an issue, that of picketing the Wharton. We know they're sexist; we know they discriminate against blacks in general, against Lesbians; we know they send paintings to warmonger ambassadors in constituencies across the globe. Let's achieve our own unity together here or we won't get anything done. We have one overriding commonality between us that crosses race, art, and sexual preference. We ARE women. Look at us. We are WOMEN, aren't we? And as women, in this room, at this moment, we have a bond. Our strongest bond. No matter what color we are or who we get into bed with, I tell you as a solid political group we constitute the only discriminated-against *majority* in the world, and I for one don't give a damn if we're Third World or Sappho or Robert E. Lee's great-granddaughter. Nuthin, I said NUTHIN is going to alter our womanness. Now, sisters, let us get on with the business of unity. Let us move solidly on that Wharton Museum, picket that museum, using slogans that include all of our felt injustices. Hear! Jesus Mother, I'm black. Don't you think I'm going to have This Museum Discriminates Against Me on Sex and COLOR on my sign. So now we've set one month from yesterday—Saturday—as the date. I think we're agreed that's a good time. The Wharton'll be jammed with people with that retrospective going on. So let us do it. Let us picket together and come before the pigs in full feminine strength!"

Applause and cheering. My mouth had dropped open. My mouth rarely dropped open. It meant I was impressed. I was impressed. Having never thought of myself as a political body, I had not thought to consider what I had access to or not on the basis of my genitalia, though I often felt discriminated against by men—and women I considered surrogate men. Hearing something for the first time, put in such an articulate and passionate way, was more than emotionally moving—I felt no need to weep upon the grandeur of words—I was more than dumbfounded, I was stupefied. Evidently she served as a kind of joint to attach the different groupings of women within the larger body, a kind of messianic quality. And Fernanda, for whom praise was pulling teeth, spoke reverentially of her.

"That's Agnes Day. Really a fine poet. Charismatic, isn't she? My God."

"Yes, she is."

OWA broke down into separate groups, divided by art, in which we discussed tactics for the picketing. I had never picketed anything—had a cross burned in front of my door, but that was small-time. I enjoyed myself. I suppose I should have been terribly down-serious. After all, my rights were at stake, right? But women or no women, the meeting still contained the human quality of flying egos foisted upon the political circus. So what now? I did not have that detachment any more. What was being said on the basis of discrimination made fucking sense. Why not picket, Shylah! Better than hanging around Longview or going to a movie or pondering how hopeless the world ever shall be, to pervert the Bible. We talked of getting space large enough to hold a kind of monster group show of women's art. Something on the grand scale. How much money it would take—resources, a building, advertising. Somebody mentioned a revolutionary takeover of the Museum of Modern Art—which was hissed out as inappropriate daydreaming. But what if— I could imagine myself with grenades and a flamethrower, stumbling over fatigues. We compared our loft sizes. Since mine was particularly roomy, I offered it for a meeting of core-group artists two weeks from that day to discuss a group show. I OFFERED IT. Shylah, you're crazy. I didn't know anything about meetings and organizing. And I agreed to design the flier, scribbling down the information and participants. I would have to assume I'd get leave from Longview for my own meeting. I said I'd mail the final design off Tuesday, special delivery, to Brent Adelman, one of the painters I'd shown with. She'd have it offset. When we broke up and I went searching for Fernanda, my mind was mulling around undigested information—sudden glut and excitement after its long sleep.

"Jesus, Shylah, you're still in the hot house. Don't you think your political consciousness is a little sudden?"

"So maybe that's the way I am. Anyhow, I look forward to it. What time is it anyway?"

"Six-thirty and if we're going to get you back by your curfew, we better haul ass."

"Fernie, you are a blessed angel. You indulge me."

★

"How was your first weekend out, Miss Dale? You appear in high spirits. I take it you felt good about being in the city?"

"Yes, terrific. Revelatory, you might say. I didn't drink anything, of course."

"That's quite a cut on your lip."

"Well worth it, Dr. Saint. Hello, pussycat. I did see Larry, at first because of bad timing. I had gone over to his loft to see Aardvark, thinking he'd be away. He appeared just as I was about to leave. We had dinner together, I'd say my lip represents Larry's coming to terms with the end of the marriage. It's, well, you know, people have different reactions to realization. The bastard really popped me one, huh? You see, it's the first time I've seen him respond. I mean, really respond. See, it cheered me up. I mean REALLY cheered me up. Isn't that goofy?"

"Why is it goofy?"

"Well, it's the first time he became flesh and blood. Some fucking coping mechanism he has. Hallelujah. Anyhow, I felt so good the next day, Sunday, knowing I'd be getting a divorce without contest, that I walked all the way uptown and back, then went to this political meeting of women artists and writers. Hell, I never go to political meetings, and there we were, both Fernanda and I, lapping it up. And I bought it. Suddenly I'm designing a flier and I've offered my loft for a weekend meeting two weeks from now, You're not going to campus me or anything, are you? I mean, it's O.K. to get involved, isn't it?"

"Certainly, if you think you can handle it. Commendable. How did you feel about meeting with a number of other women?"

"Uh, fascinated, sort of, and well, I thought some of, you know, the people were tooting their egos, well, that was bullshit, but basically what was being said made sense to me. I usually am so estranged in groups. Um, just the connection, I could be, uh, loving again, and it wasn't necessary to be tied down to one person or in one institution to give in that way. Just being with the women in some way, well, vindicated me. It was infectious; even Fernanda got into it."

"But you say you didn't have that feeling of estrangement. Why do you feel this is so?"

"Well, uh, I guess I let go of something puritanical inside I didn't know existed. I mean, ultimately, I thought, why torture myself. See, nothing can happen in a pure state. Purity is static. Right? And Larry hauling off and socking me one acted as a catalyst. So why grovel in the old injustice suck? Know what I did after he hit me and left? I laughed, God, rolled on that filthy floor and laughed."

"Feels redemptive, letting go, then?"

"Oh, yeah, absolutely. Of course, now that HE wants the divorce he'll go rough, I suppose. So I called my lawyer. You know, I'm here under his financial auspices. That's sticky. Larry's thoughts all along were put her in a nice cushy sanitarium and after a few months she'll be brand-spanking healthy and go away with me to Greece and be O.K. wife again. Poor bastard."

"Well, I think it's a healthy sign you called your lawyer and are looking out for yourself. Does getting a divorce remind you of being in any similar situation?"

"Well, this is certainly different from my mother's divorce, if that's what you mean. She hardly greeted the prospect with a sense of humor. Oh, that reminds me of something. The lawyer—her lawyer, I mean—happened to be an old friend of both Daddy and Mummy. I can remember sitting in the waiting room while Mummy went in the office. Then Daddy came in and he too entered the office. And I could hear him through the door. There's this scene between them in front of the lawyer, so I ran in despite the secretary's trying to restrain me. Shit, how long did they expect me to wait outside—always that feeling of being cut off. So anyway, I arrived in time to see Daddy slug Mummy. But he was sober this time. He never hit anybody when he was sober. And the lawyer took him by the scruff of the neck and kicked him out. Mummy wasn't hurt much. Funny, I remember pitying him—so humiliating for him, being removed that way. Overpowered for once. I remember thinking that. The lawyer, this beefy Irish fellow, put his arm around Mummy. God, how sad. Bastard that he was to us both. The father shamed before the daughter. Sad as that Christmas when his own father died and he wept openly, and when I went up to hug him, he pushed me away and said he wanted to talk to my brothers alone."

"Can you tell me a word that best defines what you felt then?"

"Hard. I, uh, pained, of course. Unworthy. I guess that's the word that sticks in my mind. Unworthy because I wasn't allowed to be with my father when he cried."

"Can you relate those feelings to what happened this weekend with your, with Larry?"

"No!"

"Try. Is there a similarity?"

"Christ, you're such a fucking psychic nitpicker, Saint. Well, there might be a similarity between my father's violence and Larry's striking me. I guess that realization of how ridiculous and sad and funny we all are. And Mummy. I remember her as being very resolved that day. For once Daddy couldn't get his way. And since they met in the lawyer's office in the morning hours, both of them were sober. God, were they sober. And Larry and I were sober. Struck me as just ludicrous though, Larry's deciding HE wanted the divorce. There's no parallel there, or maybe there is; whoops, I guess there is. Oh wait, you know what else he said to me? He said, 'Die on your own time.' Larry said that to me. And that's what happened to Mummy. She didn't make it after all that shit of getting away from my father. I don't know, maybe she wanted to be abused, it had gone too far into habit. Oh please, Dr. Saint. I don't want to wind up dead. Not like that. Not that fucking repetition. I can't stand this repetition. No, I am not my mother. I am not her. I—oh Jesus. Please, please."

"Tissue?"

"I'm O.K. I just can't—I just can't—I, um, I just cannot—you know—suicide—I don't want to kill myself. I don't want it to be the same thing over again. It's horrifying. Patterns, how much we are of patterns. I had myself convinced when I took the Seconal that I wasn't consciously planning my own demise."

"But it sounds as if something inside you, your own fear of suicide, wouldn't allow you to admit to your self-destructive needs. Which probably aggravated them. We all have some sense of the self-destructive about us. Sometimes it's the binding of that urge that makes us become more so. Surely you are not your mother, but you have clear memories of her you've been sitting on for a long and painful time. Getting a grip on them, Miss Dale, frees you. Good, let's see you in group tomorrow, our time's up."

False elation. Remembering Mummy, the psychic mess of that period, brought my spirits crashing, though I was still feeling generally hopeful. Nalani revived me by her jokes at supper that night. Afterward we went off to the work room and talked while I began designs for the flier.

"Shylah, I started work on a novel Saturday."

"Nalani! No more Deirdre the Dragon. What's it about?"

"Who knows. Does it matter really? I'm just writing it. Sort of reportage, I made her an ex-nun, my main character. I haven't much idea about pertinent novelistic events yet. It's enough that I've gotten myself out of lollipop land for a while."

"Have you got a title for it?"

"*Sojourner*, I think. Do you like it?"

"Sure I like it. Isn't there another book by that title out? Oh hell, what's the difference? I like it. I like it."

"And something else. I'm leaving Longview weekend after next."

"So you're going out into the big hairy world. How'd you like to stay at my loft for the weekend? There's this meeting of women artists going on, that's what I'm doing the flier for and then I had to go and donate my space for the meeting. Might be interesting for you to sit in or whatever. Want to?"

"Oh, I don't know. A big group—I'm not a painter anyway."

"Doesn't matter. Just thought it would be helpful, bring you out. Interesting at least."

"I'll think about it, Shylah. Maybe that's a good idea."

"I'll introduce you to my friend Fernanda; we'll have dinner one night. You know, the poet I told you about. Come on, Nalani, can't hurt."

"Yes, so right. A little shot of feminism for the shaky Lesbian. Why not?"

★

A heavy snowfall turned Longview's pruned grounds into a white, solid expanse. I spent more time outside, walked around, often alone, occasionally with Nalani. During the week preceding the weekend of the meeting, when she left for good and I had three days at the loft, new women came in to replace the two who had recently gone home. I welcomed them as I had been welcomed, made note of their fury in remembrance of myself. My insomnia was gone. I had written Alice and Daddy that I wanted to visit. Though God knows why. I had good reason to poison him. But my feelings had reversed somewhere along the line. It had to do with that mortality thing. I worried about my father now, but a vague, frustrating worry. I did want to see him. If only for curiosity. I could not believe that he was dying. So I wanted to be there. I wanted to see him. Then there was that something that made me keep forgetting that I had a father and that my father would die without having been a father to me. The forgetting frightened me.

★

"So he's divorcing me and taking the kids, says I'm unstable—I got the papers and . . ."

"Aren't you going to fight it, Kathy?"

"No, why should I? They all hate me. I don't want to be there any more. I want to join with Guru when I get out of here, become part of it, you know what I mean, Nancy."

"How can you just do that; that's horrible, I . . . Hey, Shylah, what's the matter with you? Hey, don't cry; why are you crying, Shylah?"

"No, I, uh, so pitiable. Leaving, just dissolving things. So angry, my father, I keep forgetting my father. I don't want to remember. I, uh, I received a letter from my stepmother—she says he's been very ill. I don't know. I guess he's dying. I can't stand to think about it. When I was a kid he wouldn't let me around him when he was upset or anything. I don't know how to comfort someone who can't stand me. Christ, the old bully's mortal; he's so untogether he's dying. Can you beat it? And I just realized it and I don't know what to do."

"Have you telephoned your parents, Miss Dale?"

"No, Saint. I wrote them yesterday. I'm afraid to call. I wrote them I'd like to visit. I'm so afraid Alice will find an excuse for not having me or something like that. Jesus, though, I mean I've known about it since the weekend before last and it just hit me. I even forgot about it, makes me feel so ashamed."

"Shylah, sometimes you mystify me. Why should YOU feel guilty? Your father's been so maniacally destructive in your life and I don't see why . . ."

"Because, Louise, I don't know why, 'because.' Because he's my father. It doesn't seem to matter to me, his being so prickish. I hanker to see him, it's a feeling I have. When I go in this weekend, you know, after the meeting, maybe I'll try and call him then. Christ, I was really up for this thing, I mean the meeting, meeting other women artists, and now the idea of feminist politics when Daddy's dying—aw shit—I don't know, guess I feel, uh, conflicted about my entrance into public life and Daddy—I can just guess his feelings about his daughter and feminism."

"Why can't you have both?"

"I, uh . . ."

"Shylah, this is the first time in group you've, you've become a part of us, you've shared."

"Oh, uh, well, I'm kind of embarrassed. Where's the Kleenex box, please?"

"Maybe if you just tell your father you'd very much like to see him?"

3 1 8

"But we've never spoken that way to one another. I've never been able to just tell him anything. And Kathy's speaking about her divorce and giving up her kids and everything seems so devastating that we should—that nothing lasts, you know."

"So you think you'll phone him this weekend?"

"Yes, I guess so. It's not worth the agony. I'll call. I can't NOT call him, that's all there is to it."

★

There were close to three hundred of us in my loft, roughly figuring—a three percent return on the three thousand fliers. I thought we were doing O.K. Even Nalani's old lover showed up, whom I found rather cold for my tastes, the lover that is. Nalani held up rather well. Brent Adelman got Binet and his Soixante-neuf Gallery to donate space for a week for a reasonable kickback in any sales. After all, it was good publicity for him—ironic, the old satyr sponsoring anything so women's libby— We managed to raise six hundred dollars among us, not very much but a kind of working publicity budget. We talked about tactics for the mass picketing of the Wharton. They liked the flier, though few realized that the information for our meeting had been encased in a giant vagina—so if they saw it just as a hairy valentine, so much the better.

Afterward, Nalani and I went out for dinner. I'd call my parents later. The meeting, its excitement, had shrouded or once more delayed thoughts of Daddy— speaking to that voice over fifteen hundred miles of wire. Nalani rose to the occasion.

"Shylah, look, I'll sit beside you when you call. Try not to build it up, O.K.? Sometimes just the attempt to communicate is enough. Finish your ravioli."

"I'll try, O.K. What did you think of the meeting? I think it went very well. And you were so gregarious, I was a bit surprised."

"I enjoyed myself, really much more than I expected. I liked being in the group. And seeing her, you know—my ex-lady friend—didn't seem so insurmountable— Frankly, I felt nothing about her. Guess I didn't like her that much anyway."

3 1 9

"So let's get out of here. If I'm going to make that call, I should get to the phone before the anxiety becomes intolerable."

"Hello, is this Alice? Uh, Shylah. Yes, I got your letter—I've been away for a while or I would have responded earlier. Oh, you did, I'm glad you got it. Hi, Daddy. Oh, two extensions, I see. Are you feeling better, are you O.K.?"

"Hellooo, Shylah girl. Well, ah've known more active days. Kinda quiet down here without you. How you doin, girl, huh? Shit, answer the door, Alice, want to talk to mah daughter. They got this damn minister—comes every friggin day, hangs around like a mortician. How y'all been, baby? Yer old dad thinks about you."

"You ought to try writing me sometime."

"Ah never was much of a writer, as y'all know. How's that artist husband of yours—he treat you good, Shylah?"

"Oh sure, fine. He's a peach. Alice wrote you were very sick in the hospital. You're taking it easy, I hope. I, uh . . ."

"Ah'm back, angel, just the preacher. So glad y'all called. Ah was just fixin to call you, wasn't ah, Daddy? Listen, dear, mah mother's eighty-fifth birthday's comin up in May and mah brother and ah planned a kind of reunion up Ohio way. Now, how would it sit with y'all to come down here for the month; we can all visit for a week or so, then ah'd fly up there for three weeks or so and you and your daddy would have the time to yourselves. Ah'd lahk it if you'd look out for him a bit, make sure he takes his medicine, stays away from the girls . . ."

"Ah'd, uh, ah'd love to see you, Shylah girl— Pay her no mind though, ah'm doin fine—don't need no nursemaid for Christsake, Alice . . ."

"Yes, of course. May. Sure I'll come down. We haven't seen one another in quite a while. You're sure you don't want me to come sooner? Daddy, you really are feeling better?"

"Don't you worry, honey, your old man ain't through yet. Just shut down to second gear, that's all. How them brothers of yours?"

"Oh fine, I saw them for Christmas."

"We got a nahce note from Zoe's wife, Ava; they had a little boy. In't that mahrvelous—your daddy's a grandfather."

"Yes, terrific."

"Well O.K., y'all write us now and ah'll write a long letter—goodbye, angel."

"Bye, Alice. Take care of yourself, Daddy, O.K.? I look forward to May and seeing you."

I hung up the receiver. My father's voice in the distance of telephone quavered, old. But sick-old, and I detected mellowness. What was it? OH, my name. He had called me by name. I had expected the drunk slur, the distance, and there was none of that. Threw me, the sobriety, the sober warmth.

Two months until May. I'd be out soon enough, certainly well before May. Before, I had nestled comfortably into Longview, my safe seclusion, the false insular womb. Now the idea of returning there after the weekend, with Nalani gone—I hated it. I wanted to go now. I wanted to see my father and Lime again. My curiosity had peaked with the vibrato in his voice.

★

The OWA march on the Wharton Museum and my blossoming political activism were a qualified success. One thousand of us Johnny-come-lately feminists with our slogans and work clothes and shiny, committed faces would have impressed a Roman legion. Naturally we embarrassed the museum; naturally the press and television were there to interview us, publicize our demands, and record for posterity a verbal breakdown of Wharton's one equivocating spokesman. And yes, we were promised a show of women artists within the year and the hiring of women in high administrative posts, and oh no, they would never think of discriminating against black women in particular and certainly never against radical Lesbians. I got my first participatory view of how power folds with a bellyache, that is, against media-covered public opinion. I saw it as I had perceived Larry and me in the final funny death throe. In our other demands—"that of stopping the flow of art to American constituencies abroad and of stopping the war in Vietnam and

3 2 1

of ending sexual and racial discrimination now"—we failed; managed a strong kick to a lead bucket, but failed. The nature of the process. I was no purist. I was thinking of my father at least 50 percent of picketing time.

Saint and I had set a two-week date on my departure from Longview's palatial tit. Our talks, or my talks and her questions, had reversed themselves into the future: how did I feel about seeing my father? how did I feel about the divorce? how did I feel about myself as an artist? My rabid young lawyer, Tom, had gotten a much larger cash settlement than I had initially demanded, reminding me that I had never had any idea or thought to inquire of my husband just exactly how wealthy he was. I had been married to a millionaire without it occurring to me. Such was the nature of our marriage. So much for practicing up on my typing skills.

And Aardvark died. Larry grieved over the phone. Never a salty drop for us, so the dog caught the tears. He had broken leash on the Bowery and that was it. A nice fat oil truck had left his skull flattened. I mourned for a day, then tucked the memory of Aardvark away with the other worthwhile moments of living cut short. Animals belonged in the country where catastrophe was relative and usually more organic.

★

"Well, Miss Dale, you leave us. Any feelings about it?"

"Not a lot, I'm fairly even these days. In a way, I guess from where I am now, I'll miss most the yoga and daily swimming and being fed. The regulation living of Longview. Look at me. I haven't been in such good shape in a while—well, O.K., minus the kidneys. My mind's on starting a painting from the sketches I've done and going back to Lime, seeing my father and Luanne. Oh, that reminds me, a letter from Alice yesterday confirming everything and on the bottom of the page Daddy wrote something—I mean, in his own hand. You know, that's the first time I've seen his handwriting, addressed to me, that is, you know, other than his signature, since I was a kid."

"Did it surprise you?"

322

"Saddened me. I remembered the bold strokes he used to have. This was a kind of scrawl—he must have been shaking like crazy. Just a few words, he said. I memorized them— 'Dearest Shylah, Come safely. Mother and I are laying out the red carpet—all love, Dad.' Sentimental, huh? But—sure—I was moved. I think he knows he has to be taken care of. After thirty years of hard drinking, it must be excruciating to be so vulnerable, to be dead sober all the time."

"What do you expect him to give you while you're there? By that I mean, what is it you want of your father now?"

"Just the chance, I suppose, to be there, care for him; some communication. Who knows, probably it'll just be a mellower version of the same. I'm prepared for it. It's a test for me, I think. Also, I need Lime again. I want to see the island, to see Luanne and Stanley, to see the ocean there."

"And your divorce?"

"I'm a shit load richer than I thought I'd be. Larry's generous side came through—oh, you know—I never even fathomed what our finances were—never knew how fucking rich he was. Just didn't occur to me. Now I'm delighted, since I'll be paying directly for once. I need to learn about money, huh? I'm not going to mention the divorce to my father. Seems pointless unless he asks; think I'm going to try not rocking the old boat, see how it works."

"Have you any thought on your actions that brought you to Longview?"

"Jesus Christ, have you another year to listen? What frightens me most is the pattern. You know—repeating *her* pattern— Mummy's pattern of self-destruction. I think just talking has helped a lot. OWA, being with women in an organized group, setting up structure—seeing how it works—I'm still somewhat estranged from, what would you call it, 'activism,' but now I'm, uh, I'm drawn to it just the same. The good outweighs the bullshit."

"Will you be seeking therapy, someone to see on a regular basis when you return to the city?"

"Uh . . . I can't tell. I don't think so. At least, not the way I feel now. It would be sort of frivolous and wasteful to depend entirely on outside help, don't you think? I want to try other things."

"I would say that sounds quite sensible. Well, Miss Dale—oh damn, can you beat that, the ashtray again, I've got to organize this desk, whoops, there we go— Well, Miss Dale, best of luck to you then. I know my cat will miss you. You're leaving this evening? Just be sure to pass by the admitting office and sign yourself out. Let me know how you're doing, will you?"

"Yes, of course, Saint. Do yourself a favor, huh, and get someone to attack that desk top and empty your ashtrays. I'd hate to see a good shrink go up in smoke."

"Not a bad idea, Miss Dale, I'll give it my attention. Tomorrow."

BOOK THREE
MAY–JUNE 1969

"And hast thou slain the Jabberwock?
  Come to my arms, my beamish boy!
O frabjous day! Callooh! Callay!"
  He chortled in his joy.

'Twas brillig, and the slithy toves
  Did gyre and gimble in the wabe:
All mimsy were the borogoves,
  And the mome raths outgrabe.

"Jabberwocky"
Through the Looking-Glass
Lewis Carroll

16

I spent money. A first spree in preparation for my trip to Lime and under my own signature. Larry's partial settlement check had come through, shooting my bank balance up to five figures. Money with my name on it, money I didn't have to ask for, my money, my signature. The dollar world that had paid for me without my signature, without my judgment, too often without my awareness—now mine. It would be my carefulness, my mistakes, my squanderings, my luck, my budget, my priorities, and all the manicured hands of bank executive daddies, executor daddies, and ex-husband daddies with their overblown John Hancocks marking my life could withdraw and pick me clean from their nails.

I bought a car, deciding to drive down to Florida rather than fly. It was a sprightly little yellow Volkswagen convertible, four years old and in mint condition. I shopped for a week before buying it from the agency, peered into a dozen engines I pretended to understand—when I understood nothing more about a combustion engine than how to turn a key and ignite it. Nevertheless, driving was a pleasure for me. I liked to drive and, from all I'd seen, was far better than average at it. My entrance into paper work was disorienting at first though, filling out forms, waiting in the endless welfare-like lines at the motor-vehicle department—the registration—the insurance—and the outright sadism of civil-service workers who sent me three times to stand in the wrong lines. Of course it would have been eminently more practical, less time-consuming, to have flown and taken the bus down the Keys from Miami. But I wanted the adventure, I wanted the show of independence, and fifteen hundred miles of regional Americana, the motels, mountains, and McDonald hamburger stands made for a reasonable debut.

Two days before the date I had arbitrarily set to leave New York, I withdrew two thousand dollars in cash (beyond the bank check for the car) and went shopping. To spend lavishly from my own resources—I plowed through every shop that took my interest, bought gifts for Daddy and Alice and for myself—new jeans, boots, shirts, sleeping bag, air mattress, tent, fishing rod and tackle, skates, a mess kit, books, new mattress for the loft, and just for the hell of it challenged the women at Elizabeth Arden's to a haircut, oil treatment, and shaping—emerging four hours later preened, massaged, and curled in my new safari suit and cowboy boots. Lastly I brought Fernanda and Nalani together for a dinner at Mother of God's, a restaurant suggested by one of the women at OWA. We spent the evening laughing over our ex-conship from the madhouse, over art, and over a dish listed on the menu as Mother of God's Courageous Tongue. I picked up the tab, to all of our surprise, overtipped, mentally ascertained that I had a thousand dollars left in my bag, hugged them both as I would the last survivors on earth, and went home to a full-bodied sleep in my new Mother Hubbard and mukluks.

★

It was dawn, six-thirty on a late-April morning when I packed my car methodically, making sure to place my father's ginger candy and the bronze stallion figurine along with the Italian shawl for Alice on top of my gear in the trunk. Sweater-weather spring. By midmorning it would be warm enough to put the top down.

I took my time. Once out of morning traffic, which kept me

inching across the George Washington Bridge for forty-five minutes, and across the boggy aspects of New Jersey, I cruised at sixty, watching the landscape as it thinned or fattened, and stopped for coffee every few hours. The sun held; I put the top down, skirted one skunk in the road, continuing on until late afternoon, when I crossed the Virginia state line, the first taste of South, with its long stretches of greenery and laurel.

The Dixie Side Colonial Inn. First of the big motel complexes along the highway that promised restaurant, bar, free ice cubes, color TV, and a little Mason-Dixon hospitality—not particularly in my favor as lone female figure driving something as reprehensible as a New York State–licensed, foreign-made car. But the garish façade suited my tired eyes. I parked and walked into the part marked OFFICE.

"Hello, dahrlin, what can ah do for you all?"

"I'd like a room, please. Do you have a pool?"

"Shore do, but it's not yet in service. Couple weeks, ah expect. If you'd just fill this out, ah'll give you 206, raght nahce view. Where you heading, miss, uh, Dale?"

"Florida. The Keys."

"By God, they got the best damn fishing down there. The wife and I were just in Marathon last year this time. Maghty pretty place."

"You don't say? Yes, it used to be my home below Marathon. Just visiting my folks."

"Well, ah surely hope you have a pleasant stay. We have a quality restaurant here. If you should need anythin, you just pick up the phone, hear. Room service till midnight."

"Much obliged."

I took my key, grabbing the overnighter before the bellhop could, and walked the grillwork outside stairway up to room 206. More firsts: I had never stayed in a motel or hotel alone and under my own auspices before; I had never fit the key into the lock or investigated a room to my tastes. Just the standard two double beds, undersize bathtub, glasses on a tray all carefully covered with little waxy bags bearing the name of the place, likewise stationery and that precious paper seal over the toilet.

The room-service menu had the limited number of entrees

standard to American taste of Southern vein—fried shrimp, chicken, steak, and lobster tails. I took a chance on the honey-batter Southern fried chicken, yams, and collard greens, which arrived half an hour later, accompanied by a sallow-faced busboy with flowers in hand, from the manager, he said, from the manager's garden. Southern chivalry in late-April bloom. I returned to my love affair with the color TV, listening to the soft slur of a local newscaster. Virginians spoke a genteel, modified Southern which became increasingly colorful and devil-may-care of dropped endings the farther South you went. Here, the sounds were delicate, faintly musical, like the weather—zephyrish, warmer; noticeably warmer, but not yet heat.

In Georgia I stopped to buy pralines for myself and pecan pies for the folks. It had been a fitful night at that motel, one in which I considered turning around and heading back for the city. I had dreamed I came upon my father in the dining room and he did not recognize me, did not remember having a daughter, cut me off when I tried to speak. Terrifying. I had begun to expect the old rejection pains. And what could I say to him? I didn't understand why I wanted to see him. Why come down? Why confront the wall again? In my mind I had forgotten these things. I had built up the fantasy of warmth, on his few scribbled words, on his voice over the phone. Because he was dying, because I could not let go, because I wanted it out of my mind. Victim. Stupid bitch victim. Daddy, please recognize me. At least recognize me. Nerves. By the Georgia/Florida border I had consumed the whole box of pralines, culminating in a bout of diarrhea in a tiny gas station manned by unfriendly crackers. There I clutched the broken-down doorknob with my hands, praying they wouldn't grab me off the leaking toilet.

I felt less ponderous all around after my catharsis, drove hard, and made the first slew of palms and shrubs native to the fringes of subtropicana. Outside New Smyrna Beach I pulled in at a camping sign, paid my three dollars, and awkwardly pitched my first tent. The uniformed conservation man at the park entrance let me in, but only after shooting me his hairiest eyeball. I had probably been his only lone woman camper, something rarely seen or done in these parts—something I had forgotten again. I camped in an area well populated by families with kids, close enough so some stray redneck hooligan passing by would stand off from any sudden assaults. Still, the feeling kept me wary. Fathers, Shylah. What blind spot in nature gave us fathers? Rape and fatherhood, and did men who stalk women have mothers? Could mothers be hunters? Shut up and enjoy the silence, Shylah. Turn off. Enjoy the night, night among trees, leafy, loving bedposts, clear tonight— wasn't the small wind worth the risk? I slept well with my clothes on. The dreams had stopped.

I woke early, sun hitting off the lower trunks of pine—pink-gauzy as spider webbing, and hot, a bug sound of heat in the air. I headed out, stopping at Cocoa Beach outside Cape Kennedy for breakfast.

South. Miami by noon, the vast labyrinth of overpass and shopping center, cars pulling boats, frantic tourists, palm-lined Highway 1 and farther past the familiar landmarks, Seaquarium, Monkey Jungle, Orchid Jungle—towns like Perrine, Cutler Ridge, Homestead, Florida City, then down the stretch of endless twenty miles, two-lane-highway sameness until Jewfish Creek, the little drawbridge, and the first signs of Key Largo, as if I had never been away.

Broiling. Ninety degrees or so and a hard sun. My armpits leaked sweat down the sides of the jersey top and my backside matted slick on the vinyl seat covers. Salt air hit me full face in blasts from either side. A high. Six years, was it six years, almost, since class lunacy on Peacock Island? Stanley. Stanley, I'll hunt you out. Who was left? Tavernier, Islamorada, Craig, Marathon, islands and bridges, the seven-mile bridge, then the small road off Highway 1 and the bridge-fill to Lime, double rows of palm trees, frangipani and bougainvillea lighting up from stone fences.

My father sat in the deck chair facing the water. I lit a cigarette and gathered odds and ends into my purse. Waited, looked around. The house had not changed, maybe a little cleaner from a recent painting but the same; the front yard was somehow fuller though, better attended, new shrubs, freshly pruned. Mid-afternoon in Lime, siesta time, too hot for much activity, a good time for gin-and-tonic and a nap. Distant whir of speedboats coming into the marina.

The back of my father's neck. I held the view, watched him turn the pages of a magazine, knew it was he, knew by the angle at which he held his head, and knew from the slack of neck hanging over shirt collar that he had withered, changed harshly—the collar now dwarfing him. Father, please. Daddy.

"Shylah. That you? That you, girl? So skinny. Oh baby girl, that you?"

"Hello, Daddy. Yes, it's me, it's Shylah."

He stood as I came to him, fragile in his hulk, the large head with its reddish complexion now outsized for his body. Yet he kept it up, the sprightliness, the cocky walk.

We embraced; I put my hand to the side of his head, holding it there as if to sustain the balance. And he looked at me, something we almost never did, look at one another. I saw myself in him then, the nose, the broad, distinct jaw, the dimple. The loss of weight had brought his features out, made them more defined, more accessible to me. I noted the age marks as well, lines in the leather-worn cheeks, hanging flesh, and Adam's apple at neck, the delineated upper palate. A kind of first sight in silence, holding each other under afternoon torch. The tears. The broken promise of tears.

"Son-of-a-bitch, look at me, will you, cryin on mah little girl's shoulder. Y'all sit down, honey, and tell me all about yourself. Goddamnit, Shylah, you're one hell of a fine-looking woman."

"Uh—I—uh—wait—just let me catch my breath . . ."

"Well, did you bring any of your, uh, paintings down?"

"Well no, they're too large really to move around without taking them apart. I brought some photographs though, taken at this show I was in recently, an exhibit of women artists and . . ."

"Well, let's see them."

"I've got them in my purse somewhere; here—they're rather, uh, abstract, Daddy. You know, they don't look like, uh, much."

"Hmm. Ah see, you a modern artist. Well, I can't raghtly say I understand them, but they shore are lovely colors. You know me, ah lahk pictures of boats and the lahk."

"Well, I brought some sketching materials down. I'll do a boat for you on the high seas; you like that, an old-fashioned sailing boat, right?"

"Would you do that? Goddamnit. Tell you truthfully, Shylah, I kinda think you ought to try commercial art. There's a lot of money in it, y'all want a career. How's your husband, he good to you?"

"Umm, oh fine, yes, very good— How are you feeling, Daddy? You've lost so much weight, my God."

"Oh, can't complain. Course they took away everything I got, mah bourbon, pulled mah teeth—see, these damn things are false—gall bladder. Ah still got a lot in me though, goddamnit, still going strong. Don't listen to Mother or that Episcopal know-everything priest. They sit on me lahk buzzards. Don't you pay them no mind. You lost a lot of weight yourself, girl. You been sick?"

"No, no. You know how it is. City women stay skinny. It's the fashion. And I can't stand my own cooking."

"Well, sheeit, kid, ten pounds can't hurt you. Ah'm goin to get after you to eat, Shylah girl, you gonna settle down and give me a grandchild one of these days, by Jesus, y'all gotta be in shape."

"Well, maybe a little of this healthy island living will do the trick."

"How you stand that city, Shylah? Ah always hated it. People there downraght mean. Jesus, mah whole life changed when I came down here. Well, of course you know that."

"Yes, I know that. Right down to your late-blooming accent. And it's hard to leave the island. I've been homesick for it, off and on."

"Well hell, honey, tell that husband to move down here. We even got a gallery, and there's all those artists in Key West."

"No, I don't think he'd be willing to move from the city. It's not just culture, it's the dollar thing, you know, hard to make a buck in art unless you're there. Anyhow, I'm here for the month."

"You want some help unpacking the car? Tomorrow's laundry day, you got any dirty clothes? Alice is just at the store. Say, can ah get you a drink? Ah can still make 'em even if ah can't drink 'em."

"No, um, thanks, I'd love a Coke though. What a change—into this heat, I mean."

Daddy loped through the door and into the kitchen as I went around front to the car, taking from it my suitcase, the ginger, gifts, pies, etc., through the front door and into my old room. My room. Inside too the house had retained its sameness. Even my bedspreads were the same.

What had passed in that few minutes, encompassing Daddy, the island—I could not assemble then, could not get beyond mental fragments. I tended to the business of unpacking as if there had been no separation, no hate, no childhood, no illness. The sounds of Lime, the sweetness of smell, were saturation enough. And Daddy returning with the Coke—a wave of crooked posture, false-tooth smile, bright-eyed like I'd not seen since earliest days.

"I brought you and Alice some things, Daddy. I remembered how you like ginger candy—oh, and this—I hope it's a decent addition to your collection."

"Jesus, honey, where'd you get this stallion? Fine-lookin workmanship, real old piece too. Why, Shylah!"

"They have a slew of antique stores in the city. I saw that in one window and thought it might go with your others."

"Certainly does, ah'll be a son-of-a-bitch, this is a real collector's gem. Goddamnit, Shylah. Y'all must have spent a fortune on your old dad. You shouldn't have been so generous, baby, just wunnerful, uh huh. Ah'm gonna put it in the glass case raght now. Ah'll be goddamned. Oh, here they come; Alice's back—wait till she sees this—and she got Bobby Jay with her, oh brother."

"Why, precious, you look just boo'ful, doesn't she, Corky? Soo good to see you, Shylah. Mah Lawd, you're awfully slender. Look who's here, Bobby Jay."

"Alice, you look very well. Wonderful, in fact. Hello, Unc—Uh, Bobby Jay."

"Been a raght long time, Shylah. Y'all lookin good."

"Thanks."

Bobby Jay excused himself and left, still angry from six years ago. Terrific, I hoped it kept him up nights. A reprieve. Now my father, stepmother, and I stood awkwardly in my room, clothes half unpacked. Strangers in a way, covering the strangeness with endearments. I brought out the Italian shawl for Alice and the pecan pies. Some little twinge of the sardonic bitch fluttered inside—I had given her something I knew to be elegant and expensive. Alice's taste had never developed beyond bargain-basement conspicuous consumption—right down to her Cadillacs—all those pretensions—whoever heard of tipping 8 percent? Oddly enough, she looked better than when I had last seen her—the gauche grow younger. No, I still disliked her; moreover, I still distrusted her.

Daddy shook a little standing there, a slight feebleness causing me to look his way, to the trousers that hung too loosely and the short-sleeve shirt with too much space between the sleeve opening and the suddenly slender, freckled arms. Conversation was beyond me, and when Alice suggested I finish unpacking and take a bath, freshen up, as she put it, and meet them out on the dock, I said yes, that was what I wanted to do. Late afternoon and the same cast on the streak of sunlight that hit the window slats, remembering the four-thirty prism effect, that had not changed, not lost or gained perceptibly.

I changed into a dress, one of those nondescript shirtwaist things that would hide my armpit hair—the fuzz on my legs was light enough to be innocuous. Hardly forthright, but so what. I just couldn't handle a lecture on feminine hygiene and forbidden hair. Not now.

"Alice, delicious. Turtle steak, my favorite. They're not scarce down here?"

"Not off the Keys, honey. It's still pretty cheap. Have another piece of the pecan pie; that's just the sweetest thing, bringing all those goodies. And this lovely shawl, real classy. Ah see you must have spent a fortune . . ."

"Looks good on you. Daddy, are you all right?"

"Just tired. Lot of excitement today, sugar."

"Corky, it's not so early anyhow—after ten. Whyn't you go lie down? Shy and ah'll take care of the dishes."

"Alice, goddamnit, ah'm not your little boy. O.K., girls, the old man's gonna bite the dust for a few. It's all that damn delicious food, enough to give an honest man the gout. Naght, girls. Shylah, shore is good having you here. Y'all got everythin you need; yah, you got everthin you need. Well, naght, you sleep late tomorrow, hear, plenty of time, naght."

"Good, I hear the shower water runnin. We'll go off tomorrow just you and me for a few hours, angel. He needs care, you see, but ah've found it best to be real subtle about certain things. Raght now his health's been O.K. but sometimes he has a little problem with memory and sometimes he'll upchuck his meal before he can really get it down. Well, ah'm sure he'll be O.K., but, you know, he isn't going to be with us that much longer, though sometimes ah'm given to wonder—what ah mean is, his health is fragile. But we know that, don't we, huh, Shylah? Your daddy still wants to think he's a bull; course from a wife's point of view, that hasn't been the case in years. The drinkin, Shylah, it's the drinkin. Oh well, what was ah sayin? Oh yes, it's just that there are certain things ah wanted to make sure you understood. We'll talk more about it tomorrow."

"But he's not senile . . . He doesn't act that way. He's been sick, sure, but his mind is strong."

"No, uh no, ah didn't mean to suggest that he was. Just we gotta be careful of him."

"Yes, right. Care full."

"Ah 'spect you'll be wanting to run around a little, see Luanne—gee, she's a lovely young woman, and that daughter of hers. Well, y'all just have some fun and see your friends. Ah won't be leavin for a week. Now, you got everything you need for a nahce rest?"

"Thank you, I've brought some books to look through. I'm looking forward to seeing the island a little tomorrow. Good night."

A night without the hard grate of distant cop cars yowling or the traffic or junkies screaming or fears of intrusion. Just night, where every sound had the quality of a pair of arms or a rocking

chair—constant movement—palm frond, ocean, breeze whoosh-
ings—old friendly seductions of my mind by Morpheus. Dear
God, I had lived here once.

★

My bedside clock said six. I was awake, not groggy awake but
wide-eyed and excited, wanting a walk and the outdoors. Alice
and Daddy snored as I dressed and carried my new rubber flip-
flops to the door; then, opening the screen inch by inch, slipped
out. Dewy. The front yard had an early wetness that clung to
the mat grass. Hibiscus had not yet opened petals to the day but
stretched from their bush stems like multicolored Havana
cigars. I decided to walk the short distance over to the marina,
where the guides would be just taking off with their parties; I
could get an early-morning cup of coffee in the café there. The
sun, once it was full off the horizon, heated up the morning
quickly. By eight I'd have my first sweat. The marina had seen
improvements—the docks bigger, more boats to be seen and
more varieties of boats. Two buildings had been added and the
café expanded. I recognized two of the local guides taking bait
boxes down to their crafts. At the end of the largest yacht dock,
a full-sized schooner sailboat, one of those mahogany and teak
jobs, sat elegantly alongside the standard cruisers. Magnificent
and new. It couldn't have been local, perhaps in from Nassau. I
walked to the end for a closer look. *Tikopia.* That was her name.
None of her crew about yet. Nice life—to move around in her,
to live under her massive sail. *Tikopia. Tikopia;* the name stuck.
An island in Micronesia, off Santa Cruz; I remembered it from
an anthropology textbook I had once read. I wondered if she'd
sailed around the world. Of course she had; boats aren't built
that well to sail only one sea.

Walking back to the café, hibiscus now open, frangipani glint-
ing red-orange, clear and hot again, I had an appetite for grits.
The café had suffered from redecoration—where before it was
shipside-quaint, now it was Southern-nouveau circus—lots of
red-and-gold-mottled plastic booths and then the bamboo
counter with tiny lights. I opted for the counter, looking at the

3 3 7

six or so other customers around. Four were tourists, one guide I knew as local but couldn't remember his name, and one other, rather slovenly, plump running to—fat—I said it to myself like a swear word and caught myself—

"Shylah, M-Moose, that you? Ah can't hardly—it's me, Stanley—c'mon, let's take a booth."

"Uh, Stanley? I, uh, Christ—oh, man, Stanley. It's so good to see you. I thought—oh well . . ."

"Natalie, ah think we're gonna take a booth, y'all mind?"

"Nope, Stan, y'all want to give me your orders now?"

"Coffee, a large order of grits, and may I have that with extra butter and toast?"

"Ah'll have the usual."

"Your usual takes half mah damn icebox, boy. Hokay, Stan, got it."

We sat down opposite each other at the closest of the booths. Jesus, he must have weighed in at a good two hundred and thirty pounds, and though tall, he couldn't handle weight, not that kind of weight. There was a softness to him. Insidious softness eating him up. Something broken. And it wasn't just the weight, his bearing had changed: limped now and had a stoop.

"Stanley, I, uh . . ."

"Yah, ah know, you've changed too, Shylah, looks lahk in your favor; you look good, woman—Jesus. Guess all that city life appeals to you, don't it, Moose?"

"Tell me about what you've been doing, will you? You know, I'd ask Luanne every time I wrote or phoned her about you."

"Oh hell, nuthin, ah guess, do a little guiding, sometimes pump gas at night up the road."

"I heard you were in Vietnam and got married."

"Yah, the great story of mah life. Infantry, that's what ah was in. Stupid war, Shylah, really stupid; half the damn time we didn't know who the hell we was shootin, least ah didn't. Oh, there isn't much to say. Then Soiee, ah met her in Saigon on a kind of R and R— Second time I went back our group was taken, you know, captured, not for long— Crazy, most my buddies got it, lots of butchering; then when our guys came through, it was all close fighting, they returned the favor. Whole damn village practically, lots of kids—Jesus, lahk dead dogs in the road. Did me in, Shylah— Ah just sort of forgot a lot for a while, lay up at a hospital, then got a medical discharge. Anyhow, I married Soiee, we'd been going around together, she had cousins and stuff, but her folks were dead. Real young, about fifteen, you know, but, uh, mature. Women over there have it even worse than the guys—so we came back here. Ah've thought about movin up to Miami but this is the only home I know. But it's been rough on her, conches don't cotton to foreigners, you know how they are. She doesn't have no friends, we kinda stick real close. Ah think she wants to go back to Nam, least she had her cousins."

"But you both get along, I mean, together. Don't you?"

"Well, it's hard, lahk at first it was O.K., you know; now ah guess it's just that we're together too much, don't do nuthin but watch TV and eat. Mah dad won't speak a word to us, that's another thing. But hell, ah figured things'd sort themselves out after a while, once people got used to her. What'd you expect, Shylah? You thinkin 'bout the old days, ah can tell; you got that look."

"Yeah, well, I don't . . ."

"Best time in the past, there was nuthin lahk us. Ah got a lot of memories."

"For Christsake, Stanley, you're only twenty-five!"

"Yeah so what about yourself, Shylah? Tell me about what you're doing. You got married?"

"Yes, I got married, and I'm in the process of divorce—my husband and I haven't lived together in over a year. My parents don't know that though, so it's just between us. Daddy, uh, my father, he's been quite sick."

"Yah, ah heard, drinkin finally got to him, huh?"

"Apparently. Anyhow, Alice's going North for a month and I'm going to be with him."

"You crazy! You and your old man never got on. How, you gonna handle him for a whole month?"

"It's different now, Stanley. For one thing, he isn't drinking. We had a, uh, a warm reunion—I'd like to see if we can keep it that way for once. Jesus, I am his kid after all."

"You and your old man. Pretty weird; ah remember how he

used to chase me out of your house 'cause Bobby Jay Leads was comin over—all that shit."

"Well, think of it as making us more passionate—all that conflict."

"Christ, Peacock Island, too much, huh?"

"The best, Bear, the best."

"Well, look, ah gotta go, ah can see my party out there by the boat. Guess ah won't be seeing much of you, huh? Jesus, ah can't recall—what is it, six years?"

"Six, right. I'll be seeing you, Stanley."

Stanley waved and left through the double doors. I dawdled over the remains of the coffee, watching him gas up and put the bait on his boat. I was right about thinking he'd always *be* to this island—but not this way, not that massive hulk of self-defeat. And I had spent a chunk of the driving time down here fantasizing fucking him. I thought I'd see him hard-muscled from the boat, a little more relaxed within his body, less clumsy but a quiet guy, steadfast, maybe building his own house, something like that. So much for romantic prophecy and daydream—so much soap. He seemed trapped by the island now, rather than a free spirit living on its shore. I walked up to pay—the waitress smiled evenly and said he'd taken care of it. Of course. He would.

★

"Well, lambie, you must have gotten up at dawn. What'd you do, go for a walk? Where?"

"Down by the marina; I wanted to see the boats. There's this seventy-foot or so schooner docked there, the *Tikopia*, you know anything about it?"

"Ah do indeed, belongs to five men, sailed all over the world. Marine biologists or zoologists, whatever they call them. They make films and test fish, sharks, whales, all kinds of sea life. Whole series on TV narrated by Hugh Downs or one of those big announcers. Nahce fellows, real hard workers; think they're doing porpoise and shark runs down here off the reef. Lot of money in that boat."

"I noticed. Looks only a few years old. Hi, Daddy, sleep well?"

"Ah shore did, honey."

"What would you lahk for breakfast, baby?"

"Just coffee would be fine; I ate some grits at the café."

"Hell, that's no breakfast. How 'bout some nice Canadian ham and eggs?"

"No thanks, can't eat that much in the morning; coffee's fine."

"Imagine you'll be poppin over to see Luanne; y'all know where she lives?"

"Yes, she told me. Nice area, or at least it was as I remember."

"Sort of different now; they cleared away a lot of the mangrove brush, built it up with prefabs, tore down a lot of the old hurricane houses, seems a shame—damn houses were the only ones left in one piece through Donna. But, you know, they aren't pretty enough to sell nowadays. Anyhow, some small ranch houses over there now with patios."

"Hmm."

"You see Stanley over at the marina? He guides there, you know—hardly recognize him—gotten heavy, kinda morose."

"No. No, I didn't see him."

★

It was after one when I drove the VW the two miles over to Luanne's. Alice and I had gone to the Quick Pig shopping center toward Marathon, where she could efficiently combine food buying with her talk on Daddy's needs and non-needs. My mind was on the women walking the aisles, the special foods one buys, native to the Keys, like conch and turtle chowder, concentrated Key lime juice, green bananas, the cacophony of Southern accents, the shifts and shorts and sandals and straw handbags of Florida living. Familiar faces, Alice saying hello and reintroducing me to the parents of kids I'd gone to school with; then loading food into the back of the Caddy and more chatter with locals. It occurred to me I'd be a topic of conversation in their homes for a couple of days. Island entertainment.

3 4 1

Pleasurable gossip. Shylah's return. Rumors. Struck me funny. Some new mystery for them to grow weary of and then they could go on to the next Gothic scenario at the bowling alley or over rum.

Luanne's house looked as if it had been lifted and plunked down complete and with no thought by a giant crane. It sat there, too close to the little road, pink and white, slightly L-shaped. A load of laundry hanging on the line separated her house from the next—its duplicate but for the color, which was avocado and white. Car was outside. I assumed that meant she was home. I parked in front of it, picked up the print material I had bought her from Design Research—hoping she still went in for designing and making her clothes. I had bought enough material for an army. Felt slightly daft to knock on her door knowing that practically nobody knocked on doors down here; the thing was to walk in. If someone didn't want company coming, he'd lock the door or put out the see-y'all-later sign, but only then.

"Ah'm in the kitchen. Y'all come back here— Uh, who is it?"

"Your great-grandmother."

"Wha . . . mah Lawd, SHYYYYLAHHHH. Jeeesus. Ah knew you was comin down, but not so soon. God, wait till everybody hears you're here. Have to have a big party, get everybody together. Tell me all about yourself. Whatcha been up to? God, girl, y'all too thin. Hey, wanna nahce Roman Coke?"

"Just a Coke, thanks, you have the rum."

"Ah never knowed you to be one turn down a drink. You haven't been sick or something?"

"Yes, kind of, but I'm O.K., fine. How's Loosie?"

"Pain in the ass, but ah love her; she's doing real well in school. Here, see, that's her in her class picture."

"Beautiful. Looks like you, Luanne—same shape face, something of Harry in her looks too, nose and mouth maybe."

"Ah'll say one thing for Harry. He shore could make beautiful babies. You ever want one for looks, Shylah, ah give you the keys to the jewelry box. Don't suppose he's gettin it up much these days anyway. Jesus, what a mess. But Jack and me getting along fine. Loosie loves him; he's affectionate with her. That was the worst of it—Harry didn't give Loosie any attention. Hell, she wasn't minding her teachers or me, and runnin her mouth all the time. It's been hard gettin things back to normal. Anyhow, tell me about the big city and you— You a star or anything, Shylah?—we always said you'd be famous some way or other."

"Hardly. My husband's the famous one—at least among artists— You know, we traveled a lot, met well-known people. Exciting for a while. Doesn't take long for the glitter to feel like Brillo. I think it's lonely. So here I am—feeling ecstatic in your living room. I haven't told Daddy and Alice that Larry and I split up, so I'd rather you not say anything. Oh, that reminds me, I took a walk by the marina early morning and . . ."

"Ooh, did you see the *Tikopia*? Y'all ought to see the guys who live in it. Shylah, that's it, they'd be perfect for y'all. They're all terribly intelligent—bookish—but good-looooking— mah Lawd. Know a pissload about the ocean."

"Yes, I did see her, but it was too early for anyone to be up—so what was I going to say?—oh yes, I saw Stanley, Luanne. Guess I haven't come out of the shock—Christ, the way he looks and carries himself, so defeated. What the hell happened anyway?"

"It's that damn Soy Sauce. He shoulda married one of his own kind— Ah know, ah know how you feel about such things, Shylah. See, it's complicated. When we heard he was discharged and comin home and that he'd married a Vietnamese girl, we were all set to give them a big welcome, you know, even her. Lahk the girls—Selma Anne and Bubbles and some others—we thought we could kind of take her under our wing and stuff. Make things real easy for them. So we had this big welcome-home party, the inn donated the liquor for it, everyone was there. That was what did it. The welcome-home party. He was skinny then, you know, lahk bone-skinny, and limped. So we all extended ourselves purple to her, to both of them. She wouldn't do anything with us, Shylah—it wasn't just the language, cause she knew English—lahk she wouldn't leave Stanley for a minute, she clung to him; she wouldn't let the guys, you know, really talk to him, interest him in anything. Lawd, she had

3 4 3

changed that boy; he had no sense of humor left, real quiet and kept his head down. Then one of the guys started talking about Nam and how the North Vietnamese were really pigs and went against all the rules of war, that they enjoyed killing babies and eating them— Well, Stanley, man, he went completely out of his gourd, tried to kill him, beat the shit out of him; took six guys to pull him off. Stanley was yellin 'bout how America had no business being in Asia, that half the U.S. Army's on heroin—on and on and on—that we were the villains. Ah mean, to take on that way even if he had a point—Charlie was just trying to sympathize with him; lucky for Stanley he didn't press charges. That was the end of it though. He and Tokyo Rose barely speak to anyone. Polite, you know, but well, she doesn't want to see anyone. We still tried to get them out with a bunch of us, but no go. Mah Lawd, she is really the rudest girl ah have ever met. So we figured she just sort of made things worse for him. Stanley's old man's fit to be tied. Won't speak to either of them . . . all they do is sit home and eat. She stays nahce and skinny but he looks lahk the Goodyear blimp. Ah 'spect it went hard on you, seeing him so down, Shylah, y'all loved each other so much. Things'd be perfect if you'd married one another, huh?"

"Wasn't in the cards. So look at it this way, Luanne, she was so young and uprooted here among strangers. My God, you all probably terrified her—you sure as hell terrified me when I first came among you. It takes time. And Stanley. I don't know what to say. See, he was such a gentle person for his size and strength, I can't see him surviving intact the killing and craziness he went through. Let's change the subject. You look great, Luanne, you know that, with your hair long, really great."

"Ah feel good, got sick there for a while, but Jack, he's been good for mah health all around. Now listen, how 'bout a party Sunday, no one works Sunday. Look, I'll get Bubbles and Selma Anne over here now, we'll work something out. A luau over on Peacock, Shylah— Happy days. Lemme get mah hands on that phone . . ."

The girls. Selma Anne, Bubbles, Rosemary came in three cars, but it was essentially the same rubber-banding of the clique as in high school. Both Bubbles and Selma Anne had their youngest in arms; neither baby could have been over six months. Rosemary, my fellow miscegenist from the exotic days of Nassau senior trip, had no children. A freak. I thought briefly that a woman on Lime without children by twenty-five must be slightly risqué, if not a subject for pity.

Selma Anne had grown heavy with her childbearing but otherwise looked eggish as she always had, older but eggish. With Bubbles, memories of that extreme delicacy of face, short-lived now. Still quite pretty but lined; she appeared old. We were all twenty-five or less, but these women all seemed older than I. Maybe having children, becoming mothers, maybe that made women older, or maybe not older but a quality of "settledness" I didn't feel about myself. Rosemary, though, was Rosemary— still the animal—loose; Rosemary would hang loose right into the grave. Good exchanging hugs with the comrades of high-school adventure. A time to reminisce and discuss the importance of having the proper social function fitting for our reunion.

"Lawd, y'all look so good, Shylah. You got any kids now? Tell us all about New York. Jesus, ah can't believe you're back—how long you down for, huh?"

"About a month, Selma Anne. Daddy's not been too well . . ."

"Ah know, we heard about it. That's too bad. He got so thin— guess you both did."

"Rosemary, no kids?"

"Hell no. Ah ain't havin them until ah'm thirty, no matter what the conches want to think. Having too much fun as is."

"How'd you lahk to have a practice run with mah four? Getting out lahk this is a big luxury, but at least ah got two mothers-in-law and that nursery school Miz Charlene runs. Anyhow, it's tubes tied for sure this time."

"Me too, three's enough. So how's the feel of the Keys again?"

"O.K., things have been happening too quickly really to assimilate. It's changed some, built up some—still lovely. Never doubted it."

"You still drawin, Shylah? Maybe you don't get much time to any more?"

"Not quite, Selma Anne. I paint, yes . . ."

"You sell em? Do y'all—do you draw girls lahk Keene. Ah've got one of those on mah wall."

"No. Different kind of painting. Yes, I'm beginning to sell occasionally now, not as much as I'd like, of course."

"Guess your husband's rich, huh, so you don't have to worry?"

"He's pretty rich; he's also an artist."

"Is he, uh, good-looking?"

"Hmm, hard to say. To me he was. I don't know. Not like the handsome tan guys down here."

"Was? Shylah, you ain't gettin on with him, ah can tell; he'd be down here with you if y'all was getting on."

"Well, see, my father doesn't know. Uh, no, we haven't been together in a while. So much for marriage. Come on, girls, let's talk about us, not my bad news."

"Well, ah'll tell you one thing, 'bout the only faithful wife down here is Luanne, that's cause she's still technically a bride."

"Bubbles, shut up."

"Why, she's raght. Christ, this island's full of it. Hey, do you smoke?"

"What? Grass? Once in a while. I like drinking better."

"That's the newest pastime. Everybody gets together and smokes."

"What—booze isn't enough now, eh, Roseberries—never saw the Keys as anything but peopled by bottle babies. If I'd known I would have brought some down . . ."

"You got it the wrong way round, Shylah. Works the opposite. We're gettin all the stuff from Colombia, Cozumel, Jamaica, and what with the sailors, Jesus, it's easy down here."

"How 'bout this party, huh, girls; let's get it together."

"O.K., Luanne, you're the one so organized. What do we do? Ah'll bring the grass, and ah volunteer mah special three-bean salad."

"Ah can probably get Johnny bring the lobster and some smoked fish. Business been awfully good."

"Ah'll do a conch salad and dessert. Now all we gotta do is call everybody. Guys can bring the liquor and stuff."

"How much of the class is left, Luanne?"

"Hard to say, Shylah. We got one dead, as you know. Cindy left, bunch of the guys are working the Bahamas now—'bout little over half."

"I'd like Stanley and his wife to come, really. At least, I'm going to invite them, make the effort."

"Shylah, y'all know they won't come. Ah don't think ah can stand to be around her."

"Well, try, Selma Anne."

"Anything you say, majesty. It's your party. Ah'd lahk to see this one."

They had aged and I hadn't. But I had changed, or at least I perceived things differently, and here in this room, I saw them, as with Luanne, as having remained constant. New dressing but the same talk, the same subjects, and most importantly, the same priorities, same plus children now.

Driving back to the house, I speculated on what made the difference. I had a feeling it lay in endurance. Mine was low— theirs high. Of course there were changes—changes that filtered down from TV and the conglomerate of American standards. Like they swore more, they talked about their extramarital sex life now; I guessed it had finally been at least covertly institutionalized. I wondered if they got more out of it. I wondered if playing around just meant having intercourse with more men or if they experimented, if they actually did more with their bodies now or just lay prone a little more openly. Now and then I saw an occasional prosperous-looking black tourist. Their motels must be integrated— No more crosses? New stimuli to be sorted out— Down on Lime the change would always come like the water one knew was gradually eating the boundaries of shoreline—almost imperceptibly and begrudgingly. And Luanne. I loved Luanne. In that there was more than nostalgia. In that—something still and expectant— something bound to the island—endurance.

17

Daddy stood before one of the azalea bushes with pruning
shears as I drove into our yard. So he was the cause of the new
gardenlike aesthetic. I had never known him to take an interest
in horticulture on any level before. We had usually had hired
locals to keep up the yard, a nursery man to add or subtract
bushes twice a year. He seemed to be shaping it, not cutting in
deeply—sort of snipping the bush the way a barber might trim
the hairline behind the ears of a man's head.

"You a good driver, Shylah?"

"I guess so, I like to drive well enough."

"Gotta be careful around here. A lot a crazy kids on the highway drunk on marijuana."

"Yes, I'll remember. Hey, you've taken an interest in the
yard. All those hedges and loose bushes are shaped now. God,
you did all of this?"

"Yup. Ah lahk to get the exercise, you know— Hear you were
over to see Luanne."

"Oh yes, and Selma Anne, Bubbles, and Rosemary were over.
Talked about throwing a kind of reunion on Peacock Sunday—
you know, the old classmates."

"Well, that's nahce, glad to hear they're throwing you a shindig. Say, ah got some people thought you should meet. These fellows from the *Tikopia*. We're having a little cocktail hour, Mother and I; they're coming over, and Admiral Wilty and Gladys, few of the locals, around six. Thought you maght enjoy it. Then we're going to celebrate a little at the inn. Ah haven't been out for a while, thought we maght combine things. You don't have anything planned, do you, sister?"

"No, sounds great. Perhaps I could get on board the *Tikopia*. I've always loved big schooners."

"That's about as nahce a one as ah've seen. Those guys were just on TV, matter of fact. Last week, was it? Last week."

"But I thought you were sort of recuperating. Isn't this a little much . . ."

"Nah, don't let the old lady put me under the stone yet, sister, not yet. Thought it'd be nahce for you to see some new faces. These fellows damn smart. So, hmm, you lahk what I've done with the yard?"

"Yes, very much so. Did you put in the new lime trees as well?"

"Yup, blight took some of the shrubbery. The place was beginning to get that bald look. Coleus too, see that next to the garage?"

"Uh huh."

"Shylah, ah, uh, hope you enjoy yourself down here. You mustn't think you have to stay around your old man when you want to be out or anything. Y'all look a little pekid, sister, lahk you could use some fun. Ah don't know about this life of yours. Guess I don't have any cause to wonder, huh?"

"Yes, well, mostly I'd like to see you. If you're feeling up to it, one day maybe we'll take a little boat trip or something. I ought to be able to get my hands on one around here."

"Ah'd lahk that, maybe a little fishing. I, uh . . ."

Alice was calling me from the door, and as I walked over, I could not forget the sight of my father pruning azalea. How, what? Bizarre. Maybe tender. I had not had waking time alone yet—not enough of it at least—something I wanted: to walk around alone—to maybe get out on the water—to have things settle down. I walked in the bedroom and put on my white bikini and a shirt over it to hide the hair until I had submerged. Besides, it was late afternoon and for once quiet dockside—I could dive into the water I'd not felt for six bathtub years. I had forgotten how warm it was . . . and thick with salt. Surrounding flats formed a natural protective pool against the larger predators. I swam out a bit to the first sandbar, then back to shore. The bottom was mucky around here—my feet as they touched made the grayish stuff rise around me. There were far clearer places to take the water, lagoons and off island. I could wait. Enough to splash around, have the salt dry and tighten the skin. I gave the water the benefit of an hour, then went in to change.

I dressed carefully for the evening, made order of my hair, put jasmine oil in it, dressed in white. I felt erotic from the water and from anticipation about the *Tikopia* and its crew. And slightly annoyed. I couldn't see why I felt that way, like a slightly inspiring itch. And told myself: be a bitch, be a handsome bitch—be intelligent in that way if you can.

They stood as I entered; how nice, I truly liked being stood for, all inequity (under the table) aside. I shook hands with each of them while Daddy bragged about what a witty, intelligent, creative, and unique young woman I had grown into and how we had not seen each other in so long and what a treat it was to have daughter back with Dad. It was a little weird having praise from a man who had sneered at my tits in company when I was sixteen.

Tinker Sjögren, the last of the five men introduced. Perhaps it was the change of climate that gave me that twinge, made me desire him, know him before hearing him speak. I requested a beer, glancing around to ascertain if I had kept whatever sense of myself I had. I guessed I had. He was, not "handsome," wrong word, "essential." Something essential about him—the fifty lines or so that creased the tan face, bushy eyebrows, large dark eyes, slightly broken nose, largeness. Then, when he did speak—his voice, sort of craggy—and he didn't say, "How do you do," he said, "Peculiar how spelling affects the beauty of a word. Sheila's a kind of hard name, very raspy, but Shylah, that's something else again. There's an island that sounds like it, I think it's off the coast of Ireland." A better than average compliment—impressed as it flattered, though a little heavy on the gravy.

We sat and talked, the Wiltys showed up, and the Dodsons, both far too conservative and uninspiring conversation partners for the erudite seamen, who maintained a nonchalance in keeping with their pleasant banter. Admiral Wilty, however, preferred talking about Skinny Wainwright and the war, Mrs. Wilty about their new interior decoration, the Dodsons variations of the same. Daddy, entertaining without liquor, appeared vulnerable, lighthearted, certainly; not as bombastically witty. People weren't rolling with mirth like they used to. He made no more outrageous comments. He listened more; I guess he gave more—that posture of attention. And his voice had less power, no longer boomed when he gestured, the sound coming out kind of uneven and blending with the others' talk, rather than paralyzing it. "What are you smiling about, Shylah?"

"Your name. I'm wondering why they call you Tinker, Tinker."

"Want to give it a guess?"

"I'd say offhand because you invent things. Am I right?"

"Well, sort of, that's a flattering way of putting it. I fuck around is more the truth, making a hell of a lot of noise when I decide to fix the plumbing or anything."

At dinner we were next to one another at the long table—musical-chairs-style—as we had simultaneously aggressed toward the other's company. Heat. When animals have heat for one another. I can't remember what we spoke about, it must have been superfluous, but comforting to hear the voice just the same, see the teeth, the sound of food going down. Anything under heat. Any movement at all.

"I'd like very much to board the *Tikopia*. I walked down to the marina at dawn this morning—appropriate time, don't you think, for viewing your baby, at least from the exterior? It's pretty majestic."

"O.K. inside too. Yes, you'll see it—this evening, if you like. Want to drive down with me and have a drink on Boca Chica first? There's this new pub I thought you might enjoy as much as I do. Or are you obliged to stay home tonight?"

"No, no, I'd like to—I'm sure it would make Dad—my

father—happy. He and I were talking about the *Tikopia* this afternoon."

"Then tis done, madame."

"Tis done in kind, monsieur."

★

Driving down past the familiar landmarks and lights on the
curve of islands, bridges, star and moon reflections varying on
the depths of water. We had entered each other's silence like
expert musicians. And again the reunion to island night sky, the
most constant lover, cure-all to terror and sleeplessness.

The Captain's Deck, new, on the water, quiet and vaguely
exclusive. I saw why Tinker had taken me to this place. It fit
him—massive oak and a ship's mast in the center of the bar. We
sat outside on a kind of porch overhanging the water, raised on
hurricane stilts.

"I suppose you'd think I was bullshitting you if I said that at
this moment I don't know quite what to think, but—what am
I?—I am enamored of you. You might be absolutely horrific. I
may be having a breakdown in judgment. But I find you, uh—
what do I find you?—I find you exquisite. Do you think I'm full
of shit? You see, I'm trying to be, uh, frank. I know your father
said you were married so I . . ."

"I'm not actually. I mean I'm in the process of finalizing a
divorce. But he doesn't know it. Thanks for the tropical chivalry, though—and I hope to Jesus you aren't married."

"Thank YOU for your honesty. No, not married. Once very
young and widowed young, no children, now age forty-five,
lived with three subsequent women, all delightful and smart,
all doing far better without me—I have bad habits, like wearing
dirty socks. You're an artist, yes?"

"Yes, a painter. Tell me about what you do. Tell me you work
with porpoises—you do, don't you, Tinker? You smile like
one—such high-consciousness mammals, huh?"

"Yes, I do, as a matter of fact, among other mammals, such as
whales. Those are my two chief areas of interest. Sharks too, for
that matter, but that involves other areas of study. And yes, I
believe in the ethics of dolphins. It's pure anthropomorphism,

3 5 2

straight out of Walt Disney. I like their style. Any other rationale I could give would be a complete hype. Want to go play
with the porpoises, lady?—we can, you know, we can go tomorrow. I'll find some excuse. We could take the small Chris-Craft.
Half the fellows are going to Miami anyway; it's meeting and
lecture time at college level, and just this once I don't want to
go. Let them handle it. Are you a porpoise?—ah ha—you ARE a
porpoise; I dreamed you up. Years of research have finally paid
off. It's science fiction—the ultimate porpoise— Tell me, have I
grown sleek and gray? do you see the beginnings of fins? are
my teeth slowly turning to points?"

"Perhaps I'm your fairy god-porpoise here from Neptune to
help you in your research, turning your glass of bourbon into a
whale."

"Not here, we'd never be allowed back in this place. Do you
want to see the *Tikopia* tonight? Honestly, Shylah?"

"Honestly yes. But it presents complications, doesn't it? Like
matters of decorum and will power. I don't know if I could
leave you from there, if you know what I mean. I think it would
be wiser all around if I see you in the morning, Tinker, but I
don't want to move. Not just now. I just want to sit here; this is
the first at-home, relaxed moment I've spent since my arrival.
You know, I had this crazy feeling, like a premonition, about tonight, something about meeting you. I guess I fell into a little
psychological coquetry, but when I met you, I kind of blew
it—you took away my power of flirtation. Oh, listen, I forgot, I
really should see the *Tikopia* for a moment tonight—after all, I
assume my father will be full of questions and I suppose I
should keep my credibility— Could you give me a quick noc-
turnal tour? Oh yes, I forgot to ask—*Tikopia*, that's an island in
Micronesia, an atoll actually, isn't it?"

"Yes, a small one off the Solomons near Santa Cruz."

"Were you there? you all traveled the Pacific?"

"Sailed. Yes, last year, and once on her maiden voyage. We
were studying sharks for a time and doing some testing in the
Mindanao Deep off the Philippines."

"Did you study electrical fish, all those prehistoric monsters
of the fathoms?"

"Uh huh. You know something about that area, don't you?"

"Only from books. I studied Oceania in college. My pipe dreams—I'd love to go there. What do you call yourself when you do these things—your title, I guess that's what I mean?"

"Depends on what I'm doing. I was trained in marine biology, but I got interested in—what would you call it—uh, behavior of aquatic mammals—a type of ethology. Intelligent creatures of water habits always fascinated me. For instance, porpoises, back in evolution, their prototypes were land mammals—why would a land mammal go back to the sea to evolve when so much of evolution comes out of the sea rather than the reverse? Five years ago my colleagues and I got enough private backing to buy a seaworthy boat and stock it with the necessary paraphernalia for study—we had, frankly, good publicity on it. *National Geographic* is always good for getting someone a government grant, and the interest coming out of Cousteau's work— So we got popular, too much so; it's hard enough, with the five of us afloat, without having reporters and cameramen along—and there was the additional pressure of having data that would be helpful politically—so we kind of cut it out. We still get support, but we're not so maniacally favored any more. Last year we followed the Atlantic coast down from Iceland. Whales, their movements and so on. Then here; we've been in Lime for four months now. I like it. It's kind of a respite for us. Four of us live in southern Florida anyway, around Coral Gables, so it seems a logical place to make port, far enough away from Miami and innocuous enough, but with all that the Pennekamp reef has to offer. This part of the South Atlantic is very rich in sea life. Anyhow, in that time I've kind of gotten to know Corky, knew him before he went into the hospital and now. Quite a difference in one man over a few months. It must have been a shock for you, Shylah."

"Everything's a shock. We had never gotten on well before. It had its effects on me. But without his bourbon, it's as if I was getting to know someone I'd known all my life as someone else. Confusing. Alice says he's really much sicker than he appears; I mean, his liver is pretty well shot—he's pushing sixty anyway. Shit, I don't think I can go on with this conversation—do you mind?"

"Uh uh. Except to say that I think you are of him more than

354

you feel you are. There's a dreaminess you share. Kinda show biz sometimes. Well, later for that. Come on, I'll drive us back to the ship so we can keep up appearances."

I had placed the tips of my fingers over the back of his hand, which was resting on the table. It had begun as a simple enough gesture, friendly, warm. I thought of the word "nestle."

We were absentmindedly nestling. Rough. I felt the dried and calloused fleshy pads at the knuckles and down. Dried and strong from working in saltwater and under heat. I had never been a devotee of the soft, elegant hand school of romance—because mine too were rough and dry from turp and holding brushes, scouring paint off the fingers. I believed in the roughness of hands—their innate honesty, no deceptive softness, tender-hard—easily felt and direct—touching that hand like reading the lines on his face. I did not want to withdraw.

Except that it was Tinker who moved, taking my hands to his face, around where the cheekbones cliffed near the ears, and moved his own hands, once sure I would not move mine away—up my arms to the back of neck in like gesture, and I drew him with them, like potholders around soup tureen to be sniffed first—to hold off a little sensing heat, then to cool and to touch. Careful kissing. We would not eat each other up. Not yet. The sensitive parts of my body were in love with Tinker Sjögren. I assumed that was the gist of the expression "to be in love" not "to love deeply." But the explosion—that had to do with surfaces, and my surface wanted his.

Outside the car we embraced, my head at the niche between neck and shoulder, his head over me and raised, secured there with my hand, almost maternal. In the car, too small for passion, we made a few clumsy swipes for each other before Tinker started the engine and drove the twenty miles or so with his hand on my leg, my arm on his shoulder. Two of the men were at the boat, drinking on deck, one with a telescope—hazy now, deceptive for stargazing. Inside, one large living–workroom, galley adjoining, sumptuous in the free use of teak and mahogany, yet functional, furniture and pillows doubling as life preservers or holds—beds, tables, collapsible—that kind of space conservation.

"What do you think?"

"I think it's a feat to live this close for long periods of time. And the ship's a feat."

"You're right, she is a feat. But we're no professional sailors. We rent houses if we're in port for any length of time. You know the old Paloma place? We have that now. Usually one or two of us sleep on the boat—it varies. Some of the guys have lady friends in Miami, so naturally some sense of privacy peculiar to our species begins to function."

"Yes, I see."

"You see a great deal."

"You know what I'm thinking . . ."

"Approximately. No, tell me, what are you thinking?"

"I'm thinking I better get back to the house; let's go, Tinker."

"In the case of discretion and first meetings. Me too, Shylah. We could just fall down and make love for the next month or so."

"Yes, we could."

Daddy was snoring fitfully when I returned. Alice sat in the living room reading *Good Housekeeping*.

"Hello."

"Hello, dear. Enjoy yourself?"

"Very much so. How's Daddy?"

"O.K. Talking in his sleep about the war again. He does that when he gets excited. We don't entertain that much any more. I think he wanted to show you off."

"Yes, I got that impression. I liked it actually, being shown off, or whatever he was doing."

"He's changed, honey, that's what being sick does."

"Yes. I thought perhaps while you're away I might drive him around a bit, go sightseeing or something—whatever I can interest him in—when he's feeling up to it."

"Twice a week you'll have to take him to Key West Hospital anyway. Dr. Damrosch sees him Tuesday and Friday. He's on progressive medication, stabilizing drugs and so forth—they do blood work on him. Damned expensive. That Tinker, somethin else, in't he? Quite a man. He and your daddy been friends since he came down."

"Yes, I can see why. Tinker's fond of him. I think it's the humor."

"Well, they're a lovely bunch of men, those *Tikopia* boys. Ah'm glad y'all met them. Maybe they take you out."

"Yes, perhaps tomorrow in the Chris-Craft. That is, if it's O.K. with you. Tinker's going out for the hell of it. Or do you think it's too much . . ."

"Hell, ah'm no one to lecture. Seems a bit peculiar, you and Tinker alone. You being married, for one thing. But these are the Keys, times are different. And you look lahk you could use a day lahk that. Ah think it's O.K., Shylah, for you to do your socializing now— You got that party over at Peacock they're throwin—when's that, day after tomorrow? You'll have plenty time close to home after ah leave— You O.K., honey? Y'all really thin, your skin's kind of mottled too. You haven't been sick or anything?"

"Well, I've been off my feed for the last couple of months, you know how these things happen. I just need a day out on the water. A little tan."

★

"Buy you a cup of coffee, Tinker?"

It had been simple deduction to ascertain that the others had either slept in the rented house or places unknown. There was only his rented VW dockside, not the Ferrari or other cars they had. Funny how I had taken stock of these signs of occupancy last night. So it was just him last night. Or had he told me that? I couldn't remember. I had woken again at dawn, put a swimsuit on under my chinos and blue work shirt, walked barefoot to the awakening marina and onto the boat. I found him asleep on one of those roll-up foam pieces on the deck, a sheet thrown over him, outlining the crack in his ass. I was tempted to take it off, the sheet, I mean, curious to see him that way, but didn't. It was enough I had invited myself into the privacy of his sleep. It was his option now.

"Hmm, Shylah—Shylah in the ridiculous, plushy dawn. I love you. Coffee? First us, yes?"

"Yes, us."

Tinker wrapped the sheet around him as he got to his feet and followed me below—down to his berth.

"You live by day, don't you?"

"Yes, and don't you?"

"Yes, and this is the way to begin—in the morning. Do you know how many people know each other only in the night? Deceptive, isn't it? I distrust the evening—even last night I distrusted it, you know, and I think it was because of all the enforced romanticism of night. Night's a kind of cosmetic. Hmm, Shylah; hmm, Shylah by day . . ."

Tinker had given up disrobing me—too slow and ineffectual with buttons and snaps, the bikini top that fastened like a steel trap—I took his hands away and tended to it. We were both quite naked now and rolling on the berth, first heat of day in drops of sweat on armpits and close bellies—too small, the berth; we went out to the living area, threw pillows on the floor, followed by ourselves— I was feeling more affectionate than sexy at first, busied myself kissing his feet, licking and sucking on his toes—he was toying with my calf like a lion with an outsize ostrich femur, until he grew impatient of playing children; we moved to one another, my head then turning over and stretched back on the pillow, his tongue sliding from my lips down my chin and neck, hands pinching gently back and forth on nipples, his legs flexing against my thighs, my hands to his ears. He sucked my breast, and moved the other hand down, stroking curvature of pelvis to hip, then around to cunt. Pushing the lips open, fingers dilating inside at vulva's edge, occasionally brushing clitoris until I was rigid. Arms stretched to reach breasts; his tongue licking me, lapping at the petals, pushing the clitoris around, positioned like a body floating.

"Why? Why not?"

"No, come inside me. I don't want to come yet, please; if you lick me any more I'll come and it'll be over . . ."

"I'll excite you again, sweetheart. You can go more than once, lucky lady."

"No, I can't, once. Let's please, love . . ."

"Yes, you know, yes."

3 5 8

I grasped the edge of his buttocks, as if to aim him, while he pushed between my legs, until my cunt unstuck and gave and I could feel that weight and width of cock filling me—making for joy and nostalgia and tears and loss, always the crystal of loss—inexplicable in this union. He sensed that, I think he sensed it, holding me closely, then kissing me close-mouthed on my cheeks and mouth so as to reassure, while I moved with him and for him, until I grew rigid and selfish, forgetting everything except that pleasure when everything is accounted for and orgasm—I had been shaking with it, the rhythm of me vibrating, taking him more into it, pushing him into it. He came as I had just finished—my body then especially sensitive to the pulsations of cock when seed leaves it. We rolled apart for a moment, gasping, letting the air and juice and sweat leave our bodies, letting them rest apart to return in embrace, to be satisfied in the morning with the day—breakfast first, cigarettes, beer after swimming—in the heat having these things before us.

There's a special kind of intelligence that operates in fucking. I felt Tinker was a gifted man.

"What are you thinking, sweetheart?"

"I'm thinking how intelligently we make love."

"Maybe we'd come out the same on an aptitude test. Do you know what?"

"What?"

"I don't know what. Just what. Look at us, aren't we something? Jesus. Come on, how about a shower together and breakfast— We look like we just emerged from the sea, all glistening. You smell so good—maybe a shower would just take it away."

"No, Tinker, let's take a shower—the people in the café may not share our high opinion of our smells—"

"It's really imprudent to talk love to a woman, anyone, you just met and made love with, isn't it? I love you, Shylah."

"Yes, Tinker, I think it is imprudent. I love you."

In the shower, too small to turn around in without assistance from each other, I washed him with the Lava soap, scrubbing his back and below with my hand. And around, over the pubic hair and base of cock, avoiding the prepuce with stingy hole, first rinsing my hands, cupping water and splashing it on him to remove the sticky traces of come and matted hairs, while he pushed my head back under the water, hair wet and matted down sides of back, soaping carefully my breasts and belly, lifting each one to clean underneath the downslope, until the water turned freezing; then final rinse and scrambling for the two beach towels and into the abrasiveness of cloth pants on softened flesh.

It was after ten when we wandered into the café, sat down for breakfast at one of the plastic booths. The locals at the counter were guzzling beer. We ate quickly the eggs and hominy and sticky buns, then ordered, to take out, two lunch boxes and two six-packs of beer. Their inboard on the smaller of the two docks waited for us, impervious to the weathered guide boats flanking it. We walked with the dockmaster, who gassed us up, handed over casting rods and bucket of bait, ice chips for the styrofoam container—all the paraphernalia that comes with boating on the dollar-for-dollar luxury level.

Tinker cast off and I started her up, guiding the boat out the memorized channel, feeling the hard technology pleasure from the past. Once out past the last of the channel posts I stripped down to my bikini.

"Where are we going, anyway? You want to take the wheel?"

"You look like you're enjoying it. Sure. Past Pirates' Sandbar. You know where that is?"

"Only vaguely. No, I'd sort of just like to look around. Here, skipper."

Tinker took the wheel while I stood behind him, holding the tapered yet full waist, looking into the windy panorama of ocean and horizon, then turned back to view the receding line of land and bridges.

"You don't shave."

"No, does that bother you?"

"On the contrary, I was thinking how great it is, those tufts under your arms. This shaving mania of women in America and deodorant—it's fucked up. I guess the women's movement, God bless their angry souls, has made it easier for a little variety with equality."

"So you don't mind the women's movement . . ."

"Shit no, not in the positive political sense. I mean, it's not very pleasant to have someone scream all men are inherent biological travesties, that's what I got at this reception one time—but well, you know how it works, all the things get thrown up in the air and when they settle down and everybody is comfortable with it, the pieces won't fit into hard political rhetoric but will be a matter of course and feeling. You know. Men will hopefully not be dry-eyed Spartans and women won't be ripped off of potential—all that business. I'm not a big group person anyway—I think in terms of us. One person makes a connection to another. I try to be fair, Shylah; besides, I love women, I don't want a world where we're segregated and at each other. My mother, she's been dead a couple of years now, was a dynamo; so was my father. I know I had it soft. Both of them were superdedicated biologists—quiet and affectionate people, absentminded, disorganized, but they loved me. I had it lucky that way."

"I was afraid you'd be freaked out by my hair."

"You didn't give me much credit."

"As you say, night is a cosmetic. I'm in love with you, or I think I am. I've never met anyone I was attracted to so quickly. It terrified me—couldn't you tell?—the unreality or fear of unreality. I don't want to kid myself again."

"You're coming out of something. Yes, I bet you're usually more, um, more arrogant."

"Yeah, a real pisser— No, you're right—I, uh, spent some time being, as they say, down in the mouth. Got very disconnected. But I— Right now that arrogance you speak about, I feel it coming back in waves and you . . ."

"And me. Comes and goes. Perhaps we timed each other perfectly. I've been lonely for a—what can I say—a woman of consequence in my life for a long while. Being with men on long trips twenty-four hours a day is both a help and a hindrance. Our work is so physical—what I mean is, physically exhausting—it helps. I just didn't think that much. Even so, I found myself wanting to, uh, do things for them, be motherly, if that's possible. I like to cook so I'd cook for them, listen to their problems—shit like that. I guess it took the burden off my own loneliness. I'm not complaining, I think I have it damn good— my life, that is. It's true I haven't struggled much. I love what I do, I'm attached to it—says more than working at a straight job, ass-licking and ass-sitting. I haven't been all that successful with women; my younger comrades are better endowed all around, more articulate and contemporary, I guess. Of course, I say this with a certain amount of embarrassment."

"Oh, cry me a river, Tinker. You're a prize, if that's what you want to hear. So O.K., so they are more loosely gregarious—and younger. But anyhow, I'm turned on by pensive people—I should think that would work as an asset—women wouldn't feel so threatened, because you don't come on. Besides, you're funny, I think you're funny. Hey look, porpoises. God, look at them . . ."

"Oh Shylah, Shylah, Shylah . . ."

★

Supper. I cooked, grateful for a chance to do something. My sunburn bothered me, made sensations psychedelic out of pain. Daddy and Alice and Tinker sat out, dockside. I watched them talking while the orange and purple and red of sunset went on beyond, watched them from the window next to the stove, where I poached snapper and sautéed string beans. They were laughing, Tinker and Daddy trading gestures. Watched the movement of hands—Alice's on knitting needles, which occasionally stopped when she would glance up, smiling. In the refrigerator I searched for the Key limes for the fish, wading through my father's soda pop supply, enough to give a birthday party for a class of fourth-graders. I was in too much discomfort to wear a dress; a shirt was thrown decorously over my bikini top. My head itched from the saltwater. I smelled the thick richness of summer-heat sweat coming from me. He had done this, Tinker had, made me animal again—I owed him. I felt I owed him. But more, it was how my father had become, tradition of anger, element of vulnerability and change. I wanted to tend him. Why? Stirring garlic into the beans, adding oregano, I fantasized my father and Tinker and I going off on a permanent voyage, a kind of triangle, ménage à trois. My father loved me back. He loved me back. He let me care for him. I fed him, rubbed his back—I made him live forever. He wasn't dying, not my father—temporarily encumbered from years of sauce, but not dying. Swung back to earlier thoughts, that was all. He could start up again. He wouldn't have to prove anything because Tinker and I would give him so much care he'd bloom. Shit. The beans had burned a bit. Shylah, cut the daydreaming. I pushed the mixture with a slotted spoon onto an open serving dish, took out the poached fish, unmolded the rice set with mandarin oranges and cheese, yelled from the door.

"Hey, you all. Dinner. The sunset won't get cold, but this will. Come on, hustle, hustle."

Look at them marching in for chow. Why, Shylah, you're a mother. You are. You're a mother.

"In't sweet of the lamb to cook all these gourmet things. Mah goodness, why it looks so boo'ful, uh huh. Corky, take your white pill, come on."

Up yours, Alice, I wanna give the old man his pill . . .

"Thank you, Alice, do my best."

"How's your sunburn, daughter? Looks lahk you're the sunset."

"Worth it. One day of torture for that golden brown we white girls aspire to."

"Now, Shylah, things have changed down here. Ah've met this colored major. Lovely folks, aren't they, Alice? Why we even went out for dinner . . ."

"Oh shit, I shouldn't have said it—Tiiiinker."

"Mah daughter, the civil-raghts queen—sheeit, ah remember. Oh hell, you know, folks is basically decent down here, we're just slower to change things over— Besides, ah still say they smell different, they do."

"Diet's different in part, Corky. There's always that thing about how the Orientals thought Caucasoids were animals because they smelled so . . . the Emperor used to cover his nose with silk, all that. Hmm, Shylah, the fish, it's terrific, it's, uh—what's the taste?"

"You like it, Tinker? Grated parmesan with ginger."

"It's real delicious, honey. Ah usually go for plain food, but this is very tasty. You know, your friend Tinker here's a gourmet. 'Member, Alice, he came over this one night, Shylah, y'all would not believe the cooking gear he brought with him, cooked us up a seafood jambalaya—absolutely delicious."

"I was so drunk that night on Corky's bourbon I barely knew what went with what."

"Oh, that reminds me, Luanne dropped by early afternoon. You best call her. Got that party on Peacock tomorrow. What's the matter?"

"I forgot about it. Oh hell, I'll drive over there after dinner."

"So whatcha think of mah daughter, Tinker?"

An awkward pause—too late for lip-biting, we blew it. They must have known. I laughed, Tinker laughed. Alice chuckled, looking back and forth, looked to Daddy, who shook his head as Tinker blurted something about "Great fun, just like the old man, hail daughter." He made a hysterical liar. If my father brought it up in future, I'd tell him about my marital status. He and Tinker got on so well, what was the sense in lying?

★

I found that I was not so interested in my old friends from the class of '63. Affinities had changed. I thought I would envy them. But I did not envy them. The responsible world. And motherhood . . . I didn't understand motherhood. I liked holding babies. I understood tenderness, affection, but not reproduction, not what it meant to spin out a biological piece of my own flesh.

And I was fucking bored on Peacock—old times or no. Liquor would have, I suppose, made the difference. Since I couldn't drink and they were drinking Zombies again, the plane of pleasure upon which I operated and the plane of pleasure upon which they operated were necessarily different. I felt my responses were forced and artificial. I wanted to be high and I was stone sober in every direction. We did no nude swimming this time around, because of the children, I was told. Something about the hypocrisy of that statement irritated me. Everything irritated me. Stanley and Soiee had refused my invitation. I couldn't blame them and I didn't blame my conch friends, but still it irritated me.

From a physical point of view, I enjoyed the changes in my classmates, particularly the boys, now young men. To me the girls had always been women, grown at fourteen, with the differences being in flesh texture, a line here and there, and the business of their motherhood—the extensions of themselves, their maternal professionalism, their corporate wombs.

Almost to a number the men were strong, muscular males, tan with the benefits of making a living directly off the sea. Crabs had changed the most—he no longer smelled like a sulphur swamp, skin scarred from acne but no more pus-y monsters on his cheeks and neck—and two years in Miami had moved him to have his teeth capped. Fact was, he had turned out aesthetically above average in our class, and more secure—with his older, doting wife and motel business.

My sunburn smarted under the additional exposure. It got in the way of small talk and appetite. Besides, I had lost the desire to flirt or prattle. Six of the men were single, between marriages rather, and attractive. It would have been pleasant now that the fear of them I had had when we were in school had vanished. But the motivation had vanished as well. How complimentary we had all become to one another—"Shylah, you look terrific"—"Shylah, ah always really admired you"—"Grasser, you never looked better"—"Jack, I hear you're doing quite well as the new hot-shit guide"—easy banter. The bond of class identity—second kin—that would be there. The priorities had changed; as with other animals, we had grown apart. I found it irritating and hard on me. That gulf. I accepted it. I accepted the growing apart, but it was an irksome revelation to have, on a speck-size island having sworn off hard booze with a blistered ass in the presence of revelry.

By dusk we had arrived back at the marina. My classmates were smashed and singing third repeats of school songs; their kids had begun the cycle of crankiness before sleep and the urge to join them in drink had depressed me to the edge of tolerance. I made excuses about not hitting one of the local bars, made excuses about getting back home, and practically sprinted for my car when we docked. The class reunion had wound up being an obstacle course—the first test of Shylah staying off the demon rum. Jesus. I craved my lover, my father, my sometime home, transitory but tangible at this moment. And Luanne was aware of it. Luanne was still the connection. I would see her, watch her with Loosie, talk. A constant connection. When we parted, walked to our separate cars, it was understood.

18

"Coming for dinner, love?"

"Just as soon as I tie this fucking thing up. There. Hmm, Shy, give us a squeeze. Shall we cook together? Look at all these conches I'm boiling up. I thought we could marinate them later."

"Yes, I know. Well I know, Tinker. The stench of whelk flesh dominates the whole marina. What's that you're doing?"

"Dating some fossils taken near Tavernier. Look at this one. Nice huh? See, you can make out the outline of that little critter. Alice make her plane intact?—speaking of fossils."

"You're a real bitch, Tinker."

"You also, darling. How's Corky? Hey, you know what, Shylah . . ."

"No. C'mon, put down the instruments and rope; you're not working and you know it."

"You're right. I'm being the coy fellow. You see through me to my Jell-O heart. I do love you."

"I love you more. What were you going to say?"

"Uh, what was I—oh, Corky. You and me. I figured it out. Our ménage, I mean—daddy, surrogate daddy, daughter, surrogate daughter, lover, surrogate lover, sister, surrogate sister . . ."

"Yes, it occurred to me. Do you mind? Do you mind that I'm

enjoying it, that I'm happy, whatever that means, and probably becoming ridiculous—because I'm so well loved and fucked and tan and unartistic and all that. I never had that before. Be healthy, angel. Daddy hasn't got that long; we're playing house with time—but you. You and me—you're not my father, Tinker—I know you think I'm pulling that—not so—I'm just enjoying the benefits of all of it. You are my whole roast, is that good enough?"

"The whole roast? You're an Amazon. Fuck me; then we'll go over with the reeking conches to Papa Bear's house. I'm very healthy, Shylah. I know. I know. You're afraid I'll die on you. There's nothing I can do about it. Death is individual and indiscriminate—O.K., so if it will reassure you, I promise to love you and let you love me back while I've got any control over my mind. Does that make it better?"

"Yes, it makes it better. It's not everything, but better. You forget the hate in human nature. I've made some new sketches for the series, I'll bring them out tonight."

"I'd like to see them. I wish to hell you had some of your paintings down here, not just the photos. Well, what do I know about art."

"Suck me off?"
"Suck me off too."
"Turn around, ooh, hmm, wait, too fast, I'll come on your nose."
"Shylahhhhh, uhhhh . . ."
Only for him would I swallow come. I had gotten better at it—I felt it was ritualistic. Communion. All that protein the sex books talked about was so much shit to me. I liked cocksucking to a point; then I got scared I'd choke to death and start gagging. But not with Tinker. I could romanticize about Tinker's sperm and get into it. I guess I was like everybody else in that I had always imagined sperm to taste like a combination of the corpses of fish and formaldehyde—that it is, in fact, more nuance than taste, snotlike; I could hardly be a fucking princess about it, though the conditioning reticence was there. Besides, it made him glow. We were both horrendously oral anyway,

with our kissing, talking, smoking, his drinking and my craving for it. Smooth Tinker. Nice Tinker.

★

"Catch. You can cut the lime."

"Where'd Tinker go?"

"At the store buying coffee for us."

"Guess y'all are quite the couple. Mind you, ah lahk him a lot, always have . . . Shylah, don't lie to me, you aren't getting on with that husband of yours—ah know it—don't y'all bullshit your father, girl . . ."

"No, as a matter of fact. We haven't been together for some time. It's a finished thing."

"Well, why the hell didn't you tell me? Aw hell, ah guess ah haven't been in touch much, huh?"

"I felt, uh, that it would upset you. I'm much better off, really, much. Are you terribly disappointed?"

"Ah never did trust men who paint for a living, they're crazy, unstable types—always wanted you to have the salt."

"Like Tinker?"

"Fine man, that Tinker. You better hurry up and settle down again, Shylah. Maybe you move back down here?"

"No, not now. I want to be in the city. Someday maybe to come down, maybe to have a place. I don't know, Daddy. Anyhow, I'm happy you're not upset. Did you take your pills? Alice said a half hour before dinner. It's about that time."

"Shylah. Your mother and me, it was hard for, uh— See, your mother gave you a great deal of attention. Ah, ah'm glad you grew up so well— Ah'm sorry, hard for me—when she died, you know, when y'all came down. Rough, huh. Ah see so much in you, Shylah girl, ah know ah've been a son-of-a-bitch. They, that damn doctor and preacher, they just as soon throw the spade over the grave—hell, ah'm not dead yet— Do you hate me, Shylah? Shylah, you don't hate me any more . . ."

"No, I don't hate you. Never did. Never, never, aw shit, take your pills, Daddy."

"Yes, ma'am, ah'm taking them, see—"

3 6 9

Both Alice and the doctor had said I could expect Daddy to be throwing up some of his dinners . . . that his system would often reject food rapidly . . . to check if the vomit contained blood, and if it did, to get him to Key West quickly. But I had not yet seen evidence of his illness. The slowness, the shakiness, his fragility from the effects of sudden weight loss upon a big frame, but he had shown no sign of pain, nor had he vomited suddenly or collapsed. And because of that a part of me believed in the return of his health, that I was witness to improvement, not degeneration.

We had been laughing through dinner, talking up the poker game we'd play after, eating conch and lobster, I drinking my fourth Coke of the day. He gave no warning—the lump of undigested food that spat forth from his mouth, spittle, phlegm dribbling from lip surprised him as much as us. He did not seem in pain, but the vomit kept coming— I supported the convulsing shoulders—Tinker held a saucepan under him like a trough. And there was no blood, just the stamp of his sickness made visible—something I saw as proof he would die, that something sucked on his belly from the inside. He shook his head at me, the eyes in inexpressible confusion. I knew he felt castrated by this, felt the horror of obvious helplessness, felt there could be nothing worse for him than revealing pain to daughter. It had stopped now and I motioned Tinker to help me get him on the bed. I felt the old man's shame, for he had urinated in the khaki pants. I wanted to reassure, to tell him I still found him strong, to hold him again—and did not. I could not solve or lessen discrepant pride—it had had fifty-eight years to suckle. I was not his mother.

I left the bedroom to get him a Coke. The seizure had stopped as quickly as it had begun, leaving him wide-eyed, almost restless lying down. I felt perhaps he would want to change his soiled clothes and it was best to have Tinker help him. To not be so much the nurse, something I desired and knew he did not desire. He wanted his daughter without need, as his daughter wanted him with need. They were not my patterns to change. There had been other worthwhile changes instead. We could bide. We could bide in our opposing ways now, one to the other.

"Thank you, Tinker. He O.K.?"

"How do you feel? It's O.K.; he's asleep for a while. Vomiting like that for anyone's pretty exhausting."

"Frustrated. I'm frustrated I can't cut out the element of shame in him. To make him feel that it doesn't matter. That's the pain—you know, Tinker—seeing him feeling he's lost his balls. Which to Daddy, goddamn him, are his brains. Oh, by the way, he knows about us. He asked and I told him I'd split from Larry. He took it lightly enough; I was surprised actually. Maybe he loves you as much in his way as I do. Shit, this is a crazy way to live. I'm fucked up."

"You're O.K., Shy. What's troubling you is that you are new to all of this, us and him, I mean; the pressure of loving and being loved, taking care. Sometimes it's burdensome to you. I'm relieved that Corky knows what your situation is, by the way. I hate that kind of petty dishonesty. Besides, I don't like making love to you, then sleeping alone. Let's share a bed here, Shylah. I think under the circumstances Corky'd more than accept it; he'd get something out of it. What do you think?"

"I think you're right, of course. I hadn't thought to broach the subject with him—I mean, having you sleep here. In any other circumstances, he'd pull out the Episcopal manual, but I think he's up to it. We'll both talk to him in the morning."

"I think this is as good a time as any to tell you an idea I had this morning. I want to take the *Tikopia* over to Bimini for a few days, do some diving over there; it's a good area for lemon sharks. Why don't the three of us go? I know your dad should not, from a medical point of view, go anywhere, leastwise to sea—but I also know I've been promising him a trip since before his illness. My own feelings are, don't restrict him. It's not the time in hours, it's what he can do, what he wants to do, and he's been hinting about—what can I say?—a swan-song voyage."

"I've got to take him to Key West tomorrow. I'll mention it. I already know what the doctor's going to say, but I don't think he'll balk too much. Maybe he can get me some emergency medical supplies I can take along in case. We'll figure something out. Yes, I think it'd be great for all of us. God, yes, let's go. You make things lovely for me, Tinker, you make them new and lovely."

★

I had asked Luanne to come with me when I drove Daddy down to Key West Hospital. His tests and examination took the better part of an afternoon, so it would give us a chance to shop and talk over a beer. She appeared to me a walking proof that sometimes motherhood at the age of fifteen can be a glorious way of living through puberty. Contrasted to Selma Anne and Bubbles, she looked eighteen, slender, energetic, and always there was that part of Luanne that could not be married to any-thing—a kind of independence within the limited island life that brought out an endless supply of ideas and activities for ex-citement's sake . . . we were each other's hidden sides.

"Y'all changed, Shylah. Guess returning to Lime made you see how different things are for you now, huh? Lahk, ah sensed it, sensed you when you talked to the guys on Peacock. Distant lahk. Ah know it's tough with your old man being so poorly, hard to see him sick and stuff— Y'all even loved him then— even with all that shit he gave you when we were in school."

"Yes, I do. Think I'm a masochist? And there's Tinker also. It's all happened before I've had a chance to grasp being here, settle in."

"He's quite the man, Shylah— Ah knew the minute you said you'd met them there'd be somethin coming of it. Can't live lahk a nun, girl, you aren't the type. Your Tinker reminds me a little of mah Jack. Jack's so strong, you know, lahk, ah lahk him—ah never really lahked a man before—it's always romance or nuisance—leastwise with Harry it was that way—and ah played around after the divorce lahk ah'd just invented screw-ing— Ah don't care the man have diamond balls on him, it's shit unless you can lahk him, you know, talk to him as well. Lahk us, you know, Shylah, be able to talk lahk we do."

"Yes, I seem to have found out the hard way. We better be getting back to the hospital, I've got to talk to the doctor. Daddy and Tinker and I are going over Bimini way, something the world of medicine won't sanction, I'll bet, but hell, I think the old man should do what he wants. I believe in that. If it comes to him suffering the final hemorrhage aboard ship, then so be it; he'll die where he wants to die really, with loved ones on water, not in some fucking sterile hospital."

"Look, Miz Dale, y'all know how precarious his health is—you had that sample of it last night. Now, ah understand that it's his desire to go. Don't expect me to condone it from a medical point of view. If he starts hemorrhaging way out the hell and gone in the Caribbean, it's over. Ah'd have to say you were responsible for that."

"O.K., so now I have the official word from the AMA. You're vindicated all right. Just give me what's necessary in case he has an attack. He wants to go. He feels it's worth it and I respect anyone's decisions over his own life. I agree with Daddy. And you're saying I'm a murderer if he dies on board. What would you rather—keep him half alive in some hospital hook-up so he can exist more hours to be duly noted on some death certificate—because he won't really be living—there'll be no pleasure. He has just as much right to control his life as you or any sane adult. It's his choice. Goddamn you, it's his choice."

"O.K., O.K., simmer down, Miz Dale. Ah see you're a strong-willed girl besides bein a raght pretty one. Yessir, ah can surely see that. Tell you what ah'll do, ah'll give you what ah've got on hand here, and fill these at the dispensary. Probably you won't need to use any of this, but just in case. Pray you hit smooth seas, girl!"

Stupid asshole Florida cracker doctor. No wonder Daddy dreaded these visits. Laying on all that God-complex paternalism—"Why aren't you in bed, Mr. Dale? Did you take your pills, Mr. Dale?"—he did all right, my father, joking or pissing and puking—for his moments of life he did all right.

★

"Tinker, Tinker, where are you?"
"In the galley. Hi, Shy, how'd it go?"

3 7 3

"O.K. Bullshit doctor laid it on. Hi, everybody."

"What the doctor say?"

"Lots of scare tactics about Daddy—how unwise it was—that it was on my head if he suffered an attack."

"But you stuck to it, kid. You're a fine scrapper, I'm proud of you. Fuck doctors. It's the old man's choice and you kept the faith. We're all set for tomorrow, just to go shopping for food; thought we'd all go. By the way, weren't you pleasantly surprised he didn't kick up a fuss about me moving in; as he put it, shacking up under his very nose. See, the old man can bend with the times; underneath it all he's just as much a sponge for romance as the rest of us."

"Yes, delighted. I think he even liked the idea—it's playing house and Swiss Family Robinson and all that. Hmm, you feel good. What is this? Everybody getting stoned? Give me a toke of that joint. I wanna get high—cocksucking doctor—you know what that prick said to me?—he said I was a strong-willed girl as well as a pretty one. Incredible. He hangs a murder on my head just about, then gives me that cutesy big-daddy baloney. That kind of chauvinism ought to be a felony, you know, where I could at least threaten to have him brought to court. Oh oh, I'm stoned, I can feel it; where'd you get this shit anyway?"

★

We were the Three Musketeers in Banlon Bermudas strolling the aisles of the Quick Pig supermarket. Daddy, pushing the cart, felt everything in his boat-shopping mania—felt the fruit, the steak, the Cokes, wine, beer, and gave nod to neighbors, passers-by. Tinker and I brought up the back. What a strut. The prominent islander, the king of the Quick Pig. Maisie, the check-out lady, was beside herself, called over the owner in glee as she rang up the preposterous hundred-dollar slip on Daddy's food purchases. "Where y'all goin, Mr. Corky, the damn moon? Oh, you don't say, out on the *Tikopia*, in't that raght nahce; glad to see y'all lookin so good, suh, yes indeed." My father's splurge in supermarket buying. We could have fed the whole fucking island.

We cast off early morning, seven or so. I slept little the night before, even with Tinker's comfortable body next to me. It was too much at times. Unnerving. Two men coming and going, shooting up my brain with death and sex—and from the security of sanitarium living with females. Despite my decision I was terrified, terrified that Daddy might die, that he might suddenly dissolve before my sight, give way, guts and shit and blood pouring out onto the deck, and that I would watch the inside of him spill upon me and view the rattle, unable to give anything further. I did not want to watch death again; in my deepest self it had attained a human form and I would kill death, I would do murder upon the specter of death—the only enemy worth girding against—hairy old Goliath.

★

"Corky, you been at the wheel for ten hours now—you'd think you were lashed to it. Come on, let's knock off for the evening. That's the anchor thing right there—no, to your left. Shall we go out and enjoy the sunset?"

Sundown on the ocean was ritual. Rather like turning on the six o'clock news. It must be viewed with concentration in the best possible comfort and with reverence to the state of nature. As with the most basic of functions, such as birth, sex, elimination, and eating, sunsets gave us religion, bondage to nature, and beauty, personal and yet expansive. They also afforded the Southern drinker a pre-empting, rose-colored, alcoholic view.

Our first day upon the water had been calm. Daddy took the wheel, checking directions with Tinker— I lay out in the sun and sketched a seventeenth-century galleon from a picture I had found and cut out from the Sunday *Miami Herald*— something to later frame for Daddy as I had promised that first day. With assurances that he would remain at the helm, I stripped down to the skin, getting nipple burns, gazing out at the expanse of water, occasional break of island or flats.

Tinker brought us Cokes now as we sat out under the red/black/orange of last sun, streaks of refracted light making

3 7 5

brilliant the glass and chrome about the boat. We spoke little. Daddy puffed on cigarettes, smug, well-worked, and happy from the revival of physical concentration. Tinker slugged his bourbon, alternating that with stroking my arm. He had an erection and I had that sensitized sugary feeling between my legs. All that lapping of water against the hard frame of the boat. And sunset being so cosmetic to skin color—it softened us with pinks—visual well-being. I thought of that summer in Provincetown before I met Larry, the big animal let out of the net and put back in the jungle.

Tinker and Daddy began discussing the calmness of the day, discussing events in a kind of *Farmer's Almanac* and two-boys-planning-mischief-behind-a-hill way. Their noises—to take and mull the palpable sound, to take it in, to stretch like a leopard with my nipples on fire, a glorious haze.

And if he turned to blood. If he should die now, should turn and shrivel, the brief crystal agony—sunset was down.

Twilight, and I went in, turning on lights on the way to the galley. Something to do, business of preparing dinner. I had had a bellyful of reflective joy for the moment.

★

"Come on, Tinker, don't make me laugh while you're fucking me—you'll fall out."

"Sorry, you're tickling me, sweetheart."

"Turn over, I want to be on top. What's that noise—wha . . ."

"Sounds like your father."

"Something's wrong, stay here; hand me my robe, will you."

I checked Tinker's watch. After midnight, the sounds from his cabin, a voice. Daddy lay under the sheet, twitching. His legs moved as if to run; he was speaking in streams, a nightmare. I felt the pillow—soaked. And sweat replenished itself in small stand-up drops upon his forehead and below his nostrils. Daddy fighting the war again, in the trenches—"Jack's hit, get your head down, son-of-a-bitch, don't, goddamnit. Give him back a leg, will you? Corporal, where's Shylah? Where's the nurse, don't let him bleed, will you. Jack, you son-of-a-bitch."

He hit the bed with his hand, sank into moans and unintelligible phrases, face contorted, lips pursed.

3 7 6

"Daddy, wake up. Come on, for Christsake, you're having a dream. Wake up, Daddy . . ."

"NOOOOO . . . Shy, Shylah. Jesus."

"It's O.K., it's O.K., just a nightmare. Something about the war. Come; here, I've got you. See, everything's fine."

"Jesus, Jeeesus."

"Here, some water, drink it. Let me get you a towel."

"Let me have a cigarette, will you? They're over in my shirt pocket. Thanks, honey."

"Do you remember the dream?"

"Oh, the war, but you were in it. Goddamnit, you were right there walking around in a damn combat zone. Just a little dream; that's cause ah overate, ah guess."

"Who's Jack?"

"Just a man in the war, funny guy, slow. Killed in action. Some war, huh. Ah'm O.K."

"Rest easy now, the war's over. That one at any rate."

I went back to our cabin. We did not resume lovemaking but waited; I waited until I heard the snoring come from his cabin, then lay in Tinker's arms awhile before dozing off.

"What was that all about?"

"Nightmare. A really bad one. I wonder what brought it on."

"His youth, Shylah. Probably coming back to him more now—things he hasn't let himself think about awake. Just as well. Look, you—we're going to see sharks tomorrow—that ought to take your mind off things. Keep you busy."

"What am I doing to be kept busy?"

"Keeping an eye on fins while I go in."

"You're out of your fucking mind."

"No, I'm not. I have to do some camera work. There's a knack to all this, you'll see."

"Well, if it's so bloody safe, maybe I'll just go in with you."

"Uh uh, I've got to have someone in the boat, I mean, besides Corky. We can do some regular diving short of Bimini; I've got tanks and stuff."

"O.K., O.K., I don't want to talk about you swimming with sharks or think about my lover in the teeth of one. Hold me. God, I'm tired. And I will go diving. Why the hell'd he have to have such a dramatic dream now?—everything's going so well."

"Don't worry, Shylah. You worry too much. You can't control everything. Hmm, you might think about us, that I love you; you might ponder the implications of us, you know."

"I have. I have thought of that. I have, Tinker."

"Good night, Shy."

"Night."

★

"Shark!"

"Yes, I see, three of them. Lemons too. O.K., I'm going in—it's O.K., I know what I'm doing. Help me with this stuff, will you."

"Goddamnit, boy, y'all sure you know what's wise, huh?"

"Positive. Stupid creatures. Lemons aren't known to attack much. Only danger is their unpredictability. Slow fuckers though, I'll be fine. Only thing is, Shylah, you want to make sure the rope is steady. Once I surface I may have to make a hasty exit, you know what I mean?"

"You're not bullshitting me, Tinker, you really know how to do this safely? I know people swim with sharks down here all the time. But it pisses me off if you're just showing off with risk."

"I'm not. It's an inappropriate time for risks. I've no reason to. If I felt this was really dangerous, I wouldn't chance it, Shylah. I told you I'd be careful, remember?"

"Yes, O.K. Tinker?"

"What?"

"Show me how to go down with, uh, with them in the water. I want to learn. It'd help me overcome certain, uh, fears."

"O.K., later. I believe you. Now, all set—I'm going over."

Dumb bastard. Who else but a callow neurasthenic type would allow her lover to dive into shark waters? Though I knew what he said, about the risks, about the ultimate narcosis and stupidity of the lemon shark, to be true—still, playing paparazzi with sharks underwater was not my idea of safe science. He stayed down for half an hour or so, my eyes immobile upon the patch of water where he had dived in. A fin split the waves a little farther out. I remained close to the movable stairs and the rope, just in case. I noticed a pole underfoot, made mental note of its potential as a weapon. Daddy came up behind, limping slightly, put hands on my shoulders.

"He's a fine one. Don't you worry, he'll be O.K."

"Oh, the hell with it. I know the dumb asshole'll be all right. Makes me nervous, that's all. Remember, I've been living in New York City for the past five years. We don't have sharks, just muggers and graft. I'm out of practice. There's Tinker! Hey . . ."

"I'm fine, see, everything's O.K. Not even a toe missing. Help me off with this shit, please."

"How'd it go?"

"O.K. Couple of ones I could get in close range."

"And I get to accompany you next time, I mean it. I want to go down."

"Why, Shylah? Why the first time you skin-dive since high school do you want to go in shark waters?"

"Because I'm a coward."

"I hadn't noticed."

"I am. I hate sharks."

"So why go down?"

"Then the fear will be over. I won't mind you doing it. Don't you see, it'll be put in perspective like everything else."

"Yes, I'm sorry, I wasn't putting it together. So we'll go down. Give me an hour and we'll go down."

It wasn't that deep. Sixty feet or so, some absolutely first-rate specimens of sea shells and coral on the floor. Just once. I felt if I could do this, with the sharks, I'd be somehow lighter for it, freer. Something about potency. I should be more levelheaded, more even in my decision to have Daddy with us on the boat despite the doctor's warning, despite the guilt—that is, an act of courage surrounds what a person does in all of her dealings. I carried a net bag for the shells, picking them up where I found them, avoiding the brighter reds of the fire coral. A baby barracuda was staying close, which didn't bother me. It was harmless enough under these circumstances and indescribably moronic-looking in the way it hung in the water puppetlike. Tinker had not taken the camera down this time, contenting himself to do as I did—look for things on the floor, scavengerlike—for me shells, for him fossils. I picked up the underwater sign language quickly enough.

They were there, after the first ten minutes or so, an old huge nurse shark, massive, a toothy shipwreck in its gray hulk wandering about, that obscene overbite, as if the species were deformed mutants. Then two others, lemons, one coming closer until it completed a circle of us, close enough so that I could see the configuration of gills and teeth. I pointed up. Tinker shook his head. Of course; if you stay on the bottom you're safer than when you're in mid-water. I had forgotten. The shark nosed its way in toward us, big enough, seven feet or so; that was big enough, wasn't it? I had been there and that was it for me. The water empty again of shadowed forms, we swam to the surface, Daddy helping us off the ladder.

"Look, look at the shells. Lovely. Aren't they delicate?"

"What about those sharks . . ."

"Two, no three, one lemon shark close in. Enough to scare the shit out of me."

"You appeared calm, Shylah. That's the important thing."

"As I recall, you were doing the fencing. I just tagged along. But, you know, I gave them more credence in fantasy than they're worth. Ugly, yes, but I wasn't so horrified. Got a beer, Daddy?"

He brought us both beers and for Tinker a bourbon chaser, a Coke for himself—poor old man. To be driven to Coca-Colas—it must have been like busting rank after so many years of counting coup with liquor.

"Ah'm gonna cook steaks tonight, y'all. It's mah turn. Haven't felt this good in a long while. If you want salad, you gotta make it though; never said ah could make any of that shit."

"I'm tired. You tired, Tinker?"

"I am a little. A short nap, I think. We'll see you in an hour or so, Corky."

"You're so sexy underwater, you know that? Did you ever make love to a woman that way, underwater, I mean?"

"I tried. It's too difficult, to keep an erection, and then women's vaginas seal off in water. What are you doing with your tongue, Shylah? That's marvelous; that's what seeing sharks, up against death and all that, that's what it does to you, hmm?"

"Yup, I'm picking up from our coitus interruptus last night, remember. Oh, come on, don't bite my stomach, that gets me crazy; please, Tinker, please please . . . He'll hear us, come on— Shit, so he hears us, so what, hmm . . ."

Sucking on me, my breasts, then sucking the clitoris, fingers moving in and out of asshole and cunt, I'm knitting his hair—his ears with my hands, coming, coming, over him then, sitting down on his cock, long, friendly friend cock, splitting the cunt with my fingers and putting him up inside me—bending back like a ballerina as it guzzles at the mouth of womb—pulsates—I feel it come and I grip with cunt, fold over, lie with head under his arm. Quietly, because the father watches out for sharks above-deck, thinks us asleep, or has his own story to tell.

★

Without warning, and after our quiet supper, Daddy began again—the nausea and sudden, trembling sweats. And later he slept restlessly through the night (me not at all) while the boat rocked on choppy, wind-blown waters. We were all awake early the next day. Daddy took Coke and plain toast in the morning and mercifully kept it down; then he joked some with Tinker, but there was a noticeable effort.

"Tinker, let's head back. He had his day. All of us did. The weather looks shitty. I think it's enough."

"We are, Shylah, no sense in staying out with this gloom. Don't worry too much. He hasn't puked today, probably just weak."

I went down to tell him, hoping he'd agree, he wouldn't feel punished for being sick.

"The sky's rotten. Let's cut this a day short. Tinker agrees. And you're not feeling well. Let's bring her back, Daddy."

"Y'all just goin back cause you got a sick old man on board . . ."

"No, look at the water, it's so damn choppy. What do you say?"

"Oh, ah'll be all raght, honey. Ah suppose we had that damn

fine day yesterday. Ah guess it should end on the up, huh, daughter? Goddamnit, let me take the wheel; ah'm O.K., just a touch shaky; just let me get out of this damn bed. Can't fight the weather, ah guess. Shylah, you don't think ah'm taking you away—you really *want* to go back early?"

"Yes, like you, I guess. We had our day yesterday. I don't see any let-up in the weather. I think so."

"Hand me mah pants; ah'm gettin dressed for this."

Daddy had rallied enough to take the wheel for the last half of the trip back, Tinker and I looking over the specimens we'd brought back from diving. By the time Lime was in view, rain squalls were hard upon us, water spattering decks like a spoon beating on a tin pan. But we had made it and I hadn't killed him, had I? I did O.K., Daddy. Tinker and I. We'd get him back to the doctor.

I wanted that drink, could have used one, and caught myself rolling over the slogan on my tongue. Opened a Coke instead, and waved at Stanley nearby on the dock.

"Rough trip, Moose?"

"Yes, on the way back. Sorry you couldn't make it to that re-union we had on Peacock. It was deadly without you."

"Wise up, Shylah, it would have been deadlier with me."

He walked away then, all hanging flesh and dejection. Christ, Shylah, why can't I shut up? I hated myself for saying that to him. Tinker and Daddy were tying up and checking *Tikopia;* I had already taken our gear to the car. I sensed the dying of everything. Every fucking thing. Around me and myself, the ground dying underneath, Daddy, Stanley—my own impotence, that was a kind of death.

Nothing's permanent. Even planets have no immortality. And there was something else I'd have to face. Tinker. Tinker and me and impermanence. Too tired. Tinker, I don't want to lose you, dear God.

19

"When?"

"In a week. I knew we were due to go down the South American coastline sooner or later. I hadn't expected we'd get clearance this quickly."

"It was what we avoided discussing all along. So here it is, right? Even if you weren't going, I have only two weeks left here myself. We'd have had to part for a while irregardless."

"Shylah, believe me, I had no idea the *Tikopia*'d be going this soon. For once a university bureaucracy acted with speed, after all their fuck-ups. We could have used the time to plan; I could have stayed with you for a while in New York . . ."

"How long?"

"At least through the summer, four months, I'd say. Oh God, you know, this is crazy; I'm not going to do battle, I'm looking forward to it, except right now I'm miserable. Christ, four months, how are we going to arrange our lives, Shylah, tell me. I can't ask you to move, to follow me around, nor can I set up housekeeping with you in New York. It's the old cliché again. Well shit, I'm no millionaire, but I'm reasonably well off. We haven't talked dollars before—what do you say we commute? I can't take you on the *Tikopia* for the summer, you wouldn't go anyway. After this, uh, what now? Should we find a place together, figure out where and how while we're apart? I guess that's what I'm saying. Or what do I do? I'm confused."

"Jesus, I don't know. There's nothing to do. You live on a ship and I live in a loft, at least for now. Daddy's dying, you're leaving, and I'm going back to the city. What the fuck else is there to say, Tinker? What do you want me to say, damnit, Tinker?"

"We could get married. Why not? Maybe that's my generation talking—but at least let's live together. I don't give a fuck where, just to spend time together, to have some spot we both share."

"Christ no, not that, marriage—I don't know what—no, I, uh, I can't lose you, it's just as well we'll have time apart. We'll figure something out. Four fucking months. I can't think about it."

"I know, baby, I know. When we're through, I should think mid-September, I'll um—I'll fly to New York. In the meantime, you know I'll write, when I'm not jerking off, that is. I worry about you though, you need mending time. And I have a feeling it'll be a final goodbye to Corky— Oh God help me, Shylah, I can't leave you, I can't . . ."

He turned from me in his weeping, turned his head away, facing out the window of the car, where we sat in the supermarket parking lot. Something about being outside of where we had bought so much food prepared by us for us, domesticity cut short, in the land of cars and couples—kids screaming and running about. It gave his weeping, our particular tortures, an ironic poignancy.

"Please, please, love, don't turn from me, please. God, Tinker, look at me; show me some trust, will you? If we can keep ourselves busy, you see, we have so much—we can wait, can't we? We'll see each other soon enough. Maybe by Christmas we'll have a home in mind, some place we can be together. I have some money, you know, enough. We could buy a house somewhere, on Lime or any fucking where. Tinker, we have it now. I don't want to lose that—oh Jesus, what about Daddy?"

"I'm afraid to tell him—I mean afraid of my own reaction, not his. Be with me when I do, O.K.?"

"I will. Look, cheer up, it's only four months, please; come on, let's go buy supper."

"I'm feeling so, so weak, Shylah. Jesus, I don't know if I can say goodbye to the old man without breaking down again."

"Then fall apart; you're not a fucking general, you've a right to honest tears."

"Yes, I know, darling. I have problems with that. There is that sense of decorum that makes us socialized males all such dry-eyed monsters. You must be aware of that in your father."

"Sure. Where'd it get him—the fucking bottle. How do you survive without daily tears? It always puzzled me about men. Where does it come out?"

"Power, I suppose. See, Shylah, I'm your weeping lamb."

"Here's some Kleenex, lamb."

"Everybody becomes in part your child, aren't I right, Shylah? You're a mother. I can't understand why you don't have kids."

"Maybe you'll knock me up someday, maybe that'll happen."

"Yes, maybe I will. Are my eyes dry?"

"Like the Mojave Desert. Never have I seen such virile pupils."

"When should we tell Corky, Shylah, when?"

"Tonight. I'm tempted to say, not until you leave. But he'd feel slighted that we were protecting him again. Tonight."

"O.K., tonight. I think I'll tie one on while I'm about it."

★

Daddy sat in his special rocker next to the quad-band radio. The last trip to the doctor had not been encouraging. He was suffering again. Not constantly but sometimes, in his sleep, his gut again. The doctor had for the first time prescribed morphine-based compounds in case it got bad. We kept an uneasy peace; we spoke in terms of pain cycles, diet, special considerations, the side effects of various medications. He slept badly now; I thought I detected a gray cast about his tanned face in the mornings. And each day I found myself growing more delicate around him, more awed by the battle and the futility of it, and the way he kept himself alive. I knew his weakness, the increased dosage of dope gnawed at his pride; he was fighting off his own depression. So I watched him curse the priest when he came courting the coffin—Daddy's favorite sport had always been throwing four-letter words at the clergy. I watched him shake violently, walking out for breakfast in the morning until he grew stronger with the day. I did not want to tell him about Tinker's leaving. I did not fully understand how men handle these things without becoming pudding. I worried about the strain of that departure and my own departure after Alice came back. I could stay on, I knew that, summer was a quiet time. But I wouldn't stay on. I'd leave the old man dying. Wife was first bond. I'd go back and paint and he'd die. I was losing myself in premortum grief.

"Hi, Daddy. How's it going?"

"Fine. Alice called. Ah gave her your love. Luanne called. Did a little puttering in the yard. Give your old man a kiss."

"Hmm."

"Where's mah boy?"

"Stopped off at the *Tikopia* to pick himself up a bottle of bourbon for the house."

"Funny thing, a man accepting his daughter's lover. You two unmarried and all. Ah know, ah know, things are different. Hell, your mother and I slept together for years before we were free to marry, but in those days it was all done secret lahk. Damn well fooled your grandmother; ah used to sneak out at dawn. Ah guess people knew. But as ah said, it was different then. Ah'm too old to accept free love, honey. But ah see you two around— ah try not to think too much—getting all soft in this. Guess ah failed you and her—your mother. Jesus, ah loved that woman though, we had our moments—you know, the war—stealin time, that was what we were doin. You, too. You learn from us, Shylah. Stay together, that's all there is; don't make those mistakes, don't abuse. He's a fine man, that Tinker. You settle with him, Shylah."

"Yes, I probably will. We have a problem of geography to work out though."

"Goddamnit, girl, ah don't understand you; you can take your paints with you, how come you gotta be there, up Nawth with all those crazy colored boys on the loose. Jesus, you some kind of career girl or something? In't a home the best?"

"I do what I do. I'm not about to stop. We'll work it out."

"Well hell, honey, you don't see the man but once a year, he gonna leave you, that's just too much to ask."

"He's going to be out on the water a great part of the time, Daddy. At least for a while. I have work to do for a show I'm going to be in in late fall. It's important to me that I complete my new series. I want to show it. You understand."

"No. Maybe a little. Look, ah'm not gonna be here to see that these things work out; ah want for you to have a nahce life, you understand that, Shylah?"

"Things never entirely work out and you know it. I'm doing what I feel I can do and I think so is Tinker. We have so much at this moment. Let's not think about other things."

"You know, angel, you have a point. We have it now."

★

I had time before Tinker came back, before we would sit with Daddy and tell him of the *Tikopia*'s sailing date, time to make a quick trip to Luanne's. I had seen so little of my friends, most importantly, not seen enough of Luanne since coming down; they had called and I had returned their calls, but the privacy and needs of the three of us had quenched any desire to go beyond us. Luanne had acted middleman to this breach of island sociability, putting it down to my father's medical needs, which of course no one would swallow—it was after all so bizarre—sworn enemies, old Corky Dale and Shylah, taking care.

"Hello, Luanne, you busy?"

"Hell no. God, Shy, ah never get to see you. Oh, it's O.K., really, ah know you got all that shit goin on over t'your place. You wanna beer?"

"Please, and to see you. Where's Loosie?"

"At play rehearsal, school thing, you know. Lawd, ah'm glad you stopped by, ah phoned, you know . . ."

"Yes, we were at the market. I've wanted to invite you all over for supper, but Daddy—his health is kind of precarious, he has problems keeping food down."

"Ah gathered. Mah folks said you dropped by."

"Yes, just for a half hour or so. Kind of a courtesy call. They look very well."

"We're a healthy clan, you know that. Anyhow, thanks—ah'd of never heard the end of it if you hadn't paid your respects and all that . . ."

"I figured."

"Hey, you know what?"

"What?"

"Selma Anne brought over a copy of *Life,* mentions your name; there's this picture of you next to a painting. Y'all didn't tell me, ah would've bought a copy."

"I didn't think to tell you. The article about women in the arts, yes."

"Lawd, shows y'all picketing, some cop hitting some girl, all that stuff. Some of the paintings aren't paintings though—sort of hard porn, in'it. Yours isn't, but that big photograph-lahk painting of the couple screwing—though it's kind of vague—*Life* won't print anything lahk that real close up, will they?"

"Hardly."

"You always were one for causes. Ah look to you to see what's gonna happen down here in a few years. Lahk with the Negroes, and when you pierced your ears, and the dress you wore to the prom. You not a Lesbian or anything, are you?"

"Uh uh."

"But you lahk, uh, women's lib, huh?"

"Sure, it's the only sensible thing. I don't want to be told my work isn't worth shit because I've got a 'female sensibility' and all that."

"Well, ah certainly believe in equality, but ah don't want to stop being a wife and mother."

"Come now, Luanne, you've been running the show from one vantage point or another since I've known you. This just acknowledges your power. God help us if anyone tried to deny you your maternal instincts."

3 8 8

"You ever made love to a woman?"

"A couple of times."

"Mah Lawd, ah've always been curious about that. But y'all have always lahked big masculine guys."

"One doesn't necessarily threaten the other. Oh, for Christsake, Luanne, you're not going to get uptight that I'll suddenly lunge for you."

"Shit no, ah'm just curious. All those times we slept together. Ah guess if ah hear these things from you it's enough, you know. All the exciting things."

"Yeah, I know. You like me to take the risks and report to you. And I like you to be maniacally secure and in control of your island, so I can have the, uh, stability. You know that's always been the way with us."

"Ah guess sometimes ah wonder what would have happened if ah hadn't quit school and had Loosie, but had finished and gone on to college lahk my parents wanted. Ah got pretty depressed about it all when Harry and I were busting up. Sleeping around helped a little, and going on trips. Loosie started showing the effects though, since Harry wasn't visiting her and ah was runnin around. Anyhow, Jack solved those problems."

"You're incredibly strong, do you know that, Luanne, you are. It's always been your choice to be here. And it looks like a good one—at least for you—wouldn't you say?"

"Well, ah've always had this wild desire to, you know, to demonstrate mahself in some way."

"Maybe you already have."

"What with Selma Anne and Bubbles—they'd think ah'd turned Yankee—you know how it is. Ah started reading those Flannery O'Connor stories you sent me, ah couldn't put the books down; and *The Group* too, McCarthy raght?—so ah was reading all the time for a while. They 'bout lost their minds that I was reading so much—said ah'd been invaded by your spirit— shit lahk that. So you know what ah've been doing? This is just between us, Shylah, O.K.?"

"O.K."

"Ah've been writing this book. Ah type lahk a couple pages a day when ah can. Ah know it sounds crazy . . ."

"A novel, Luanne?"

"Yup, it's probably not worth anything. Listen, when ah finish it, can ah send it to you, will you read it?"

"Of course. Send me a copy though. Keep your original, you don't want to lose all that work. What's it about, Luanne, can I ask? I'm so curious."

"Y'all promise not to . . ."

"Yes, of course. Now TELL me."

"Well, ah got the idea from reading *The Group*. Actually, it's lahk make-believe and stuff, but it's about us, sort of. You know, the island and stuff. We're the heroes though, and there's this murder and then everyone's screwin around, and, well, just lahk a lot of other books now."

"How far into it are you?"

"About page 200, ah figure ah got another hundred to go. In'it crazy. Ah've been trying to tell you since you been down, but we haven't been alone enough. Not even Jack knows; he asks what ah'm doin and ah just say ah'm writing letters or keeping a diary or whatever. Mostly ah work when he's not around. And ah haven't told the girls or anything. Ah'm afraid they'd guess who the characters were and take it personally."

"You amaze me. Can I read some of it now?"

"No, wait till ah finish and retype it. It makes me too embarrassed, you know."

"O.K. Don't start getting shamefaced about it though, Luanne, or you won't be able to finish it; just write. Move your ass on it, O.K.? I want to know what my character's all about, how you portray us."

"Will you send me one of your paintings? Ah know it'll be abstract or something, but ah'll hang it, honestly."

"Sure I will. They're awfully large canvases, Luanne. I'll have to find you or paint you a smaller one. Listen, I've got to get back, it's closing in on five-thirty. See you soon. A novel. Luanne, you're a veritable Fanny Burney."

"Who?"

"A woman who wrote a best seller under her father's unsuspecting nose. See you later."

"Maybe tomorrow huh?"

"If I can, maybe tomorrow."

Shylah, don't romanticize this for Christsake. The book probably sucks—all Southern-belle-ishness or some such. I never
doubted her genius, just her grammar; but why not? While Bubbles and Selma Anne read confession and movie magazines and
popular astrology, Luanne went through everything I sent her,
asked for books as presents, asked me to suggest authors. I had
forgotten her passion for reading, had forgotten her often vicari-
ous living, her powers of observation. Weren't writers observ-
ers? I felt that of Fernanda, that she lived vicariously through
me at times and that she observed instead of felt much of what
was her life. Luanne had both qualities though, she had emotional perception— Oh Luanne, I hope to hell you're a decent
fucking writer— What can I say to you if it's rotten? I'd pass the
buck, I'd use Fernanda's opinion and not offer my own. I'd be
the coward, no, I wouldn't be the coward; if she made it long
enough, it could maybe be another *Peyton Place*—all value
judgments aside—she'd make money off our asses. Luanne.

★

Tinker and Daddy sat together at the dining table. Tinker had
told his news—I knew it by the cerebral browish look each
wore, knew it by the manner in which they puffed hard on cigarettes, Tinker clutching his bourbon glass too possessively. And
sunset had begun—yet they weren't glancing in the direction of
the sliding-glass panels; they looked to each other. Pained me
to know they were talking about Tinker's trip without me there.
Slighted. The information was to pass from both of us. The
sphere of intensity had been their own, not ours. Please don't
leave me, don't do that to me, don't switch it off.

"Shylah, come, ah didn't see you there."

"I was watching you both. You told him, Tinker. I thought we
were going to be together when you told him."

"Shylah, I couldn't sit with Corky without telling him. You
weren't here; sometimes things just work that way. Please don't
feel put out."

"I'll get over it. We'll miss him, Daddy, won't we?"

"Just lahk you, Shylah, he's gotta leave. That's what y'all said to me this afternoon."

"Yeah, I'm biting my tongue."

"Why, you can come down when he gets back—so we'll be together again. Alice too; that'll be something to look forward to."

"Don't start protecting me now, goddamnit—goddamn you, Daddy . . ."

"Ah'm sorry, girl. You know horseshit when you hear it. Can't fool a cavalryman's daughter, not even about that."

"No, no, not about that. Turn around and look at the sun go down—there's your full-blown, passionate sky. Lovely, especially tonight. Go on, look at it, turn around, Daddy . . ."

"Sometimes it almost hurts, doesn't it?—looking at that—it almost damn well hurts, these mushy sunsets."

"I'll start dinner."

"Shylah."

"Yes, Daddy?"

"You and Tinker. You go off for a while tonight. Take in a movie or something. Have a night to yourselves."

"Well, I . . ."

"No, ah know what you're worried about. Ah'll be fine for a while. Haven't had much time to myself. Y'all go off and enjoy yourselves lahk any other courting couple. Mind, ah still have a little self-sufficiency in the old blood."

"I think I'd like that, Corky. We could stop in a few places in Key West, I think it would be O.K. Yes, sweetheart?"

"Yes, all right. Later after supper."

★

We had driven to Key West around nine. He was right, my father, he needed something to break the time together—just an evening to himself. I worried. True, he had eaten well, taken medicine, seemed comfortable, wasn't spitting or anything. But it was unpredictable with him, when the attacks would begin and how long they would last. We stopped at Sloppy Joe's, old hangout of Williams and Hemingway, where I had always liked the rough, open-air bar, stand-up, belly-up drinking tactics. Tinker ordered a drink while I used a nearby pay phone to call Luanne. It seemed a simple enough way of getting someone to check on him. I asked her to stop by the house at ten-thirty, pretending to visit me. So a little deceit; that way he'd think nothing of it, or if he were in the middle of an attack, she'd be able to help.

"Well, Shylah, my date for the evening, what would you like to do?"

"Get a fancy motel room with a swimming pool for a couple of hours."

"Are you serious? Marvelous idea. Do you know of any?"

"We passed some on Highway 1; sure I'm serious. I called Luanne to drop by the house in an hour or so, all quite underhanded, just to make sure he's O.K. He wants us out by ourselves, so why not a motel room—we have the privacy of a luscious, depraved, plastic motel room—it's off-season anyway, there won't be anyone around. I can scream and moan, be an animal without Daddy in the next room, and we can swim. How's that?"

"Bathing suits?"

"I've still got mine on underneath. You can swim in those blue jock undies you've got on. Come on, nobody's going to bust you. We're an all-American illicit couple. We'll pay in advance."

"You're giving me a hard-on."

"I hope so. We might as well make love a lot for the time you have left. Not that desire works that way, but I won't see you for four months. It's like life insurance."

"Anything, Shylah, anything at all."

The Sea Horse Motor Lodge, two swimming pools, tennis, miniature golf—vacancy, poolside apartments. I had been right in my prediction—the fifty or so units were empty except for five or so. May was off-season slow, hardly worth the electric bills. We took one of the poolside rooms—sliding doors, hot and cold running everything, electric sliding floor-length drapes covering the view to the pool, a queen-size bed. All the Ameri-

3 9 3

can trappings of sterile room versus sexy expanse of mattress.

"Let's swim first, Tink . . ."

"You go ahead, I'll watch. I feel like—well, look, I'm inhibited wearing just these things."

"They're little ones like a French suit, and look, Tinker, not a soul is around. Come, I didn't expect that nonsense from you."

"I'm a conformist, Shylah, you know, the type that likes to be as anonymous as possible."

"Bullshit, you've been splattered across TV and *National Geographic;* you give lectures, get interviewed. How unanonymous can you be? Look, there isn't anyone in sight, and who the hell's to care if there were."

"O.K., you're right, I'll be O.K. once I'm in."

Someone had left one of those large beach balls next to the pool, which I commandeered for a game of dive-and-catch. Neither one of us was any good at the latter, but the exercise and the feeling of being alone in a vast expanse of Americana-run-wild plastic was adventuresome. It took our minds off things. The few remaining hours we had in the room became a honeymoon. Soaked until our skins puckered, we rolled around on the bed, in and out of towels, until we tired of horseplay and lay facing each other, side by side, naked and silent.

"What are you thinking, Tinker?"

"I'm thinking the only poem I ever cared to half-remember. It's anonymous. You must know it."

"Recite it to me."

"Western wind when wilt thou blow?
The small rain down can rain,—
Christ, if my love were in my arms
And I in my bed again!

"I think that's how it goes. I used to say it quite a bit to myself after Angelica died, and later at sea, when I was particularly lonely for that kind of love and companionship. It comforts me, somehow."

"Then recite it to yourself when you're away, and I will also. I know the poem."

3 9 4

"Hm, it's a crazy life we're going to lead if we remain together. We'll be seeing each other on the wing for a while. You're very young. Are 'we' really so important to you?"

"Yes, yes, 'we' are, and you?"

"Yes, and it frightens me; you are the part of me that is my love."

I stroked his face and eyes, kissed his neck, wept in the cave of armpit, held him fast to me, loved him out of body in motel splendor, came for myself and for him, helped him help me give him pleasure, wet on the plastic bed in the plastic room. I clutched at the muscles of his legs between mine, hands on ass dimples, tongue, cock, his eyes, blessed the silences. Tinker, so full with you.

Home, with Daddy sleeping, healthy grumbles and snoring. We tiptoed into our room, undressed, slipped under sheets, kissed, held, turned over, touched distantly my hand upon his ass, his to my thigh, slept soon.

★

The next few days I saw little of Tinker. The *Tikopia* was in the process of being outfitted with new scientific stuff from Miami, and getting a scrape-and-varnish job. He commuted daily to Miami, talking to university foundation members, bringing back new equipment. The other men were visible now, assembled around the work that had to be done. I tended to Daddy as much as was allowed, ran through sketches, lay out in the sun, caught crawfish, wrote letters to Fernanda, talked to Luanne.

And Daddy showed strain. Brooding did not become him— he'd look away or stammer. Something would be torn from him, and for once there was nothing to control it with. He had begun to grasp hold of his dying; the wound had opened and he could do nothing but hide. We kept a distance then, distance from pain. Pain and inequity. I had something he couldn't have. I might live. I might see Tinker again. A basis for hope. For Daddy, hope was this moment and what surrounded him. For Daddy, compromise was akin to amputation—acceptance would not come within his habits of living. I pitied him this, I pitied him the rigid cavalryman code, and I kept to myself and waited.

★

"Hello, everybody—Tinker below?"

"Sure is, Shylah, come on board."

"Jesus, it's spotless. What is all this boxed stuff?"

"Instruments, sounding gear, canned goods."

"Hi, Shylah, am I glad to see you, Christ."

"Are you busy? If you are, I'll leave."

"God, terribly, but I can't do anything more right this minute. Let's take off for a while. How's Corky?—I really haven't seen him in days."

"Terrible. We both are. It's a fucking wake."

"Don't start that. Come on, I need a drink; let's go to the inn and get lunch, O.K.?"

"O.K."

But neither one of us could eat. Tinker's nervousness and my depression grated on us. We opted for sitting at the half-deserted thatched bar, he belting double bourbons and me with my goddamned beer.

"Now when?"

"Day after tomorrow, around seven. Get a good day out if we start early; hope the weather holds."

"I propose a last supper for Daddy, you, and me. I hope to hell we survive it."

"I have the advantage, darling. When we get busy we really get busy. It keeps me from thinking. Man's great escape, right?"

"Fucker. I'll be generous, O.K., so I'm glad you can escape. Work your ass off, it's your job."

"Don't think about it. You're on a tension wire right now. Don't you think I know it?"

"You're drinking a lot; that much, tension or no tension, I noticed."

"Look, so get off my ass, Shylah. I've never *not* wanted to leave on one of these things. It's painful, and you're not making it . . ."

"Neither are you. Oh Christ, I don't want to fight with you. I can't take any more in, I can't . . ."

"Shh, baby. You're usually the one with the strength. Shylah, don't turn from me, please, dear God . . ."

"I'm O.K. Really, Tinker, get on with what you're doing. Working late?"

"Until about eight at least."

"Let's get out of here; I think you better get started on whatever and I have to pick up the mail and run errands."

"Shylah, I love you so much."

"Yes."

★

Tinker was late that night returning and Daddy barely spoke, appeared to be dreaming, but in a depressive sort of way. I sponged off his face and took to massaging his shoulders, while he did his best to look down or away, but not at me, not in the eye—what dogs do when they want to maintain peace, and what we humans do when we feel guilt or shame or inferior. And there was nothing to be done on that score but wait out his misery and my own.

★

Early. Six or so when Tinker rose for his last day in dock. I got up with him, making us coffee, Daddy snoring in the other room. A clean wind blew up through the open window slats, gusted in one side of the house and passed out the windows of the other. Outside, between the house and the telephone poles, the giant webs of garden spiders glinted wet and pastel in the apricot first sun. Cool today, a pleasant day for manual work. Tinker drove off and I walked around the yard, squashing a small scorpion after musing over the wisdom of mercy with barefoot children about. The spider, fierce-looking and harmless, caught my attention again, climbing around, expanding the huge web, elegant meanderings.

Sounds of children getting ready for the seven o'clock arrival of the island's old school bus, tourists from the nearby motel getting together their rented tackle and rods for that day with the marlin as loudly and abrasively as their enthusiasm would vent. I took the mushroom basket from the stoop, made a rectangular tour of the front property gathering Key limes, guava, and picking the plain brown balls that opened into ambrosia from the sapodilla tree. A couple of coconuts had fallen last night; most were still green, but these seemed ripe enough for eating. A belt-buckle-size palmetto bug fell on my T-shirt, positioned itself like a hideous scarab pin to my left breast. I let it remain there an instant until it began traveling and the thought of its crunchy frame on my bare skin made me swipe it off onto the mat grass.

I would not think about Tinker. I would not wallow; I'd catalogue the day, the smells of him upon my skin, the stray chest hairs on my arm.

The school bus had stopped. I looked over to the road, heard the familiar squeal of brakes, the chatter of children's high-pitched tongues, watched them board and the bored expression on the lady who drove the bus, hearing the ancient brown seats creak for new blood and the engine build up as it passed by and continued its journey over the slender bridge that separated island from main stretch of Highway 1.

Someone nearby had already made the first swimming pool dive of the day. Somebody else—a woman's laughter—joined the anonymous body. The island seemed a natural conductor of sound—or was it the water as conductor and island as receiver?

The screen door banged shut from the ocean side of our house. Daddy was up. Jesus, what a stork in his Black Watch plaid Bermudas and short-sleeve shirt, all hanging gut with pencil-thin extremities, the gawky, outsize feet, bulging knees. He walked around toward me, past the giant cobweb, catching for a moment the refracted light upon himself. Daddy, my father.

"Hello, baby. Tinker off for the day?"

"Yup, he'll be back mid-afternoon. Want some breakfast, how about it? I have all this fruit, see."

"Yes, but hell, not fruit, eggs and ham. God, ah'm hungry. Y'all hungry, kid?"

"I could eat. You sleep O.K.?"

"Sure. You? Well, ah should ask, you got that man next to you."

"Not for long. I'll make us some breakfast."

"Wait. Don't let him go. Shylah, don't . . ."

"I can't do that."

"No, that's not what ah mean—he be back. For you, he be back."

"Yes. And I'll be back for him. It works both ways. Nice, huh? Nice between us. Don't worry so, Daddy; I'm flattered that you do, but it detracts needlessly from your own pleasure. Jesus Christ, really, I love him; I love Tinker, isn't that enough? Let's go in and eat."

After breakfast I stopped over at Luanne's, coaxing her into supermarket shopping with me, then to help pick out a new dress at the Tropical Bandanna. Something to wear, festive. I wanted to be festive for the last supper.

"Mah Lawd, when y'all stop shaving those armpits, Shylah? Is that women's lib too, or you got an allergy to razors, or what?"

"I like it."

"All that damn hair. Jesus, ah never grew mine an inch. Jack'd deeevorce me for sure; y'all best get a dress with sleeves. Tinker lahks it, ah mean, he doesn't mind?"

"Nah, he likes to stick his nose in it."

We had squeezed ourselves into the same fitting room to try on Miz Lurene's latest gear from Miami. As it had been our custom in high school, and although the other two dressing rooms were vacant, friendship meant closeness and each would be slighted in each other's presence if we were not in touching range. I had picked out three white cotton dresses to try. White, the impracticality of it, its purity—the color, though it was absence of color, color of mourning in the tropics. I had always favored white. White was ritual, love, and terrific with a tan. I chose a modified minilength piqué, fit tight at bodice, tight enough so that I could get away with no bra down here. Sedate but alluring. Also disguise. White was disguise.

I viewed myself in the triptych full-length mirror, studied the tan, the bleached peach fuzz of leg hair, reds in my head hair, sun wrinkles in my face—I had changed; I hadn't thought so, but I had. The soft ingenue cuteness had gone, leaving my face more angular, older. I liked it, liked discovering me in the mirror and seeing a difference. A comfortable face at last.

We left with my purchase and the groceries, driving back in Luanne's Pontiac to her house.

"You know, I love the idea of you writing a book. You really won't let me see it?"

"When it's finished. Didn't think ah'd ever do anything lahk that, did you?"

"Sounds reasonable in a way, from what I know of you."

"You think of yourself as grown up, Shylah?"

"Nope; well, when I looked in the mirror I got some sense of change. Mostly I see myself as growing older, not up. Inside, I'm still short."

"What does that mean, short?"

"Small. I don't know. Looking up."

"Ah see myself as never being small, now. Lahk ah played house when ah was four, and now ah'm twenty-four and ah'm still playing house—just that everything is larger."

"Makes sense. All that 'responsibility suddenly descending' upon us is a categorical parental hype. I always felt the responsibility in a way."

"Real hard for you to have him leave, in'it?"

"Yes. But I like the idea of testing the endurance of love by time. It's my outrageous romanticism. What we have now is so unreal, closeness and death and passion against this tourist backdrop of leaving. It's too quick, too facile. Something, every breath, everything leaving. God, I envy you your stolid husband and Loosie, and this house that you clean to immaculate kingdom come. Not always, but today I envy your ability to stand still. Jesus, it must be a virus."

"You still cutting yourself down . . ."

"Not so much any more. Just that with you I'm aware of what it means to live like I've been living, knife-edged, thinking too much, grappling for more or wider or bigger of something always indefinable. I think of you as bound and growing and me as unbound and exploding. And Tinker, loving him, you know, in a domestic way—makes me wonder if we could survive together."

"Well hell, be practical. You gotta have something to survive together for. Y'all can't live on sex and supper all the time. Get knocked up, Shylah. When y'all get together in the fall, get pregnant. That's what all that other stuff's about anyway. We aren't out of it yet. Every damn thing has a function in life; it has to add, not just feed on itself. Lahk with you, your art is lahk your baby, and you have it by yourself—makes it hard to last with a mate, because you don't really share the love with him and make a product. Well, that's just mah opinion, comes from bein a mother."

"Hmm. Who knows, Luanne? Perhaps I enjoy less. Maybe I'm a masochist. Sometimes I question my acceptance of Daddy at this late date. That he was an absolute prick when I was a kid doesn't matter to me. What's with us now, getting to know things and understand them, caring for him? I'm sheltered by it at last, I have such tenderness for him."

"Honey, your daddy is dying; he's your kin, Shy. You'd be loving him no matter what."

"I don't think so— You really believe that? Christ, it doesn't leave much leeway for personality attractions or anything. See, I always wanted it to be, uh, you know, to be friendly between Daddy and me— It's partly his charisma; beneath the blood I enjoyed him, his humor, that personality thing."

"He has that about him, ah'd be the first to admit. But you've always had trouble, Shylah, accepting people's faults as well. Y'all get turned off by so much."

"True, intolerance. Oh well, my bare breast is tired from beating it. You like my new dress?"

"Yes, of course, looks great on you— Ah can't believe you spent seventy-five dollars on a dress."

"I can't either. It's because I'm putting on the dog. I've got to get back, clean up, bake a pie, let out nervous energy. Anyhow, I'll see you soon. We'll have supper together or something. Alice gets back in a week or so."

★

"Where? I don't see it. Come on, Daddy, there's absolutely no way a shark could get into the swimming area—you probably saw some kid out there snorkling and . . ."

"Goddamnit, don't sass me, Shylah—when ah say ah saw something, oh, it's out there all raght . . ."

"O.K., whatever you say. So how'd he get in? I thought it was impossible."

"Yup, it is impossible—there ain't NO way that shark—Jesus, he's seven feet at least—no way he could've navigated the flats unless the son-of-a-bitch was hauled—someone put it there . . ."

"Oh, ridiculous. Who would haul a shark into a bathing area? Besides, look, the water's clear out there—I'd be able to see the shadow from here. Easily. Honestly, Daddy, there's nothing out there—see. Look, I'm filthy, let me just get changed and cleaned up a bit; Tinker should be home pretty soon—he said he was going to try and knock off early. Take a nap or something, O.K.? Your eyes are just playing tricks on you—honestly, there's nothing bigger than a rock lobster in there . . ."

Weird, I mulled over Daddy's fantasy while letting the shower water relax me. Alice had said his mind was still strong . . . oh well, everyone has a pet delusion of some sort now and again. And then the craziness of Tinker's leaving. I threw on Daddy's terry-cloth robe, skirting the water puddle left outside the shower curtain, and proceeded to unload the food and the new dress from the car, things I had forgotten to do with the shark threat and all— We'd feast on meat tonight—a leg of lamb, always the roast on official occasions, potatoes for strength, greens for the eyes, wine for the spirit, and Coca-Cola for my father.

★

"Hello, darling, resting?"

"Yes, for a bit. What time is it, Tinker?"

4 0 2

"Four."

"Already? You're through until you leave? Tell me you are."

"I am. Nothing more to do. What's this Corky was saying about the water off the dock being sabotaged by a shark. He was pissed. Jesus, was he pissed off. Just saw him, though I didn't see the shark. He's dreaming, isn't he? No fish could get over that sand fence."

"Yeah, dreaming. I guess he's more upset than I thought. He thinks someone hauled it over, maybe through the boat channel."

"You've been swimming there every day . . ."

"O.K., Tinker, there's no shark out there—you'd be able to see it. Look, forget the paranoia. Sleepy?"

"Yes, move over, let's catnap together. Wait a second, I tripped on my own enthusiasm—I stink, ooh."

"Yes, you really do. What were you working on, slapping your underarms with bait?"

I heard the shower running and joined him under the water. I had no wish to speculate on the providence of sharks when Tinker would be leaving fifteen hours hence. Instead, I preferred to wash him, taking the round soap in hand, scrubbing from the neck to shoulders, down back, underarm, and into crack of ass. Baboons groomed each other, and likewise I groomed him with the soap, under the water, and he me, though I was clean—and, as if excused, we made love under chrome faucet, towel-dried each other, and took our nap, though he could sleep and I could not. The shark. What'd my old man have to go out and dream that up for . . .

I was up, dressed in my new white dress, with two young frangipani orchids tucked into the upsweep of hair. Daddy sat in his chair outside—his sundown and now shark-watching chair—reading *Adventuresome Male* magazine. I could see him from the kitchen window occasionally glance up and out, checking for dorsal fin. I put the roast in and methodically cleaned and scraped the potatoes. I would rather we had eaten at one of the local restaurants on Tinker's last night, it'd take the strain off me, but Daddy's inability to keep food down stopped me from suggesting it. Still, the atmosphere in the house—preparing last meal, last rites, last this, last that—shit—Shylah, stop it. Stop thinking.

My mind turned back to the shark and Daddy's vigil out there with his army binoculars on the table. It didn't seem to matter that much to me, but to him it had become intrigue. In that amount of space the shark could have been easily caught and hauled back. Things like that do sometimes happen down here. But Tinker had not seen it, I had not seen it.

I thought of paradoxical things, my body relaxed in love, orgasmic and suntanned, well taken to care. I thought of Tinker lying there on his side, the breath creasing his lips; I thought of my father's late fatherliness; I thought of Longview and Dr. Saint and dying without dying and the asphalt streets and all the dead dogs in my life and Larry negotiating with my lawyer through his for an equitable settlement, whatever the hell that was. I'd be back there in a couple of weeks with summer upon me and no real plans except maybe to visit Fernanda for a while. I knew also that I could stay—what I did not say was that I chose to leave. I would not wait death out—I wanted my loft surrounding me, to be about my work. For Daddy there was Alice; for me there had never been an Alice. Forgive me, Daddy, I won't be here to watch you die.

"Hi, what can I do?"

"You're awake."

"I can't sleep. Shylah, Shylah my love, I need a fat drink. Where's the bourbon?"

"Down there. Don't get drunk, huh, not tonight."

"Jesus, don't give me that crap— No, forgive me, forgive me, I won't, I promise. Marry me? Sail away with me? Be eternal?"

"Now you're doing it. Here, sweetheart, check the lamb, will you?"

"Lambs, Lamb of God, that takest away. Jesus, it's the insanity of all this—it's getting me down. Would you ever want children, speaking of lamb, Shylah?"

"If I can, yes. Yes, two; right, we'll have two and one nursemaid."

"We'll throw them in the brine with the porpoises when they're babies, right? We'll have champion swimmers."

"Of course, anything. Go tell Daddy to come in. Let's eat soon, yes, ten minutes or so."

"Hmm, O.K., you look exquisite. That dress, it's new? White. Appropriate white, purity and mourning and love, yes. Beautiful, the beautiful lady . . ."

"Don't make fun of my efforts. Hard, isn't it?"

"Hold me, Shylah, hold me very tightly."

"You're so huge, I can't squeeze any harder."

"I have something for you, I want to give you later after dinner, O.K.? We'll go for a ride, yes?"

"Yes, of course."

I brought the food to the table, opened wine and Coke, and put them into glasses; went into my bedroom to see myself in the full-length round mirror. I'd drink a glass of wine, just one tonight, despite my liver, all that shit—I'd wish the evening to stay as it was now, clear and warm.

"Sit down, men, before the meat gets cold."

"You're eating meat, Shylah, I thought you were going to give it up."

"Not tonight; it's blood and I crave blood—must be the shark."

"Ah wanna know who put the shark in the goddamn bathing area."

"It'll keep, Daddy."

"Ah put up a no-swimmin sign. Private property, but you never know when one of the local kids is going to jump in lookin for crawfish. You leavin early tomorrow, son?"

"Seven in the morning. Best to start off early, I think."

"How long will it take you to reach South America?"

"Oh, two weeks to Venezuela the way we're going. We'll be there for a month or so in those waters."

"Y'all gonna write, aren't you?"

"Yes, every chance."

"You aren't gonna forget mah Shylah, are you?—y'all ain't been shacked up for nuthin."

"Daddy dear, stow it."

"No, comes a time when . . ."

"I mean right by your daughter, if that's what you mean, Corky."

"Well, these new women, ah'm of a different generation— But, hell, you get down to it, things are the same, women and men still the same, less you want to live lahk a hermit. You want to live lahk a hermit, Shylah?"

"No, though I think we're all hermits in some way or other. Pass the potatoes."

"You all dressed up, daughter; hell, y'all look lahk a woman for once. Ah used to know this French whore who kinda serviced us back in the war. She had hair lahk you, Shylah. God almaghty, did she have hair, had a line of it from tit to pussy and under everything, Jesus . . ."

"Daddy, do me a favor and shut the fuck up. You've been in a piss-mean all afternoon . . . Oh God, Tinker, get me a pan, will you? It's O.K. I know, I know, I've got you, puke it up, Daddy, you're among friends. Puke it up."

"Ah din't wanna be sick tonight, aw goddamn, ah din't wanna be sick."

The end of the feast—mangy, half-carved leg of lamb and flower in the bowl. Daddy's arm around Tinker, who was supporting him, taking him into the bedroom— Dearest, don't die, don't you fucking die on me, prick father— Tinker, don't leave. God, let me stay sane and sober. You went back on me. You turned in pain.

I got a sponge and wiped the table clean of vomit, the spew that had missed the saucepan, removing the plates of food while Tinker tended to him, to the tears and sweat. What a way to begin this. Why don't you leave, Tinker? I can't stand the waiting, I can't stand the long moments. Look at him, look at him. I want to get out of here, to get away from the first and last paternal tendernesses. It's too late, you bastards.

★

"Shylah, I'm so . . ."

"Nothing, nothing. Don't say it. I know. Is he O.K.?"

"Upset. And you wanted this to be so special. The dinner and your dress and all."

"So I wanted it to be special, the goodbye feast. Just fell apart, that's all. The intention was there."

"He's going through, as best he can, both dying and loss of others. It's too much to ask of anybody that they suddenly become evolutionary in their thinking."

"It's this fucking funeral-parlor-filled-with-love routine that I can't stand any more. Are you hungry, Tinker, did you get enough to eat?"

"Yes, how about dessert?"

"You get it—it's in the refrigerator. I just want to see if he's all right."

Daddy lay like a turtle cadaver on the outsize bed, shaky and confused, his head propped up by pillows.

"Guess ah spoiled your dinner, huh, daughter?"

"What's the difference? Cleared the air in a funny way. Too much tension."

"But ah wanted us all to have a good time tonight, makes me angry."

"Who the hell cares if you puke up a little leg of lamb or not? We have so much now. Please don't get that look in your eyes, Daddy; don't feel you've been shamed. I need you. Please don't pull away just because you can't be the bull all the time."

"Guess even that goes, huh, daughter?"

"Good riddance. Would you like a little tea or some Coke? Do you think you could keep some dessert down? We could join you."

"Just a Coke, yah, ya'll can attend the dying man's bedside; goddamnit, ah can't lick everything."

★

We stayed the night by the bedside, talking, sometimes silent, my father refusing to sleep and us unable to leave him. Around

4 0 7

five-thirty the last of Venus had been replaced by a pink haze over the ocean. Then the real feast, all of us haggard, my white dress discarded on the bed for shorts and shirt. I made breakfast with everything—eggs, ham, corn bread, grits, papaya juice, coffee, and we took it out, out to the dock table, to sit for the last time and eat and be there, Daddy looking for that ominous fin. It did not appear. It would not appear. I felt it. The tension between us, the foreboding, would not appear again either.

Mornings have that emerald quality of reflection. The cast being green, delicate lime, to match the name of the island. Perhaps that was why, though they said it was for the Key lime bushes, perhaps that was why the name.

Daddy did not come to the marina. I drove us down, Tinker having surrendered his rental car the previous day. In the last minutes they embraced, Daddy repeating my gesture of holding the head with one hand. They kissed, on the mouth; then slapped backs like sad bears. Daddy was the first to break it, looked out to the water, maintaining, maintaining.

"Shylah, I've not yet given you what I said I had for you last night. It's corny as hell; these things are symbolic and I'm not going to say it isn't. Here."

An emerald ring, marquis-cut and surrounded by aquamarines, unusual and old in its mounting. I had told him once that I had a fondness for both but otherwise was not much given to jewels, didn't wear any, no wedding band ever.

"I went by a place on Lincoln Road when I was in Miami the other day. I had avoided giving you a ring because I thought, well, I thought you would react negatively."

"I love you, Tinker. I can't escape ALL the symbols in the statement. I'll wear it, you'll see; I'll have it on, come October."

"Still interested in the possibility of the domestic life between us?"

"When we started sleeping together, from the first time to the last, my diaphragm has been in the suitcase I came with. There's a vote of confidence for the continuation of the race through Tinker out of Shylah, and vice versa."

"I'll call you ship to shore, in the evening, around six or seven your time."

"We better get to the *Tikopia*, don't you think?"

"What time is it?"

"Six-thirty."

The men working on deck waved. We had agreed I would not wait there for it to leave but say goodbye then. I was begging for the torture to be over. He had work to do. I put my hand to his face, felt around the jaw to lips, nose, eyes, until it rested on one cheek. We kissed, close-mouthed, almost abruptly—parting was never sexy—and clung. The last stamp of body for a while.

"Please be careful."

"Yes, and you also."

"I love you very much, Tinker."

"Not more than I, you. Stay healthy and, Shylah—DON'T drink."

"Bye, angel."

"Love."

I got back in the car, driving it to the marina café, and parked in back. He wouldn't be able to see me or the car from here. I was cheating a little. I'd go have a cup of coffee until they left, just to see it off, just to see it go.

I watched Tinker, watched him standing at the bow, the long wisps of hair blowing slightly, the *Tikopia* sailing out of the small harbor and into the channel. He looked toward the café for a moment and I wondered briefly if he knew I was behind the slats of the window watching, watching him until the boat rounded the dock and I saw nothing but guides preparing for their party's day out bonefishing.

Stanley came up behind me. "They off?"

"Yes."

"Funny how our lives are so different now, Shylah. You ever think of that?"

"Yes. I've got to go, Stanley. I'll see you around."

"S'long, Moose."

I went back to the house then and slept, in a dream saw Tinker leave again, and woke up glancing at the bedside clock—it was after three, and I heard the clip-clip-clip of my father's pruning shears from the window. I rolled over thinking I'd not get up, went off in a daze of daydreams, when the clip-clip-clip ceased to invade the afternoon sounds and the screen door slammed.

"Daughter, come out here!"

"What?"

"Look."

In his arms was my stepmother's largest vase, the kind that's flat, like a large carrot and olive dish, and in it were jasmine, hibiscus, frangipani, azalea, and tuberoses set at angles to one another, forming a kind of layered design.

"Ah picked them for you."

"You did this?"

"And arranged them mahself—kinda pretty, huh?—'member when you were little—oh, ah guess you were too young to remember— Anyhow, you lahked flowers so much you used to steal 'em from the neighbors' gardens. They'd be after us to beat your ass—oh Lawd— Your mother and ah didn't know what the hell to do—you'd be stealing from them—you know those neighbors—we always thought they were assholes anyway. Then, just as we'd be about to spank you—ah mean we had to do something—you'd come out with these all nicely put-together bouquets and you'd say they were presents for us—that you'd arranged them yourself. God, you were a funny kid . . ."

"Oh yeah, I do sort of remember that . . . Hmmm, these are lovely—I mean really, the way you put them together. Jesus, wait a minute, let me wake up, will you—I've still got sand in my . . ."

"Maybe you don't lahk them any more? Ah didn't . . ."

"No. No, Daddy . . . no, they're terrific . . . I mean I just can't get over that you picked them for me."

"And there's more . . . See, ah dressed up the whole house—for you, daughter."

"My God. Yes, Daddy . . . I see the flowers."